30130505633349

Slough Library Services

✔ KT-426-965

Please return this boo
date shown on your receipt.

To renew go to:
Website: www.slough.gov.uk/libraries
Phone: 03031 230035

LIB/6198

Slough
Borough Council
www.slough.gov.uk

H16/

THE BROOKLANDS GIRLS

It is 1919 and the Maitland family are still coming to terms with the aftermath of the Great War. After her brave work as an ambulance driver and nurse close to the front, Pips is restless and without purpose. Determined to enjoy life after the years of misery, and to help her forget a broken love affair, she seeks excitement in the London parties and balls of the Roaring Twenties. But when faces from the past reappear, Pips is posed with a dilemma. Can she ever trust a man's promises and allow herself to love again?

THE BROOKLANDS GIRLS

THE BROOKLANDS GIRLS

by

Margaret Dickinson

Magna Large Print Books
Gargrave, North Yorkshire,
BD23 3SE, England.

British Library Cataloguing in Publication Data.

A catalogue record of this book is
available from the British Library

ISBN 978-0-7505-4780-2

First published in Great Britain by Macmillan,
an imprint of Pan Macmillan

Copyright © Margaret Dickinson 2019

Cover illustration © Colin Thomas by arrangement with
Colin Thomas

The right of Margaret Dickinson to be identified as the author of this
work has been asserted by her in accordance with the Copyright,
Designs and Patents Act 1988

Published in Large Print 2019 by arrangement with
Macmillan Publishers International Ltd.

All rights reserved. No part of this publication may be reproduced,
stored in a retrieval system, or transmitted in any form or by any
means, electronic, mechanical, photocopying, recording or otherwise
without the prior permission of the Copyright owner.

Magna Large Print is an imprint of Library Magna Books Ltd.

Printed and bound in Great Britain by
T.J. (International) Ltd., Cornwall, PL28 8RW

Pan Macmillan does not have any control over, or any responsibility for, any author or third-party websites referred to in or on this book.

For all my family and friends for their love, encouragement and help through many years.

The Maitland Family

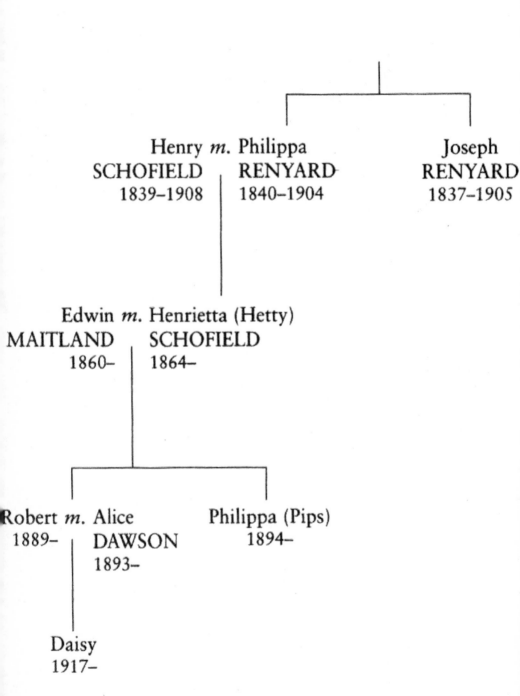

Henry *m.* Philippa
SCHOFIELD · RENYARD
1839–1908 | 1840–1904

Joseph
RENYARD
1837–1905

Edwin *m.* Henrietta (Hetty)
MAITLAND · SCHOFIELD
1860– | 1864–

Robert *m.* Alice
1889– | DAWSON
1893–

Philippa (Pips)
1894–

Daisy
1917–

The Dawson Family

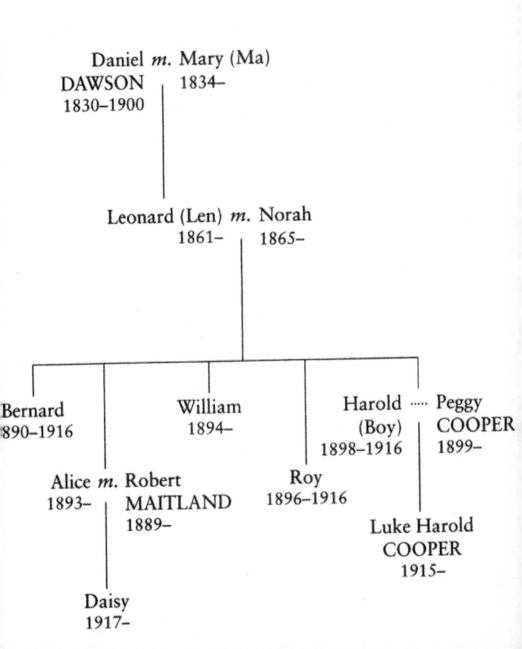

Daniel *m.* Mary (Ma)
DAWSON | 1834–
1830–1900

Leonard (Len) *m.* Norah
1861– | 1865–

Bernard
890–1916

William
1894–

Harold ····· Peggy
(Boy) | COOPER
1898–1916 | 1899–

Alice *m.* Robert
1893– | MAITLAND
1889–

Roy
1896–1916

Luke Harold
COOPER
1915–

Daisy
1917–

ACKNOWLEDGEMENTS

As always, this is a work of fiction; the characters and plot line are all created from my imagination and any resemblance to real people is coincidental.

Once again, I am very grateful to James and Claire Birch, of Doddington Hall near Lincoln, for allowing me to use their beautiful home as the setting and inspiration for this story, and also to the members of their team, who have been so helpful with my research.

My love and thanks to my nephew, Charles, his wife, Hilary, and my great-nephews, Alex and Matthew, for taking us to Brooklands Museum and for all their help with research there.

My sincere thanks also to Mike Hodgson, of Thorpe Camp Visitor Centre at Tattershall Thorpe, Lincolnshire, who acted as a guide on one of our coach trips to Belgium. He has so generously shared his knowledge and expertise in answering all my questions, then and since.

Thank you, too, to my 'first readers': my brother, David, my niece, Helen, and my friend, Pauline.

I wish to give special thanks to my wonderful agent, Darley Anderson, and all his team, to my brilliant editor, Trisha Jackson, and to everyone at Pan Macmillan.

A great many sources have been used in the research for this novel, most notably *We Danced All Night* by Barbara Cartland (Hutchinson & Co. Ltd, 1971); *Singled Out* by Virginia Nicholson (Viking, 2007); *The Great Silence* by Juliet Nicolson (John Murray, 2009); Brooklands: *The Official Centenary History* by David Venables (Haynes, 2007); and *Brooklands: Cradle of British Motor Racing and Aviation* by Nicholas H. Lancaster (Shire Publications, 2009).

One

Doddington Hall, Lincolnshire, July 1919

'I'm bored out of my tiny mind.'

Robert Maitland watched his sister pace up and down the long drawing room. She was tall and slim and vibrant with auburn hair and bright green eyes. She was strong and determined, if a little wilful at times, but he loved her dearly and wouldn't change her for the world. Almost three years earlier during the battle of the Somme, her daring had rescued him from no-man's-land and, though he had lost his right arm, she had undoubtedly saved his life.

'The trouble is, Pips,' he murmured with a fond smile, 'you have anything *but* a tiny mind. Of course you're bored. There's nothing for you to do. Not now,' he added in a whisper.

The war, in which they had both played such an active part, had been over for seven months and yet only during the last few days had it been formally declared at an end with the signing of the Treaty of Peace at Versailles on 28 June.

'You know, I'm not entirely happy with the terms of this agreement,' Robert murmured, jabbing his finger at the newspaper lying on the table in front of him.

'Then why don't you write to Lloyd George and tell him so? I'm sure he'll listen to you.'

'Less of your sarcasm, sister dear.' He smiled and then added more seriously, 'No, I'm concerned at the conditions they're imposing on Germany. President Wilson had the right idea, but other countries concerned seem to want to exact revenge. And a punitive revenge at that.'

'Understandable, I suppose, when you remember how poor Belgium and France suffered under their occupation. And they are going to be dealing with the aftermath for years to come.' Pips paused in front of one of the windows overlooking the grounds at the rear of the hall, where the Maitland family lived in the small village of Doddington. 'Oh Robert, what am I going to *do* with the rest of my life? If only I'd been allowed to train as a doctor like you, I'd've had something to come back to.'

Robert grimaced. 'Fat lot of good that did me.' He touched the stump of his right arm. His brown eyes were dark with regret and his strong chin hardened as he thought – as he did so often – of what might have been; what should have been.

'You could still practise, you know,' Pips insisted. 'I really don't know why you don't.'

He sighed. 'Pips, we've been over and over this so many times. I can't face the pity in people's eyes – and their doubt that I can do a good job.'

'You don't have to be a "hands on" doctor.'

Robert laughed wryly. 'Impossible, wouldn't you say? But a GP has to be able to examine his patients.'

'You've still got your left hand. You've learned to do all sorts with it. Why not that?'

'I'd be afraid of missing something. We're not talking about my rather untidy left-handed writing, Pips. People's lives depend on a thorough examination and I wouldn't be able to do some examinations thoroughly.'

Pips was thoughtful for a moment, then she nodded. 'Fair enough, but Father could do any you couldn't. He's not ready to retire yet. So much of a doctor's work is listening to people, diagnosing them or sending them to a specialist. It isn't *all* about physical examinations.'

Robert's career had been carved out for him; to qualify as a doctor and then to join his father's general practice in Doddington and the surrounding district. But shortly after he'd qualified, war had been declared and together with a friend from medical school, Giles Kendall, Robert had volunteered to join an independent flying ambulance corps, organized by one of his father's old friends, Dr John Hazelwood. It was an ambitious and daring plan to go right to the front to treat casualties as quickly as possible. Anxious not to be left behind, Pips had volunteered to go with them, taking her lady's maid, Alice Dawson, and Alice's brother William along too. Always near to the fighting, they had all been in constant danger, but only Robert had sustained a permanent injury when risking his own life to save others. The war had put an end to his promising career – or so Robert believed.

'You could go back to nursing,' he said now, trying to divert the attention from himself back to his sister. 'Get properly qualified.'

Now it was Pips who pulled a face. 'It'd be so

tame after – well, you know.'

He chuckled. 'So, you want another war, do you?'

'Of course not. How can you even suggest such a thing?'

'Sorry,' he said, at once contrite.

They exchanged an understanding glance. They had always adored one another and, in recent years, they had been through so much together – seen and dealt with such terrible sights – that now they were even closer, if that were possible. But there had always been an undercurrent of rivalry between them, at least on Pips's side. She had envied the things her brother had been allowed to do that she had not, just because she had been born to a strait-laced mother, who still held on to her Victorian ideals.

'The war changed Mother's outlook a lot,' Pips murmured, smiling gently. 'I still find it hard to believe that she let me go to the front, but even so I'm sure she wouldn't approve of me becoming a nurse in peace time. I think – now it's all over – she expects me to slot back into my place of being a dutiful daughter and find myself a respectable husband.'

'Beautiful though you are, Pips, that is not going to be easy. Most of the "suitable husbands" of your generation are lying in Flanders fields.'

'I know,' Pips whispered huskily.

There was a pause between them before Robert said, more briskly, 'So, what *are* you going to do, because you need to have something to occupy you?'

'I don't know. I just don't know.'

18

'It's the silence, Pips, that gets me. I'd thought I'd relish the peace and quiet after the constant sound of gunfire, but I don't. I feel as if it's just a lull between the shelling and it's all going to start again. But it doesn't.'

'The whole country's silent – grieving, I suppose. There's hardly a family in the nation that hasn't been touched by the loss or injury of loved ones.'

'I expect there'll be memorials going up all over the country. People will need a focal point for their grief when they couldn't have a proper funeral. They've no sense of closure.'

'And even for those who do have proper graves out there, a lot of their relatives will never be able to visit and, of course, those who were never found – blown to bits or lost in the mud – well, there's nothing to commemorate them, is there?'

'There should be.'

Pips watched her brother as he sat gazing out of the window. She wondered if he were seeing the flat Lincolnshire farmland before him or the mud-filled trenches, littered with bodies, the barbed wire and the stretch of land between him and the enemy; no-man's-land. He was still as handsome as ever with a broad forehead and strong chin, brown hair and eyes. But those eyes that had once sparkled with ready laughter were now dull. Pips longed to be able to help him but, right now, she didn't know how any more than she knew what to do with her own life. For both of them, after being so needed, a chasm of uselessness lay before them.

There was silence between them until they

19

heard a scuffling outside the door and a piping voice shouting, 'Pips? Pips?'

Pips's face lit up and her boredom disappeared in a trice.

'I'm here, darling. I'm coming.' She ran down the length of the room and opened the door to sweep the eighteen-month-old little girl into her arms and swing her round. The child squealed with delight. Then, still carrying her, Pips waltzed back down the room to where Robert was sitting near a window.

'And here's Papa too.'

Alice followed her daughter into the room and came towards the three of them, smiling.

Lady's maid to Henrietta Maitland and Pips, Alice had accompanied her young mistress to the front to nurse the wounded. Secretly, she had loved her young master for years, but it had only been in the horror of the trenches and after his injury that Robert had come to rely on her totally and had realized that he had fallen in love with her. He could not, he'd declared, face the rest of his life without her. War had swept away the conventions of Victorian and Edwardian society and, although shocked at first, Henrietta had come to love her daughter-in-law. Alice, with her sweet nature, had trodden the rocky path between her former work colleagues and being a member of the family with tact and diplomacy. Now, she was loved by the family and servants alike, and there was no denying that Alice and Pips were the only ones who could handle Robert's dark moods. Even his father, Dr Edwin Maitland, didn't know how to reach out to him when the horrific memories of the war clouded Robert's mind. Strangely, it was the Dawson family – Len Dawson in particular – who still had difficulty accepting that his daughter had married 'out of her class', as he put it.

'It's *Aunty* Pips, Daisy,' Alice admonished oently new, but Pips only laughed.

'I don't care what she calls me,' Pips said.

'She has the pair of you twisted round her little finger.' Alice gave a mock sigh. 'So it's left to me to administer discipline.'

'Discipline? She doesn't need any,' Pips laughed. 'She's perfect.'

Alice pulled a face. 'Except when her cousin Luke comes to play with her. And Peggy's bringing him this morning.'

'Yes, he does try to boss her about a bit,' Pips agreed. 'I suppose, because he's two years older, he thinks he's in charge. But then she retaliates and stands up for herself, even though she's only little. I'll watch them, Alice, don't worry. I've nothing else to do.'

'What about me?' Robert pretended to sulk. 'What am I going to do?'

But Alice forestalled him. 'Your mother wants you downstairs in the parlour. She wants to go over the estate's accounts with you.'

Robert grimaced as he pulled himself up. 'Not my favourite pastime, but I suppose beggars can't be choosers. Like Pips, I can't pretend I've anything else to do.'

Brother and sister exchanged a glance. They were back to the start of their earlier conversation.

21

Two

Doddington lay approximately five miles west of Lincoln. It had one main street and lanes running from it into the surrounding countryside. The hall was a magnificent Elizabethan mansion with an estate of gardens, park and farmland, which provided employment for many of the villagers. Completed in 1600, the house was a symmetrical building, topped by three turrets with leaded cupolas. Its large front windows overlooked the long drive towards St Peter's church, where the whole village worshipped, were baptized, married and buried.

'Now, you play nicely with Daisy, Luke, and don't give Miss Pips any trouble,' Peggy Cooper instructed her son when she brought him to the small room that had been set aside as Daisy's playroom. Luke grinned up at Pips, his eyes sparkling with mischief.

Peggy Cooper had given birth to her son when the boy's father, Harold Dawson, Alice's brother, had been unable to come home from the front to marry her before he'd been killed on the Somme, leaving the young girl to bring up her child alone. But she was not entirely alone. Although disappointed at first, her family had stood by her and the Dawsons too had supported her. Peggy's mother, Bess, was a formidable woman, recognized by all as the village gossip, yet beneath her

22

ample bosom beat a heart of gold. Although she had not lost a close family member in the war, her daughter's unexpected pregnancy had, for a while, become the subject of village gossip. Eventually, though, her friends and neighbours had rallied round and supported the girl, following the example set by Henrietta Maitland.

'Peggy's not the first nor, sadly, will she be the last to bear an illegitimate child before this dreadful war is over,' Henrietta Maitland had remarked prophetically at the time and now the girl worked at the hall as a part-time housemaid. Peggy was small in stature, with a sweet face and fair hair, but her blue eyes were always sad. Even when she smiled, the sorrow never quite left them.

'My word, Peggy, that cheeky grin is just like his dad's,' Pips said now as she ruffled the boy's curly brown hair. 'Right, what are we going to play today? It's fine enough for us to be outside, if you like.'

'Robin Hood,' Luke answered promptly. 'I'm Robin Hood and Daisy's Little John.'

'And who am I, then?'

Luke gave the matter consideration before his grin widened even further as he said, 'Friar Tuck.'

Pips roared with laughter and patted her flat stomach. 'Not quite the right shape, but never mind. We'll pretend.' Then she held out a hand to each child. 'Come on, then. Let's go and find Sherwood Forest.'

'That's your orchard, Pips.'

'*Miss* Pips, Luke,' Peggy said.

'Right, then,' Pips said, 'you'd better show me where we live. Where's the Sheriff of Nottingham's castle?'

'The gate house.'

'My word, you have got it all worked out.'

'It's their favourite game, miss. Luke's even persuaded Sam to make him a bow and some arrows and a little one for Daisy – though she's not quite big enough to use it properly yet.'

'Right, off we go. We'll see you in the kitchen for lunch, Peggy.'

For all of them now, it was little Daisy who brightened the Maitlands' lives and who made them all hope and plan for the future, just as Luke carried the ambitions of the Dawson family. Losing three of his four sons to the war, Len Dawson now looked upon Luke as heir to his modest business as village carpenter, wheelwright and blacksmith. The fourth Dawson brother, William, was considered by Len as the black sheep, who had brought shame and disgrace to the family when he'd refused to enlist at the start of the war. Even now, Len would not have his name mentioned in the home. But William had gone with Alice, Pips and Robert to the front to act as a stretcher bearer, thought by many to be just as dangerous an occupation as being a soldier.

'I want to save lives, not take them,' William had persisted stubbornly. Serving with the flying ambulance corps for the duration of the war, William had fallen in love with a Belgian nurse and had made her country his home. Both Alice and Pips wrote to him regularly and received letters in return. Secretly, they would let William's mother, Norah, and his grandmother, always known as 'Ma', read the letters. But never a word was said to Len.

Later that afternoon, Pips walked down the lanes
from the hall towards the Dawsons' home, with
Daisy in the old wicker baby carriage that had
carried both Robert and Pips as infants. Luke
skipped along beside her. As they neared the cottage, they could see Ma Dawson sitting outside
the front door, smoking her clay pipe and watching the world go by. Even in winter she would
spend some time of each day out of doors. Only
rain or snow could keep Ma housebound. Somewhere in her mid-eighties, Ma Dawson was
considered the matriarch of the village.

'Nah then, Miss Pips. Brought that young
scallywag back to us, have you? Has he behaved
himself?' But she was smiling as she said it. Her
fondness for her great-grandson was obvious.

Today, Pips had brought Ma's great-grand-
daughter to visit her too. 'She's coming on.' Ma
nodded towards Daisy. 'Just like her mother, isn't
she?' Daisy favoured Alice in looks and colouring
with a sweet face, black hair and dark blue eyes.
Ma gave a toothless grin. 'But I reckon she's got
some of your spirit, Miss Pips. As she gets older,
we'll have two of you to deal with.'

Pips laughed. 'Oh, I'll keep an eye on her.'

Ma cackled with laughter. 'That's what I'm
afraid of. She'll be following you into mischief,
I'll be bound.'

Pips sat down beside the old lady and murmured, 'Is the coast clear?'

'Aye, he's at his work, but don't say owt in front
of the young 'un. Not any more. He's getting a

mite too sharp. Tell you what. We'll go inside. I'm sure you'd like a cuppa. Bring little Daisy. She's too young to understand owt yet. Luke can run up to his granddad. Luke,' she raised her voice, 'go and find Granddad.'

The boy scampered up the lane towards the workshop where they could hear Len at his anvil.

'How's Mr Dawson managing? With the work, I mean, now that he's on his own.'

Ma pulled herself stiffly to her feet. 'He's taken on Sam Nuttall, one of the few lads to come back to the village from the war. He's shaping up quite nicely. But it'll never be the same as if it'd been his own lads back home again and working alongside him.'

'Of course not,' Pips murmured. 'And how are you all – coping?' This time, her meaning was clear. Three of the Dawsons' four sons had been killed on the Somme within days of each another.

'Len doesn't say much. Being a man, he keeps it all to himself. But it's Norah I'm worried about. It's as if she thought they'd died just for the duration of the war, you know. And now she expects them to come back.'

'And what about you, Ma?' Pips asked softly.

The old lady was silent for a moment, before she said slowly, 'I've lived a long time, Miss Pips. I've seen a lot of folks die afore their time through illness or accident. And I've lived through wars too when families lost their menfolk. I don't mean you don't feel it any the less or that you get hardened to it, but you learn to deal with it.'

'But this is a bit different, isn't it? It feels as if a whole generation of men from all classes of society has been wiped out.'

'Aye, your age group, Miss Pips. From the highest in the land to the most humble, we're all united in sorrow. And it's going to be hard, especially for the young women of your age. Where are you young girls going to find husbands now?'

Pips smiled thinly but did not answer. It was a grievance she heard almost daily from her own family.

'Let's just hope that President Wilson was right when he said that it was "the war to end all wars",' Ma said. 'And we must make the world a safer place for Luke and Daisy and their generation.'

Pips sighed heavily. 'It's going to take a while. There's a lot of unrest and unemployment as the troops are coming home.' Then she grinned. 'But now women – at least some women – have been given the vote, things should get better. We might even get a woman prime minister one day.'

Ma cackled with laughter. 'I don't doubt it, but I don't expect I shall live to see that happen, Miss Pips.' Then she lowered her voice. Now that Luke was out of earshot, she asked, 'You've had a letter from William?'

Pips nodded as she lifted Daisy out of the baby carriage and they walked slowly round the side of the cottage and in through the back door. Passing through the scullery into the kitchen, Ma sat down in her favourite chair by the range, where the fire burned winter and summer.

On the mantelpiece above the range were two photographs. One was of Bernard and Roy together, both in uniform and grinning at the

27

camera, taken just before they had been posted abroad. The other was a grainy picture of Harold as a young boy. Both frames were edged with black cloth. 'We don't have a picture of Harold in his uniform,' Ma had told Pips once, 'seeing as how he ran away to join up because he was underage.'

'Oh Miss Pips, you've brought little Daisy to see us.' Norah Dawson greeted her, reaching out for her granddaughter. 'Now, I wonder if I can find a piece of your favourite cake.'

Daisy chuckled and wound her arms round Norah's neck. 'Cake – cake.'

The three women smiled.

'Miss Pips has had a letter, Norah.'

For a moment, a fleeting look of fear crossed Norah's face as she glanced at the door.

'It's all right, duck. I've sent Luke up to his granddad. Best he doesn't know about the letters now. He might tell Len. Innocently, of course,' she added swiftly.

Norah bit her lip nervously. 'But Len might bring him home. He won't want him in the way.'

Ma waved her hand dismissively. 'He'll sit him well out of the way at the workshop. Besides, Sam'll keep an eye on him. He's very good with the little lad.'

Norah relaxed a little, but still murmured, 'I'll make sure the back door's closed. That way, we'll hear if anyone comes in.'

When the three women were settled with a cup of tea and Daisy was sitting on Norah's lap munching a piece of sponge cake, Pips drew the letter out of her pocket and handed it across the table to Norah. She read it swiftly and then again more slowly, now reading it aloud to Ma:

'*Dear Miss Pips,*

I'm settling in very well here and there is a lot of work to keep me busy. Brigitta's grandparents, Mr and Mrs Dupont, treat me like a son and I'm slowly learning the language too, though they speak excellent English.

Now, I have some wonderful news. With Mr Dupont's kind permission, I proposed to Brigitta and she said "yes". We are to be married in the autumn – October – after harvest time, though what sort of harvest we'll manage, I don't know. Although we weren't too badly affected here, it will take a long time to get back to normal, never mind the poor folk who have lost almost everything. If you get the chance, please tell Mother and Ma that I am very happy. Of course, I wish they could be at my wedding, but I know that won't be possible.'

Norah paused for a moment as her voice cracked with emotion, but then she took in a deep breath and carried on, though her voice trembled a little.

'*I know they would love Brigitta and I hope you will tell them all about her. Thank you for the photographs of both Daisy and Luke. Perhaps one day I will be able to meet them. I hope they grow up to be good friends with each other.*'

Norah glanced up. 'You've sent him photographs, Miss Pips?'

Pips nodded. 'I hope you don't mind.'

'Of course not. It's kind of you to write to him. Please – when you write again, give him our love.' She gestured towards her mother-in-law and Ma nodded.

'And – and tell him,' Norah went on hesitantly, 'I see now that I was wrong. I got caught up in the patriotic fever of the time along with the boys and look what's happened. We've lost all three of them. Only William had any sense and we've lost him too, though it's some comfort to know he is happy. Of course,' she added swiftly and a little nervously, 'I'm only speaking for myself and Ma. Len will never change the way he feels.'

'Won't he?' Pips asked gently. 'Are you sure?'

Norah gave a deep sigh. 'Positive. He will never forgive William. Not as long as he lives, so there's no way we could go to the wedding, even if we could afford it.'

'When we get a definite date, I will take Alice and perhaps Daisy too. William should have some members of his family there.'

Norah's eyes filled with tears. 'Oh would you, Miss Pips? That would be wonderful.'

As Pips bade her farewell, Ma murmured, 'She's a remarkable young woman.'

'Yes, but I wonder what she will do with her life now. I fear she'll never find a husband.'

Ma snorted with contempt. 'We thought she'd found one in Dr Giles Kendall, didn't we? The young feller that Master Robert had met at medical school and who went out to the front with them. Though he turned out to be a wrong 'un, didn't he? Running off with another nurse out there. But don't you worry about Miss Pips, Norah. She'll find summat to do with her life, never fear.'

As Pips walked home again, there was a little more spring in her step. William's happy news had given her something to plan. She was determined that at least she and Alice would go to Belgium for his wedding in a few months' time. Daisy, too.

About Robert, she couldn't be sure.

Three

Early in September, Henrietta said, 'Basil and Rosemary are dining with us on Saturday night.'

Before the war, it had long been a tradition in Henrietta's family to have a dinner party every Saturday evening and she had continued the ritual. The war had interrupted that but now Henrietta felt it was time to try and get back to normal as much as possible.

Pips clapped her hands. 'That's wonderful. It seems ages since we saw them both.'

'Basil was so busy in his post as consultant to the War Office and even though it's over now, I expect there are still things he's needed for. Anyway, he's home at the moment, so they're coming.'

'I do like old Basil, he's a darling.'

A portly figure with a florid face, a grey handlebar moustache and a booming voice more suited to the parade ground than a genteel dining

31

room, the major was nevertheless always such fun. He was Pips's favourite dinner guest. His wife, Rosemary, was an elegant and charming woman and Henrietta's best friend. Together they had done a great deal of fundraising during the war, sending welcome gifts out to the troops, especially to the flying ambulance corps where Henrietta's family were serving.

On their arrival, the major held out his arms to Pips and kissed her soundly on both cheeks.

'My dear girl. How lovely to see you. I hope you're sitting next to me.'

She hugged him in return. 'Of course. Would I sit anywhere else?'

The talk was general during the first two courses, but over dessert, Pips asked, 'Are you still working as a consultant for the War Office, major?'

'At the moment, yes, but there is talk of the numbers employed being seriously reduced. It's to be expected, I suppose, now we're no longer at war.'

'But they'll still need to keep the department active, surely?'

'Sadly, I fear that will be the case, but I expect an old duffer like me will soon be put out to grass. They'll want a younger man – probably one who actually served at the front – to take over that sort of role in the future.' The major smiled. 'But more importantly, my dear, what are you going to do with yourself now?'

Pips wrinkled her forehead. 'To be honest with you, major, I'm not sure. But I must *do* something. My usefulness in life has suddenly gone from one extreme to the other.'

Major Fieldsend patted her hand. 'You'll find something, my dear, I'm sure.'

Pips leaned closer. 'The first thing I'm going to try to do is to take whoever I can persuade to go out to Belgium to William Dawson's wedding.'

He chuckled. 'Good luck with that.'

'I think I might need it, major,' Pips said with heartfelt irony.

'So, are we going, then, Alice?'

'Going, Pips? Going where?'

'To William and Brigitta's wedding. It's next month, you know, and time's getting on. We ought to be making arrangements. Booking the ferry and other transport. Sorting out passports for us all. That sort of thing. I'm not sure what we need for Daisy, but I'll find out.'

'Oh, I don't know if I should go. I don't like to leave Robert...'

'Surely, he'll come too?'

Alice bit her lip and shook her head. 'No, he says he can't face going back there. At least, not now. It's too soon.'

'Oh phooey.' Pips flapped her hand impatiently. 'I'll talk to him.'

'Try, by all means, Pips, but I don't think even you will be able to persuade him.'

Pips picked up her skirts and took the stairs two at a time to the Blue Drawing Room on the first floor. It was a long room, with windows looking out over the rear gardens. On either side of the white marble fireplace, ornate cabinets held Hen-

33

rietta's precious china and, in the centre of the room, a chess set was laid out, with a chair on either side; this was where Robert and Pips played against each other with fierce rivalry. Family portraits of Henrietta's ancestors adorned the walls and at the far end of the room there was a large embroidery frame. Alice was a clever needle-woman and now she had the task of repairing the tapestries that lined the walls of Henrietta and Edwin's bedroom. There were comfortable sofas and chairs dotted about the room, but Robert was sitting near the window, yet again gazing out of it into the far distance.

'Never mind sitting there,' Pips said as she came into the room. 'You should be out touring your estate.'

'The estate works perfectly well without my interference.'

'Oh for goodness' sake, Robert! It isn't interference. You're going to be in charge of all this one day...' She waved her hand to encompass the hall where they all lived, its grounds and the farmland beyond. 'Mother won't live for ever.'

Robert managed a smile. 'I wouldn't be too sure about that.'

With a sigh, Pips sat down beside him. 'You've got one of your black moods, haven't you?'

Listlessly, Robert said, 'I suppose there's no other way to describe it. Then I feel guilty because it's affecting all the family. Especially Alice.'

'Alice loves you devotedly, she'll never give up on you. Nor will we, but I have to admit I haven't her patience. I itch to tell you to "snap out of it", but I know it's not that simple. And poor Mother – she longs to help you but doesn't know how. And even Father – a doctor – doesn't know what to do.'

'I know,' Robert said gloomily. There was silence between them until Robert asked, 'You don't think it's affecting Daisy, do you? I couldn't bear to think that.'

'No, I don't. At the moment, she's too young to understand and, as she gets older, she'll just think her daddy can be a bit grumpy at times.' Pips leaned forward and added gently, 'If it would help to talk about it, you only have to–'

'No, no, I can't. None of us can.'

'Sam Nuttall does.'

Robert looked up at her. 'Does he? Does he really?'

'Yes, but he tells folks all the good bits – the camaraderie, playing football behind the lines, visiting Talbot House in Poperinghe on a few days' leave, cooking breakfast in the trenches, even about using the empty tins of Ticklers jam to make hand grenades.'

'But I bet he doesn't tell them about the soldiers sleeping in waterlogged trenches, with rats as big as cats nestling under their armpits. Or about the dreadful wounds men suffered, how they were left for hours, days sometimes, in no-man's-land where their wounds became infected and it was impossible to save them. Or about thousands being mown down by machine guns on the first day of the Somme as they climbed out of the trenches or being blown sky high by mines and their bodies never recovered.'

'No, he doesn't tell them all that, though I've no doubt he remembers it all,' Pips said gently, 'just as you do. Just as all of us who were out there remember. But he visits the Dawsons and tries to bring them some comfort to think that their three lads had some good times too.'

Slowly, Robert turned to look at her. 'How do you cope with it, Pips? You saw the same dreadful sights that I did.'

'But I didn't get wounded, did I?'

'You got shot in the back of the leg rescuing Mitch Hammond from his crashed aeroplane. You could have been killed.'

'So could you.'

'Yes, perhaps it would have been better...'

'Don't you dare say that, Robert Maitland. Don't you ever let those words pass your lips.'

He grinned sheepishly, feeling the black cloud of despair beginning to lift a little. Though he loved Alice fiercely and she was kind and patient and considerate, it was Pips who challenged him and could often bring him out of his despair like no one else could. And now there was Daisy too. His adorable little daughter could lift his spirits just by running into the room.

'So, why are you here? Did Alice ask you to come?'

'No, it's something else entirely,' Pips said, bending the truth a little. 'William gets married next month and I think we should go.'

'You and Alice, you mean?'

'And you and Daisy too.'

'Oh no, not me, Pips. I couldn't, but you could take Daisy. I'm sure her uncle William would love to meet her.'

'Could you really not try, Robert?'

He shook his head and said huskily, 'I wish I could – for Alice's sake – but it's too soon. I don't know if I'll ever be able to face it.'

'But you'd allow me to take Alice and Daisy?'

He chuckled, the last shreds of the dark veil falling away. 'Allow? Since when did you need anyone's approval to do something? Not since you were about ten years old, I think. I must ask Mother.'

'Don't you dare! She'd say five! Besides, you're wrong. I sought her approval before we went to the front.'

'Yes, you did, but if she hadn't given it, you'd have gone anyway, wouldn't you?'

'True,' Pips admitted as she stood up. 'And now I'm going to the Dawson household to see if Norah will come with us.'

Robert gave a bark of laughter. 'You've no chance there.'

'Oh Miss Pips, I couldn't possibly. Len would never forgive me.'

'Your own son's wedding, Mrs Dawson,' Pips said softly.

'Miss Pips,' Ma spoke up from her place by the range, 'don't upset her. You know she can't go. You take Alice and little Daisy and tell us all about it when you come back. When *he's* out the way, o' course. And you can take messages to William from me an' Norah. Take some photos too, if you can. You'll do that for us, won't you?'

'Of course I will, but–'

'There's no more to be said, Miss Pips.' Ma's tone was firm and brooked no more argument.

37

Four

'William – and Brigitta. How wonderful to see you both again,' Pips greeted them with open arms. 'And just look who I've brought with me.'

She turned aside to usher Alice and Daisy forward. 'This is your niece, William.'

'Hello, Daisy,' William said gently, not wanting to rush the child, but Daisy, as always, was beaming with delight and stretching out her arms to be taken into his.

'She's adorable,' Brigitta said, gazing at the little girl. Then she seemed to remember that she was their hostess and drew them into the warmth of the farmhouse to introduce her grandparents.

'It is so good of you to come for William,' Mrs Dupont said in perfect English, though she had a strong accent. 'You are very welcome. We have your rooms ready.'

'We don't want to impose upon you,' Pips began. 'We can easily stay in Pop.' She used the name that the soldiers had used for the nearby town of Poperinghe.

Mr Dupont chuckled. 'My wife would be offended if you did.'

'We certainly don't want to offend you, so thank you, madame, we'll be delighted to stay with you. And if there's anything we can do to help you...'

'The wedding is only two days away.' Mrs Dupont's eyes twinkled. She was small and round, but quick and lively in her movements. 'There is much to do.'

'Then let's get going. We're not frightened of hard work.'

The older woman's face sobered as she nodded and said seriously, 'I know that. I remember.' Then, shaking herself from bitter memories, she said, 'Sit down, sit down. Eat. It is all ready. What will the little one have?'

The 'little one' ate heartily everything that was put in front of her, but by the end of the meal, Daisy's eyelids were drooping with tiredness.

'I will take you upstairs,' Brigitta said to Alice. 'We have borrowed a cot from a neighbour. It is beside your bed. You don't mind sharing with Pips, do you?'

'Heavens, no,' she laughed. 'We shared a tent for long enough.'

'And I'll help you to clear away, madame,' Pips said.

'Thank you. I'd be glad of your help.'

The two women chatted as they washed the pots and Pips asked, gently, about life in this area of Belgium now.

'Do you know, Pips, that every building in Ypres has been destroyed? Even the water systems, drains, sewers – everything. Some of the more wealthy people have already sold their properties and have decided never to return. Others, who can afford to, will stay away until rebuilding is done, but for many...' she shrugged – 'it is their home, what else can they do but come back to this area?'

'So, is that what they're going to do? Rebuild

Ypres as it was?'

'Pips, we have a wonderful king in Albert. Do you know, he never left the country? All through the war he remained in the Allied-held part and, now, he is the prime mover in the reconstruction of devastated areas. Since earlier this year, he and his ministry have been providing prefabricated huts in a safe area to the north-west of Ypres as temporary living accommodation for those re-turning and, of course,' she laughed, 'for all the builders arriving here to find work. And they'll find it.'

'It will always be a place that people will want to visit. From abroad, I mean.' Pips placed the plates she had dried carefully in a pile. 'They will want to see where their loved ones are buried – or where they perished, even if they have no grave to visit.'

Mrs Dupont nodded. 'I've heard that there are a lot of visitors arriving already, seeking answers and some kind of comfort. But to answer your question, there is a lot of discussion about what should happen to Ypres.' She was silent for a moment before continuing. 'You've probably heard about the suggestion that it should be left in its ruined state as a constant memorial – and a reminder,' she added bitterly. Then, more strongly, she went on, 'But the locals – including my husband and me – do not agree with that and discussions are still going on. There's also been an idea to have what they're calling a "zone of silence" somewhere near the ruined cathedral, I believe. But we don't agree with that either. We think,' Mrs Dupont smiled wryly, 'though I don't expect anyone will take notice of us, that the town should be rebuilt as it was and that a memorial should be built on the outskirts large enough to hold all the names of the fallen in the Ypres Salient who have no known grave.'

'My goodness! That's ambitious. There'll be thousands of names.'

Solemnly, Mrs Dupont nodded. 'But it would mean such a lot to their families, don't you think, that their boys are not forgotten? Even though their resting place will probably never be known, at least their names will be remembered.'

'I agree. It's a marvellous idea. I hope it happens. But what about your farm? There must be a shortage of food.'

'We were lucky. We didn't get much shelling here so we are able to grow some crops again now, but many of the farmers returning to the areas that were badly shelled are having to salvage what they can.'

'And I suppose it will be quite dangerous. There'll still be unexploded bombs, ammunition and all sorts of equipment just left there. To say nothing of all the trenches which have scarred the land.'

Mrs Dupont sighed. 'It will be a huge task. But warehouses are being opened to feed the folks who are returning until the land can be used again.'

There was a pause before Pips asked quietly, 'And William? How is he settling in?'

Mrs Dupont's smile was warm and genuine. 'He's a lovely young man and we couldn't be happier that he is to marry Brigitta.' Her smile faded. 'He has told us all about his family and we are surprised at their – oh, what's the word in English?'

'Attitude?'

'That's it. We can't understand how anyone can disown their own son.' She shrugged. 'They should respect his decision. He was a very brave young man to do what he did.'

'I know. But his father was – is – very opinion-ated and the patriotic fervour in Britain at the outset of the war was unbelievable. His mother and grandmother have changed their opinion somewhat now, but they are ruled by Len.'

'It's very sad. For all of them, not just William.'

'He'll be happy here with Brigitta.'

'Oh yes. And he's been tending the local war graves, especially the nearest one – Lijssenthoek cemetery.'

'So, where are they to be married?'

'In Poperinghe. It'll be a very small wedding, but we hope to keep a few of our traditions.' Mrs Dupont smiled. 'Come, let me show you some-thing.'

They moved back into the living room where Mr Dupont was now dozing by the fire. Mrs Dupont beckoned Pips through into the front parlour and closed the door quietly behind them. From a small table she picked up an embroi-dered handkerchief. On it were four names.

'This was my mother's name' – she pointed to the first one – 'then mine, then my daughter's – Brigitta's mother – and now, Brigitta has just embroidered her own. The bride carries it on her wedding day and afterwards it is put back in its frame and hangs on the wall. It is a treasured family heirloom and all the more precious because we lost both Brigitta's parents when she was very young and we brought her up.'

'What a lovely idea, madame. What other traditions are there?'

'One is that as the bride walks up the aisle, she hands a single flower to her mother and they embrace.' For a moment, her face was sad. 'Of course, that will have to be me. As they leave after the ceremony, both bride and groom go to the groom's mother and hand her a flower. The bride and she embrace to show that the bride accepts her new mother-in-law–' Mrs Dupont paused for a moment before adding, 'We are sad that William's mother was unable to come, but I think it will be in order – if she is willing – for Alice to receive the flower. After all, she is representing William's family, is she not?'

Pips's voice was husky as she said, 'I am sure Alice will be delighted and honoured, madame.'

The wedding was a simple one, with few guests. Brigitta had one attendant, one of the nurses who had lodged with her grandparents during the war, and William had asked one of the farm labourers to be his best man. He and William also worked together tending the graves of the fallen and had become good friends.

From the front pew on the right-hand side of the church, Alice, Daisy and Pips watched the ceremony. The little girl, as if recognizing the solemn occasion demanded her very best behaviour, was quiet but enthralled by the proceedings, especially when William and Brigitta sat in two large chairs near the altar.

'They are King and Queen for a day,' Pips whispered to her. As the wedding Mass ended, William kissed his bride and then led her down the aisle. They paused beside Alice who, with tears of happiness in her eyes, accepted the flower Brigitta handed to her and kissed her new sister-in-law on both cheeks.

Outside the church, Pips unhooked the Brownie camera from her shoulder. 'Now, I must have some photographs...'

The families, now united, returned to the farmhouse where Pips and Alice had helped Mrs Dupont to prepare a wedding breakfast. The three of them had been up since dawn; only the bride had been excused from the work on her special day.

The eating and drinking and the merriment went on until it began to grow dark when, shyly, Brigitta went upstairs with Alice to the bedroom where she was to spend her wedding night with William. The farmhouse was a long building and the young couple had been given two rooms on the first floor at one end; a bedroom and a sitting room.

'I don't really believe in young couples living with their parents,' Mrs Dupont had said to Alice and Pips as she lifted her shoulders in a helpless shrug. 'But, with things as they are, we have no choice. At least at the far end of the house, they will have some privacy.'

Daisy had been in bed hours and so it was Pips who took a walk in the deepening dusk with

William. 'We shall go home tomorrow,' she told him, 'but I am so glad we came. It's wonderful to see you so happy, William.'

'I'm a lucky man,' he said huskily. 'I never thought someone like Brigitta would love me.'

'You underestimate yourself, William. She's a lucky girl too. You'll be a marvellous husband and perhaps, one day, a father too.'

'I hope so,' he said softly. There was a pause between them before he added, 'Please give my love to Mam and Ma, won't you?'

'I will,' she promised.

'And keep sending me pictures of Luke and Daisy.'

'Of course.'

He hesitated again and Pips prompted, 'Come on, William, what is it you want to say? I can see there's something.'

'It's about Ma, really. She must be a big age now.' He smiled wryly. 'If – when, I suppose – anything happens to her, will you let me know?'

'Yes, I will. Would you come home?'

He hesitated. 'If I thought he'd let me see her, then, yes, I would.' There was no need for William to explain to Pips that he was referring to his father.

As they turned to go back into the house, William took her hands into his. 'Thank you, Pips, for all you have done for me. I'll never forget you. You've always treated me with nothing but kindness and understanding.'

Once, working as a young man on the estate, William had idolized Pips, but now he was a grown man and he had found a true love that, to his amazement, was reciprocated. But Pips would always have a special place in his heart.

'Oh phooey,' Pips said and they both laughed at the expression she had used all the time he had known her.

'Give my best regards to Robert and to your parents.'

'I will, William.' She touched his cheek. 'Just be happy, that's all we want.'

Pips, Alice and Daisy left the following morning in a flurry of goodbyes and good wishes. Daisy was in tears, stretching out her arms to William and clinging to him until Alice had to prise her away from him.

'We'll come again,' Pips said. 'I promise.'

Mrs Dupont wiped the tears from her own eyes as she kissed Daisy and hugged Alice and Pips. 'You will always be welcome.'

As they journeyed home, Pips said, 'What a lovely family they are. He'll be happy, Alice.'

'I just wish...'

'I know.' Pips clasped her hand and murmured, 'I know.'

The families back home – the Maitlands and Ma and Norah Dawson – were eager to hear news of the wedding and when Pips's photographs were developed, they pored over them.

'She's such a pretty girl,' Norah murmured.

'She is. You'd love her, Mrs Dawson,' Pips told them when Len was safely at work. Luke too was out of the house. They made sure that the little boy overheard nothing about their trip.

'He's too young to understand. He wouldn't mean no harm,' Ma said. 'But he's a chatterbox, bless 'im. And if Len got to hear...'

'My only worry is that Daisy might say something to him,' Pips said. 'She's full of her trip to Belgium.'

Norah shrugged. 'Ah well, can't be helped. We'll just have to deal with whatever happens. We've not talked about you attending the wedding in front of Len, but I'd be surprised if he hasn't heard the gossip already. But all that matters to Ma and me is that William is happy.'

The three women exchanged glances. 'He said I was to be sure and give you his love. He is happy, Mrs Dawson, very happy, though of course he misses his family. He'll make a good life out there for himself.'

'I'm glad,' Norah whispered and Ma nodded. 'But I don't expect we'll ever see him again.'

'You never know,' Pips said. 'Life takes some unexpected turns sometimes.'

She took her leave, promising, 'I'll bring his letters to show you every time he writes.'

It was all Norah and Ma could hope for now.

Five

'Philippa,' Henrietta greeted her as she entered the hall, carrying Daisy. They had been out for a brisk walk. The little girl's cheeks were pink from the early November cold. Pips set her down and Daisy

47

ran towards the kitchen, shouting, 'Biccick'.

Fondly, both women watched her go. 'Cook will find her a hot drink and her favourite biscuits, I'm sure,' Henrietta said. She turned back to Pips. 'There's a letter arrived for you with a London postmark.'

Her mother was the only person who called her by her full name. Henrietta Maitland – grey haired, but still slim and energetic – held out an envelope to her daughter.

'Really? I wonder who it's from.' Pips took it and tore it open. 'Oh, it's Milly,' she said, scanning the letter to read the name at the end. 'How lovely.'

Henrietta frowned. 'Who – might I ask – is Milly?'

'Haven't I mentioned her before, Mother? I'm sorry. She's–'

'Come into the parlour. We're just about to have elevenses before your father sets off on his rounds. You can tell us both all about her.'

With a small smile, Pips followed her mother obediently.

When the three of them were sitting comfortably in the room known as the Brown Parlour, where the windows looked out over the rear gardens and the panelled walls were adorned with family portraits, Henrietta poured coffee and handed round biscuits.

'Now, dear, tell us about this Milly. Who is she and how do you know her?'

Edwin smiled at his daughter over his spectacles, his kindly eyes full of mischief. Ever since his marriage to Henrietta, who had inherited

48

Doddington Hall from her childless uncle, Edwin had been the local doctor. At almost sixty, he was still active and always wore a morning coat and a top hat on his rounds. His brightly coloured waistcoats were a cause for amusement amongst both young and old. He was greatly loved by all his patients and not one of them dared to think about the time when he might retire. They'd all believed that when that day came, Master Robert would be there to take up the reins, but now everyone wondered if that could ever be.

Pips took a deep breath. 'When Giles and Rose left the corps...' It seemed strange to speak of the young man whom she'd loved and thought she would marry. 'Dr Hazelwood sent out a husband-and-wife team, Matthew and Grace Wallis. He was a qualified surgeon and she an experienced nurse. Shortly afterwards, their niece, Milly Fortesque, arrived.' She smiled fondly at the memory. 'We all thought – including her uncle and aunt, I might add – that she was a scatterbrain, who would throw up her hands in horror at the first sight of blood. But she surprised us all. She was shocked, of course, at the injuries we all encountered, but she was so courageous and her lively spirit kept us all entertained. She was as much a tonic for the wounded as any medicine. She's a wonderful mimic. She really should be on the stage.'

Henrietta frowned. 'Is that what she is? An actress? Or a music hall star?'

'No, Mother,' Pips said patiently, but she could not resist a swift glance of amusement at her father. 'She's the daughter of a wealthy businessman of some description. And please, don't ask me what he does, because I don't know. All I *do* know is that he promised to set her up in a flat of her own in London when she returned from the war. And evidently' – she waved the letter she still held in her hand – 'he has kept his promise and she's asked me to go and stay with her.'

Henrietta's face brightened. 'Oh, she sounds a nice girl. Perhaps she could introduce you to her circle of friends. And will you be chaperoned?'

This time Pips dared not catch her father's glance for fear she would laugh and she had no wish to hurt her well-intentioned mother. One of Henrietta's priorities had always been to see Philippa happily married and raising a family in her role as a dutiful wife and devoted mother. She had scotched Pips's ambition to train as a doctor like Robert, but the war had disrupted her plans and now, with the loss of thousands upon thousands of young men, there was a scarcity of the type of husband Henrietta wanted for her daughter. But perhaps ... Henrietta refused to give up hope entirely.

'Mother dear, I'm sorry, but I think chaperones went out with the war.'

Henrietta sighed. 'So much is changing and not always for the better.' She paused and then asked, 'Shall you go?'

'Yes, I think so.'

'You sound doubtful,' her mother persisted.

'Well...'

'If you're worrying about Robert ... I freely acknowledge you and Alice are the only ones who can help him when he gets one of his dark moods.' Henrietta waved her hand helplessly. 'Even your father and I can't reach him. But Alice can manage him, I'm sure. You mustn't put your own life on hold, Philippa.'

Pips nodded but said nothing. It wasn't Robert who concerned her. It was her adorable niece, Daisy, whom she couldn't bear to leave.

A week later, Pips replied to Milly's letter.

I'd love to come to London, but may we leave it until the New Year?

Milly wrote again by return:

All right, though I'm sorry you won't be here for all the parties my friends and I hope to have around Christmas and New Year. It's high time we all had some fun. But be warned, Pips, if you don't come in the New Year, I shall come up there and kidnap you...

Pips showed the letters she'd received from Milly to her brother and to Alice.

'She sounds like a bundle of fun,' Alice said. She and Robert had left the front before the young woman's arrival. 'You should go, Pips.'

'I will, but I want to be here for Christmas. I've got such a lovely surprise lined up for Daisy...'

'Let's hope this year will be better than last year,' Robert said. 'No one felt like celebrating, not even families who hadn't actually lost anyone in the war.'

'Sadly, there weren't many of those,' Pips said. 'But at least the soldiers should be home this year.

Last year there were so many who hadn't been demobbed in time. They were getting very disillusioned and fearful that there'd be no employment for them when they did finally get home. It was appalling after all they'd been through.'

Robert rattled his newspaper. 'Have you read this in the paper? The King is to host an evening "Banquet in Honour of The President of the French Republic" on the tenth of November followed by a remembrance event to be held in the grounds of Buckingham Palace the next morning. And he – the King, I mean – has written a letter to all his peoples of the Empire suggesting that there should be some sort of commemoration to honour those who gave their lives. Listen, I'll read an extract:

'To afford an opportunity for the universal expression of this feeling it is my desire and hope that at the hour when the Armistice came into force – the eleventh hour of the eleventh day of the eleventh month – there may be for the brief space of two minutes a complete suspension of all our normal activities. During that time, except in the rare cases where this may be impracticable, all work, all sound, and all locomotion should cease, so that in perfect stillness the thoughts of everyone may be concentrated on reverent remembrance of the glorious dead.'

Robert looked up. 'What d'you think?'
'I think it's a wonderful idea.'
'Lutyens built a temporary wooden-and-plaster cenotaph for the Peace Day Parade in July, but there's been such a call for something more

permanent that there's going to be one built in Portland stone on Whitehall. It'll be the country's official national war memorial.'

'I must certainly see that,' Pips murmured. 'And I expect there'll hardly be a town or village throughout the land where there *won't* be some sort of war memorial erected. I'll ask Mother what's going to happen here. No doubt she'll have given the vicar his instructions for the eleventh of November.'

Brother and sister exchanged an amused glance.

Doddington village church, set close to the hall, was packed on the morning of 11 November.

'I think the whole village is here,' Robert whispered from the Maitlands' family pew. 'Even Len Dawson's sitting at the back.'

'Really?' Pips craned her neck, but over the sea of heads, she couldn't pick him out.

Robert had been reluctant to attend. He rarely mixed with the villagers now and dreaded being the focus of their pitying glances, but even he couldn't find a convincing excuse for his absence on such an occasion.

As the hour of eleven stuck, the whole congregation stood, bowed their heads and fell silent. After two minutes, the vicar mounted the steps into his pulpit and looked out across the upturned faces. He couldn't remember ever seeing his church so full and, for a moment, he felt as if his words would be inadequate. But he caught Henrietta's steely gaze and knew he must continue. He cleared his throat.

'Dear Friends,' he began, 'we meet today to

remember all those whom we lost in the recent terrible conflict. We give thanks for those who returned, perhaps maimed in body or spirit...' deliberately, he kept his gaze away from Robert, 'but who, nevertheless, did come back. As a community, we should do our best to help them in any way we can to put the horrors behind them and to build a new life, whatever that might be...'

Outside the church, as the villagers stood in small groups chatting, Robert tried to hurry away, with Alice and Pips walking on either side of him, but Sam Nuttall stepped into his path and, tactfully, held out his left hand to shake Robert's.

'Master Robert, it's good to see you. When can we hope to see you back in harness alongside your father?'

Automatically, Robert took the man's outstretched hand, but hesitated over his answer. 'Um – I don't think that's going to be possible, Sam, do you?'

The young man feigned a puzzled frown. He – like everyone else there – had heard of Robert's reluctance to try to take up his interrupted career once more.

'Why ever not? Ya can hold a stethoscope in your left hand, can't you?'

Robert gave a sarcastic laugh. 'I suppose so, but what about examining folk? Have you any bright ideas as to how I could do that?'

'Actually, I have. Your dad's getting on a bit now and although he's still as sprightly as ever at the moment, he can't go on indefinitely. Folks round here were safe in the knowledge that you were going to take over from him. But now...' He left the words hanging for a moment, letting them sink into Robert's mind and take root. 'You see,' Sam went on boldly, 'we don't want a stranger taking over the practice entirely, but I don't think we'd mind if you had a young doctor to assist you.'

Robert stared at him and Alice and Pips glanced at one another.

'Now why,' Pips murmured, 'did we never think of that?'

'It's a brilliant idea.' Over dinner that evening, Pips relayed Sam's idea to Edwin and Henrietta. 'Don't you think so, Father?'

'It would be one solution, I suppose, but it depends on what Robert thinks.'

'Oh phooey,' Pips said, and, quoting from Shakespeare, added, '"He thinks too much; such men are dangerous".'

Robert laughed. 'Ah, but I haven't got the "lean and hungry look".'

'That's because you sit around too much doing nothing,' Pips shot back, but it was said with affection and the whole family laughed. 'Robert, honestly, you ought to do something. Mother's not ready to hand over the reins of the estate quite yet and besides, I don't think you'll ever be ready to take them, will you?'

Robert grimaced. 'It's not what I'd planned. Oh, I know I'm the heir and all that, but I'm hoping that Mother will stick around until Daisy is old enough to take over.' He grinned. 'That'd be just perfect for me.'

'In that case, then,' Henrietta said spiritedly,

'you ought to find something else to occupy you.'

Robert turned to his wife. 'Alice, darling, what do you think?'

Alice smiled into his eyes and said softly, 'I think it's an excellent idea, but you must be the one to decide. We'll all support you, you know that.'

'Actually, Pips is right,' Edwin said quietly. 'Give it some serious thought, Robert. I'm not ready to hang up my stethoscope just yet, but if you were to ease your way back into the work, when I do begin to feel I ought to take things easier, we could get a young doctor who could assist you.'

'Preferably an unmarried one,' Henrietta murmured and glanced archly at Pips, but even she, this time, was joking.

Pips caught her eye and laughed. 'You never know, Mother. You just never know.'

Six

'Mr Dawson.' Pips stood in the wheelwright's workshop as Len packed up his tools for the day. He glanced up and glowered at her.

'What d'you want?'

'I wondered if I might have a word with you?'

'What about?'

'Your two grandchildren.'

'What about 'em?'

'They're very close. They play together a lot.'

He regarded her sullenly. 'No harm in that, is there?' His lip curled. 'Unless, of course, you

56

think young Luke isn't fit company for the heir to the estate.'

Pips sighed and then, determined not to let him get the better of her, she put her hands on her hips. 'Oh for goodness' sake, Len Dawson, stop being so prickly. They play nicely together and Luke is so caring and protective of little Daisy. We're very happy for them both to spend time with each other.'

'So – what's the problem?'

'There isn't one really. I just wanted your opinion about something. I would like to get a tricycle for Daisy from Father Christmas and wondered if you would be happy for me to get one for Luke too. I presume he still believes in Father Christmas?'

For a brief moment, Len's face softened and Pips caught a glimpse of what the man could be like if only he would let go of his bitterness and resentment against the world.

'Aye, he does, but it's his mam you should be talking to, Miss Pips, not me. You should ask her permission.'

Gently, Pips said, 'But you're the man in his life, Mr Dawson.'

Len nodded. 'Aye, sadly I am.' He paused and then added, 'The only thing I would say is that I wouldn't want him to get the idea that Father Christmas is – well – wealthy. We won't always be able to give him such a grand present in the future.'

'I will always treat them equally, Mr Dawson. I can't speak for the rest of my family, but knowing them as I do, I think they will feel the same. They are first cousins, after all.'

'Aye well, as you know, I didn't hold with Alice marrying above 'ersen.'

'She's a wonderful wife to my brother,' Pips said softly. 'I don't know how he would manage without her.'

Len shrugged and seemed to be struggling with a decision. 'I'll show you summat.' He beckoned her. 'Come through to the back.'

He led her out of the workshop, across a small backyard and into a shed. He removed a tarpaulin to reveal two identical wooden go-carts. 'I made 'em one each.' He glanced at Pips and for the first time in a long time, Len Dawson smiled. It made him look ten years younger. 'Like you, Miss Pips, I wanted to treat them both the same. They're both my grandchildren even if one was born on the wrong side of the blanket and the other's the daughter of a toff.'

'They're wonderful,' Pips said, inspecting his handiwork. 'What fun they'll have with those.'

'Not as grand as a tricycle,' he murmured.

'They're better. You've made them yourself – with love.'

Len cleared his throat. 'Aye, well. 'Tis the least I could do. But don't you go telling Norah and Ma. I want it to be a surprise on Christmas morning.'

'Of course I won't, but maybe I'd better think of something else to get them.'

'No, no. A tricycle each'd be grand. Kids can't have too many toys.'

As Pips walked back to the hall, she smiled inwardly. Were two little children beginning to thaw Len's cold heart?

'Has Jake sorted out a Christmas tree yet, Mother?'

Jake Goodall had worked at the hall for several years. At the age of about twelve, he'd run away from a boys' home for orphans, where he'd been raised, to look for work. Finding him sleeping rough, Henrietta had taken pity on him and had employed him. He had been too young to volunteer during the war, besides which he would never leave Henrietta, who had his undying and lifelong devotion. He was still small for his age, but wiry and deceptively strong.

'Yes, he's bringing it into the hall this afternoon. I was thinking you might like to decorate it with Daisy.'

'And Luke? She'll want Luke to help.'

'Of course.'

'I'll ask Peggy to tell him to come to the hall tomorrow afternoon. We'll do it then.'

'I'll ask Wainwright to get the decorations ready for you. We'll all come and watch.'

The whole family gathered in the Great Hall the following afternoon to watch the tree being decorated and to offer unwanted advice as to where each decoration should go. The room, where the family always dined, was long with antique oak chests, tables and chairs. Mahogany china cabinets held valuable heirlooms and the front windows looked out over the driveway, down to the gatehouse and beyond. To the left stood the village church.

'Luke and Daisy, you do the lower branches whilst I climb up the steps to reach the top.'

'Oh, do be careful, Philippa,' Henrietta said worriedly. 'Shouldn't you let Jake do that?'

'I'm fine, Mother. Alice, will you hold the steps?'

The two children ran around the tree deciding where to hang each shining bauble.

'You do the branches at the very bottom, Dais,' Luke instructed. 'I can reach a bit higher.'

'I can do it.'

Luke – two years older – grinned. He was at least six inches taller than his cousin, but the kindly boy said, ''Course you can, Dais. But if you can't, then I'll lift you up.'

'Are we putting candles on, Mother?'

Henrietta shook her head. 'Too dangerous. It sparkles quite enough with all the baubles.'

Pips put the finishing touch on the topmost branch – the fairy – and climbed down. 'Well, if we ever get electricity at the hall, Mother, I shall insist we have lights on the tree.'

'If it's safe, then, yes, I agree.'

'You've done a wonderful job, children,' Edwin said. 'You too, Pips. Now I feel as if Christmas is really here.'

'My birfday tomorrow,' Daisy said. 'Cake.'

'And it's my birthday three days later,' Luke said. 'Me gran's making me a cake and said I could ask if Daisy can come to tea with us on Thursday. Would that be all right, Aunty Alice?'

'Of course. And you must come to Daisy's birthday tea tomorrow, Luke. Pips, if you're walking back home with Luke, please would you ask Mam if she and Ma would like to come too. And Dad too, if he'd come. They'd all be very welcome. Peggy has already said she'll stay on after her normal hours and help.'

Luke whispered something to Daisy and at once she said, 'Can Sam come?'

For a moment, Alice looked startled and turned towards Henrietta for approval, but the older woman merely smiled and nodded. 'Of course he may. Are there any other friends you'd like to invite? Other children from the village, perhaps?'

Luke shook his head. 'No, ma'am. Just Sam.'

Henrietta smiled and ruffled his hair. 'Very well, then. But I think it's high time you called me something a little less formal than Mrs Maitland or ma'am. How about Aunty Hetty?'

The boy looked up at her. 'Are you my aunty?'

'Not really, but we are connected...' She waved her hand towards Alice. 'Your real aunty is my daughter-in-law, but "aunty" is a courtesy title given to older ladies.'

He glanced at Pips. 'Like I call you "Aunty Pips"?'

Pips nodded.

He turned back to Henrietta, grinning. 'Thank you – *Aunty Hetty* – I'd like that.'

Robert chuckled. 'You're very privileged, Luke. Only my father ever calls her "Hetty".'

Henrietta brushed it aside saying, 'I just think Henrietta is such a mouthful. Besides, I prefer Hetty.'

Later, Henrietta asked, 'Why do you think Luke wants Sam to come to Daisy's party?'

Alice volunteered an answer. 'Luke spends a lot of time at my father's workshop and I think Sam

61

is very good with him. Besides, Sam was good friends with Harold. He talks to the boy about his father when it's perhaps too painful for my parents and Ma.'

During the month of December, 1919, the Maitlands and the Dawsons began to try to put the horror of the war and their terrible loss behind them. Not that they ceased to remember or to think about their loved ones, but all of them tried to move on.

The birthday parties of the two young cousins seemed to set the tone for Christmas and by the day itself, the children's excitement had reached fever pitch. Pips and Alice took Luke's tricycle down to the Coopers' cottage late at night after they knew Luke would be in bed.

'I hope he's asleep.'

'You must be joking. I used to stay awake deliberately to see if I could see Father Christmas.'

Alice chuckled. 'And did you?'

'Not once, but years later, my father told me that he once had to sit up until almost two o'clock in the morning before he could fill the stocking at the end of my bed.'

Two burly shadows loomed up in the darkness. 'Hello, Miss Pips – Alice.'

'Oh, Sam, it's you – and me dad. You startled us. Whatever are you doing sneaking about at this time of night?'

'Same as you, I expect. Helping Mr Dawson play Father Christmas, though we've left the reindeer at the end of the lane.'

As the clouds drifted away from the moon for a

moment, they could see that both Len and Sam were each carrying a very bulky parcel.

'Whatever have you got there, Dad?'

'It's a go-cart. I've made one for Luke and one for Daisy too. You didn't tell Alice then, Miss Pips.'

'Heavens, no. The secrecy's all part of the fun, isn't it?'

'We've brought Luke's tricycle. Do you think he'll be asleep yet?'

'I shouldn't think so,' Sam said. 'But we've instructions from Peggy to leave the go-cart in the shed at the back. We can leave the tricycle there too. Does Peggy know about it?'

'No.'

'Then I'll tell her tomorrow, though I think she might guess where it's come from.'

Like thieves in the night, but ones who were leaving gifts, not stealing them, the four left the presents in the Coopers' back garden shed and crept away. Further up the lane, Sam said, 'I'll bring Daisy's go-cart to the hall, Alice. I was going to anyway, and was going to go round the back to find Jake.'

'That's probably the best idea, because that little madam will still be awake,' Alice said with feeling.

'If she's anything like me,' Pips said airily. 'Then she certainly will be.'

Without the terrible memories of their elders, the two children were wild with excitement on Christmas morning and thrilled to find that they had the same main presents as each other.

The weather was fine, but frosty, so Pips was able to spend a happy Christmas morning teaching both children how to ride their tricycles and go-carts.

'Come on, Robert, you're coming outside with me. Mother and Alice are supervising the Christmas luncheon preparations in the Great Hall. They don't need either of us.'

Soon the grounds around the hall were filled with shrieks of laugher with Pips chasing after the two youngsters, whilst Robert watched, laughing at their antics.

'How did Father Christmas know to bring us both the same presents?' Luke asked.

'Because he's very clever. He'll know you and Daisy are friends and play together. He would want to treat you both the same.'

'Oh.' The four-year-old boy was serious for a moment. 'Me granddad ses Daisy prob'ly won't always be my friend.'

'Why's that, Luke?' Pips asked gently.

'He says she's – above us. We're only a working-class family and one day Daisy might be the owner of the hall.'

Pips hesitated, unsure for once what to say to the little boy. She didn't want to say anything against his grandfather, yet she was silently furious with Len Dawson and his bigoted beliefs.

Feigning deliberate casualness, she said, 'Well, our families are connected, aren't they? You're Daisy's cousin, aren't you?'

'Am I?'

For one awful moment, Pips wondered if she had put her foot right in it. Maybe no one had ever explained the exact relationship to him. Then, to her relief, Luke himself said, 'Oh yes, me mam told me that Harold Dawson was me dad, but he got killed.'

'Yes, that's right and Alice – Daisy's mam – was your dad's sister, so you see, we're family.'

'So, you don't think that one day, when she grows up, Daisy won't want to be friends with me any more?'

Mentally crossing her fingers, Pips said brightly, 'Heavens, no!'

She could only hope that her declaration would prove to be true.

'It's all about the children now, isn't it?' Robert said over dinner on New Year's Eve. Christmas had been a happy time for the Maitlands and even the Dawson and Cooper families, concentrating their energies on Luke, had managed to celebrate rather than be overwhelmed with grief as they had been the previous year. Time would never heal the raw wound of their loss, but they were all learning to cope.

Even Robert's moods seemed to have lifted. 'And you're all right,' he went on, 'I should get up off my backside and do something useful. I don't want Daisy growing up thinking she had an indolent father.'

'Such language, Robert,' Henrietta admonished softly.

'I apologize, Mother. That's what the trenches do for you. Niceties and drawing-room language didn't seem to matter out there. So, Father,' he turned to Edwin, 'a new year – a new start. Perhaps I should begin to help you in the practice, if only a little. What do you suggest we do?'

'We'll open up the room we had fitted out as your surgery before the war and then–'

'It's all ready,' Alice said quietly. 'Sarah and I have been cleaning and dusting it regularly.'

Robert laughed. 'Looks like I've no escape, then.'

Edwin smiled at his daughter-in-law over the top of his glasses. What a blessing she was to the family. 'Well, then, I suggest you ease yourself in gradually. Take on a few patients and see how it goes. I will, of course, continue to carry out any necessary physical examinations that are difficult for you.'

'All right. I'll start on Monday. What about home visits?'

'Jake has learned to drive my car. He could take you.'

And so it was all arranged and Robert at last had something to look forward to each day. There were still times when the memories crowded in and a black mood descended but as time had gone on, these occasions became more infrequent.

And the locals, playing their part, flocked to his surgeries.

Seven

An unusually mild, but wet, winter turned into spring and with it, in the middle of April, came a surprise visitor.

'Dahlings!'

Shown into the Great Hall where the family were sitting down to dinner, the visitor flung her arms wide as if to embrace them all. Edwin and Robert politely rose to their feet, though they had no idea who she was.

'Good Heavens!' Pips smiled as she, too, rose and hurried down the long room. 'Milly!'

The two young women embraced each other affectionately.

'I got your letter saying you would come in the New Year, but when I heard no more I thought, Well, "if the mountain won't come to Muhammad..."' Golden curls framed her pretty face and her bright blue eyes twinkled with merriment and mischief.

Pips turned and, with her arm still around Milly's waist, drew her forward. 'Now, I must introduce you to everyone. I'm forgetting that you don't know anyone else here.' But before introductions could be made, Henrietta, ever the thoughtful hostess, rose.

'You are very welcome, Miss – er...'

'Fortesque – but *please* call me Milly.' She went towards the older woman with her hands outstretched. 'I must apologize for arriving unannounced and so late too. Mummy would scold me for being so impolite, but I just couldn't wait a moment longer to see Pips.' She turned and beamed at Pips. 'I *have* missed you.'

A small smile twitched at the corner of Henrietta's mouth. Normally, she would have been appalled at such thoughtless behaviour but Pips had not exaggerated when she had told them that Milly was 'absolutely adorable'. To her surprise,

Henrietta found herself saying, 'I will see Cook. Please join us. We have only just started.'

'Oh I couldn't impose, really...'

'I insist. You haven't eaten, I presume?'

'Well, no, but...' Now Milly was flustered and her cheeks turned pink.

'It's all right, Milly dear,' Pips said, giving the girl's waist a little squeeze. 'Mother wouldn't offer if she didn't mean it.'

'And you must stay with us,' Henrietta went on. 'Or have you already booked into a hotel in Lincoln?'

'No, no, I just thought I could find somewhere later...' Her voice trailed away and now she looked acutely embarrassed. 'I don't want to be a nuisance.'

Edwin now moved from his place and held out his hand. 'I am Edwin Maitland. Pips, take Milly upstairs. Perhaps she would like to freshen up first and then you must come and sit near me. You are most welcome, my dear.'

Milly was fast recovering her composure. She clasped Edwin's outstretched hand in both of her own. 'You must be Pips's father. She said what a darling man you are.'

Edwin chuckled whilst behind him Henrietta said drily, 'Well, I won't ask you what she said about me.'

The whole family laughed as Henrietta left the room to seek out Cook to provide another meal for their unexpected guest.

As Pips ushered her upstairs to a guest bedroom, Milly said, 'Your mother's very kind, but I don't want to impose and put her to any trouble.'

'We always keep a guest room ready, Milly. Please don't give it another thought. Now–'

'Oh, I forgot – the taxi. He's still waiting outside. I must go down...'

'Don't worry. I'll see to that. You freshen up and then come down.'

'You're all so sweet,' Milly murmured.

Pips ran back down the wide staircase. 'Father, have you any money handy? The taxi Milly arrived in is still–'

'Wainwright,' Edwin addressed the butler, who, as usual, was still hovering, 'perhaps you could...'

'It's all right, Wainwright,' Robert said, getting up again. 'I'll take care of it.'

When he'd paid the taxi and Henrietta had come back to say that a meal for Milly would be served shortly, the girl herself arrived back in the room and took her place near Edwin, who sat at one end of the long table.

'Now, my dear, I must make the introductions.' He gestured towards Henrietta sitting at the opposite end of the table. 'You've probably guessed that this is my wife. The handsome young man to her left is our son, Robert, and on his left is his wife, Alice. The only person missing is tucked up in bed and, I hope, fast asleep. That's Robert and Alice's daughter, Daisy, on whom, I may say, the whole family dotes.'

'I know,' Milly said candidly. 'Pips's letters are full of news about her.'

Pips pulled a face. 'Oh dear. Do I bore you? I do go on about her a bit, I suppose.'

'Not at all. She sounds adorable. I can't wait to meet her and it's most *awfully* kind of you to ask me to stay, Mrs Maitland.'

Henrietta smiled and inclined her head in acknowledgement.

'How are things in London, Milly?' Pips asked. 'You got your flat, then?'

'Oh yes, Daddy was as good as his word. It's in Hampstead and I can have all my friends round and throw wild parties whenever I want.'

'And do you?' Robert smiled across the table at her as he picked up his fork in his left hand and began to eat. Milly's clear blue eyes rested on him for a moment but then she glanced away as if she was afraid he might read her sympathy in them. The wounded, who had returned from the war, didn't want pity, she knew that.

'Do I – what?'

'Throw wild parties.'

'Oh yes,' she replied swiftly – a little too quickly, Pips thought. 'All the time. And then there's the theatre and opera and the ballet. Oh, there's so much to *do* there. That's why I've come to see you.'

Robert chuckled. 'To get away from it all for a while.'

Milly's eyes were wide with surprise. 'Heavens, no! I want Pips to come and stay with me and have lots of fun too.'

There was silence around the table. Milly gazed at them in turn. 'Oh dear, have I put my foot in it? I didn't mean to imply...'

Edwin and Robert spoke at once.

'Of course you haven't, my dear.'

'You're right. Pips is always saying how bored she is now.'

'Life is very different back home, isn't it?' Milly said, her face suddenly serious. 'After all we went through. And you three...' she nodded towards Alice to include her – 'were there so much longer than I was. I don't know how you coped.'

'You were wonderful, Milly,' Pips said. 'Even though you hadn't much nursing experience, you were like a ray of sunshine and a tonic for all of us when you arrived. We'd all got rather jaded by then. You were rather thrown in at the deep end, but the soldiers loved you.'

'It'd do her the world of good to stay with you for a while, Milly,' Robert said quietly. 'What d'you say, Pips?'

Pips laughed. 'I'll start packing. I'd love to come, Milly. But first, stay a day or two with us and I'll introduce you to the countryside.'

'That'd be lovely. Even though I'm a city girl at heart, I do love the countryside. But I must be getting back home soon and I do so want to take you to Brooklands.'

Robert glanced up. 'The racing circuit? But I thought it had been closed during the war.'

'As soon as war broke out the owner handed it over to the Government and the RFC moved in and the flying schools were taken over for military training. Racing virtually stopped, though there was at least one meeting where all the competitors took part wearing their uniforms.' She giggled. 'It was called the All-Khaki Meeting, but they did allow the public in to see that.' She paused and then, seeming a little hesitant, went on, 'Daddy's – um – with Vickers and, amongst others, they had a flying school there before the war.'

'Vickers? I thought they were armaments and aircraft manufacturers?' Robert asked.

'They are. Before the war they manufactured at a factory in Kent, but they tested their aircraft at Brooklands. In 1915, they started actually making aircraft at Brooklands too in what used to be the Itala factory there. And now, it's opening up again as a racetrack and a meeting is being planned for the last week in May. You'll love it, Pips.'

Robert chuckled. 'I'd be careful, if I were you. She'll be wanting to take part.'

'Perhaps she can,' Milly said airily. 'The Brooklands Automobile Racing Club don't allow women drivers, but some of the smaller private clubs, who use the circuit, do.' She smiled coyly. 'My friend Paul runs a club there – The Whittaker Racing Club – and he allows women to race.'

At the far end of the table, Henrietta cast her glance to the ceiling.

'It's so *quiet*,' Milly said as Pips showed her the croquet lawn, the orchards and all the well-kept gardens. 'But it's lovely,' she added hastily. 'I'm surprised you haven't got soldiers recuperating here.'

'We did have for a while towards the end of the war and for a short time afterwards. But, of course, once they were well enough they went home to their families.'

They walked in silence across the croquet lawn and beneath the trees in the orchard.

'Your brother – Robert – is he coping?'

Pips linked her arm through Milly's. 'That's one of the reasons I wanted to bring you out here, so that we can talk without being overheard.'

Milly laughed. 'And there I was thinking I was being given a privileged guided tour.'

'Of course you are. That as well.'

There was a pause before Milly prompted, 'Go on.'

'Robert's the reason I've held off coming to see you in London. Daisy, too, if I'm honest. I wouldn't want you to think I don't want to come, because I'd love to. It's just that it's been very difficult.'

'Tell me.'

'Over Christmas and New Year we all encouraged him to join Father again in the practice. We believed he could still treat patients even if he couldn't do some of the physical examinations.'

'But your father would do that.'

'Exactly.'

'So?'

'He did make a start in early January and we all thought he was doing so well for a couple of weeks. But he still gets black moods sometimes and during the third week he took a day off. Then in the next week it was two days and so on, until he decided that he couldn't face it any longer. So now, he's back sitting in the drawing room upstairs most of the day, just staring out of the window at God knows what.'

'Seeing dreadful pictures from the past, I expect,' Milly murmured. 'It's what we're all trying to blot out, Pips, but we each have a different way of dealing with it.'

'But he's not dealing with it, is he, if he just sits there wallowing in it?'

73

'Is there no one who can help him?'

'I don't want to sound conceited, but I can usually drag him out of his moods and so can Alice, though she has a different way of handling him. She's so calm and gentle and loves him devotedly. He couldn't have chosen a better wife – even though our mother didn't approve at first.'

'Really? Why not?'

Pips laughed wryly and explained what had happened before Milly had arrived at the front.

'But I remember William. He was still there, wasn't he? He was so brave working as a stretcher bearer. He was lovely. Is he back home? Can I see him again?'

Pips shook her head. 'He stayed in Belgium. He's married Brigitta.'

'Oh, the nurse.' Milly clapped her hands. 'I'm thrilled to hear that. But how did Robert and Alice come to marry, especially if your parents didn't approve?'

'It was only Mother. She has rather grandiose ideas sometimes – about what is proper, I mean.'

'She's like my Granny Fortesque. She can't accept how the world is changing either. It's hard for them, but I think your mother is a dear. My granny would have thrown up her hands in horror if a flighty young piece had arrived unheralded and without a proper invitation on her doorstep as the family were sitting down to dinner. But your mother never turned a hair and made me feel welcome. But you still haven't answered my question about Robert and Alice.'

'Alice had loved him for years, but Robert only realized his feelings for her out in Belgium. When he was wounded, she brought him back home and – he just refused to let her leave his side ever again.'

'How romantic,' Milly breathed. They walked on in silence for a while until Milly asked, 'So, what *is* he going to do? He's not the sort of person to be happy doing nothing, is he? Not for ever.'

Despite her frivolous outward appearance, Pips thought, Milly could be remarkably perceptive.

'Mother's training him to take over the running of Doddington Hall and its estate, but his heart's never been in it. He just says he'll keep things ticking over until Daisy's old enough to take over.'

'Mm. It must be hard on all of you. D'you think a trip to London would help him? He'd be most welcome to stay with me. And Alice, too, of course.'

Pips shook her head. 'It's sweet of you to offer but just now he won't leave home. He won't even go into Lincoln. We even had a job to persuade him to come to church on Remembrance Day last November.'

'But at least you're going to come, aren't you? If you don't, I'll kidnap you like I threatened, but this afternoon you must take me into Lincoln and show me your wonderful city. By the way, are we anywhere near a little place called Ashford-in-the-Water?'

'In Derbyshire?'

'I think so.'

'It's about sixty miles away by road, I think. Why?'

'Oh, just a thought. Mummy has a distant relative who lives there, Martha somebody, and they say she has a daughter who looks just like me. I just thought it would be fun to see her and find out if it's true.'

'We could go, if you like. I'm sure Father would let me borrow the car. Or Jake could take us.'

But Milly shook her head. 'No, no, it's a long way. And besides, we might not be welcome.' She laughed. 'Mummy says Martha is rather a tartar.'

'Well, if you ever want to go, let me know and we'll take a trip there.'

Two days later, the two young women left Doddington to journey to London. Pips had to hold back the tears when she kissed Daisy 'goodbye'.

'We'll miss you, Sis.' Robert hugged her. 'And I'll miss our games of chess. Who's going to beat me now and keep me in my place?'

Alice hugged her too. 'Don't stay away too long. Daisy will miss her Aunty Pips.'

'Don't say that, Alice, or I won't go. I wish you could come too.'

Alice stood back and held her sister-in-law at arm's length. 'Oh no. This is where I want to be. Where I've always wanted to be.'

'I know,' Pips said huskily, as she blinked back the tears. Pips rarely cried and she wasn't going to start now. 'But I'll soon be back. I can't imagine there'll be anything to keep me in London for very long.'

Eight

Life in London was a world away from what Pips was used to. Strangely, there was an air of frenetic excitement.

'Everyone's trying to blot out the past,' Milly explained, as the taxi took them from the station to her apartment. 'There hasn't been much fun for the last few years, so we're making up for lost time.'

Pips gazed around her, taking in all the sights; the buildings and parks she'd only heard of or read about but had never seen. Even the fashions were different here in the capital. She smiled. Such changes took a while to reach the country-side. Then her smile faded. On one street corner, she saw a soldier, still dressed in his uniform, but now it was tattered and stained. One sleeve of his jacket hung limply and emptily by his side and he was holding out a tray of matches. On another corner, another soldier was singing 'It's a Long Way to Tipperary' and rattling a collection box under the noses of passers-by.

Pips's eyes widened and she gasped. 'Oh my – how can that be?'

'What?' Milly asked.

With a shaking finger, Pips pointed at the soldier. 'He's – he's lost his arm. In the war, by the look of it, but why is he reduced to – to such a menial occupation? And that one, to begging?'

For a moment, Milly's face was grim. 'There're a lot of them on the streets, especially in the West End. The "land fit for heroes" is a broken promise. It's never going to happen.'

'But – but why?'

'Why d'you think? The Government have no money. I expect we're deeply in debt as a nation. Mainly to America, so Paul says. And as more soldiers are demobbed, unemployment will rise.'

'But the women who've been doing men's jobs whilst they've been away will surely go back to being just housewives, won't they?'

'Married ones, yes. But what about single women – and there are going to be a lot more of those now. They need to work. And the widows too.'

Pips frowned. 'Yes, I hadn't looked at it like that. I'd thought that we'd look after all our returning heroes. Aren't they given any kind of pension after all they've done?'

'My friend, Paul, says that the dependants of military personnel killed in the war receive a pension and also anyone who was wounded and couldn't continue service.'

'Obviously what they receive,' Pips murmured, 'is not enough.'

'I'll throw a party,' Milly said, as they sat over a leisurely breakfast the next morning. 'I'll introduce you to *all* my friends.'

'That'd be nice,' Pips murmured.

'You don't seem terribly enthusiastic.' Milly sounded hurt.

'Oh Milly – I'm sorry. Of course, it'd be lovely.'

'But ... I feel there's a "but". Are you missing home – and especially Daisy – already?'

'No, it's not that. I can't get the picture of those soldiers selling matches and begging on the street corners out of my head. That could be my brother. Is there nothing that can be done?'

Milly put her head on one side and regarded her friend thoughtfully. 'You haven't really left it behind either, have you?'

'Have you?' Pips countered, a little more sharply than she intended.

But Milly had never been one to take offence and she didn't now. Instead, a frown wrinkled her smooth forehead. Quietly, she said, 'I try not to think about it. Like I said yesterday, we're all trying to forget it.'

Pips leaned forward. 'But we shouldn't. Oh, I don't mean we should wallow in self-pity and never-ending grief, but we should try to build a better world. Think of all those wonderful young men who gave their lives so that we might live in freedom. They'd want us to go forward, but they'd also not want us to forget their comrades, those who did come back, albeit with their lives shattered. Not everyone has a loving family like Robert to care for them. I see that now. And what about poor France and Belgium – and even Germany, if it comes to that? Their lands are laid waste. They've nothing.'

Milly gave a wry laugh. 'You sound just like Daddy. You should meet him.'

Very seriously, Pips said, 'I should like to very much.' Then realizing she was appearing ungrateful towards her charming and attentive hostess, she forced a lightness into her tone and said, 'But in the meantime, what about this party? What can I do to help?'

The following two days were spent in a whirlwind of planning and preparation and sending out invitations for the coming weekend.

By eight o'clock on the Saturday evening, Milly's apartment began to fill up with her guests. By ten, it was bursting at the seams.

'Pips, this is my friend, Paul Whittaker.'

Pips shook hands with the fair-haired young man. His face was open and honest with a firm jawline and twinkling blue eyes.

'I'm delighted to meet you, Miss Maitland. Milly has told me all about you.'

'Not everything, I hope. And, please, call me "Pips"'

'Shall we go and help Milly hand round drinks?'

'Yes, let's.'

They each took up a tray and began to move around the room.

'It's getting very noisy. What about the neighbours?' Pips asked Milly as she dispensed drinks and handed round canapés.

Milly, a little tipsy but by no means drunk, giggled. 'They're all here, darling. No one's going to complain. By the way, there's someone I want you to meet. He's just arrived, but I think you might remember him...'

Milly took her hand and weaved her way through the crowded room. 'Here she is,' she said triumphantly to the dark-haired young man who was leaning on the piano with a drink in his hand.

'Good Lord! *You!*'

'I'm flattered that you haven't forgotten me, Miss Maitland.' Mitch Hammond's dark brown eyes twinkled saucily at her.

Pips grinned. 'Unfortunately not.'

'Aw now, don't be like that. I told you I'd see you again, didn't I?'

'You did, but if I remember correctly, I said, "Not if I see you first".'

'Well, you didn't – thanks to Milly's popular parties. I arrived late on purpose so I could sneak in without being noticed.'

'Mitch is friends with my Paul. They were both in the RFC and then the RAF and now they go motor racing and flying together.'

'Motor racing?' Pips's eyes lit up. 'Oh yes, I remember now. At Brooklands, you said.'

'There's a meeting at the end of May. Like to come?' Mitch's steady gaze dared her. 'I'm sure Milly plans to go to support Paul.'

Despite her reservations about this brash young man, Pips found herself nodding. 'I'd love to.'

The party was a roaring success. Pips had never laughed so much since before the war. All the bitter memories were swept away, even if it was only just for this evening.

Milly was a clever mimic and, with her friend Paul playing the piano, she imitated the Edwardian music hall acts; Vesta Tilley, Nellie Wallace and Marie Lloyd. The only time that Pips was reminded of the war was when Milly sang Marie's song, 'A Little of What You Fancy Does You Good'. Milly had sung this saucily to the wounded soldiers. It had brightened their day and lifted their spirits.

The party didn't break up until three in the morning, but, as Milly had said, there were no complaints from neighbours for they were staggering home to their own apartments.

'I'm so glad my mother can't see me still in my dressing gown having breakfast at eleven in the morning,' Pips laughed the next morning when they both surfaced. 'She'd be horrified.'

'Mummy wouldn't mind too much, but I shudder to think what Granny Fortesque would say.'

'Tell me about your family. Have you brothers and sisters?'

Milly shook her head. 'No, there's just me. Shame for my parents, really. I'm sure my father would have liked a son to carry on the aircraft business after him.'

'Oh yes, I remember you told us that he's with Vickers.'

'My parents live near Weybridge. Very close to Brooklands.'

'How exciting.'

Milly nodded. 'I'll take you to meet them.' She smiled teasingly at Pips. 'Daddy will love you. He likes a daredevil.'

'By the way,' Pips added, 'I've never asked you about your aunty and uncle. Dr and Mrs Wallis. Are they well?'

Milly giggled. 'Don't let him hear you calling him "doctor". He's a Fellow of the Royal College of Surgeons and is entitled to be called "mister".'

'Oops, sorry.'

'But, yes, they're both very well. A bit lost – like

we all are – now the war's over. It was only because of them that I went out to Belgium, you know. When they volunteered to join Dr Hazelwood's flying ambulance, I begged them to take me too. Luckily, the great man said "yes", even though I wasn't trained.'

'You had other qualities, Milly. You were an asset to the corps.'

'Sweet of you to say so, darling. Now, what are we going to do today?'

'Not much, if you don't mind.'

Milly chuckled. 'Where's your "get up and go"?'

'It's got up and gone,' Pips joked. 'I'm not used to such late nights. We country folk must seem very staid to you. Boring, too.'

Milly laughed. 'No, never boring, Pips. Just – different.' She sighed and added, with a flash of insight, 'Not empty headed like me and most of my party-loving friends.'

'Don't say that. How many of those at your party did some kind of war work?'

Milly wrinkled her forehead. 'Most of them, actually. All the chaps were in the forces and a lot of the girls did something. Peg worked in munitions. Did you notice her long-sleeved dress? She was wounded in an explosion at the factory and her left arm was burned. And three of them worked in the canteen on an army base.'

'There you are, then.'

'But we're not clever like you, Pips. Mitch told me that you are a wizard chess player.'

'Robert and I play a lot together, that's all.'

'You're far too modest.' There was a pause before Milly added, 'So, are we going to Brooklands next month? Paul has offered to take us.'

'Oh most certainly. I'll write home and tell them I'll be staying until the end of May.' Pips paused and then, with her head on one side and her eyes twinkling, she asked, 'Do you think they'll let me have a drive round the track?'

Milly's face was a picture.

Nine

'Now, the next thing we're going to do is to take you to a dance at the Grafton Galleries.'

'Really? Where's that?'

Milly giggled. 'Grafton Street, silly. It's a huge underground art gallery and *so* respectable even your mother and my Granny Fortesque would approve. D'you know, when dances are held there, they cover up any nude pictures they might be exhibiting? To spare the blushes of us single girls, I suppose.' Her tone sobered as she added, 'Little do they know about the times we had to cut men's clothing off to treat their wounds.'

'But I haven't brought an evening dress,' Pips said, steering the conversation away from Milly's dark memories.

'Then we'll just have to go to Selfridges and get you one or two.'

'One or two?' Pips almost squeaked.

'Or more.' Milly laughed at her friend's horrified face. 'You can't wear the same dress two nights running.'

'Just how many of these dances are we going to go to?'

Milly waved her hand airily. 'Oh several, I hope, and then there are the parties you'll be invited to now you're staying with me.'

But when Milly took her to the large department store, even Pips, never used to spending money on fancy clothes, was caught up in the excitement.

In the ladies' department they were pampered and spoiled by the attentive assistants, who scuttled backwards and forwards bringing dress after dress to the changing room.

'Pips, darling, just look at this divine dress. It's the latest fashion.' Milly twirled around, showing the backless dress, cut to the waist.

'Oh my, that's very fast, Milly, don't you think?'

'Well, I abandoned my whalebone corset in the war. Didn't you?'

'Yes, but–' Then Pips laughed and asked, 'Whatever would your Granny Fortesque say?'

Milly giggled. 'Or your mother. But they won't know – unless we tell them. Do try one on, Pips. You're so tall and slim, it would look magnificent on you. Try the dark green one. It will be perfect with your hair colouring.'

They left the store armed with several packages.

'And we must have our hair done tomorrow morning. We'll call in at my hairdresser's. I'm sure Pierre will fit us in. I'm thinking of having my hair bobbed. It's all the rage, you know.'

The underground room was packed, but Paul and Mitch soon found their way through the throng to the girls. They were dressed, as were all the men present, in black tailed coats and white ties. All the women – just like Milly and Pips – were in lovely ankle-length evening dresses.

'Right, can you do the one-step?' Mitch shouted above the noise of the live band.

Pips shook her head.

'Then I'll teach you. Come on.'

'There's hardly room to move, let alone dance,' she protested.

Mitch only grinned. 'All the better. No one will notice that you can't do it properly.'

'Oh go on, then.'

He led her into the centre of the floor and proceeded to teach her the steps. Afterwards, Pips had to admit that he was not only a good teacher, but also great fun to be with. As they sat out the next two dances, at one of the tables set around the side, he fetched her sandwiches and cake. Handing her a bright pink drink he said, 'Sorry, no alcohol.'

'Oh my!' Pips laughed. 'Are we following America's example?'

In January that year, America had passed a law prohibiting the making and selling of alcohol.

'I certainly hope not. Besides, whatever would it do to Scotland's economy if they banned the making of whisky? No, I think it's just here. You can't blame them. Get a few rowdy drunks and the place might get smashed up. And I'm sure there are some valuable paintings here.' He nodded towards the walls. 'Even if some of them are covered up.'

They laughed together, easy in each other's company. As the music changed to a lilting waltz, Mitch said, 'Ah, now you must be able to do this.'

'Yes, actually, I can.'

They danced until Pips's feet began to ache. 'I'm not used to this,' she said, slipping off her shoes beneath the table and rubbing her feet.

'Then you'd better get used to it, darling,' Milly trilled, 'because Mitch is taking us to another nightclub now.'

'But it's almost two in the morning.'

'And this, my darling Pips, is London.'

Everyone stood as the band played 'God Save the King' and then made their way up into the night.

'Shall we walk or get a cab?' Paul said. 'It's over a mile away.'

'Oh, get a taxi, I think, especially if Pips's feet are hurting already, but we'll begin to walk in that direction just in case – ah, there's one.'

Mitch flagged down the vehicle and the four of them clambered in.

'Good evening, Mr Hammond. Or should I say, "Good morning"?'

Mitch squinted at the driver. 'Good Heavens! Hello, sir. What are you doing here?'

'Earning an honest living,' the driver chuckled. 'It's good to see you again. Quite recovered from your little mishap over there?'

During the war, Mitch Hammond had served with the Royal Flying Corps, undertaking danger- ous missions over enemy territory to take recon- naissance photographs. He had crash-landed in no-man's-land and had been rescued by Pips and William under fire. At that time, Mitch's only concern had been that his precious photographs should not fall into enemy hands. It wasn't until later that he had realized he had put all their lives in acute danger. Pips had been shot in the leg, but had accompanied Mitch back to England and had arranged for the photographs to be collected by a senior member of the RFC – the very man, it seemed, who was now driving their taxi.

'Absolutely, thank you, sir. And how are you?'

'I'm well, thank you, Hammond. Sorry, *Mister* Hammond.'

'What a coincidence, bumping into you like this.'

'Not really. There are quite a few of us on the taxis – and we're the lucky ones to have found any sort of work.'

As they alighted, the driver waved away Mitch's offer to pay him. 'Have this one on me, Mr Hammond. Just for old times' sake, eh? Besides, I owe you one. I got a real pat on the back when I took those photographs of yours to my superiors. They were invaluable.'

'Well, just this once, then, sir. And thank you. Goodnight.'

As the vehicle pulled away, Pips said, 'Is that who I think it is?'

'Yes, the guy who collected those blasted photographs that you risked your life for. Damn it, you can't go anywhere, can you, without reminders popping up?'

Pips put her arm through his. 'Come on, let's find this nightclub of yours.'

Mitch led his three friends down into another

deep-underground cellar. 'You can get a drink here,' he muttered as he held tightly on to Pips as they went down the stairs. 'I think I need one.'

The room was hot and stuffy. The band thumped out the latest dance music and the laughter, if a little forced perhaps, was loud.

'This must have been written just for you,' Mitch said as he held Pips close and whispered in her ear.

'What is it?'

'"A Pretty Girl is Like a Melody".'

'But what dance is it?'

'Goodness knows. There's hardly room to dance properly anyway. We just shuffle around. Don't you realize, my sweet, innocent country girl, that dancing is just an excuse for a man to hold his girl close?'

She felt his arms tighten about her, but Pips did not pull away. She knew the incident with the taxi driver had unnerved him and she was willing, just for tonight anyway, to help him forget.

Ten

'So, what does Paul do exactly?' Pips asked Milly as they waited for him to pick them up in his car on the day of the race meeting at Brooklands. 'I do like your new hairstyle, by the way. Very chic. Though what your granny will say, I daren't think.'

Milly patted her short hair self-consciously. 'You've got a point there,' she murmured. 'Anyway, Paul. His parents have a farm not far from Weybridge and he helps them out from time to time – at harvest time and lambing, that sort of thing – but his main occupation is running a small private racing club at Brooklands. And, of course, he races his own cars there too.' She smiled archly at Pips. 'So does your admirer, Mitch Hammond.'

'You can forget any matchmaking there, Milly Fortesque, or I'll be on the next train home.'

Milly pretended to pout and then gave an exaggerated sigh. 'What a shame! You'd be perfect for each other. Oh well, it was worth a try.'

Turning the focus of attention away from herself, Pips asked, 'Is there anything between you and Paul?'

'We're good friends, that's all,' Milly said firmly. 'Oh, I know our mothers don't believe there can be a friendship between a man and a woman, but we seem to manage it. I'm not ready to settle down yet. Once you're married you're expected to conform and to have babies. Maybe one day, but not yet.'

Pips chuckled. 'My mother too. That's part of the reason I was glad to escape to London for a while, though I have to admit she's not been so bad since Alice and Robert married and had Daisy, though she did say she hoped you would introduce me to all your nice friends.' She paused and then asked, 'D'you think there can be just friendship between a man and a woman, then?'

Milly wrinkled her brow. 'I'm not sure. It ought to be possible, but the trouble is that, sooner or later, one of them might start to have romantic feelings for the other and then it gets complicated. Ah, here he is.'

Conversation in the car was impossible above the noisy engine, but once they had parked, Paul offered an arm to each girl and they walked towards the track. Already crowds had gathered and the sound of revving engines filled the air. There was a feeling of excitement and expectation.

'Let's bag a good position to watch the racing,' Paul said. 'We'll take you up to the bridge over the Members' Banking. You'll get a good view from there.'

As they walked, Pips said, 'How did this all come to be built? And why here?'

'A chap called Hugh Locke King and his wife went to Italy and watched a road race there,' Paul said. 'They noticed that there were no competitors from Britain and wondered why. Finding out that we weren't allowed to race on public roads in Britain, he decided to build a track on part of his estate. Originally, he was going to build it as just a flat oval, but it was suggested that if banked corners were constructed, it would allow greater speeds. They did this, but the increased cost almost bankrupted poor old Locke King; with help from his wife and her family, though, the project was completed and it was opened in June 1907 by the Earl of Lonsdale.' Paul laughed. 'I've heard tell that the parade round the track after the official luncheon almost developed into an impromptu race.'

'Oh my!' Pips exclaimed when they reached the bridge and joined other spectators. She gazed around her. To her left was a steep banking on the track which gave way to a long straight, running parallel to the railway – the London and South Western line – which brought racing enthusiasts from Waterloo to within walking distance of the circuit.

Paul pointed. 'At the far end of the straight, there's another banking called the Byfleet and then,' he swept his arm in an arc, 'the track goes round and comes to a fork to take the drivers either to the Members' Banking again or to the finishing straight.'

'How long is a lap?'

'The outer circuit is about two and three-quarter miles.'

Pips's eyes sparkled and her heart beat a little faster. How she longed to drive round this track. 'What's that building over there?'

'That's the clubhouse, darling,' Milly said. 'The offices of the Clerk of the Course are there.' She giggled. 'It's what they call the centre of operations and it's also used as changing rooms for the drivers.'

'And over there,' Paul butted in, 'is Test Hill, where we put our cars through their paces and, of course, the hill and the whole track are both used by the motor trade for testing their new models as Locke King probably intended all along. The car's the future, Pips.'

Pips glanced at Milly. 'You told me before, Milly, that the RFC were here in the war. Was Mitch here, then?'

'Yes, he did his basic training here and now he can't keep away. Maybe he'll teach you to fly, if you ask him nicely.'

Pips blinked. 'Eh?'

'Oh yes. Didn't you know? He's started up his own flying school here; The Hammond Flying School.'

'I supposed that was my fault really,' Paul laughed. 'I'd started my racing club, and, as you might imagine, if you know him well, Mitch was not to be outdone.'

'So, do you fly, Paul?'

'Oh yes. And Mitch races his Sunbeam too. We both belong to the BARC.'

Pips gazed around the scene before her. 'They have motorcycle races here too, don't they?'

'Don't tell her, Paul,' Milly giggled. 'Her brother was telling me that she used to ride his motor-cycle in secret before the war.'

'Did you?' There was new respect in Paul's eyes.

Pips nodded. 'I did, but I haven't liked to ride it since, seeing as he believes he can't ride it now. It doesn't seem fair. It's gathering dust – and probably rust – at the back of our stables now, I'm sorry to say.'

'If he ever decides to sell it, let me know. I'm sure my friend, Michael, who's in the motor trade, could find a buyer for it.' He paused and then asked, 'You mentioned "stables". Have you got horses, then?'

Pips's eyes clouded. 'We did have, but they were commandeered in the war. Even my lovely Midnight – a big, black stallion, who'd only let me ride him. We haven't had the heart to replace them yet. Though,' she went on, brightening a little, 'now we've got Daisy, maybe we should think about getting her a pony when she's a little older. Anyway...' she forced a smile, 'aren't you driving today?'

93

'Not until the third race. I've time to get you two ladies settled first.'

'Oh look, there's Mitch making his way to the start line. Give him a wave, Pips.'

They all waved enthusiastically, but Mitch didn't seem to notice them.

They could just see the start line in the distance as the cars lined up. When they were all in place, the starter moved backwards to stand in front of each one in turn, raise his flag and then drop it. The car would then speed off.

'Why don't they all go together?' Pips asked Paul.

'It's a handicapping system, so that the smaller-engined cars get a fair chance against the bigger ones. In some races, they have chicanes set out for the bigger cars too, to slow them down a bit. It's all carefully worked out to be fair.' He grinned. 'Allegedly.'

'Why are there two drivers in some of the cars?'

'Some of the drivers take their mechanics with them.'

At the start, Mitch was in fourth place out of the ten cars racing. By the second lap he was in third place and, two laps later, had moved into second.

'He'll never get past the chap in first place,' Pips muttered. 'He's driving like the wind.'

Pips was right; there was no way past the leader and Mitch finished in second place.

'Right, I'll have to go and get ready,' Paul said. 'If Mitch isn't in any more races, I'll send him to find you.'

They watched the second race and just before the third race was due to start, Mitch joined them. He was still in his driver's suit and his face and hands were black with oil and dust.

'Well done.' Pips grinned at him.

Mitch pulled a face 'Not good enough. What good is coming second? It's first – or nothing.' He nodded towards the track. 'Paul's race is about to start. There's a woman driving in this one.'

'Now, this I must see.'

Mitch grinned. 'I thought that'd make you sit up and take notice. Certain clubs that race here allow mixed races too. Paul's for one. Come on – let's watch how she does.'

As the cars lined up, Pips leaned forward to try to pick out the woman driver. 'I didn't think they'd let women race again men,' she murmured. 'I thought it was only in all-women races.'

'There are those too. There's a famous one called the "Bracelet Race". Muriel Denton won it on one occasion. Hers is the Napier with a number four on the side.'

Pips felt her heart pounding. How she longed to be behind the wheel of a car, hurtling round the track.

As the race ended, Mitch said, 'Muriel came in third. Not bad, I suppose.'

'Don't you dare say it!'

'What?'

'"For a woman."'

'I wouldn't dream of saying any such thing – especially about Muriel. She's fearless and is never satisfied with anything less than first place. Just like me.'

Pips's eyes gleamed. 'You know her?'

'Of course. We all know each other.'

'Would you introduce me to her?'

He put his head on one side and regarded her mischievously. 'On one condition – that you don't ask to drive her car.'

'Oh no,' Pips said airily, 'I wouldn't do that. Besides, I intend to drive yours.'

Mitch stared at her for a moment and then burst out laughing. 'The cheek of the woman! Come on, let's go and find Muriel. But I warn you, she won't be in the best of tempers having just lost a race.'

But Muriel greeted Pips and Milly with warm, firm handshakes. 'I lost power in the penultimate lap.' She grinned. 'I was lucky to finish third and not conk out altogether. Mind you, I shall be giving my mechanic a roasting.'

Muriel Denton was a good-looking young woman in her early thirties, Pips guessed, with strong features and a wide smile. She removed her leather helmet and shook her short, brown hair. 'Let's go and find a drink. I'm parched.' She hooked her arm through Pips's. 'Interested in cars, are you?'

Pips chuckled. 'I'm interested in speed. Horses, motorcycles, cars – even planes, if I ever get the chance.'

'Can you fly?'

'No – though I'd love to learn.'

'But first – I expect you'd like a tootle round this track.'

'I would. I'm working on Mitch.'

'Really? You must be honoured. He doesn't let just anyone drive his car.'

'He hasn't said "yes" yet.'

'Ah!' There was a pause as they walked a little further. 'I didn't catch your name. Milly, I know already of course.'

'Pips Maitland.'

Muriel stopped suddenly, forcing Pips to a standstill too. She turned towards the other woman with a question in her eyes. Muriel was staring at her. 'Now that,' she said slowly, 'explains it.'

'Sorry, you've lost me.'

'Pips Maitland. *You*'re the nurse, who risked her life to save Mitch when he crashed in no-man's-land in the war, aren't you?'

'Well – um...'

'No need to be modest, my dear. You got shot in the leg during the rescue *and* you brought him all the way back to England, didn't you? So, now I understand. He owes you a ride in his car around Brooklands at the very least. Come on, let's get that drink.' She called back over her shoulder as they began to walk again. 'Milly, dear, do keep up.' Then she lowered her voice to add, 'She's a sweet girl, but a little flighty.'

'Not near the trenches, she wasn't,' Pips murmured, sticking up for the girl she now regarded as her friend.

'What? What d'you mean?'

'She wasn't qualified – or even trained – as a nurse, but she was a huge tonic to the troops and to the other members of our ambulance corps when she joined us.'

'Milly went out to the front? You're having me on.'

'Absolutely not. She followed her aunt and

97

uncle – Mr and Mrs Wallis.'

'Where were you when she joined you?'

'We went to Arras and then back to Ypres for the third battle there. The one they call Passchendaele.'

'My God! Milly Fortesque was at Passchendaele?'

Pips nodded. 'She was.'

'Well, now I've heard everything. Why did she never say?'

'We don't talk about it much. None of us do.'

Muriel glanced back over her shoulder to where Milly was walking arm in arm with Paul, her tinkling laughter echoing across the ground between them. There was suddenly a new respect in Muriel's eyes. 'Well, well, well. Who'd have thought it? No wonder she wants to dance the nights away now. I just thought she was a society good-time girl – the sort they call a flapper these days, but now I understand. She's trying to forget too.'

'She saw some dreadful sights and went through some tough times. We all did.'

'How long were you there?'

'I first went out in September 1914 and apart from a couple of trips home, I was there the whole time.'

Muriel's face was suddenly bleak. 'Were – were you ever at the Somme?'

Pips nodded. 'Yes, from the end of June 1916 until the end of the Battle of the Somme, though I went home on leave then.' She said no more to this woman whom she'd only just met, but that had been a tough time for Pips. On her return after seeing Robert and Alice marry, she had been distressed and hurt to find that her lover, Giles, had fallen in love with one of the other nurses.

'Anywhere near Thiepval?' Muriel asked, interrupting her thoughts.

'Very near there, yes. Why?' Pips turned to look at Muriel and saw her swallow hard.

'My darling husband – Captain Roger Denton – was killed on the first day of the Somme – the first of July – near Thiepval. I was told that he died instantly and didn't suffer, but I know that could have been an out-and-out lie.'

'It was a catastrophe. We saw it happen. We witnessed the bombardment of the enemy lines for several days beforehand and we were there when the troops marched to the front and when the mines were exploded. And then they went over the top.' Pips was silent for a moment. 'The shelling hadn't done its work – the Germans had dug their trenches too deep. The mines did a lot of damage, of course, but not enough and when our lads began to walk towards the enemy lines, they were met with a hail of machine-gun fire. And yet our boys still kept going. Thousands were killed on that first day alone.' She squeezed Muriel's arm. 'If your husband was in those first waves, it is very likely that he *was* killed instantly. I'm not going to lie to you, Muriel, it was a slaughter, but in most cases, death – if it came – came swiftly. Though, of course, there were a lot of casualties too. We were overwhelmed with wounded. My own brother, who went out as a doctor, lost his arm trying to bring casualties in from no-man's-land.'

'You – you don't remember hearing my husband's name.'

Pips shook her head. 'We rarely got to know their names and then probably only their first names. But no, I don't remember him. I'm sorry.'

'Thank you for telling me. You've made me feel a little better. Perhaps he didn't suffer as I've been imagining.'

'Even if he wasn't killed outright, we did our best to alleviate their pain, I promise you, even when there was no hope of recovery.'

Muriel nodded. 'Thank you,' she said huskily. She cleared her throat and said more strongly, 'I'll tell you something, Pips Maitland. You can drive my car any time you want to.'

Eleven

As they left Brooklands later that day, instead of returning to London, Paul took the two girls to the Fortesques' home on the outskirts of Weybridge. The manor was a large country house, set back from the road and surrounded by well-kept lawns and trees.

Henry Fortesque was tall, with an upright bearing. He had a moustache and piercing blue eyes that seemed to bore into Pips's soul. But he was smiling as he held out his hand. 'You are very welcome, Pips. We know how you looked after our girl at the front and we're grateful. Come and meet my wife Victoria, who, I should warn you, does *not* like her name to be shortened.' He led the way into a large, sunny drawing room where a woman, whom Pips guessed to be in her late forties, jumped up from a sofa and came towards them, hands outstretched. She was an older version of Milly, with blonde, short, curly hair, a pretty, doll-like face and blue eyes. She was bubbly and promised to be full of fun – just like her daughter – but Pips guessed her zany exterior hid a steely strength when it was needed – again, just like Milly.

'My dear Pips, how welcome you are. Sit down, beside me. Have you enjoyed your day at Brooklands?'

'It was wonderful, Mrs Fortesque, thank you.'

'Muriel has promised her a drive in her car,' Milly said.

Henry Fortesque blinked. 'Muriel Denton has? Good Heavens – you must have been a hit with her. I've never heard of her allowing anyone else to drive her beloved Napier.'

Milly linked her arm through her father's. 'I think, Daddy, it was when Muriel found out that Pips had been nursing near the Somme, where her husband died.'

'Ah, that might explain it, then.'

As they sat down on a sofa opposite, the door opened and a maid carried in a tea tray. 'We always make sure we wait for afternoon tea until Milly gets here when she's been at Brooklands. Thank you, Mary, and would you tell Granny Fortesque that we are having tea in the drawing room, please?'

The girl bobbed a curtsy and left the room,

whilst Victoria handed around plates, cakes and poured tea. As she was passing a cup to Pips, the door opened and an elderly lady, though still slim and straight-backed, with white hair piled on top of her head in neat curls, entered the room. She wore a long-sleeved, high-necked dress, similar in style, Pips couldn't help thinking, to those favoured by Queen Mary. As if indeed she were the Queen, everyone rose to greet her.

'Good afternoon, Mama,' Henry said, offering her his place on the sofa.

But, with a wave of her hand, the imperious lady brushed him aside. 'You know very well, Henry, that I prefer the winged chair near the fire. If I get down onto that thing, I'll never get up again without a crane.'

Milly rushed to her and planted a kiss on both her wrinkled cheeks. *Darling,* Granny. How are you?'

Granny Fortesque – as Pips had now realized who she was – tutted quietly and yet there was the hint of a smile at the corners of her mouth. 'Always so effusive, aren't you, my dear? How they coped with you at the front, I shudder to think. And whatever have you done to your hair? Let me see.'

Milly stood meekly in front of her grandmother and submitted to her scrutiny. Pips held her breath, but, to her surprise, the older woman nodded and said, 'It's rather daring, but I must admit it suits you, Milly. I've seen pictures of girls with straight hair with this style, and I didn't like it, but because your hair is naturally curly, it frames your face. It's really quite sweet.'

When she was settled in her chair, everyone sat down again. Now Granny's sharp eyes alighted on Pips. 'And who have we here? Please introduce her, Henry. And yes, Victoria, I'll have lemon tea as usual, if you please.'

'Mama, may I introduce Miss Philippa Maitland – known as Pips. She is Milly's friend. They were in Belgium together. Pips, this is my mother, Eleanor Fortesque.'

'"Pips"? It sounds like something you find in an orange. I shall call you Philippa.'

Pips rose again, crossed the space between them and held out her hand. 'As does my mother, Mrs Fortesque.' She smiled. 'How do you do?'

'Please call me "Granny Fortesque" or we'll get muddled up between my daughter-in-law and me.'

They shook hands and Pips sat down again beside Milly's mother.

'Where were you both in Belgium? Safely behind the lines, I take it. And whatever did my scatter-brained, flighty granddaughter actually do to help the war effort?'

Pips stared at her. Did no one back here understand just what Milly had done? Had she told them nothing? Pips set her cup carefully on the low coffee table and met the older woman's steady gaze. Milly's parents were listening intently too, though out of the corner of her eye, Pips caught sight of Milly shaking her head frantically.

'Milly came out just after her aunt and uncle, Mr and Mrs Wallis, joined our flying ambulance early in 1917. My brother lost his arm towards the end of the Battle of the Somme and he and

103

Alice, who was a nurse in our corps, had gone home. Then – two more left.' Once again, she did not say that it had been Giles's departure with Rose that had left the corps depleted.

'I'm sorry to hear about your brother. What rank was he?'

'He wasn't in the army. He was a doctor with the corps.'

Eleanor Fortesque frowned. 'Then how did he become so seriously injured? Was it the shelling?'

'No, he went into no-man's-land to pick up the wounded and was hit by a sniper.'

'Pips went out to rescue him. Wasn't she brave?' Milly said, desperately trying to steer the conversation away from herself.

'I wouldn't have thought they'd have allowed you to do that.'

Now Pips laughed. 'They didn't, but because we were an *independent* flying ambulance corps, we came under no one else's authority but our own.'

'Then you were very foolhardy, Philippa.'

'But he would have died if we hadn't got to him quickly.'

'He wasn't the only one she rescued...' Milly went on, but Pips interrupted. 'This isn't about me, Milly dear. It's about you and what you did.'

'Oh Pips, don't. *Please* don't.'

Pips stared at her for a moment and seeing genuine tears in the girl's eyes, she got up and went to sit beside her on the other sofa. She took Milly's hand and said softly, 'Why not, Milly?'

'I – because we shouldn't talk about what happened out there. We – no one does. We – we should protect them.'

'Dearest Milly – I don't like to hear you described as scatter-brained and flighty.' Pips smiled. 'Perhaps, back here, you are, but out there, you were anything but that and your family and your friends have a right to know that they should be justly proud of you.'

Through her tears, Milly suddenly giggled. 'But you'll ruin my reputation, Pips. I'm an empty-headed party girl.'

'Here, maybe, but out there – never!'

'Millicent,' Eleanor said, 'I would like to hear what your friend has to say...' She met Pips's gaze with a steely stare. 'And then I shall make my own mind up as to what description you deserve. Pray continue, Philippa.'

'Oh Pips,' Milly said again and hid her face against Pips's shoulder. Pips put her arm around her friend, but had no intention of not continuing.

'Milly had no formal nursing training when she came out to the front, but she was a tonic in other ways. She lifted the spirits of the casualties and our – by then – rather jaded members of the corps. She met the wounded being brought to our advanced first-aid post and comforted them as best she could until she could pass them on to a professional medical person. Even when she was covered in their blood and exhausted after long hours on duty, she never failed to smile, give a cheery word or gently hold the hand of the dying. And the soldiers loved to hear her singing and doing her impressions of the music hall artists.' Pips raised her eyebrows. 'I expect you do know that she's a wonderful mimic?'

Eleanor gave a brief nod. 'Go on.'

'In the privacy of our tent, she would shed tears over all she had witnessed, all the terrible sights she'd seen and the ones we couldn't save, but never once did she let the soldiers see that.'

There was silence in the room for several minutes when Pips fell silent. Milly remained where she was with her face buried against Pips's shoulder.

At last, Eleanor spoke in a voice that, strangely, was not quite steady. 'Millicent, come here.'

Milly's head shot up and for a moment she looked frightened. Pips almost laughed aloud. It seemed the young woman was far more afraid of her fearsome grandmother than ever she had been of German guns and shells. As Milly rose and went to kneel in front of Granny Fortesque, Pips saw Henry and Victoria exchange a glance, but not knowing them well yet, she could not read anything in the look. Eleanor leaned forward and cupped her hands around Milly's face. 'My dear child, I owe you an apology...'

'Oh Granny, you don't need to say that.'

'Yes, I do. I have misjudged you. I am extremely proud of you as I am sure your mother and father are too. Will you forgive me – forgive us all?'

'There's nothing to forgive, Granny. Really. I really *am* all the things you said. I am flighty and pleasure seeking; a party girl – a flapper.'

'Perhaps so, but obviously, much more besides than we have given you credit for.' She stooped forward and kissed Milly's forehead, adding quietly, 'Some time – when you feel like talking

about it – I would like to hear more, but I understand that perhaps just now it is too raw for you.'

Milly nodded and then got up off her knees and
went to sit down beside her father, who, though
he squeezed her hand, said nothing. Now,
Eleanor turned her gaze on Pips.

'And as for you, young woman...'

Pips held her breath, thinking she had offended
her hosts. But suddenly, the old lady smiled and it
was like the sun appearing from behind a cloud. 'I
thank you for your temerity in standing up for
your friend against a formidable old woman. I admire you for that and you will be welcome in this
house at any time. In fact, I hope you will visit us
often. And now,' she added, getting up stiffly from
her chair, 'I will have a brief rest in my room
before dinner.'

Shortly afterwards, Milly took Pips to her room.
'Are you dreadfully angry with me?' Pips asked
her in a small voice.

'Oh *darling,* no, of course I'm not. In a way, I'm
glad you said what you did. I find it awfully difficult to tell anyone what happened out there and
especially talking about myself. I could tell them
all about you and the others, but not about me.'
She giggled. 'But now they all know – my family
and everyone at Brooklands – even Paul, and
that's why I intend to have fun now. We should
grab enjoyment while we can.'

'I agree, but I still think we should try to do
something to help soldiers who can't find work
for one reason or another.'

Milly wrinkled her forehead. 'Why don't you
find Dr Hazelwood and ask his advice? Your

father is still in touch with him, isn't he?'

Pips stared at her. 'D'you know, Milly Fortesque, sometimes you are absolutely brilliant.'

Milly fluffed her hair and laughed. 'Don't go telling anyone, darling. You'll ruin my reputation completely.'

Over dinner that evening, there was no more talk of the war, only of the future.

'Will you continue to manufacture at Brooklands, Mr Fortesque?' Pips asked.

'Oh yes. I don't know how much Milly has told you about the company.'

'Not much,' Pips smiled, 'she seems rather shy about it.'

Henry chuckled. 'I expect she doesn't want to appear boastful, but Vickers developed the Vickers Vimy, a long-range bomber that, I'm pleased to say, was not needed as the war ended before it went into service.'

Pips pulled a face. 'That's good, I suppose, but did it affect your company?'

'We thought it might but we were fortunate that we could then turn our efforts to civilian aviation. Last year – I don't know if you heard about it – the *Daily Mail* offered a £10,000 prize for the first flight across the Atlantic.'

'Of *course*. I knew I'd heard the name Vimy before. My brother and I followed the news avidly, but, please, go on. I'd like to hear it from your side.'

'Tommy Sopwith, who was also a major manufacturer of aircraft for the war effort and also at Brooklands, and his company, along with ourselves and one or two other manufacturers, entered.'

'And you won.' Pips couldn't stop herself.

Henry smiled benignly and nodded graciously. 'Winning a well-publicized event like that can be worth a thousand advertisements.'

'It was a fantastic achievement.'

There was a pause until Granny Fortesque asked, 'And what do you hope to do with your life, Philippa? Are you going to continue to be a party girl, like Milly?' She had the grace to smile across the table at her granddaughter. Now there was no censure in her tone, only a gentle teasing.

'D'you know, Granny Fortesque, at this precise moment, I haven't any idea. Like Milly, I suppose, I just want to have a good time for a while, though I can't see it fulfilling me for very long. I always wanted to train to be a doctor, like my brother, but my mother wouldn't hear of it.'

Eleanor was silent for a moment before saying, 'I can understand that, I suppose, though, with no disrespect to your mother, I don't think I would have agreed with her.' She leaned across the table and said in a stage whisper, 'I was a secret suffragette, you know. My family never knew, but I used to attend some of Mrs Pankhurst's meetings before the war.' She gave an exaggerated sigh. 'But, of course, that's all gone now that women have been given the vote – well, some of them, anyway.' She sat back and, almost tongue-in-cheek, suggested, 'You could, of course, stand for Parliament.'

Pips chuckled. 'I could, but, you see, I don't seem to fit into the views of any particular party.

I like some Tory ideals and some liberal ones, and as for this new labour party that's growing, well, I can sympathize with some of their aims too.'

'So, for the moment, you're going to continue with a life of idle pleasure.'

Pips grinned, liking the old lady more and more. "Fraid so, Granny Fortesque.'

Twelve

The promised drive for Pips around the Brooklands track took place the following weekend. They were all there: Milly, Paul, Mitch and Muriel – and she had brought along another young woman.

'I want you to meet Pattie Henderson, Pips,' Muriel said. 'She's a racer too.'

Pips shook hands with the woman whom she gauged to be a little older than Muriel, in her late thirties or maybe even her early forties. She had dark brown hair and brown eyes and a very firm handshake.

'Muriel and I – along with a few others including Milly, who, although she doesn't drive, is an honorary member – are known as "the Brooklands Girls".' Pattie laughed and her eyes twinkled with merriment. 'Are you going to join us?'

'Let's see how she drives first,' Muriel said. 'Driving round Brooklands isn't quite the same as driving an ambulance in the war.'

Pattie's eyes widened. 'Is that what you did? My

word! Well, there's one thing, Muriel, she's obviously got no fear. Come on, let's have a tootle round.'

'She can drive my car, if you'd rather, Muriel,' Mitch offered, but she waved him away. 'No, no, I'm not one to go back on my promises. Just don't crash it, Pips.'

It was arranged that Pattie should go first and that Pips should follow her track line. In a borrowed suit and leather helmet, Pips climbed in behind the wheel, her heart thudding, her palms sweaty with excitement. They set off steadily, but when Pattie saw that Pips was following her faithfully and keeping pace, she increased the speed – once, twice, three times – until they were both tearing round the track almost as fast as if they were in a real race.

Pips felt the power of the car and knew – had she been inclined – that she could have surged past Pattie, but she was not going to show off. At least, not today!

As Pattie slowed and pulled over to where their group of friends was waiting, Pips drew in behind her. They surrounded her car.

'Oh *darling* – that was wonderful. You went so *fast*.'

'You're a natural.' Mitch grinned.

'If I hadn't seen it with my own eyes,' Paul said, 'I wouldn't have believed it. It normally takes years for someone to reach that proficiency. You handled the car like a pro.'

Pips felt a rush of pride, but it was Muriel's approval she sought. As Pattie climbed out of her car and joined them, Muriel said, 'Pattie, meet the latest recruit to the Brooklands Girls.'

'So, you need to buy yourself a car now,' Mitch said. 'I've heard of one going for a reasonable price. He's a mate of mine, so he'll treat us fairly. Well, actually, he's a mate of Paul's really. Michael's his name and he lives near to Paul's family's farm. But I know him well.'

'Is there anyone you're *not* mates with?' Pips chuckled.

'Not many in the racing world – or the flying fraternity either, for that matter. That's the next thing we must do. Take you flying.'

'When?' Pips asked mischievously.

'Whenever you say the word.'

Pips gasped and her eyes widened. 'You're on – the very next time I come down to stay with Milly.'

Mitch frowned. 'Oh, are you going back to Lincolnshire? I thought you'd moved in with Milly.'

'No, it was just a holiday even though it's turned out to be quite a long one. I don't want to outstay my welcome.'

'But if you're going to buy a car and race, you need to be down here.'

'We'll see,' Pips said, carefully. She was torn; half of her longed to become part of the racing world, the other half was missing her home, her family and especially Daisy.

That evening she told Milly that she was going home.

'Oh darling, just for a visit. You will come back, won't you?'

'Well, I don't like to impose...'

'Oh phooey.' Milly flapped her hand and they both laughed as she copied Pips's favourite saying. 'Look, why don't you move in with me? I love having you here and we get on well, don't we?'

'We do, but...'

'You can pop up to Lincolnshire any time you want. So, what do you say?'

'Only if you let me pay half the expenses of the apartment.'

Milly pulled a face. 'There's no need, but if that's the only way you'll come, then, yes.'

Pips thought quickly. Though she loved her family dearly and adored little Daisy, she had to make her own life and this was something she'd love to do. She craved excitement and racing at Brooklands, and perhaps even learning to fly too, would give her plenty of that.

But just how was she going to break the news to her family – especially her mother? Henrietta would be sure to disapprove.

To her surprise, it was Robert who questioned her plans.

'It's very dangerous, Pips. I know you're a daredevil and you're bored, but this is taking things a bit too far. I wish I'd never let you ride my motorcycle now or drive Father's car in secret. And what on earth will Mother say?'

'Amazingly, both she and Father seem philosophical about the idea. They like Milly. Who wouldn't?'

Robert snorted. 'No doubt Mother thinks you'll meet a suitable young man mixing with the upper echelons of society.'

Pips laughed. 'The only eligible bachelor so far is Mitch Hammond. You remember him.'

Robert rolled his eyes. 'I do indeed. I wouldn't tell her that, if I were you. She never took to that particular young man.'

'I've no intention of telling her. And now, I'm going to find Daisy and take her to see her other grandparents. There was a letter from William waiting for me when I got back and I've promised to share his letters with Ma and Norah.'

'Not Len?' Robert said impishly, with a flash of his old humorous side, which was sadly missing most of the time these days.

'Hardly,' Pips said drily.

A few minutes later, Pips was picking up her niece and swinging her round, the little girl squealing with delight. 'How's my girl?' She set her back on the ground. 'I'm sure you've grown.'

''Gain, 'gain,' Daisy pleaded, reaching up, so Pips dutifully obliged.

'Now, we're going to see Grandma Dawson.'

'Cake?'

Pips laughed. 'I don't doubt that Grandma Dawson will have cake for you. Come along. Let's go and find Mummy and see if she wants to come with us.'

Alice agreed readily. 'Cook has packed a basket for them. She has your mother's approval, of course.'

'Oh Alice, you don't need to explain. How are your family coping? Especially after the food shortages during the war.'

'They're fine. We were lucky in the country. The

114

estate helped everyone around here and, as you know, my father grows his own vegetables too. All the villagers do, but I expect it was more difficult in the towns and cities. It's getting better now, though.' Compulsory rationing had been introduced in February 1918 and there had been queues in the towns and cities where some people were accused of hoarding. Meat rationing finished in December and the rationing of butter finished the following May. Alice pulled a face. 'But sugar's still rationed and the production of flour is still what they call "controlled". Same thing, really, isn't it?'

The two young women walked down the lane, with Daisy between them. Every now and again they swung her into the air.

'I think she's got your daredevil spirit, Pips. She scared us half to death last week. She went missing.'

'What?'

Alice nodded. 'She'd climbed up the steep stairs into the room above the gatehouse. It was Jake who thought to look there.' Alice was referring to the young man who had once been a stable boy at the hall, but who now, since there were no horses, worked as a gardener and handyman. He still had his own living quarters above the stables.

'I bet he misses the horses, doesn't he?'

Alice nodded.

'I don't think Father – or Robert – have ever thought about replacing the ones that were commandeered during the war.'

'No, only about buying a pony for Daisy when she's old enough.'

'What about Robert? Wouldn't he like to ride again?'

Alice sighed. 'He doesn't seem to want to do anything much. I really thought after New Year that things were going to be better, but he's sunk back into depression again.'

'Still getting those awful black moods?'

''Fraid so.' She paused. 'He misses you whenever you're away. He says there's no one else who can beat him at chess.'

Pips chuckled. 'Then I'll give him a thrashing tonight. He'll soon wish me gone again.'

Reaching the cottage, they were welcomed inside by the two women. Seated in the Dawsons' kitchen, with Daisy playing with a box of bricks on the hearth, the four women exchanged the local gossip.

'Peggy's walking out with Sam Nuttall. Did you know?' Ma said.

'Do you mind?' Pips asked carefully.

'Not a bit,' Ma said firmly. 'Sam's a fine lad and he's very good with Luke.'

'Clara's not too happy,' Norah said, referring to Sam's mother. 'She thinks her son can do better for himself than marry a girl with an illegitimate child.'

'Oh phooey! He'll make a great stepfather for Luke. Poor Peggy wasn't the first and she certainly wasn't the last before the war was over.'

Ma laughed wryly. 'That's exactly what I said when Peggy came to tell us and so did your mam, Miss Pips, if I remember rightly. And Harold was friends with Sam – all the lads in the village were

116

good mates. He'd be pleased.'

'What does Mr Dawson think?'

'He's all right about it. Thinks a lot of Sam, though he's forever reminding him that the business will be Luke's one day, not his.'

'Anyway, one of the reasons we've come is because there was a letter from William waiting for me when I came home and you know I always share his letters with you. Where's Luke?'

'Safely up at the workshop,' Norah said.

'Here, Alice, you read it out to your mother and Ma. I think there's something you'll all be interested to hear.'

After news about himself and Brigitta and her grandparents and how they were slowly getting the land back to as near to normal as it would ever be, William had written:

Oh, and some other news that might interest you. Work is to be done on all the wartime cemeteries, starting with three to be used as sort of 'test cases'. Architects have been appointed to design them. Forceville on the Somme is one. All the wartime wooden crosses are to be replaced with permanent white markers of Portland stone, made in Britain and brought out here. When finished, all the cemeteries will look magnificent – a fitting resting place for all our brave lads and so comforting for relatives when they visit. You'd be surprised how many families are already making the trip out here to find their loved ones. As I think you know, I have already volunteered to help care for the local cemeteries, Lijssenthoek, of course, and Brandhoek. We had to bury so many there, didn't we? I shall feel I am still helping to care for them.

117

Alice wiped tears from her eyes as she handed the letter to her mother to see William's words for herself. 'My brother is a good man. I only wish Dad would recognize it.'

'He sounds happy,' Norah said wistfully. 'Please give him our love when you write back to him.'

'Why don't you write to him, Mam? We could send it with ours.'

Norah shook her head. 'I daren't,' she whispered. 'If your father were to find out...' She glanced down at the letter once more, as if committing her son's words to memory.

William had ended, as always, by sending loving messages to his mother, grandmother and sister, even though he wrote to Alice regularly too.

But there was never a word about his father.

Thirteen

As they sat together that evening over the chessboard, Robert asked, 'What's the mood like in London, Pips?'

'It's frenetic. Everyone's trying so desperately to forget the war and have a good time and yet, for the workers, the unemployment situation is getting worse. As more and more men are demobbed, there'll be less and less work for them, even when they have got rid of all the women who did war work in the men's absence.'

'A lot of them won't like that. The women, I

mean. They had a taste of independence. Mother was only saying yesterday that a lot of girls won't go back into service now. We were lucky; our staff stayed and are still with us. Even Jake, who wasn't old enough to be called up before the war ended.'

'And did he ever get handed a white feather?'

Robert laughed. 'Heavens no. He's far too small. He only looks about fifteen now.'

'He's never known his real age, has he?'

'No, and I don't suppose he will ever find out now. He seems to know the year, but not the actual date. All he knows is that he's twenty some time this year. Mother's already decided that next year, when he'll be twenty-one, we shall have a celebration for him on or very near Midsummer Day.'

'What a lovely idea. I'll try to be here for that.'

'Check mate!' Robert said suddenly with a wide grin. 'You're not concentrating, Pips.'

'Yes, I was. You've beaten me fair and square. I think you've been practising whilst I've been away.'

'And you're really determined to go back to London, are you?'

Pips wriggled her shoulders. 'Robert, there's nothing for me to do here.'

'There's Daisy,' Robert said craftily.

'Yes, there is. But she's your child. Yours and Alice's. I'd be in danger of monopolizing her, if I stay.'

'I don't think either of us would mind. Alice would be glad of the help.'

'I'll come home very often, I promise.'

119

'So, are you coming to see this car with me?' Mitch said, visiting the apartment in July when he'd heard that Pips was back in London and had now moved in with Milly.

'Of course I'll come, but if I do buy it, where will I keep it?'

'At Brooklands, of course. You'll rent a garage. It's where Paul keeps his cars. And so do I.'

Pips laughed. 'Cars! How many has he got? How many have *you* got?'

Mitch grinned. 'I've only got the one racing car, but Paul had three at the last count plus the one he calls his run-about; the one he uses for ordinary travel. I've asked him to go with us to look at this car for you. Hope you don't mind? He's a whiz with anything mechanical.'

'So was William,' Pips murmured. 'How he would love to look after a racing car.'

The four of them set out at the weekend to visit Mitch's friend.

The car was standing in the yard outside the farmhouse. When they pulled in beside it, Michael appeared and shook hands with them all. Pips inspected it closely. It was a silver-coloured 1912 Sunbeam – the same make that Paul drove.

'They're good cars,' Mitch said. 'As long as you don't think it's too big for you to handle.'

'Oh *dahling!* Don't say that to Pips. That's tantamount to a *dare*. And you know what she's like...'

But Pips only grinned. 'We'll soon see, won't we?' She glanced at Michael. 'May I take it for a run?'

120

'Of course, but just don't go too fast. You'll frighten the labourers in the fields. And you must be sure to keep on our land. She's not allowed on the public roads.'

Mitch laughed. 'Aren't they used to you and your cars by now?'

Michael shook his head. 'The men who work for my father are, of course. We're fairly remote so when I'm repairing and testing cars, the noise doesn't reach the neighbours. At least, I hope it doesn't. Haven't had any complaints yet. Well, not many,' he added with a wide grin. 'You drive it first, Pips, seeing as it's you who wants to buy it, but then I should let Paul drive it too. He'll get a feel for how she handles.'

Pips drove, rather sedately, down the lanes around the farm and arrived back full of enthusiasm.

'It's marvellous,' Pips said climbing out, when she returned to the farmyard.

'You take her, Paul,' Mitch said. 'You're more of a mechanic than I am, though I wouldn't mind a spin when you come back.'

After both men had driven the vehicle, they, too, were enthusiastic.

'Don't you think it's great?' Pips asked them.

Michael laughed. 'A car is always "she" to us.'

'And why is that?' Pips said, adding warningly, 'And be very careful how you answer.'

'I wouldn't get into that discussion, if I were you, Michael,' Mitch laughed.

Michael stroked his chin, deliberating. 'Because we love them and spend a lot of time and money on them. That do?'

121

Pips nodded. 'Reasonable. I'm glad you didn't say because they're temperamental.'

Michael spread his hands. 'Now, would I dare say something like that?'

'Not if you want to sell me this car.' Pips did a quick calculation in her head. Each member of the Maitland family received an annual income from the estate, and all through the war years, the money in Pips's savings account had increased very nicely. Now she could afford to buy herself a car. The deal was struck and they shook hands.

'And now you need to rent a garage at the track,' Paul said. 'I'll act as your mechanic to start with, if you like, but, like I said, you can't drive this on public roads.'

'Yes, though, it's a shame. It would have been nice to have been able to take it home to give Daisy a ride.'

After several practice runs on the Brooklands circuit, Muriel declared that Pips was ready to enter a race. 'We'll enter you for the race at the end of September. Paul's organized a ladies-only race.'

The next few weeks had passed in a blur as Pips practised regularly. As she lined up at the start, her heart was pounding, her head buzzing with all the advice from Mitch, Muriel and Paul. She touched the poppy brooch she always wore. Today, it was pinned to the left shoulder of her driving suit. It was her talisman. She got a reasonable start and was happy to tootle round at her own speed in fourth place, being careful to keep to a sensible racing line. Two cars passed her, but in this, her first race, she didn't let it worry her. It was better to get the feel of the track. Even if she came last this time, at least she'd taken part. But as her confidence grew, she increased her speed and passed the driver in front of her. Now, she was in fifth place. Another lap and she was back in fourth. Well, it wouldn't be too bad, she told herself, if she could finish where she'd started, but it would be nice to gain just one more place... She felt the power of the car beneath her and gently pressed her foot on the accelerator. The car leapt forward and she flew past the next car. Now, however, she was running out of laps and the car in front of her was several seconds ahead.

The race finished with Pips in third place. Her friends surrounded the car as she drew to a halt.

'I say, old thing, that was some drive.'

'Darling, you were wonderful.'

'Third place in your first race.' Muriel was smiling. 'You'll actually get a prize. I can see we've got some real competition now. You've certainly proved yourself worthy of being one of the Brooklands Girls.'

'Your engine sounded a bit rough on the last lap,' Paul said. 'I'll take a look at it for you. Although, Mitch was talking about a friend of yours, who's a good mechanic. Perhaps you'd prefer him to look after it for you.'

Pips heaved herself out of the car. 'He used to work for us and he came with us to Belgium at the start of the war as a stretcher bearer, but he stayed there. He married a Belgian nurse. So, I still want you to look after my car for me, please. You must let me know how much I owe you.'

Paul waved her offer aside. 'No charge – it'll be my pleasure.'

'He does the same for me,' Mitch said and then tapped the side of his nose. 'But a bottle of whisky won't come amiss now and again.'

Pips laughed. 'You're on.' Then she sobered as she asked, 'I saw one of the cars up against the iron fencing on the Railway Straight. Who was it? Was she hurt?'

The two men glanced at each other. 'We hear she's all right. Her tyres lost tread during the race.'

'The front of her car's a mess, though. That'll take a bit of putting right.'

'Come on, darling. Let's get you to where the presentations are made. I can't wait to see you get your prize.'

The crowd clustered around the presentation area and when Pips stepped up beside the two women who had come in first and second place, a cheer from the crowd went up. She shook hands with them and was relieved and delighted when they congratulated her with genuine warmth; she had expected animosity but as Muriel had explained to her, although there was keen rivalry on the track, once the race was over, they were all friends again, united in their love of the sport.

When the presentations had taken place and the three women had stepped down, a tall fair-haired man was standing beside Mitch.

'You're one of Muriel's protégées, aren't you?' he said to Pips, as he gripped her hand firmly. 'And it's your first race, isn't it? Well done. We'll have to watch our backs, won't we, Mitch? My name's Jeff Pointer, by the way, and you've just beaten my sister, who was in fourth place.' But he was laughing as he added, 'I work for Mitch. I'm a pilot at his flying school. Would you join us for a celebratory drink?' He was tall and thin, with bright ginger hair and a face covered with freckles. His eyes twinkled merrily at her.

'I'd love to, but my friends are waiting for me.'

'Bring them along too. The more the merrier. I can see Muriel, oh and there's Milly Fortesque with her. *Now,* the party'll begin if Milly's here.'

'You know Milly?'

'Who doesn't?' Jeff grinned. 'She's a regular here with Paul. We've been trying to get her to learn to drive for years, but she adamantly refuses. D'you know her?'

'Yes, I do. I'm lodging with her at present.'

'Then your life will be one long round of parties,' he chuckled. 'She'll be making up for lost time now the war's over.' He frowned. 'I didn't see her for some time towards the end of the war. I've no idea what she got up to.'

Pips said nothing. Perhaps, one day, she would enlighten him, but she wasn't sure just how many more people Milly wanted to know what she'd 'got up to' in the war. She was saved from answering him by Milly and the others joining them.

'Darling, how perfectly marvellous. I'm *so* proud of you. And your picture will be in the papers. Did you see all the photographers milling around you? And well done to Pamela too...' She kissed Jeff on both cheeks. 'You must both come to my party next Saturday night. Muriel and Pattie have already agreed to come. And Mitch and Paul will be there, of course. It'll be a real

Brooklands affair.'

'I can't wait.' Jeff smiled at Milly and winked at Pips.

Fourteen

'My dear girl, how lovely to see you again.' Dr John Hazelwood came towards her, his hands outstretched in greeting. 'You haven't changed a bit.'

'Nor have you,' Pips said, smiling at the small, rotund, jovial man with rimless spectacles and a bristling moustache.

As they sat down at the table in the small restaurant where he had suggested they should meet, Pips said, 'I hope you didn't mind me contacting you.'

'Of course not. How can I help?'

Pips plunged straight in. 'I'm appalled by the sight of so many soldiers begging on the streets. I want to do something, but I don't know where – or how – to begin.'

Dr Hazelwood beamed. 'Do you remember Talbot House in Poperinghe?'

'Indeed I do. It was set up by the Reverend Clayton as a place where the soldiers could have rest and recuperation during their time away from the front, wasn't it?'

The doctor nodded. 'For a few days they could forget about the war, though I doubt they did. Well, I have opened up a house in Clapham for much the same purpose, though now it's to give

126

help and advice to those who are finding their return home very difficult. We can even give bed and board if it's necessary, though most of them just need assistance to find their own way ahead. Marigold is still doing what she does best and raising funds, though it's more difficult for her, now that the war is actually over.'

Marigold Parrott had been a valued member of Dr Hazelwood's flying ambulance corps. She had raised money, obtained equipment and supplies.

'I'll be sure to tell my mother. I know she'd want to help. But what can I do?'

'Hazelwood House is run by volunteers. If you could spare a day or so here and there...'

Pips beamed. 'It's just the sort of thing I've been looking for. I'd be delighted to help.'

Over coffee they discussed details and then Dr Hazelwood asked, 'Tell me, how is your brother?'

Pips sighed and explained, ending, 'We just can't seem to get him to do anything.'

Towards the end of the war, the Maitland family had welcomed convalescing wounded soldiers into their home. Robert had become interested in the effects of shell shock and had been encouraged to interview patients and write about his findings for medical journals.

Dr Hazelwood nodded. 'I feared as much. Your father said something of the sort in his last letter.' He was thoughtful for a moment. Slowly, he said, 'I will write to him again and encourage him to resume his work. His findings would still be very valuable.'

'Next time I go to Lincolnshire, I'll talk to him too.'

By the time they parted on the pavement out-side the restaurant, Pips's step was lighter than it had been for years. At last there was something useful she could do and yet she could still enjoy Brooklands and Milly's parties without feeling pangs of guilt.

Now she could really feel she was living her life to the full.

'Daisy! My, how you've grown!'

With a wide grin, the little girl ran into Pips's outstretched arms to be swung high in the air. 'I'll soon be free, Aunty Pips.'

'So you will. And what would you like for your birthday?'

Alice and Robert watched with indulgent eyes. After a non-stop round of parties in the city, even Pips had felt the need to return home for a few days at the end of September.

Still carrying her niece, Pips sat down near the window. 'So, how's everyone? I haven't seen Mother or Father yet. I expect he's out on his rounds, is he? But where's Mother?'

'Gone into the city to see her friend Rosemary Fieldsend.'

'How's old Basil?' The three of them smiled, re-membering the major who, as 'someone import-ant in the war office', had kept them well informed during the war.

'He's fine. A bit bored now that it's all over.'

'Your mother and Mrs Fieldsend seem to have the right idea,' Alice said. 'They're still busy fundraising, but for the wounded now. There are so many of them who can't find any work at all and the weekly compensation allowance for the injured is hardly enough to keep a family.'

Although Pips already knew that Robert was no longer studying shell-shocked patients, she decided to play the next few minutes very craftily, deciding not to mention, for the moment, anything about her meeting with Dr Hazelwood. 'You know, Robert, that's something else you could write about – the plight of the maimed. Have you done all you can do for the present on the effects of shell shock?'

Robert pulled a face and shrugged listlessly. 'I – sort of – lost interest.'

Pips stared at him. 'Lost interest?' She glanced at Alice and then back to Robert. 'Why? I thought at least you were still doing that.'

'You tell her, Alice. I don't want to talk about it.' He got up suddenly and left the room.

'Whatever's happened? I thought he'd still got that to occupy him – something really worthwhile, if he still feels he can't practise alongside Father?'

'We all thought that – even Robert himself for a while – but I think talking to sufferers and then writing about it accentuated everything. He was reliving the past every day.'

Pips was thoughtful for a moment. 'Alice, would you mind if I talked to him?'

'I'd be glad if you would. We've all tried, but he just brushes us aside. I know your poor mother feels it deeply that she can't reach him.'

'I'm surprised he doesn't listen to you.'

Alice sighed. 'It hurts me – but no, he doesn't. Not now.'

Pips touched her hand and smiled. 'Leave it with me. I'll give it a lot of thought but before I go back to London, I will talk to him. And now, Daisy, let's go out into the sunshine and teach you how to play croquet. I'm sure the small mallet I used to play with as a child must still be in a shed somewhere. And this afternoon, we'll go and see Grandma Dawson, shall we?'

With their day happily organized, Pips tried to put the matter of her brother's idleness out of her mind, but it niggled away at her for the rest of the day.

'Where's Luke?' Daisy asked as soon as they entered the Dawsons' cottage after lunch that day.

'He's picking blackberries in the back garden,' Norah said. 'Do you want to go and help him?'

Daisy nodded.

'I'll find you a bowl, duck.'

'I'd better go out and watch them,' Pips said, starting to get up.

'No need, Miss Pips. Luke'll watch her. He's very good with her. Very gentle and protective.'

'Aye, he is.' Ma nodded. 'But a bit too much sometimes, Norah. He can be a bit possessive. He doesn't like her playing with any of the other kiddies in the village.'

The three women chatted for half an hour, though Pips kept getting up to look through the scullery window just to make sure that Daisy was all right. *Maybe I'm getting possessive over her too,* she thought with an inward smile.

'How are you all?' she asked Norah and Ma.

Norah spread an old blanket on the kitchen table to do her weekly ironing. She picked up the

130

heated flat iron from the hob. 'Oh – you know.'

Ma glanced at her daughter-in-law. 'She'll not mind me saying it to you, Miss Pips, but she's lost. From having a houseful of her family to care for, she's only got her husband and an old woman to look after now.'

Norah picked up one of Len's shirts and smoothed it out. 'Everything reminds me of them,' Norah murmured. 'Even this. There should be a pile of men's shirts to iron every week but now there's only two. I wouldn't have minded if they'd come back wounded. Even if they hadn't been able to work no more. We'd've managed somehow. Len'd've worked twice as hard just to have 'em back home but...' Her voice trailed away, but after a moment's pause she spoke again, more strongly now. 'But we mustn't grumble. You've only to go into any church hereabouts and read the list of names of all those who didn't come back. We're not the only ones grieving.'

'They're starting to build a lot of war memorials and inscribe the names of the fallen on them. Have you heard if anything is planned for Doddington?' Pips asked.

The two women shook their heads.

'It'd be nice, though,' Ma said. 'It'd be somewhere for us to go – a focal point – since we haven't got a grave to tend.'

'I do know where they're buried,' Pips said quietly. 'Bernard and Roy are together and Harold is not far away. Maybe one day you could visit them, Mrs Dawson.'

Norah opened her mouth to reply, but at that moment the two children came into the kitchen

131

carefully carrying their bowls full of blackberries.

'I showed her which to pick, Grandma,' Luke said, grinning. 'On'y the ripe ones, else she'd 'ave picked green 'uns an' all.'

'Hello, Luke. My, you've grown too.' Pips glanced at Norah. 'Isn't he like his uncle, Bernard?'

'Aye, he's shot up just lately. Peggy has a job to keep him in trousers that fit.'

'He's going to be a big lad, like his other uncle – William,' Pips said, without thinking.

Puzzled, Luke glanced from his grandmother to Ma. 'Who's William?' he asked innocently.

'I put my size fives right in it. I'm so sorry, Alice,' Pips told her sister-in-law when she returned to the hall. 'I wouldn't upset your mam and Ma for the world. I remember not to mention William in front of Len, but I totally forgot they don't speak of him in front of the boy, though I should have remembered because they always make sure he's out of the way every time I take them a letter to read. Oh dear.'

'Don't worry about it, Pips. What happened?'

'Your mam just muttered. "He's a relative and he was a big lad like you're going to be." Then she gave him a mug of tea and a sandwich to take up to his grandpa at his workshop and it seemed to pass off all right. Just so long as Luke didn't ask Len who William was.'

'Dad can't go through life without William's name ever being mentioned, even if he'd like to,' Alice said tartly. Her sharpness was not aimed at Pips for her blunder, but at her father's stub-

132

bornness. 'It's ridiculous the way he's acting and so unfair on Mam and Ma.' She sighed. 'There's nothing I can do about them, but I do so want to help Robert. Have you thought about what you could say to him, Pips?'

'Sort of.' Pips grinned. 'Maybe a bull in a china shop would be the best approach with him.'

Alice laughed too. 'You do cheer us up, Pips. I understand why you want to be in London, but, please, don't ever stay away too long, will you? We all miss you so much.'

'Dear Alice,' Pips said, giving her a hug. 'And now, I will go and find Robert – just for a chat at the moment. I'll bide my time about the other matter.'

'He'll be where he spends most of his time – in the drawing room gazing out of the window.'

'And seeing scenes from the past, I expect.'

'I fear so.'

Fifteen

As the family rose after dinner, Pips said, 'I've set the chessboard up in the drawing room, Robert. It's time I beat you. I must be losing my touch.'

'I don't really feel like it tonight, Pips. I'm tired. I think I'll go up to bed.'

'Nonsense. You can't possibly be too tired for one game. You've done nothing all day.'

She heard Alice gasp and her mother say softly, 'Oh Pips...'

For a moment, Robert glared at her and then he pulled a face and shrugged. 'As ever, my dear sister is perfectly right.'

They climbed the wide stairs side by side and entered the Blue Drawing Room on the first floor. Pips had set up the chessboard in front of the fireplace and they sat down on either side of it.

'Actually,' she began, 'I don't want to play – I want to talk to you.'

'Ah, I was rather afraid you might.'

Pips said, 'Robert, what's happened? Your moods are worse than ever and more frequent.'

He sighed heavily. 'Nothing's happened. That's probably the trouble. There's nothing for me to *do* any more.'

'Oh phooey. There's plenty, if only you'd put your mind to it.' She put her head on one side. More gently she asked, 'Are you still getting nightmares?'

He nodded.

'And why have you given up your research into the causes of shell shock?'

'It just makes it all worse. Talking to the men and then writing it all down. I just never get away from it.'

'Do you anyway?'

Gloomily, he said, 'If I'm honest, no.'

'It's a shame you've given up on that work, Robert. I thought you wanted to help people. To be a doctor.'

'How can I?' he snapped.

Unfazed, Pips said, 'By doing exactly what you were doing. Researching the causes of the terrible mental anguish of the wounded. Emotional scars are every bit as bad as physical ones, but they're not seen and understood by others, so in a way, they're almost worse. With your medical knowledge and your own experiences – oh, I don't mean losing your arm, I mean everything you saw out there too – just think, if you could come up with some treatment for the condition, or at the very least an understanding of it, that would be something, wouldn't it?'

'It might be a case of "physician, heal thyself".'

'Quite possibly, but in so doing, you'd be helping a lot of others too.'

'It's just that I'm trying my damnedest to forget, not still be steeped in it.'

'You'll never forget, Robert. None of us will. Why d'you think there's this frantic effort to fill our waking hours with music and dancing – and drinking, it has to be said?'

'Is that what you're trying to do in London?'

'Of course I am.'

'And can you? Forget, I mean.'

Slowly Pips shook her head. 'No, it's impossible when every time you set foot outside the door there's an old soldier standing on a street corner, maybe without an arm or a leg – or both – carrying a tray of matches in an effort to earn money to support his family. There are some that just stand there rattling a box and making no attempt to hide the fact that they're begging. Poor devils!'

'But I thought they were paid compensation – a weekly sum – a sort of pension?'

'Allegedly – but I expect it's scarcely enough to support a man, wife and several children, especially in the cities.'

'I suppose what you're telling me is that I should count myself lucky and stop feeling sorry for myself.'

'Now, would I do a thing like that?'

'Yes.'

'You can't help remembering, Robert, I know that, but you are lucky in that you have the support of a loving family and there really is something useful you can do. You started to write about the effects of shell shock with Alice's help, if I remember. Didn't she type up your notes for you and weren't you sending them through to Dr Hazelwood? I thought he was going to get them published in the right place for you?'

'He was.' He smiled wryly. 'He's still interested. He keeps badgering me too. In fact, I had a letter from him two days ago asking how my research was going.'

Pips spread her hands. 'There you are, then. Why on earth aren't you getting on with it?'

'Probably because you're not here. Alice is a darling and I love her even more than the day I married her, but she daren't talk to me quite as bluntly as you do. And poor Mother daren't say "boo" to me.'

'That surprises me. Mother was never the reticent sort. But I expect not knowing what you – what we – went through, she doesn't quite know how to handle it. What about Father?'

'He's tried in his gentle way, but I suppose I needed your blunt approach.'

'So, has it worked?'

'All I can promise you, Pips, is that I'll have another go. I still correspond with some of the men we had here as convalescents and the Lincoln Hospital will be able to put me in touch with a few more, I've no doubt.'

'Good,' Pips said, getting up and starting to move towards the door. 'I'll be going back to London at the weekend.'

'Are there still more races before the end of the year?'

Pips shook her head. 'Only a motorcycle race meeting in October, but I have a date with an aeroplane and I want to see you back at work before I leave.'

'You're on, but where d'you think you're going now? You're not going to escape that easily. You promised me a game of chess and I want to prove that the last time I beat you was no fluke.'

Back in London by October, Pips wrote home, addressing her letter to her mother and telling her about the work she had found at Hazelwood House. She knew the news would be relayed to the rest of the family. Then she added:

I'll be coming home at the end of November in time for 'the birthdays', but is anyone coming down to London for the unveiling of the Cenotaph in Whitehall on the eleventh of next month? Milly says we can find accommodation for anyone who wants to come.

A few days later, Henrietta replied:

Your father and I will come down on the train, but sadly, no one else seemed inclined. I even asked Sam

137

Nuttall, but he says he prefers to go to the old comrades club that's opened in the city for sing-songs and reminiscences. And, of course, not one of us can persuade Robert and, without him, Alice won't come. We don't want to trouble Milly, so if you could find us a nice small hotel...

On 10 November, Henrietta and Edwin arrived in London. When they were settled into the hotel not far from where Milly lived, Pips went to see them.

'There's something else happening tomorrow after the unveiling. The funeral in Westminster Abbey of the unknown soldier.'

'Are we allowed to attend that?'

'I don't think so. The King is to follow the cortège along with other members of the Royal Family and ministers of state. I've heard that about one hundred women who have lost their husbands and all their sons – and sadly there are that many – have been invited to attend. And other bereaved mothers will be in the abbey too. I don't think we can go, though we could stand outside to pay our respects, I suppose. But tonight, the coffin is arriving at Victoria Station at about half past eight and a few of us are going down to see it. Would you like to come with us? I don't expect we'll be able to get very close as it will no doubt be guarded through the night. But it would be nice to see it, don't you think?'

Henrietta and Edwin glanced at each other and then chorused, 'Of course.'

Now Pips hid her smile. 'Mitch has offered to pick you up in his car. I hope that's all right.'

Stiffly, Henrietta said, 'That's very kind of him.'

'Mrs Maitland,' Mitch greeted her, gallantly kissing her hand. 'Please sit in the front seat. Pips and Dr Maitland can climb into the back. Here's a rug for your knees. Now, are you comfortable?'

Henrietta inclined her head graciously.

They drove to Victoria and as he parked the car, Mitch said, 'It's on platform eight, I believe.'

They were surprised how many people had come to view the casket. 'It's been organized so reverently,' Mitch said, as he offered Henrietta his arm. 'They exhumed the bodies of unknown British soldiers from various battlefields and placed them in six plain coffins covered by union flags and took them to a chapel near Arras. An officer – a brigadier, I believe – who had no idea where each one had come from, then placed his hand on one of the coffins at random. The others were taken away for reburial and the chosen one stayed in the chapel overnight. The next day, undertakers placed the coffin in a casket of oak and branded it with iron. Do you see the medieval sword on the top?'

Henrietta nodded.

'That was chosen from the Royal Collection by the King himself.'

'What does it say on the plate?'

Mitch squinted to read the lettering. *'A British Warrior who fell in the Great War 1914–1918 for King and Country.'*

'Very appropriate,' Henrietta murmured.

'I understand that tomorrow morning it's going to be placed on a gun carriage and taken by six horses to Whitehall for the unveiling of the Ceno-taph. It'll then be taken on to Westminster Abbey.'

Henrietta couldn't stop herself holding on to Mitch's arm a little tighter. It was all so very sad.

'Shall I take you back to the hotel now?' he asked softly.

'If you please, Mr Hammond. I'd be most grate-ful.'

The following morning, Mitch again fetched the couple from their hotel and took them to White-hall. Standing together, Edwin, Henrietta, Pips, Mitch, Milly and Paul watched the arrival of the coffin of the unknown warrior.

'They say that the six horses pulling the gun carriage are all war veterans,' Mitch murmured to Pips. 'Do you see they're wearing their war colours?'

She nodded, unable to speak for the lump in her throat. To her, those horses represented the sacrifice her beautiful Midnight had made.

As the carriage drew to a halt, the King stepped forward and placed a wreath on top of it. He stepped back and saluted. There followed a short service conducted by the Archbishop of Canter-bury. As Big Ben struck the final note of eleven o'clock, the King pressed the button that released the two huge union flags covering the cenotaph. A reverent silence of two minutes followed. Then, led by the King, wreaths were laid at the foot of the Cenotaph.

'Oh, it's just like the wood and plaster one,' Pips whispered. 'Same shape and everything, but the wreaths are now carved.'

'And now it's all made in Portland stone,' Paul said.

'It's beautiful,' Milly breathed and wiped tears from her eyes.

They continued to stand behind the lines of soldiers whilst the command was given for the procession carrying the unknown soldier to his final resting place in Westminster Abbey to begin.

'It's a wonderful idea, isn't it,' Edwin said, his voice a little unsteady as they prepared to leave Whitehall, 'that an unknown soldier should represent the thousands who lost their lives in battle? It'll be a focal point for all those whose loved one has no known grave.'

'I understand there are four wreaths representing tributes from our Allies,' Mitch said. 'One has been made up of laurels from the grounds of the ruined cathedral in Ypres. And I think a service here is going to be an annual event on Armistice Day.'

They walked together to the abbey even though they could not go inside.

'We'll come and have a look later in the week,' Pips said, linking her arm through Milly's.

As the crowds began to disperse at last, Edwin said, 'And now you must all come and have lunch with us at the hotel before we catch our train home later this afternoon.'

As they walked back and Mitch once more took Henrietta's arm, she said, 'You have been very kind to us, Mr Hammond, but I do hope you won't interpret this as a sign that I approve of your pursuit of my daughter.'

Mitch turned his twinkling dark eyes on her.

'Now, whatever gave you that idea, Mrs Maitland?'

'I am no fool, young man. I have seen the way you look at her and I remember when you were staying at the hall after your injury. You made no secret of your admiration for her. And it wasn't all because she'd saved your life.'

'So, you don't like me?'

Henrietta chuckled and her own eyes were full of merriment as she said, 'I'm beginning to like you very much, Mr Hammond, but...'

'Mitch, please.'

'You're what I call a lovable rogue and I don't think you're exactly what I have in mind for my daughter's husband.'

'But what does *she* have in mind, Mrs Maitland? Isn't that more to the point?'

Henrietta pursed her lips. 'Unfortunately, Philippa is very wayward. And she has been very hurt once before. I don't trust her to make a suitable choice.'

'But you want her to be happy, don't you?'

'Of course I do.'

'Then,' Mitch said carefully, not wanting to offend this lady, of whom he was growing quite fond, 'whether it's me or not, I do think you should allow her to make her own choice.'

The corner of Henrietta's mouth twitched with wry humour as she said, 'I'm rather afraid, Mitch, that she will anyway.'

The two of them glanced at each other and exchanged a look of understanding that neither of them, until this moment, had ever thought possible.

After his injury, Mitch had gone to Doddington Hall to recover. Henrietta had seen for herself his interest in Pips, but had viewed him as a brash, flirtatious playboy. But now she was seeing a different side to his nature and her feelings towards him were changing, though not, she reminded herself sharply, enough to view him as a possible son-in-law.

'So,' Robert asked his parents when they arrived back at the hall later that evening. 'Was it all unbearably sad?'

'It was sad, yes,' Edwin said, 'but there was such a dignified pride amongst all those there, that it was uplifting to see that those who were lost are being revered and remembered. I wish you'd felt able to come with us, Robert. I think you would have found it helpful.'

'I doubt it,' Robert answered morosely. There was a pause before he asked. 'When's Pips coming home again?'

'At the end of the month for the children's birthdays.'

'Not before?'

'I don't think so.'

'I don't think she cares about us now she's got all these fancy friends in London.'

The mild-tempered Edwin, for once, glared at his son and was on the point of making a sharp retort, when the sight of Robert's empty sleeve checked him. He took a deep breath and forced himself to say steadily, 'She cares very much for all of us, but we must allow her to make some sort of life for herself.'

'To find a husband, you mean,' Robert said sarcastically. 'Did Mother pick one out for her whilst she was there?'

Edwin's even temper was restored as he chuckled. 'I think she would have liked to have tried but the only two young men we met were Milly's friend, Paul, and – um – Mitch Hammond.'

'Oh him! I can't see Mother ever approving of him.'

'Probably not, but he was very kind to us during our stay. Ferried us about in his car.'

Robert snorted derisively. 'Trying to make a good impression, I expect.'

'The only person – as you very well know, Robert – that he has to make a good impression on is Pips.'

'He'll never do that, I promise you.'

Sixteen

Pips came home again for Daisy's birthday at the beginning of December. It had become a tradition that the two young cousins should celebrate their special days together, first at the hall for Daisy's and then at the Dawsons' cottage for Luke's.

'What are we getting Daisy for Christmas this year?' Pips asked the family when the excited little girl, now three years old, was safely in bed. 'A pony?'

Alice glanced at Robert. 'Now that is a good

idea. You could teach her to ride.'

Robert grimaced and muttered, 'Could I?'

'Of course you could,' Pips said firmly. 'You'll only need to walk beside her to start with.'

'But what if the pony bolted?'

'You can still run, can't you? You haven't lost the use of your legs as well, have you?' She heard her mother's sharp intake of breath at the far end of the table and, out of the corner of her eye, she saw Alice cover her mouth with trembling fingers, but Pips kept her gaze fixed on her brother.

For a brief moment, Robert glared at her and then he laughed. 'Oh Pips, what would I do without you? My wonderful mother and my darling Alice...' he glanced at Henrietta and touched his wife's arm in a fond gesture – 'are kindness itself and I love them both dearly for it. You, too, Father. But it's Pips who dares to challenge me, to snap me out of self-pity. Yes, you're right, I will teach Daisy to ride, but I'll always have Jake with us – just in case.'

Pips nodded her approval. 'Jake will be ecstatic to have a pony to care for again.'

As Pips had predicted, Jake Goodall was thrilled. 'Oh Master Robert, it'll be like old times to have a horse in the stable again.'

Robert chuckled. 'Not exactly a horse, Jake, just a little girl's pony.'

Jake grinned. 'If she's owt like her aunty, it'll not be long before she needs a horse. And, yes, I'd be delighted to help you any time you say. Have you got one in mind?'

Robert shook his head. 'I wondered if you knew

145

of any?'

'I was talking to a mate of mine after church last Sunday and he was talking about his dad needing a fresh shire horse for his farm. He knows a horse dealer near Horncastle. He might be able to help us. Shall I ask him?'

'Please do. And if we need to go and look at one, will you come with us?'

Jake's boyish face turned pink with pleasure. 'I'd be honoured, Master Robert.'

They set off two days later, Pips driving Edwin's car. Just before they reached the market town, Pips turned off down a narrow lane towards a farm set in the Wolds.

'My mate said he's a tough man to deal with. Drives a hard bargain.'

'As long as he's fair with his price, Jake, I don't mind. Anything for Daisy. But we want the best, so if you have any doubts, don't hesitate to say so.'

'I won't, Miss Pips.'

The man – Ben Rudd – was a farmer and horse dealer.

'It's a pity you couldn't wait till the Horncastle August horse fair.' The man, a burly farmer, dressed in corduroys and with bushy sideburns, shook hands with them. He cast just one sympathetic glance at Robert's empty sleeve and held out his left hand. 'Ya'd have had the pick then. Folks come from all over to the fair here, even the Romanies, but I've a couple I'd like to show you. Stables is this way.'

He led them round the back of the farmhouse into a yard surrounded by buildings. Every stable

– and there were about twenty of them, Pips estimated without actually counting them – held a horse.

'Oh my, this is Heaven!'

The three of them followed the farmer past each one, but their progress was slow because Pips wanted to stop and stroke each nose over the stable door. Following her lead, Jake patted each one too.

Halfway round the yard, Pips stopped in front of a black stallion. Pips rarely cried, but at the sight of the magnificent animal, her eyes filled with tears. 'Oh Robert – Jake – look. He's just like Midnight.'

Ben Rudd stopped and turned back. 'You have a horse like him?'

'I – had.' Pips's voice shook. 'He – he was taken in the war. Commandeered for the front.'

'Aye, you don't have to tell me about that, miss,' Ben said bitterly. 'Nearly ruined me, the war did. I expect you never saw him again?'

Pips shook her head, not trusting herself to speak.

Gently, Robert said, 'He's far too big for Daisy, Pips.'

'But you could ride him, Robert. And Jake would love to keep him exercised, wouldn't you, Jake?'

Jake hesitated and before he could answer, Robert said, 'Now, don't embarrass the lad. Of course Jake would love to have him in our stable, but I doubt I could ride a big fellow like him and I wouldn't want temptation put in Daisy's way.' He smiled. 'She's like you, Pips, far too daring for her own safety.'

Ben Rudd moved closer. 'Now, let me tell you folks summat. I'm known about these parts as a hard-headed businessman and, most of the time, I am. 'Specially with folks who try to tek advantage of me. But I can also recognize genuine folk, so I'll mek a deal with you. You can have him on a month's trial and if he don't suit, you can bring him back. I won't even tek any money off you till you've decided whether to keep him or not.'

'Oh Robert, do let's take Mr Rudd's offer. Let's at least give it a try.'

'But if he's anything like Midnight, Pips, I'll never handle him. Only you could ever ride him. Even when I had both arms, I could never manage him.'

'He's a big feller, I'll grant you that,' Ben said, 'and I dun't expect you to believe me, but he's a gentle giant. He's even good with children, though mebbe he's a mite too big for your little 'un yet. She's three, so I was told. Is that right?'

Pips nodded.

'Then she'd be better with a pony. Let me show you the two I have.'

He led the way again round the yard until he came to a larger stable in which there were two ponies.

'They're brothers. One's a year older than the other, but they're both docile.'

Pips, Robert and Jake inspected the ponies and all agreed they were both perfect. 'I can't choose,' Pips laughed. 'Why don't we take both of them, Robert, then there'll be one for Luke to ride too? You know we always try to treat them both equally at birthdays and Christmas.'

'I don't think Len Dawson would agree. He'd see it as charity.'

Pips thought quickly. 'Not if it stays at the hall and we don't actually call it Luke's. We'll just say it's for him to ride whenever he wants, alongside Daisy.'

'It's a thought,' Robert murmured. He turned to Ben. 'What's your best price, Mr Rudd, for both of them?'

The man stroked his sideburns thoughtfully, glancing from one to the other. 'Normally, I'd be asking more, but I'll be fair with you.' He named a price.

Robert, Pips and Jake glanced at each other.

'Tek a moment on yer own. I'll see if the missus can rustle up a cuppa for you.'

As the man turned away, Pips called after him, 'And your price for the stallion, if we decided to take you up on your offer?'

Ben turned, removed his cap, scratched his head and then pulled his cap on again. 'Ah, now that'd be about double the price for both ponies. But he's a magnificent animal. I'll let you have a closer look at him.' He walked back towards them and opened the stable door and led the horse out into the yard.

'He certainly is,' Pips murmured under her breath. Louder, she asked, 'What's his name? And the ponies – what are they called?'

'The big feller's Samson. The brown pony is Jingles and the slightly smaller brown-and-white one is Lucky.'

Pips went to the stallion's head and held her fist

149

under his nose for him to get her scent. Then she stroked and patted his face. The three of them walked round and round the animal.

'He's so like Midnight,' Pips murmured. 'It's incredible.'

'But not as feisty, by all accounts.'

Pips laughed. 'Actually, I don't mind if he is, but maybe it's a good thing really. For Daisy as she grows up.'

'I could never ride Midnight, Miss Pips,' Jake put in. 'But if you get this one, he'd need riding out regularly.' There was a look of longing in the young man's eyes. Then suddenly, he hesitated, but Pips guessed his meaning.

'If I'm away a lot, Jake, you could exercise him, couldn't you?'

Jake beamed.

'Right, that's settled. If you agree, Robert, we'll take all three.'

'Hey, wait a minute. We haven't discussed the price yet.'

'We're not haggling. Mr Rudd is being very fair, aren't you?'

Ben smiled. 'If you're taking all three, then I can lower the overall price a bit.'

Pips spat on her hand and held it out to the farmer. 'Done.'

As they climbed back into Edwin's car, Pips said, 'And now I have to tell Mother – and Mr Dawson.'

'Rather you than me,' Robert chuckled.

To their surprise, Henrietta was delighted that there were going to be three animals back in the stables and even Len Dawson accepted the news that Luke would have a pony to ride at the hall whenever he wanted.

'I never thought he'd be so agreeable,' Pips confided to Robert, 'but it seems that nothing's too good for his grandson – never mind where it's coming from.'

'When is Mr Rudd bringing them?' Robert asked.

'Christmas Eve. Alice and I have arranged for Daisy to go down to the Dawsons for the afternoon. That way – hopefully – neither of them will see them until Christmas morning after church. Mother says she'll invite the family to have a drink with us after the service and Jake can bring the ponies onto the front lawn for the children to see.'

Pips wrote to Milly to tell her that she was staying in Lincolnshire and inviting her to the hall for the festivities.

Milly wrote back:

Darling, how sweet of you to invite me, but I must spend it with my parents and Granny. I hope you understand. You would have been most welcome at the manor, but I know you just have to be with Daisy at Christmas! Have a wonderful time, but do come back very soon. You have to get some practice in. There's a meeting at the end of March and Muriel thinks you should enter the all-women's race...

When Len, Norah and Ma were seated in the Great Hall in front of the windows overlooking the front lawn, the maid handed around glasses

151

of mulled wine.

'Something warming,' Henrietta smiled. 'Happy Christmas to you all.'

The Dawsons, a little nervous in what were to them rather grand surroundings, returned the greeting. Luke and Daisy were at the far side of the room, telling each other what presents they had received.

'Daisy – Luke,' Pips said, putting down her glass, 'I want you to put your coats on and come outside with me. We have a surprise for both of you. Sarah...' she turned to the maid, 'please tell Jake we're ready.'

The girl nodded and scuttled away.

'Why, Aunty Pips?'

'You'll see.'

They stepped out of the house and down the front steps and waited on the driveway for a few moments before Jake appeared from around the corner leading two ponies.

'Oh – oh!' Daisy breathed.

'Now – don't rush to them. Go to them nice and gently until they get to know you. One's for you, Daisy, and the other is for Luke to ride any time he wants to, though the pony will live here so that Jake can look after them both.' Tactfully, she added, 'The ponies are brothers and I think they'd be unhappy to be separated, don't you? Is that all right, Luke?'

The boy was pink with pleasure and lost for words. He merely nodded.

'Let's go and say "hello".'

They walked slowly towards the ponies and Pips showed them how to hold their fists under the ponies' noses to allow the animals to accept their scent and then to pat their faces.

'Now, Jake has saddled them up, so how about a little ride?'

'Yes, please, Aunty Pips,' Daisy whispered, still understanding that she mustn't frighten them.

'Yours is called Lucky and the other is named Jingles,' Pips said as she lifted Daisy onto the back of the smaller animal. Jake helped Luke to mount and then they both led the children around the lawn.

'That's enough for today,' Pips said after half an hour. 'Now, Luke, I want you to promise me something. Like I said, you're welcome to come and ride Jingles any time, but you must never do it on your own.'

Luke nodded solemnly. 'I promise, Miss Pips, and besides, I'll only want to ride when Daisy's riding. And anyway, I'll be at school in the week and I help me granddad afterwards, so...' Luke, though not yet five at the time, had been able to start at the nearest primary school the previous September.

'Then perhaps we can arrange with Jake that you come every Saturday afternoon. How would that be?'

The boy nodded and stroked Jingles's neck. 'See you on Saturday, boy.'

'Eh, but it's nice to see Miss Pips riding out again on a black horse,' Ma said as she sat for a few moments outside the cottage on Boxing Day morning. 'Quite like old times.'

Sitting beside her for a brief respite, Norah

153

said, 'It is, but I'm not sure about Luke being allowed to have his own pony at the hall. He'll get ideas above his station. I'm surprised Len agreed to it.'

'Oh Norah, for Heaven's sake, let the boy have some fun. There's not been much of that in recent years. They're too young to be grieving like us. And besides, haven't you noticed, they're very carefully avoiding saying that it's Luke's pony – only that he can ride it any time he likes?'

'He'll look upon it as his.'

'I think you're wrong there. For a little chap, he's very sensible and it's not in his nature to take advantage of his privileged position as Daisy's cousin and best friend.'

'You think not.' Norah was still doubtful. 'Well, I can see trouble ahead if they get too close. It's all very well now, but what happens as they grow up? You tell me that, Ma.'

But Ma, smoking her clay pipe, didn't even trouble herself to answer.

Seventeen

When Pips arrived back in London early in the New Year, there was a letter from William waiting for her. Knowing that Pips now spent much of her time in London, he often wrote to Milly's address. He had written it in the middle of December.

'It only arrived yesterday,' Milly told her, recognizing the Belgian stamp. 'I expect it was delayed in the Christmas post.'

Pips opened the letter and then read it to Milly:

'*...I can hardly contain myself for joy, Pips. Brigitta is expecting a baby, due towards the end of March or early April. I have written to Alice too and hope she will be able to find a moment to tell Mam and Ma...*'

'How wonderful. I'm absolutely thrilled for them.'

'March is going to be an exciting month, then,' Milly laughed. 'Because Muriel has entered you for the all-women's race that Paul's arranged at the end of the BARC meeting.'

'Oh my! Then I'd better get some practice in.'

'Have you seen that huge car that Count Zborowski's entered in the first race?'

They were sitting on Members' Hill for the race meeting on Easter Monday. They had a good view of part of the track, including the finishing straight. Below them were visitors' cars of all shapes and sizes and motorcycles parked haphazardly. Men in overcoats and trilbies chatted to one another and discussed the form of the racers. A small black dog ran around, but never strayed far from its owner's side. In the distance they could see the name 'Vickers-Brooklands' emblazoned on the side of a building and beyond that, trees lined the track that curved away to the right.

'No. Where is it?'

'Over there, lining up for the start. You can hardly miss it.'

'Good Heavens! What is it?'

Mitch laughed. 'He calls it *Chitty-Bang-Bang*, but it's a Mercedes with a twenty-three-litre engine. It's a noisy beast and I don't think Paul's Sunbeam will stand a chance against it – or probably any of the others, for that matter.'

The start was noisy and Pips laughed; the big car sounded as if its engine was exploding. 'I see why it's called that now.'

'I was right,' Mitch said, as the cars sped round the track. 'There're really only the two cars in it. One or two have fallen out already.'

As they rounded the bend in front of the members' enclosure, the count's car swerved and there was a universal intake of breath amongst the watchers, but he righted it and on the far banking increased his speed to pass the Sunbeam, finishing the race in first place.

'Second's not bad for Paul in the circumstances,' Mitch said magnanimously. 'Let's go and have a closer look at this beast.'

They watched the rest of the BARC's races until it was time for the two events Paul had organized for his own club members, one being the all-women's race.

'And now, I'd better get ready for my little effort,' Pips said.

On the starting line, dressed in her brown driving suit, leather helmet and goggles, Pips gripped the steering wheel and crouched forward in her seat. All around her, the noise of revving engines filled the air and she breathed in the exhaust fumes from nine other cars. But she loved it; loved the atmosphere of this place, the excitement, the crowds, the noise and the bustle. She glanced to either side of her. Two cars away was Pattie and, beyond her, Muriel. There were three other drivers, whom she'd only met briefly, but who made up the unofficial club that had become known as the Brooklands Girls. And then there were three more women, who were strangers to her. She knew Milly and Mitch would be watching from the bridge or from Members' Hill, though Paul was somewhere close if she needed help.

The starter passed in front of each one of them, raising and dropping his flag, and they were off. It was a six-lap race, approximately sixteen and a half miles. Starting on Railway Straight she soon reached the Byfleet Banking and steered her car to a line about halfway up, passing the aviation village and then along the gently curving part of the track and round behind Members' Hill and on to the Members', or Home, Banking – but she dared not take her eyes off the track to look up at her friends. Muriel, Pattie and two others were ahead of her but she kept up a steady speed and on the second time round the Byfleet Banking went a little higher. Her speed increased as she came off it and she passed one of the cars. On and on for four more laps, again overtaking another car to finish in third place.

'Darling, that was wonderful. Another prize,' Milly trilled as she found Pips parking her car in the paddock.

'Well, I don't mind losing to Muriel and Pattie, but they'd better watch out. I don't mean to make a habit of it,' Pips said, as she climbed out of the car and removed her goggles.

Milly dissolved into a fit of giggles. 'Oh Pips, your face is black except where your goggles have been. You look like a Panda in negative.'

Pips grinned, her adrenalin still pumping, as they made their way to the area where the prizes were given out.

As they stood to have their photographs taken, Pattie said, 'You know, Pips, you really are a very good driver. Where did you learn to drive like that? You're absolutely fearless.'

'Riding around the lanes of Lincolnshire on my brother's motorcycle started it all. And then I used to drive my father's car in secret. He's a doctor and he needed a vehicle for his rounds. In the countryside he had to travel miles to do home visits.' She stopped, unwilling to talk about her service in the war, but Muriel had no such reserve.

'And she drove ambulances at the front. *That's* where she gets her fearlessness from.'

Pattie's eyes widened. 'Did you really? What a wonderful thing to have done. I ended up in a munitions factory and, though I know it was worthwhile work, Lord, it was boring.'

They posed a little longer for a few more photographs before, growing restless with standing about, Pattie said, 'Come on, let's go and find a drink. I'm parched.'

The talk in the clubhouse centred around cars and racing and though Milly didn't drive herself, she seemed quite at home amongst those who did. Muriel smiled. 'She keeps our spirits up when we lose.'

'Which isn't often,' Milly laughed, 'though I

think you've got some more competition now with Pips.'

'We certainly have,' Pattie said, raising her glass. 'Here's to you, Pips. Just don't win too often, will you?'

But Pips's first win came with the very next race and this one was not just for women, so it was a double triumph.

'Wow,' Mitch greeted her as she climbed, rather shakily, out of the car. 'That was some drive. Come on, there's a gaggle of photographers waiting for you and one or two newspapers want an interview with you. You're going to be famous...'

Robert wrote the following week:

Dear Pips,

We saw your picture in the newspaper. Mother was mortified at how you were dressed and with black smuts all over your face but Father is more concerned for your safety – as am I. Although I tried to reassure him that there was nothing to worry about and that all you do is just tootle round a racing track, I rather suspect that 'tootle' is not quite the right word for the speed you go! Daisy was intrigued with the picture, but couldn't quite understand that it was her Aunty Pips. I have to admit you weren't exactly easily recognizable. I'm enclosing a photograph of her on her tricycle. Perhaps she will follow in her aunty's footsteps – Heaven forbid! – though she's a little young yet to be let loose on my motorcycle. She's getting on very well with her riding lessons. She's a natural horsewoman – just like you were.

Pips pored over the picture of her niece and a

wave of homesickness engulfed her.

Two days later a letter from Alice told her the news that William and Brigitta had had a baby boy.

No doubt you'll be hearing from William directly, but I couldn't wait to write to you. The baby was born on Easter Sunday, so they are calling him Pascal, which means 'born on Easter' apparently. When I went to tell Mam and Ma, Dad was there, so I haven't been able to tell them yet. It's not that I'm frightened of him any more, but I have to think of Mam...

'Oh for goodness' sake,' Pips muttered. She was very tempted to travel all the way back to Lincolnshire and give the stupid man a piece of her mind!

Eighteen

'Good Heavens! What are you doing here? I hardly recognized you in civvies.'

At the race meeting in May, a distinguished-looking man, tall and straight-backed, with dark hair and a small neat moustache had pushed his way through the crowd until he was standing in front of Pips. He was dressed in a navy-blue suit, with a white shirt and striped tie. 'I was hoping to see you,' he said, smiling.

Pips moved towards him and held out her hands. He took them both into his own.

160

'Captain George Allender,' she murmured softly. 'How good it is to see you again.' As she looked into his dark blue eyes she could see the sadness was still there. No doubt he had horrific memories of the war too.

For a moment, he seemed embarrassed. 'Actually, it's "Major" now.'

'Oh George, how wonderful. When did you get your promotion?'

'In the last year of the war. In July various French, British and US forces launched a counterattack that became known as the second battle of the Marne. I was posted there with the rank of major.'

'Not before time, George.' She smiled saucily at him. 'And did you have any disobedient nurses to contend with?'

He laughed but, strangely, the amusement did not reach his eyes. 'No, but I missed you, Pips.'

'How did you know I'd be here?'

'I saw your picture in the newspaper when you won your first race back in March and when I saw that there was another race meeting here today, well, I just took the chance that you'd be here.'

'How are you? How's life in civvy street?'

This time he did not smile. 'More difficult than I could ever have imagined.'

'Of course, you must miss the army life? How are your wife and your daughter, Rebecca? Did she pursue her nursing career like you wanted her to once you left the army and could take over caring for your wife? Oh I'm sorry, what a lot of questions all at once.' She linked her arm through his. 'Come on, I've got a hamper in my car. We can have a picnic on Members' Hill and you can tell me everything. It'll be less crowded now than going to the clubhouse or the restaurant.'

They shared cucumber sandwiches and a flask of tea. 'I suppose it ought to be champagne,' Pips laughed, 'but I don't drink if I'm going racing.'

'Very wise,' George said, as he pulled out a white handkerchief and wiped the crumbs from his moustache. 'Are you racing today?'

'Yes, the last race is an all-women's event, so I'm in that.'

'I see you still have the brooch,' he said.

Pips smiled as she touched it. 'I always wear it. It's my good-luck charm.' For a moment, she was catapulted back in time to a small, muddy cemetery near Brandhoek, standing beside the grave of one of George's friends, with poppies growing all around them and he was telling her that he had fallen in love with her. And then he had given her the brooch in the shape and colours of a poppy. He had asked nothing of her, vowing that he would never be unfaithful to his invalid wife. As Alice had rightly said, he was a gentleman in every sense of the word, but in the middle of the catastrophic war, he'd wanted Pips to know that he loved her, just in case they should never meet again. No one, apart from the two of them, knew about that moment and she had pushed it into the far recesses of her mind.

There was a long silence before George said, 'Pips, there's something I have to tell you.'

She turned to face him, but he was staring straight ahead watching the cars still thundering round the track. She could tell by the tone of his

162

voice that it was something serious. 'Go on,' she said gently.

'My wife took her own life last November on Armistice Day.'

Pips gasped. 'Oh George, I'm so very sorry. I thought she'd be so much better when you got home.'

'She seemed to be – for a while. Rebecca and I tried everything. We took her to every doctor we could find. And whilst they were good – very sympathetic and understanding – nothing seemed to help. She was given so many pills that, evidently, she just stored them up – unbeknown to us, of course – and took an overdose.'

'How – how is Rebecca?'

'Very bitter. I think she blames me.'

'Whatever for?'

'For being away for so long.'

'The war was hardly your fault. And you were a regular soldier. You had to go. Besides, weren't you in the army from a young age? You were already a soldier when you married, weren't you?'

George nodded. 'Yes. If I think about it rationally, I know I'm not to blame, but it saddens me that Rebecca feels that way. There – there was some instability in Alison's family. Her mother was in an institution for several years. She died in there. I didn't want the same to happen to Alison. That's why we cared for her at home.'

'Doesn't Rebecca understand that?'

'Maybe she will in time, but just now...'

He said no more, but his meaning was obvious.

Pips didn't quite know what to say. 'George, I...'

'Don't, Pips, please don't say anything. I haven't come here to embarrass you, I promise. I still feel the same about you – that will never change – but I know there can never be anything between us. There's such a big age difference and besides...' he smiled wryly, 'I am sure by now you have a long line of young men queuing up. Unless, of course, there's already someone you're serious about...' Even the former army officer could not keep the hope from his tone. She could tell that he longed to hear her say the words: No, there is no one.

Despite the seriousness of their conversation, she sought to lighten it. She turned to watch his face as she said, 'There is someone very special...' She saw the hope in his eyes die and was sorry that she had thought to tease him. 'A little girl called Daisy. She's my niece and she's three years old. But no, there's no man, I promise you.'

'Are you still in love with Dr Kendall?'

George had been there when she had found out that Giles had deceived her. He had been the one to comfort her and take care of her.

'Good Heavens, no! He's not worth a second thought,' she said spiritedly and then added more thoughtfully, 'but I suppose the experience made me more wary. I tend to take what flirtatious young men say to me with the proverbial pinch of salt now.'

'So, how did you get into the racing world?'

Pips laughed. 'I don't think you ever met Milly Fortesque, did you? She came out to join the ambulance corps quite late on in the war just before Arras and Passchendaele.'

George shook his head. 'It would have been after I left that area, then.'

'She dragged me to London to stay with her, though I have to admit I didn't take much persuading. Through her I met up with Mitch Hammond, whom I'd met in the war too. He goes racing and flying – anything to do with speed, you could say – rather like me.'

George smiled, watching her face become animated just talking about it.

'There's a whole group of them – including women – and, well, it was just what I needed.'

'I can see that,' he said softly. 'Does it help you to forget?'

Pips sighed deeply. 'Not for long, if I'm honest, but we seem to be able to push it away for a few hours.'

'I was so sorry to hear about your brother's injury. Dr Hazelwood told me.'

'Yes, he said he'd seen you. He visited us in Lincolnshire soon after the war ended and he still keeps in touch with Father.'

'How is he now? Your brother, I mean?'

Pips grimaced. 'Physically, fine. The wound healed well after the operation. He was lucky not to get an infection, but it's his mental state that worries me. He's very depressed. My father says that in the old days it would be referred to as melancholia.'

George nodded and said softly, 'That was the diagnosis given to my wife, but Robert's case is surely very different. Not only has he suffered a catastrophic injury that has altered the course of his life – because I presume it has – but he also has the same dreadful memories that we all have to deal with.'

Pips sighed. 'He could still do some kind of medical work. We're all trying to get him to study the condition that's now coming to be known as shell shock. We had several patients at the hall with it and he did make a start on writing up notes about each of them, but he seems to have lost the impetus to do even that now, although' – she smiled impishly – 'I did give him a good talking to when I was last home and he has started to get in touch with sufferers through Lincoln Hospital, so Alice tells me. And perhaps you don't know either – unless Dr Hazelwood told you that too – that Robert married Alice.'

'Yes, he did tell me. I'm very glad for them both.' He was silent for a time before shaking his head slowly. 'I've been an army man all my working life. It's all I've ever known – all I ever wanted to do – yet going through that war, I began to doubt the rightness of being a soldier. It should never have happened and all those fine young men slaughtered – for what?'

'The world is a very different place now, but I don't think it's necessarily for the better,' Pips said. 'Country borders have changed and people have been uprooted from their homes. And the unrest that seems to be building in this country is frightening. I don't know where it will end,' Pips said. 'And to see former soldiers begging on the city streets is just appalling.'

'The authorities didn't get the lads home quickly enough after hostilities ended. And, in a lot of cases, there was no work for them to come back to. I suppose one has to have some sympathy for the Russian revolution, yet I'm not sure that the new regime is going to be any better. Different, certainly. But better? Only time will tell.'

'Oh George, it is so good to have someone to have a serious conversation with. I miss that when I'm away from home. Milly is an absolute darling and I'm extremely fond of her, but her conversation centres around the next party or dance. And as for Mitch and Paul – and the rest of their set – their waking hours are wholly centred around cars and flying.'

George laughed. 'You seem to be pretty smitten yourself. With the cars and the flying, I mean.'

Pips had the grace to laugh. 'Guilty as charged, sir.'

They sat together a while longer until George said reluctantly, 'I must go. I've a train to catch back into London. I'm taking Rebecca out for dinner this evening.'

'Sorry I can't take you myself, but let me see if I can find someone to give you a lift back to the station.'

'I wouldn't dream of it. It's not far.' He smiled. 'For a former soldier, used to route marches, it's no distance.'

Pips grinned. 'That's why it's so perfectly positioned within walking distance from the station. It brings a lot of people from London. Where are you staying?'

'We have a small, two-bedroomed apartment in Clapham.'

'You're *living* down here? In London?'

'I still have a house near York, but it seemed ridiculous to stay up there on my own. I've rented it out for the time being.'

'Rebecca's with you, then?'

'Sort of. She's at the London Hospital and although she stays there when she's on duty, she can get home on her days off.'

'Is she enjoying nursing?'

'Oh yes. Very much.' He paused and seemed suddenly ill at ease. 'I'd very much like you to meet her. Would you – would you be able to have dinner with us one evening?'

'I'd like that. Here, I'll give you Milly's address. Just drop me a note. I won't be going back home to Lincolnshire for a couple of weeks. I'm needed at Hazelwood House.' She went on to tell him about her work there.

'Perhaps that's something I could do too,' George murmured as he carefully tucked the piece of paper on which Pips had scribbled Milly's address into his inside pocket. He smiled. 'I'll see you again, then.'

Nineteen

'Are you the reason my mother killed herself?'

Pips had received George's invitation to join him and his daughter Rebecca at Simpson's-in-the-Strand for dinner. She had arrived to be warmly greeted by George, but coldly so by the stony-faced young woman at his side. Rebecca was slim with her long brown hair plaited and wound around her head. Her features were even, though the rather sulky mouth spoiled what could have been a pretty face. She had shaken Pips's proffered hand limply before turning away to march ahead to the reserved table. Conversation over the meal had been stilted and awkward and now Pips understood why. Whilst her father had gone to settle the bill, Rebecca had dropped her bombshell question.

Shocked, Pips stared at Rebecca. 'Good Heavens, no. How could I be? She never knew me.'

Rebecca frowned. 'But she might have known *about* you.'

'There's nothing to know, except that I met your father out in Belgium during the war.'

'He's in love with you. I can see it in his eyes when he looks at you. It's – it's how he used to look at my mother.'

For a moment, Pips's composure was shaken, but then she lifted her chin and met Rebecca's gaze. 'There's nothing between us, Rebecca. There never was.'

'Maybe not yet, but he'd like there to be.'

'Has he told you that?'

'No, but...'

'Then you can't possibly know. I'm desperately sorry to hear about your mother's death, but don't blame your father for it. She was a very poorly lady.'

'She was all right when I was at home looking after her.'

Pips put her head on one side and asked gently, 'Was she? Was she – really?'

Rebecca bit her lip. 'She was missing my father then.'

'And was she better when he came home for good?'

Rebecca glared at her, as if Pips was making her face truths she'd rather not face. 'I left home then. Father insisted that I build my own life and so I came to London to train to be a nurse. So, then I was the one who was missing.'

'You think she wanted you both at home? With her?'

'Yes, of course she did.'

'So why didn't you? Stay at home, I mean?'

'Oh, so now you're trying to turn the tables and say it was my fault.'

'Nothing of the sort,' Pips said sharply. 'Your mother was a sick woman and I don't think anything – or anyone – could have prevented her from doing what she did.'

Rebecca glanced over Pips's shoulder to the far side of the room. 'I think he's coming back. Please don't tell him what I said. He'd be so angry.'

'Of course I won't. But I promise you, Rebecca, there was never anything romantic between us. He was kind to me at a very difficult point in my life, that's all. Your father was – and is – a true gentleman and a good and faithful husband.'

Rebecca glared at her and Pips could see in her eyes that the young woman did not believe her. But there was nothing else she could say. If she persisted, it would perhaps seem like 'the lady doth protest too much'.

At last Rebecca blurted out, 'I don't want you to see him again.'

Pips was mystified. Whatever was the matter with the girl? She was behaving like a jealous wife, not a grown-up daughter who was forging her own life and career. Now Pips was angry. 'I rather think that's for your father to decide, don't you?' she said stiffly.

'No, I don't. He's vulnerable since Mummy's death and I've seen how he looks at you and I know about women like you.'

'Women like me?'

'Yes, women who went to the front who weren't proper nurses yet thought they could bring "comfort to the troops".'

Pips was appalled at Rebecca's insinuation, but she managed to keep her temper in check. 'I admit I was not a fully trained nurse. Although I took an intensive first-aid course before I went, my main job was driving ambulances to ferry the wounded from the front back to the first-aid posts. If you ask him, your father would verify that. There was no "comforting the troops", as you're suggesting.'

'I've no intention of talking to him about you or even mentioning your name after today. I shall do my best to prevent him seeing you again.' Rebecca rose as George neared the table. She held out her hand to Pips, who also stood up and took it.

'It's been very nice to meet you, Miss Maitland, but we must go now. I have to be back at the hospital. I'm on duty at six.'

As he joined them, Rebecca tucked her hand possessively through her father's. 'Come along, Daddy. I have to get back.'

For a moment George looked nonplussed – a little lost, Pips thought. So with an impish smile, she moved towards him and kissed his cheek. 'It's been lovely to see you again, George. Take care of yourself.'

'I'll be in touch,' he said. 'I wanted to show you around this place. It has a history as a meeting place for chess players and for holding tournaments. I thought it would interest you. Never mind. Another time, perhaps.'

Pips stepped back, nodded but said no more. As she watched them leave the restaurant, her eyes narrowed. Rebecca had certainly underestimated her. What the young woman couldn't possibly know on such a short acquaintance was that the more Pips was told not to do something, the more she was likely to do it.

Not many days had passed before Pips received another note from George asking her to have lunch with him on any day that suited her.

Rebecca has a week of night duty, he wrote, *so I'm rattling around this flat on my own. Any day will suit me.*

They arranged to meet at the same restaurant as before on a Wednesday. This time he was able to take her on a tour of the restaurant and show her the original chess set on display in the Bishop's Room.

'During the last century it was *the* venue for chess players and tournaments,' George explained. 'Matches were played against other coffee houses and runners carried the moves between them.'

Pips laughed. 'It must have slowed the games down.'

'It hosted several world matches and even the first women's world tournament. But, before you ask,' he teased her, 'during the last few years the popularity for holding chess tournaments here has declined, though I think they still hold one now and again.'

Pips chuckled. 'What a shame. I was thinking of putting my name down.'

A waiter approached them and said that their table was ready.

'I'm going up to Lincolnshire on Friday for the weekend. Mother is holding a twenty-first birthday party for Jake on Sunday in the grounds, if it's fine,' Pips said, as they sat down. She went on to tell him all about Jake and ended, 'Would you like to come with me?'

'Wouldn't that be an imposition on your mother?'

Pips shook her head. 'Not at all. She always keeps a spare room ready for unexpected visitors and I'm sure Robert – and Alice – would like to see you again. And I would *love* you to meet Daisy.'

He regarded her solemnly. 'Are you sure? About Robert, I mean? Wouldn't it revive memories he's striving so hard to forget?'

'Robert must learn to face his demons – as we all must. Perhaps you could help us a little by telling him how valuable you think his work is. That's if you do.'

'Of course I do,' George said swiftly. 'And I'd be more than happy to talk about it, if he wants to.'

'You must make him,' Pips said bluntly.

George was made most welcome at the hall and on the Saturday evening, Major Basil Fieldsend and his wife, Rosemary, were guests too. Pips had forewarned her family of the manner of George's wife's death and how his daughter was now very possessive of him, so that they were all careful in the questions they asked. Henrietta – as always – seemed to be calculating whether or not he would make a suitable husband for Pips.

'There's a big age difference between you, Pips,' she remarked as the four women retired to the Brown Parlour after dinner leaving the men to talk and drink port around the dining table for a little while longer.

'Mother dearest, George was extremely kind to me at the time Giles jilted me. We are good friends, that is all.'

'I don't think so,' Alice said softly. 'Not on his side anyway.'

'Oh Alice, don't you start matchmaking too,' Pips laughed.

Alice shrugged. 'I could see it before – out there – but, of course, his wife was still alive and I'm sure he was too much of a gentleman ever to say anything then, but now...' She left the sentence unfinished, but the implication in her words was obvious.

'Mrs Fieldsend, do come to my rescue – *please*,' Pips said. 'They're joining forces against me.'

Rosemary Fieldsend chuckled. 'My dear Pips, it is your mother's dearest wish to see you happily settled. You can hardly blame her for that.'

'What does he do now that he has left the army?' Henrietta persisted.

'As far as I know, nothing.'

'Does he get any sort of army pension or has he private means, do you know?'

'Mother – really!'

Henrietta shrugged. 'I just want to know what you might be getting yourself into, that's all, if what Alice says is true.'

Pips opened her mouth to retort, but at that moment they heard the menfolk leaving the Great Hall and coming into the parlour.

For the moment, the subject nearest to Henrietta's heart was closed.

Twenty

The party for Jake Goodall, held on the croquet lawn, left the young man with a tumult of emotions. In turn, he was embarrassed by the attention, yet warmed by it and grateful for his good fortune. Each member of the family and staff gave him presents – most of them useful gifts – but the one most precious to him was a book on horses from Pips.

The day ended with Jake stammering his thanks to Henrietta, who said, 'You are most welcome, Jake. I am so glad I found you all those years ago.'

'So am I,' was his heartfelt reply.

Only three days after their return to London,

Pips answered the doorbell in Milly's flat to find Rebecca standing there.

'You didn't take a scrap of notice of what I said, did you? Not only have you seen him again, but you took him home to meet your family. You're determined to get your claws into him, aren't you?'

'Come in, Rebecca. I'm not about to have an argument with you on the doorstep.'

Reluctantly, the girl stepped over the threshold. Pips closed the door and led the way into the living room. She was thankful that Milly was out.

'Now,' she said, turning to face the irate young woman, 'just understand this – your father and I are friends. That's all.'

Rebecca shook her head. 'No, it isn't. He told me last night that he intends to ask you to marry him.'

Pips stared at her. 'That's news to me,' she said, able to be quite truthful. There was a pause before she added, 'And what did you say to him?'

'I told him I wasn't happy about it. That he should honour Mummy's memory and not even think about remarrying. And certainly not you.'

'And what did he say then?'

'What he said is nothing to do with you.'

'I rather think it is.'

Rebecca avoided meeting Pips's steady gaze. 'He – he got quite angry. He asked me if I expected him to remain celibate for the rest of his life. Then he – he told me that Mummy hadn't been a proper wife to him for years but that he'd respected that because of her illness.'

'He must have loved her very much, Rebecca,' Pips said gently. 'Many men would have sought solace elsewhere.'

Suddenly, Rebecca sank into a chair and fished a handkerchief out of her handbag. 'He told me more about you and your family. I'm – I'm sorry for what I implied before. I realize now that you're not a–' she smiled wryly – 'a "camp follower".'

'No, I'm not,' Pips began indignantly, then her sense of humour came to her rescue and she laughed too. The tension between them eased a little.

'Are you going to marry him?'

'I really haven't thought about it. Besides, he hasn't asked me.'

'But he will. I know he will.' Tears filled her eyes again.

Pips watched her for a few moments and then asked, 'Is it because you don't like me or because you don't want him to remarry at all?'

'He's all I've got,' Rebecca whispered. 'I can't bear to lose him.'

'Why on earth would you "lose" him, as you put it?'

'You'd take him away from me.'

'Rebecca, you're his *daughter*. Nothing and no one will ever change that. He loves you devotedly. I can see that and, besides, you have your own life to build. You're at the start of your career and maybe one day you'll meet someone and get married.' Her mouth twitched as she added, 'I'm sure your father would love to be a grandfather.'

Rebecca managed to smile thinly. 'I'm sure he would, but where are all the young men that I and my contemporaries are going to marry? I think I'm destined – along with a lot of other girls of my age – to remain a spinster, don't you?'

Sadly, that was a statement with which Pips could not argue. She was, after all, 'in the same boat', as the saying went.

By the time Rebecca left, they had not become friends and probably never would, but they had cleared the air between them – at least for the moment. Rebecca would never embrace the idea of her father's remarriage and her relationship with any future stepmother – whether it was Pips or not – would always be frosty. But at least their meeting had served one purpose for Pips: by the time George took her out for a romantic candlelit supper, she was prepared for his proposal.

The expected invitation to have dinner with him came the following week and, as they reached the coffee stage, George reached across the table and took both her hands into his. 'Pips, you know how I feel about you, don't you? Will you do me the honour of becoming my wife?'

Even though she had been forewarned, Pips was still unsure of her reply.

'George, I am extremely fond of you, I think you know that, but I'm not sure that I could give up my lifestyle and I expect you would want me to become a dutiful wife.'

'Good Lord, no!' George smiled. 'That's what I love about you, Pips. Your energy, your courage and meeting life head-on. I shall probably trail in your wake, but, no, I'd never expect or want you to give up racing, though of course I'll worry about your safety.'

'And flying,' she said impishly. 'I want to take a course of lessons.'

'Now that is exciting. I wouldn't mind having a shot at that myself.'

'Really? That would be marvellous. It would be a shared interest.'

'I'm sure there'll be others.'

They smiled at each other. Their shared experiences in the horrific war united them. When the memories surfaced and perhaps threatened to overwhelm them, each would always understand the other.

'But there is one insurmountable problem,' George said.

'Rebecca,' Pips murmured.

He looked startled. 'Why would you think that?'

Pips wished she could bite the end of her tongue off. She had spoken without thinking.

George frowned and, making Pips feel even more uncomfortable, asked, 'Has she said something to you?'

The only time Pips had ever been known to lie had been in the war when she'd helped ease a dying soldier's passing. She had even, on one occasion, pretended to be the mother of a fatally wounded boy. He had gone peacefully with her kiss on his forehead. But now, she would not begin any relationship with George – whatever that was to be – with a lie.

'I get the feeling she's not happy about you marrying again.'

He stared at her for a moment and then seemed to realize that he was putting Pips in a very awkward position. Slowly, he said, 'Then I will talk to her.'

'Oh please...' Pips began, but he squeezed her

179

hand reassuringly. 'I won't let her know you've said anything, I promise.'

Pips nodded and then, after a pause, she said, 'So, what was the problem you meant?'

He smiled ruefully. 'The difference in our ages. I don't think your mother will be too happy about that, do you?'

Now Pips was able to laugh. 'I think my mother has finally accepted that I will go my own way in life. If I say I'm going to marry you, then I will.'

'And are you?'

'What?'

'Going to marry me?'

Pips's laughter faded. 'Honestly, George, I don't know. I'm very fond of you. Love you, I suppose...'

She hesitated and he said softly, 'There's a "but", isn't there?'

She sighed heavily. 'You know what happened to me before? You were there.'

'Dr Giles Kendall, you mean?'

She nodded.

'Were you – very much in love with him?'

Pips frowned and then shook her head. 'I don't think I can have been. I hardly ever think about him now and, if I'd loved him deeply, surely I would still be broken-hearted. And I'm not.'

'I'm glad to hear it,' he murmured. 'He wasn't worth it.'

'But he was my first...' She paused, searching for the right word, but there was no need for her to say more. George understood.

'That doesn't worry me, so long as you're not still carrying a torch for him.'

Pips chuckled. 'Not even a candle.' Then she sobered as she added, 'But there's still Rebecca. The very last thing I'd want to do is to come between you and your daughter. She needs you, George, and I think – if you're totally honest – it would break your heart if there was a rift between you.'

When they met again the following week for lunch at Claridge's as they had arranged, George's face was bleak as he sat down opposite her. As if unable to keep it to himself any longer, the usually reserved and rather staid man blurted out, 'You were right. Rebecca has told me she can't bear to think of me marrying anyone. It's not against you personally, just that she thinks I should be faithful to her mother's memory. But Pips, Rebecca is young. She has no idea how lonely the rest of my life will be.'

Pips waited patiently. She could sense there was more he wanted to say. He fiddled with his napkin and waved away the approaching waiter.

'She told me herself what she had said to you. About – about my wife's death. Pips, I am so sorry. I was appalled. We had quite a row about it. I think it's the first time we have ever quarrelled like that.'

'Then I'm sorry that happened, because she will blame me for being the cause of it.'

'I told her she was being very selfish and she shot back at me that she'd had to care for her mother from quite a young age when I was away playing soldiers.'

'George, she's still very young. She's lost her

181

mother in tragic circumstances, it has to be said. And I guess you've been away in the army for much of her young life and now, you're all she has left.'

'But can't she see that you would be a wonderful mother to her?'

'She doesn't want a stepmother and certainly not one who is only a few years older than she is.'

'Then couldn't you be friends?'

'We could try, but only if we're both willing. Otherwise it would never work.'

'You haven't actually said you'll marry me yet. Perhaps after this, you won't want to.'

Pips reached across the table and took his hand. 'Yes, I will marry you, George, but not yet. However, in the meantime...' She smiled and gave him a saucy wink.

George Allender, a former officer in the British Army, actually blushed.

Twenty-One

As summer turned into autumn, they met as often as they could in discreet hotels or, occasionally, at Milly's flat if she was away. When Milly had been introduced to him, she'd declared later to Pips, 'He's absolutely *adorable*, Pips, darling. But whatever is Mitch going to say?'

'It's none of Mitch Hammond's business,' Pips said tartly. Milly raised her eyebrows, but said no more.

182

One weekend, Pips and George travelled to Brighton and stayed in a hotel as man and wife under the name of Mr and Mrs Maitland.

'It sounds so much more believable than "Smith", don't you think?' Pips had giggled. 'And we daren't use your name in case Rebecca is keeping tabs on you.'

'I think she may already have guessed.'

'Really? Has she said something?'

'No, but that's exactly why I think she knows. She pointedly avoids asking me what I've been doing whilst she's been on duty and when she's home on her day off or her weekend off, she fills the time with organizing for us to go here, there and everywhere; museums and art galleries in the daytime and the theatre, the opera and the ballet in the evenings. I'm exhausted by the time she goes back on duty.'

'But it's good, isn't it? That she wants to spend time with you.'

George shrugged. 'Much as I love her, I'd rather be with you.'

Pips touched his face tenderly. 'We manage all right, don't we?'

He sighed. 'Pips, I want to be with you all the time. I want to wake up beside you in the morning – *every* morning. I want to watch you when you race, go up to Lincolnshire with you when you visit your folks. Just – everything.'

'Then tell her.'

'I've tried. Believe me, I've tried. But as soon as I do, she puts her hands up and says, "I don't want to hear it, Dad".'

He caught hold of her hand, turned it over and

kissed her palm. 'Marry me, Pips. Please.'

Pips felt herself relenting. He was a dear, kind man. She felt safe with him. He would never hurt her as she had been hurt the last time she'd believed herself in love. She loved George, there was no doubting that, but it was not the kind of exciting, all-consuming passion that she believed falling in love meant. And yet, now, what else was there to hope for? It was said by some that there were almost two million women in Britain who would never now find a husband. A whole generation of fine young men had been wiped out and with them the hopes and dreams of a generation of young women and the children too that they would never bear. The effects of the war that was supposed to end all wars would be felt for decades to come.

Pips kissed him tenderly. 'I will, George,' she breathed against his lips. 'But not just yet. Let's enjoy what we have right now. Maybe, in time, Rebecca will come around.'

As she drew back from him she could see the disappointment in his eyes and the doubt on his face. She squeezed his hand. 'I've got a practice session this afternoon. Come with me.'

'I can't. I must go. Rebecca will be home tonight.'

'Then I'll see you next week? Milly's away with friends, so you can come to her flat.'

'I presume you've told her. Does she mind?'

'Milly? Heavens no! She thrives on intrigue and romance. And before you ask, she's very discreet, although I know you probably wouldn't think so. And then, next weekend, I'll be going home. Will you be able to come with me?'

'I don't know. I'll see what Rebecca's doing.'

'Clara Nuttall, I want a word with you.'

Bess Cooper had marched down the village street from her own cottage and was now standing outside the Nuttalls' home, her arms folded across her chest, fuming with what she believed was righteous indignation.

Bert looked up from digging his vegetable patch and frowned. 'What's to do, Bess?'

'You might well ask, Bert Nuttall. I want a word with your wife. Fetch 'er out here else I'll drag her out mesen. By her hair, if I have to.'

'Eee, steady on, Bess.' He threw down his fork and stepped towards the irate woman. 'Nowt can be as bad as that.'

Bess pursed her lips. 'I'll be the judge of that, Bert. Just get her out here and then you'll hear.'

In the cottage garden a few yards away, the Nuttalls' nearest neighbour was making no pretence at not listening. She was standing near the fence gaping openly at Bess. Bert glanced at her briefly and then turned back to Bess. 'Won't you come inside? We don't want half the village to hear.'

'Well, that's where you're wrong. I want 'em all to know what your precious son's been up to.'

'Sam? Is this about Sam?'

'Indeed it is.'

'Then shouldn't you be telling me?'

'This is women's business.'

'Ah,' Bert said thoughtfully and then again, 'Ah, I see.' And now he had begun to under-

185

stand. 'I'll get her. Wait here, then, if you won't come in.'

Bess waited for five long minutes, her anger growing with each minute that passed. When at last Clara appeared out of the front door, Bess's wrath had reached boiling point. She pointed an accusing finger. 'Your lad's got my Peggy pregnant. You'd better make sure he owns up to it and marries her as quick as possible.'

Clara's mouth dropped open and, behind her, Bert sighed. He'd suspected that something like this might be the trouble. Out of the corner of his eye, he saw their neighbour cover her mouth with her fingers, but he knew it would not stay covered – or silent – for long. Before nightfall, the news would be all around the village.

He had one last attempt at taking both women indoors, to keep the matter to themselves for just a while longer, but now neither of them was listening to him. Clara moved towards Bess.

'Oh aye, and what makes you so sure it's Sam's?'

'Why, you – you...' Bess's hand shot out to grab Clara's hair, but the woman dodged backwards and, on the wrong side of the gate, Bess could not reach her.

'They've been walking out for over a year now. It's high time he made an honest woman of her.'

'Honest? That's a laugh. This is the second time she's got 'ersen into trouble. D'you really expect him to take on Harold Dawson's bastard and this 'un too – whoever the father is?'

'The father,' Bess bellowed at the top of her voice, 'is your Sam, and if he doesn't do the right

186

thing, I'll drag him there mesen.'

'Over my dead body.'

'That can be arranged, Clara. That can be arranged.'

With that parting shot, Bess turned and marched back up the street, whilst Clara went back into her home, up the stairs to her bedroom, undressed and got into bed even though it was only eleven o'clock in the morning.

Bert sighed and went back to digging his vegetable patch.

'Mrs Maitland, may I have a word with you, please?'

Henrietta looked up from her needlework to see Peggy standing hesitantly in the doorway of the parlour. Her pretty face was blotched and her eyes swollen with weeping.

'Oh my dear girl, whatever's the matter? Come in and sit down. I'll ring for Sarah to bring us some tea.'

'Oh, no. Please – don't trouble.'

'No trouble, my dear. I can see something's wrong. How can I help?'

As if her legs gave way beneath her, Peggy sank down into a chair. 'I – I have to give in my notice, Mrs Maitland.'

'Oh dear. I'm sorry to hear that. You're an excellent member of our staff, Peggy. May I ask why?'

Fresh tears welled in the girl's eyes. 'I – I'm so ashamed, Mrs Maitland. You'll be so angry – so disgusted at me.'

'Let me be the judge of that. Just tell me.'

'I – I'm pregnant.'

'And are you and Sam getting married, then?'

Peggy stared at her. 'You – you haven't even asked me who the father is.'

Henrietta smiled. 'Well, I rather think I know the answer to that one. You've been walking out with Sam for over a year. The thought wouldn't even enter my head, my dear, that your baby is anyone's other than Sam's.'

Peggy hiccupped. 'I wish his mother had your faith in me.'

Henrietta put her head on one side. 'Mrs Nuttall is not accepting that your baby is her son's?'

Peggy shook her head and buried her face in her hands. In a muffled voice she said, 'Mrs Nuttall has taken to her bed and says that if he marries me, she'll never get out of it again. She'll die there and it will all be his fault.'

'Ah, now I wouldn't worry too much about that, Peggy. Clara Nuttall has done this once before, if you remember.'

Slowly, Peggy uncovered her face and stared at Henrietta. 'Oh yes. In the war. I'd forgotten.'

'So, first of all, has Sam asked you to marry him? I presume he knows about the baby?'

'Yes, he said straight away that we must get married. I mean, we *want* to get married. It's not just because of the baby.'

'So, apart from his mother, is there any other problem?'

'The – the vicar. He's refusing to marry us.'

'Is he now,' Henrietta said tartly. 'Then you can leave the Reverend Stanhope to me, my dear.'

Pips did not see or hear from George for two weeks, so, after the race meeting towards the end of September, when she only managed a fourth place, Pips travelled to Lincolnshire on her own and walked into a furore.

'Whatever's going on?' she asked Alice. 'I don't think I've ever seen Mother so agitated.'

'There's to be a shotgun wedding in the village and your mother and the vicar are at loggerheads over it.'

'Why? And whose is it?'

'Peggy Cooper and Sam Nuttall.'

Pips frowned and shook her head. 'Why is there a problem? Sam will make a wonderful father for Luke.'

Alice nodded. 'Yes, he will. But Peggy's pregnant with her *second* illegitimate child. The vicar isn't taking kindly to the fact.'

'Then why on earth did they tell him? Why didn't they just arrange a wedding?'

'Because they've left it rather late and she's showing. And there's more to it than that. Clara Nuttall is dead set against it and has taken to her bed vowing that if her beloved son marries that slut, it'll kill her.'

'Poor Sam,' Pips murmured. 'But why is Mother involved?'

'Because she's given the vicar a piece of her mind. She says it's not for him to judge them. His job is to marry them in the sight of God.'

Pips's mouth twitched. 'Good for her. For once, I quite agree with her.'

'As she pointed out, we're all lucky that Sam came back.' For a moment Alice's face was bleak as she thought about her three brothers lost in the carnage of the Somme, Luke's father, Harold, amongst them.

'What do your family think about it?' Pips asked gently, guessing Alice's thoughts from the expression on her face. 'After all, Luke is their grandson.'

'They're quite happy for them to marry. They think it would be the best thing.'

'And Peggy's mother – Bess Cooper?'

Alice gave a wry laugh. 'She and Mrs Nuttall had a blazing row in the street by all accounts. That's how the whole village got to know about it.'

Pips grinned. 'I wish I'd been there, but I can picture it. Anyway, enough of village gossip. Where's Daisy? I've got a present for her.'

'You spoil her, Pips. You bring something for her every time you come home. She'll begin to expect it, if you're not careful.'

Pips shrugged. 'Oh phooey! And why shouldn't she?'

Alice laughed and shook her head. 'Oh Pips!'

Pips had brought home a baby doll for the little girl. It had a porcelain head and a cloth body and was dressed in a yellow lace dress and matching bonnet.

Daisy hugged the doll to her chest. 'I'll call her Matilda.'

'That's a very pretty name, but what I really want to see is how well you can ride your tricycle now. Are you going to show me on the driveway and then, perhaps, I'll take you down the lane to visit your other grandma?'

'I'll get Daddy. I have to have a grown-up – or

Luke – with me.'

'But aren't I a...?' Pips began, but Daisy had rushed away. Pips smiled, thinking how much the whole family trusted Luke to look after Daisy.

Moments later, Pips and Robert were standing near the front door watching Daisy pedal confidently down the drive as far as the gatehouse, turn competently and come back towards them.

'My word, she does ride it well. Someone must have spent hours with her.'

Robert laughed. 'Not at all. She was riding like that after only minutes.' He paused as he watched his daughter. 'She's like you, Pips, she seems to be a natural at anything she tackles.'

'And how's she getting on riding her pony?'

'The same. She's fearless.'

'And Luke? Does he still come every Saturday afternoon?'

'Never misses.'

'Then I must take them both out while I'm here,' Pips declared.

'Which isn't often now.'

'You know I can't sit about here doing nothing and, delightful though Daisy is, I can't monopolize her. Besides, I'm helping out at Hazelwood House for a couple of days each week, remember?'

'You should marry George and have babies of your own. He has asked you, I presume?'

'Well, yes, but...'

'You don't love him?'

'Oh I do, I do.'

'I hope you're not still hankering after Giles Kendall. If ever I was wrong about someone, it was him. I thought he was a decent bloke.'

'He was,' Pips said swiftly. 'In many ways, he was a fine man. Never forget that he helped to save your life, Robert.' She sighed. 'But we were thrown together in such unusual circumstances; maybe it was never going to work.'

'That didn't excuse him for taking up with that nurse who joined the corps after Alice and I left.' There was silence between them as they watched Daisy turn the tricycle around and pedal off again.

'So why are you hesitating about accepting George? Is it the age difference between you? I know Mother is a little anxious about it.' He chuckled. 'Although I think her desire to see you safely married overrides even that. How old is he, by the way? Do you know?'

Slowly, Pips said, 'Not exactly. Somewhere approaching fifty, I'd guess. It doesn't worry me unduly, it's just...'

'What?'

She sighed. 'I want to *live* life to the full. I don't want to be – restricted. There's so much I still want to do.'

Robert was serious now as he said, 'You think George will reach the pipe and slippers stage long before you're prepared to live a quieter life. Which he will, if I'm honest.'

'I don't think I'll ever reach the "quieter life" stage. He's promised he won't stop me doing anything I want to do, but saying it and doing it are quite different.'

'Oh, I think he'd keep his word. He's a man of honour.'

'But it might hurt him and I wouldn't do that for the world.'

'I think you'll hurt him more if you *don't* marry him, Pips. It's obvious he adores you.'

'And then there's Rebecca.'

'His daughter?'

Pips nodded and went on to recount all that had happened between her and Rebecca. As she fell silent, all Robert could say was, 'Ah, well, I think you do have a problem there.'

They watched Daisy turn the tricycle round again and come hurtling back towards them, calling out as she neared them, 'Aunty Pips! Grandma's. Cake.'

Pips and Robert laughed. 'She's a little minx,' he murmured fondly. 'She knows that today is Mrs Dawson's baking day and there'll be scones, fresh out of the oven and then smothered in cream and jam. Off you go. I'm sure you want to catch up on all the latest village gossip and there is certainly some to be heard at the moment.' As he turned away, Robert said over his shoulder, 'Oh, and by the way, I'm continuing my research into shell shock. It's still hard, but getting easier.'

'Now *that* is the best news I'm going to hear today.'

Twenty-Two

Ma Dawson was on her usual seat outside the front of the cottage, her pure white hair covered by her lace bonnet and a black shawl around her shoulders against the autumnal nip in the air.

'Nah then, Miss Pips. Home for a while, a'ya?'

'Just a few days, Ma. How are you?'

'Not so bad for an owd 'un.'

Pips put her hands on her hips as she smiled down at the elderly woman. 'And just how old would that be, Ma?'

Ma grinned. 'Ah, now that'd be tellin'. Like I allus tell the young'uns. As old as me tongue and a little bit older than me teeth. Mind you, I ain't got any o' them left now.'

Rumour had it that even Ma wasn't quite sure exactly how old she was but she must be approaching ninety now, Pips reckoned. She'd married her sweetheart when he'd returned from the Crimean war and so she must have been born sometime in the mid-1830s at least. Her husband had learned the trade of wheelwright and carpenter from his uncle and had passed on the trade to his son, Len. It had been Len's dearest wish to see the village industry, which now also incorporated the smithy and undertaker's trade, pass in turn to his sons. But now, he focused all his hopes on his grandson, Luke.

'Is everyone all right?' Pips asked tentatively.

'As well as they can be, Miss Pips. Poor Norah still seems to be expecting the lads to walk in through the back door, though I have to say, Len is coping better now he has little Luke to focus on.'

'And what's this I hear about Sam and Peggy?'

'Ah well, now, that is causing a bit of a to-do.'

'I can't understand why Mrs Nuttall's acting up.'

'Funny woman, is Clara Nuttall. You mebbe

194

won't remember, 'cos I think you was away by then, but when Sam volunteered, Clara took to her bed. It was only your mam, me and Bess Cooper that persuaded her to get up and help out with the knitting and sewing for the troops. And she's done the same again this time. Just taken to her bed and refuses to get up until Sam promises not to marry Peggy.'

'And will he?'

Ma laughed. 'I dun't reckon so, so it looks like Clara might have to stay there this time.'

'Luke?' Daisy tugged at Pips's skirt. 'Where's Luke?'

'Ah, bless her,' Norah said, appearing round the corner of the cottage carrying a tray with three cups of tea on it. 'She idolizes Luke. He's with his grandpa, lovey. Shall I take you up there to see him?'

Pips sat down beside Ma to drink her tea, her eyes still on her niece walking up the road beside her grandmother. 'So, when's the wedding fixed for?'

'That's just the trouble. Vicar won't marry 'em. 'Specially since neither of them are regular churchgoers. Not since the war, that is.'

Pips was solemn. 'Yes, it's tested a lot of people's faith. I can understand that.' There was a pause before she added, 'They could always get married in the register office.'

'Oh, now that would finish Clara off and no mistake.'

'D'you think I could help in any way? Perhaps I could have a word with Mrs Nuttall.'

'You can try, duck. We've all had a go. Even

195

your mam went to see her. She managed to prise Clara out of her bed last time, but not now. She's adamant. You certainly couldn't make things any worse than they are now. That is a fact.'

'Right. No time like the present, as they say. I'll go this minute. Will you and Mrs Dawson look after Daisy until I get back?'

'Luke'll mind her.' She nodded up the lane to where Norah, Luke and Daisy were walking back towards them. The boy was holding her hand. 'He's very good with her. Very protective.'

'Well, they're cousins, aren't they?'

'That's true, but I don't think they understand things like that at their age. They just know that they like each other and are friends.' She didn't voice Norah's concerns about what might happen when they grew up.

When the two youngsters were playing happily together in the Dawsons' back garden, Pips walked further along the lane until she came to the cottage where Bert Nuttall, his wife Clara and their son, Sam, lived. Sam was safely at his work alongside Len Dawson in the blacksmith's workshop – she had seen him as she had passed by – and Bert Nuttall would be working on the local farm where he was a wagoner.

She tapped on the door and, when there was no answer, she opened it and walked in. The interior was dark, but Pips knew the layout. She stood for a moment in the narrow passageway.

'Anyone home?' she called.

After a moment a querulous voice asked, 'Who is it?'

'Pips Maitland. May I see you for a moment,

Mrs Nuttall?'

There was a pause before the grudging answer came. 'If you must. I'm in me bedroom.'

Pips opened the door to find the woman in bed, propped up against the pillows. The room was dingy, the curtains drawn against the daylight. Pips crossed the room and opened them. 'How are you today, Mrs Nuttall? I'm sorry to see you're not well. Is there anything I can do for you?'

Clara glared belligerently at her visitor as if the entire blame lay with Pips. 'You can tell that stupid son of mine that he's not to marry that slut.'

Pips arched her eyebrows. She perched herself on the end of Clara's bed. 'Now why would I want to do a thing like that?'

'I reckon he left all his sense out in Flanders.'

'At least he came back to you, Mrs Nuttall,' Pips said softly.

Clara avoided meeting Pips's steady gaze and wriggled uncomfortably. 'I know, I know, and I'm grateful. Truly I am. Not a day goes by that I don't thank the Good Lord for his safe return. But...'

Pips waited.

'It's him wanting to marry that Peggy Cooper, who had Harold Dawson's bastard. You'd've thought she'd've learned her lesson, wouldn't you? But no. She goes and gets herself pregnant again.'

'It takes two, Mrs Nuttall,' Pips said mildly.

Clara glared at her. 'How do I know this one's my boy's? It could be anyone's, for all I know.'

'Really?' Pips widened her eyes as if enjoying a juicy piece of gossip. 'Are you saying that Peggy is the village whore?'

Clara winced. 'Miss Pips, really! I never said that.'

'You implied it,' Pips shot back, though she kept her tone calm.

Clara wriggled her plump shoulders again. 'It's just that I would have liked a nice girl for my Sam. Not – not someone who's already got a kiddie and now another one on the way.'

'Does Sam say the child is his?'

'Well, yes, but he would, wouldn't he? He wants to marry her.'

'So, let me get this straight,' Pips said, pretending to be confused. 'After Harold was killed, Peggy has had several boyfriends, has she? And now she's latched onto your Sam to be a father to her child – children, I suppose – even though you're not sure this one is his?'

'No, no, I never heard about her taking up with anyone after young Harold was killed – not until my Sam – but she wouldn't let it be known, would she? She'd keep it secret.'

Pips threw back her head and laughed aloud. 'Oh, Mrs Nuttall. There are no secrets in this village. You should know that.'

Clara plucked at the edge of the sheet. 'You think so?'

'I don't *think*, I *know* so.' She leaned forward towards the woman, who was so obviously genuinely distressed. 'Mrs Nuttall,' she said seriously, 'your boy – along with countless others – suffered untold horrors out there in the trenches. You're extremely fortunate that he has come back unscathed. Even my brother, who was a doctor and shouldn't have been anywhere near the danger area, didn't escape injury, did he? And as for poor Harold – he was brought to our first-aid post. He was terribly injured, but we were able to tell him he had a son. He sent a message to Peggy saying that he was sorry that he'd shamed her and that he'd have married her if he could have got back home. But I think he knew – even then – that he wasn't going to make it.'

Clara bit her lip, but could think of nothing to say.

'If Sam has found happiness with Peggy, then please, let him – let *them* – be happy. Believe me, he deserves it. And Sam and Harold were friends, weren't they? I reckon Harold would be tickled pink that Sam is going to be a father to Luke.'

'Vicar won't marry them,' Clara muttered, though Pips had the feeling that her defences were crumbling.

'Ah, now, my mother's working on him, but if he's adamant, then what about a chapel some-where or a register office?'

Clara flinched as if the very idea was anathema to her.

'Mrs Nuttall,' Pips said gently, 'I'm as sure as I can be that Peggy's baby is your grandchild.'

Clara stared at her as if that thought had never filtered into her stubborn head, so firmly had she closed her mind against the girl.

And now, Pips played her trump card. 'And you don't want your grandchild to be born out of wedlock, do you?'

'So,' Ma greeted her as Pips walked back into their cottage. 'How did it go?'

199

Pips put up both her hands to show her crossed fingers. 'Too early to say yet, but I've certainly given her something to think about. I think the main stumbling block now seems to be the vicar, but let's hope my mother can work her magic.'

Ma chuckled. 'I have no doubt she will. Vicar's only a man, after all, and even I wouldn't hold out long against Hetty Maitland.' Ma had known Pips's mother since she'd been a little girl in pinafores and was the only one of the villagers bold enough to call her 'Hetty', apart from Luke, who had now been given special permission to call her 'Aunty Hetty'.

The three women laughed as the two children came running into the cottage.

'Right, Daisy, time we were going home. Say goodbye to Luke.'

To their surprise the little girl planted a kiss on the boy's cheek. Far from being embarrassed about it, Luke only grinned.

'Aunty Pips, don't go.' Daisy wound her chubby arms around Pips's neck. 'I don't want you to go away again.'

'Darling, I've got a big race meeting later this month and I must practise. I have to go back, but I'll come home again soon.'

'Can I have a ride in your car?'

'Sorry, darling, but it's a racing car and I'm not allowed to drive it on the ordinary roads.'

The little girl pouted for a moment, but then her sunny nature reasserted itself as her quick mind thought of another treat with Aunty Pips. 'Then next time you come, will you take me riding?'

'Of course.'

'Promise?'

'I promise,' Pips said solemnly.

When she arrived back at Milly's flat, there were two letters waiting for her; one from Milly saying she would be away for the weekend and the other was from George.

My dearest Pips, I'm so sorry I wasn't in touch before you went north to visit your family. Rebecca came home ill and I really hadn't the heart to leave her alone in the flat. She's well again now and back at work, so when can we meet?

Was it always going to be like this? Rebecca coming between them, coming first in George's list of priorities? And then she castigated herself for being mean. The girl had no one else to turn to when she was ill and, of course, George had wanted to care for her. Wouldn't she go running home if one of her family needed her care, even though there were plenty of others there to help? She sighed. She really must have a serious talk with George before she could give a definite answer to the question he asked her repeatedly.

He arrived the following weekend. 'Rebecca's on duty until Tuesday,' he said as he unpacked his suitcase, put his clothes in the drawer, which Pips had left empty for him, and hung his suit in the wardrobe. He smiled as he turned to face her. 'So, what are we going to do?'

'I have a practice session tomorrow.'

For moment, a frown flitted cross his face but then he seemed to force a smile and nodded.

'May I come along too?'

'Of course, but, George, we need to have a serious talk. I could see – just now – that you aren't happy about my – er – pursuits and yet you said you'd never try to change me or stop me from doing what I want to do.'

'I won't,' he said swiftly. 'It's just that I felt I'd let you down last weekend and I wanted to make it up to you now by taking you wining and dining.'

Pips shook her head. 'I'm not that sort of girl. Oh, I don't mind the odd dinner out, wearing a posh frock and all that goes with it, but it's not really me.' She moved closer to him and put her hands on his shoulders. He slipped his arms around her waist. Softly, she said, 'I do love you, George, but I really think that before we get married we should get to know each other a little better and, then, there's Rebecca.'

'Yes,' he said soberly, 'there's Rebecca.'

Twenty-Three

With only three meetings left before the end of the season, the Brooklands Girls and their friends decided to make a party atmosphere at a meeting in October.

'After the Autumn BARC meeting,' Muriel told them, 'there's going to be a long-distance race organized by the Junior Car Club. It's the two-hundred-mile race, so none of us are competing that day. We'll be able to relax and enjoy ourselves.'

'That's a first, isn't it?'

Muriel nodded. 'On two counts. It's the first for small cars and also the first long-distance race since the war.'

'There'll be a huge crowd there, then,' Pattie said.

'Ah, but they won't all be able to get into the clubhouse, will they?'

'True.' Pattie grinned. 'So, what are we to do?'

'Take hampers and champagne,' Milly suggested. 'And be sure to bring the gorgeous major with you, Pips. If it's fine, we'll have a party on the hill, if there's space. If not, we'll take over the clubhouse.'

'The Clerk of the Course will *not* be amused,' Muriel said.

'Leave him to me.' Milly waved her hand. 'He's a friend of Daddy's.'

'I don't think I've ever seen quite so many people here,' Pips said, when they arrived at the meeting in Paul's car. 'The bookies will do a roaring trade today. There are men, women and even some children. Daisy will love this when she's a bit older. I must bring her.'

'Coming to the end of the season, they've all had the same idea as we have,' Milly said. 'At least we've got a fine day. Even the sun's trying to shine. Let's see if we can find a place on the hill to start with.'

They commandeered a spot on Members' Hill and sat down to watch the race, well wrapped up against the October chill. Pips introduced George to Muriel and Pattie, but Mitch seemed to have disappeared.

'The race will last over two hours,' Muriel explained as she sat down next to George and pointed out the places of interest around the circuit and told him a little of its history. 'Now, they're going to start in a minute. Let's get that champagne opened. Major, would you do the honours?'

'Call me George, please.'

Mitch joined them just before noon as the cars lined up at the Fork Start. The noise was deafening and there was no chance to introduce him to George. Even the cheering crowds could not be heard against the roar of four rows of pounding engines.

Pips stood up to watch. 'I can't count them from here, but there must be about forty cars taking part.'

'It's a terrific advert for small cars,' Pattie said.

'Not so good if they break down, though,' Muriel said wisely. 'They'll do well to last the seventy-three laps.'

'They're off!'

'The three Talbot-Darracqs are in the lead already.'

'Hardly surprising after the practice results,' Pattie said. 'Don't the drivers look smart in their white driving suits?'

'The two Bugattis are having a go at them, though,' Pips murmured.

The three Talbot Darracqs took the first three places, as expected. There was more racing, but once they'd seen the presentation of the cup to the winner of the two-hundred-mile race, the friends retired to the clubhouse.

'So, who's the guy who's in love with you?' George was trying to speak lightly and to smile, but his mouth was tight as they walked towards the clubhouse.

Pips's eyes widened. 'What on earth are you talking about?'

George nodded towards Mitch. 'The good-looking, dark-haired chap. Ex RAF, I'd say at a guess.'

Pips followed the line of his gaze. 'Oh him? That's Mitch Hammond.'

'Ah. The guy you pulled from his plane wreckage in no-man's-land?'

'The very same. He runs a flying school here and he's one of Milly's set. There's a whole clique of them.'

'I don't doubt it,' George murmured, his gaze still on Mitch.

Pips moved closer to him. 'George, you're wrong. We don't even like each other.'

'My dearest Pips, for an intelligent woman you can be remarkably blind sometimes.'

'Oh phooey!' Pips laughed and linked her arm through his. 'Come on, let's go and join them in the clubhouse and forget all this nonsense.' She hugged his arm to her. 'I think you imagine every man is in love with me.'

'They probably are, my darling,' he answered, his tone quite serious.

They spent the following few days at Milly's flat, but when she arrived home from her parents' house on the Tuesday, a little earlier than they'd expected, George said at once, 'I'll leave.'

'No need, darling,' Milly said. 'I don't mind you being here. As long as you don't mind Paul being here too.'

'It's your apartment,' George began, but Milly laughed and flapped her hand.

'If it doesn't bother you two, it certainly doesn't worry me, though what my Granny Fortesque would say – and Pips's divine mother – I daren't think.'

'I'd make an honest woman of her tomorrow – I think you know that – but she seems to be hesitating.'

'She adores you, George, but I think, like me, she's not ready to settle down just yet. We're having too much fun.'

'And you and Paul?'

Milly shrugged. 'Funny you should ask me that, George. I told Pips that Paul and I were just friends, but it seems he's got other ideas. And now he's proposed. Several times, actually.' She giggled deliciously. 'And so have a few others. I'm very fond of him, but I'm not ready. Not yet. I want to cause a bit more of a stir. By the way, I don't know if you're up for it, but I've organized a party for tomorrow night and there's going to be a midnight scavenger hunt. It's a new idea someone's come up with. We all put five shillings into a kitty for the winners and you have to collect a variety of things from around the city.'

'You really are one of what they're calling the flappers, aren't you? Defying all the conventions of the time by wearing short skirts, bobbing your hair – drinking and smoking – and generally

206

shocking the older generation.' He smiled. 'So will Pips be roaring through the city's night-time streets?'

'I do hope so.' Slyly, she eyed George. 'But if it's not your sort of thing, I'm sure Mitch would keep her company.'

'I'm sure he would,' George said drily. 'But there'll be no need. I'll be with her.'

Milly hid her smug smile.

For Pips, London at night was an exciting place, but she could sense it wasn't quite George's idea of fun as they drove around the city in the back of Paul's car following the set of demands that had been devised by Pattie and Muriel.

'We can't possibly do that,' he protested. 'Collect a policeman's helmet? We'll be arrested.'

Milly, in the front seat beside Paul, giggled. 'Well, the other items aren't much easier. Someone suggested a blonde hair from an actress, though we could probably get away with one of mine.'

'That'd be cheating,' Pips said primly, then laughed. 'But it might be the only way.'

'Someone suggested we should steal the door knocker from Number Ten.'

'No! What about the policeman who stands outside?' George protested again.

'One of us could lure him away,' Milly said.

'I don't think you'd manage that.'

'Never mind,' Pips said. 'Let's go for something a little easier. I don't expect we'll win anyway. It's not like racing. It's not the winning that matters, but the taking part.'

'Let's try for a commissionaire's hat from the Savoy...'

'Or a nameplate from somewhere...'

Back at a coffee stand near Hyde Park Corner in the early hours of the morning, they compared their trophies.

'I declare Muriel the winner. How*ever* did you get a policeman's hat without being marched off to Holloway?'

Before Muriel could answer, Pattie piped up, 'She cheated. It was someone who comes to Brooklands and he *gave* it to her.'

'But won't he get into awful trouble?'

'Yes, if anyone finds out, but hopefully they won't, if she returns it to him before he goes on duty at six, like she's promised.'

'Then you'd better get a move on, Muriel. It's half past five now.' Milly yawned. 'Come on, Pips. I'm exhausted. Time for bed, I think.'

The following morning, Pips told George, 'I'll be going up to Lincolnshire tomorrow for Sam and Peggy's wedding on Saturday. Would you like to come with me?' She chuckled. 'It'll be separate bedrooms again, I'm afraid. I wouldn't wish to offend my mother's sensibilities.'

'But I'm not invited to the wedding, am I?'

'Not exactly, but anyone can go to the church service.'

'So the vicar has capitulated, has he?' George smiled. He'd heard all about the contretemps over the wedding.

'No one holds out against my mother for ever.' Pips laughed. 'I understand she told him that he

208

ought to be grateful a young couple still wanted to be married in church. Since the war and the dreadful flu epidemic that took so many lives, many have lost their faith. They're weary of listening to your patriotic sermons, she told him.'

'Did it affect anyone close to you? The flu, I mean?'

Pips shook her head. 'My poor father was run ragged attending to patients. It came on so suddenly. Someone could seem perfectly well in the morning and be stricken by the afternoon. There were two deaths of elderly people in the next village, but no one close to us, thank goodness, though several were very ill. But to answer your original question, she – my mother, that is – is holding a wedding reception at the hall for them, so you can come along as my guest.'

'She's a very generous woman. I heard all about her magnificent fund-raising for the troops in the war. My own men were so grateful for all the gifts you personally brought to the trenches – especially at Christmas time – and I expect most of them were from her.' They exchanged a sober glance, for a moment, reliving their time out there.

'So, will you come?'

'Of course. Any excuse to be with you.'

'And Rebecca? What will you tell her?'

'I'll think of something.'

'Don't lie to her, George. I don't want our relationship built on lies.'

He sighed. 'Then I will tell her the truth – the whole truth – and she can begin to learn to deal with it.' He took her in his arms and, with his mouth against her hair, murmured, 'I mean to marry you, Pips, and no one – not even Rebecca – is going to stand in my way.'

Only now did Pips realize that he truly loved her.

Twenty-Four

'You're most welcome, Major Allender,' Henrietta greeted him when they arrived at Doddington Hall for the wedding. Ever perceptive, she had quickly noticed a subtle change in their relation-ship, the way they looked at each other, the way he'd put his arm around Pips's waist as she'd climbed the shallow steps to the front door; steps that Pips had run up and down for years without mishap. Yet to the observant mother, the simple protective action spoke volumes and opened up her hopes again.

The only 'fly in the ointment' for her was the difference in their ages, but Henrietta sighed inwardly. With such a shortage now of suitable young men, how could she raise such a piffling objection? He certainly had all the other qualities she sought. He was a highly decorated officer from the war. He was charming, courteous – a true gentleman – and obviously very much in love with Pips. Perhaps, after all, Henrietta began to hope her wayward daughter would really settle down and forget all this motor-racing nonsense.

'Please, call me George,' he murmured, as he glanced around the Great Hall. Already the long dining table was set for the wedding guests. It looked to George as if the whole village would be attending. Perhaps they were, if Henrietta's generous reputation was to be believed. 'This must be giving you a lot of work. Is there anything I can do to help?'

'That's most kind of you, but we're fortunate here, we haven't lost any of our staff like a great many of the country houses have. We still have everyone we had before the war – apart from William, of course. Even though some of the younger ones went to do war work, they were glad to come back to us afterwards.' She laughed. 'I was quite surprised, actually; I thought the girls would like the city life, but no, they've come back home.'

'It's a beautiful part of the country. I can't blame them. I must try to see more of it with Pips whilst we're here.'

'Ah now, we have a little surprise for her, which you will hear about at dinner tonight. We shall be eating in the Brown Parlour tonight as it's just family. This,' she waved her hand towards the grand table, 'is being prepared for the wedding breakfast tomorrow and I don't want to cause the servants any more work than is necessary.'

George smiled to himself. Henrietta Maitland was a remarkable woman. Who, in her position, he wondered, would be so thoughtful towards their staff. 'Now he began to see from whom Pips had inherited her altruistic motives. He warmed to his hostess and realized that she could become a very useful ally in his pursuit of her daughter.

'Philippa, we have a surprise for you,' Henrietta

211

said as the dinner came to an end and Wain-wright moved silently about the room, serving coffee. 'You tell her, Robert, because it was your idea really.'

'We've bought another horse for the stable. His name is Boxer. Jake and I went back to see Mr Rudd at Horncastle last week. We thought it would be nice to have two horses rather than just the one alongside the children's ponies. Only, at the moment, Daisy is forbidden to ride him, so no putting her on his back. And certainly, she's not to go anywhere near Samson.' He glanced at George and added casually, 'You're very welcome to use Boxer any time you come here because I don't think you'll get the chance to ride Samson – not when Pips is around. She loves riding him.'

Before George had time to respond, Pips clapped her hands. 'Oh how lovely!' She drank her coffee quickly and got up. 'I must see him this very minute.'

'Oh, isn't it a bit late now...?' Henrietta began, but Pips was halfway out of the room. George smiled indulgently, finished his own coffee, begged to be excused and followed her.

As the door closed behind him, Robert mur-mured, 'Well, I think that went well, don't you? I don't think he guessed that we'd bought another horse for him to ride out with her, do you?'

Edwin chuckled. 'Of course he did, Robert, my boy. But if it's something to please Pips, he's not going to argue, is he?'

'Oh dear, I hope he doesn't see it as charity in some way.'

'Of course he won't. It's only for him to ride.

It's not *his* horse. Besides, Jake is in his element having the stables almost fully occupied again.'

The following morning, Pips and George took both horses out for a ride. They galloped across the open fields, the wind streaming through Pips's hair. Soon she was urging her mount, Samson, forward towards a hedge. She sailed over and carried on, but George pulled his horse up and found the nearest gate to follow her. Jake had warned him not to try anything too ambitious. 'We're just finding out what Boxer can do, sir, and we've not tried jumping him yet.' He'd grinned. 'You might find yourself trailing in Miss Pips's wake, though.'

George smiled as he dismounted, opened the gate, led the horse through and then closed the gate. As he remounted, he couldn't even see Pips, but he trotted on. He'd catch up with her somewhere.

'Boxer is wonderful, Robert. He'll be perfect for Daisy to graduate to when she's old enough.' Unseen by anyone else, Pips gave her brother a broad wink. She had guessed the reason for the arrival of another horse in the stables.

'Have you seen this in the paper?' Robert said, pretending to ignore her gesture.

'Not this morning. I've been too busy. What is it?'

'The British Legion have adopted the poppy as their emblem. The idea came from an American woman, but it was taken up by Earl Haigh: we should all wear a replica of a poppy for Armistice

Day here and wreaths of them can be laid at all the war memorials and the sales will go towards funds for helping the wounded.'

'What a marvellous idea,' Pips said, fingering the poppy brooch on her left shoulder. 'Very symbolic, I'd say, wouldn't you?'

'Most apt,' Robert murmured, without looking up.

In support of one of their own, the whole village turned out for the wedding.

'We'll be overrun, Mother,' Pips said, but Henrietta only smiled. 'I expected this might happen. Everything's in hand. We won't run out of food. Several of the villagers have contributed pies and puddings and even vegetables from their own gardens. Isn't that thoughtful? There's been a veritable stream of visitors to the back door. And at least all the rationing has finished now.'

'Doesn't Cook mind others providing things? I'd have thought it would have wounded her pride.'

'Not a bit of it. She understands their need to feel involved – to feel they're giving something to the bride and groom after all they've been through. They all stood by Peggy when she was left an unmarried mother.'

'They took their lead from you, Mother,' Pips murmured.

Henrietta waved aside the compliment. 'And, of course, they're all thankful to see Sam safely back home.' Henrietta regarded her daughter. 'But, from what I hear, it was you who changed Clara's mind.'

'Oh phooey. She'd have come round. She

wouldn't have missed her son's wedding.'

'I don't know so much. I haven't forgotten that the Dawsons – apart from Ma – didn't come to their daughter's wedding when Alice married Robert.'

Pips couldn't resist teasing her mother just a little. 'Well, you were in two minds for a while.'

'Philippa, I hope I'm always honest enough to admit when I've been wrong. And I was wrong about Alice. She's the perfect wife for Robert. She can deal with his dark moods far better than I – or your father, for that matter – can.'

'And you're wrong about something else, too. Norah did come to their wedding. She sneaked in at the back at the last moment and hurried out before they set off down the aisle. I saw her.'

Henrietta's eyes widened. 'Did she? Well, I'm glad to know that.'

The wedding was a pretty village affair on a bright autumn day. Charlie Cooper escorted his daughter proudly up the aisle to stand beside a blushing Sam whilst Clara shed tears in the front pew. But seeing – and hearing – the villagers' support for her boy soon helped to dry them.

After the service, when everyone had gathered in the gardens at the hall, Bess declared to anyone who would listen, 'Have you heard? Mrs Maitland's found them a little cottage on the estate. Needs a bit of doing up, mind you, but Sam'll manage that. His dad and my Charlie will lend a hand. Len Dawson's even said he'll help. Thinks a lot of Sam, does Len. Mind you,' Bess let out her loud laugh, 'he's made it quite clear that Sam'll

215

never get his business. That's for Luke to inherit, he keeps saying. But Sam's content.' She eyed Pips. 'And when can we expect to hear wedding bells with you, Miss Pips?'

Pips laughed. 'Don't hold your breath, Mrs Cooper. There aren't enough men to go around now.'

Bess's face sobered. 'You're right there. Our Peggy's been lucky, but I don't reckon Betty'll ever get wed. Not now.'

There was silence between them as they both thought about Roy Dawson, who'd been Betty Cooper's sweetheart and who'd perished at the Somme. Bess Cooper was not an educated woman, yet she had a wealth of wisdom and common sense. She was a force to be reckoned with in the village and probably the only two people who 'outranked' her were Ma Dawson and, of course, Henrietta.

'We've lost a generation of young men, Miss Pips,' Bess went on, 'haven't we? But not only that, we're left with a generation of spinsters and we've lost the babbies they'll never have now.'

'Yes, it's a tragedy all round,' Pips murmured, but as her gaze alighted on Luke and Daisy sitting together on the grass, she smiled gently and said, 'Our hopes now rest with the youngsters we have got. We must cherish them and trust them that a war like that is never allowed to happen again.'

'Amen to that, Miss Pips. Amen to that.'

'This is perhaps going to be a rather unusual bridegroom's speech,' Sam said, as he stood at the end of the long table in the Great Hall. The villagers crowded into the room. 'First of all, my wife and I' – his face reddened, but he was encouraged by the ripple of applause – 'would like to thank Mrs Maitland for her generosity in asking us all here today to this beautiful setting and to everyone who has contributed, because I know you have. We'll never be able to thank her – or all of you – enough. We would also like to thank our parents for their help and support. They – and all the villagers – have supported both of us through some very tough times.' His glance rested on Luke. 'But there's one other person that I want none of us to forget today. Luke's dad, Harold Dawson. Not only did he love Peggy very much, but he was my mate too. We grew up together and I want to add to the solemn vows I made to Peggy in church that I will try to be the best stepdad to Luke that I know how to be.' His glance now took in the members of the Dawson family standing together to one side. 'We'll never forget Harold and we'll always tell Luke all about him.'

Norah wiped tears from her eyes, but Ma smiled and nodded her approval. 'Well said, lad.'

Sam rounded off his speech with more thank-yous and a toast to Peggy's sister, Betty, her only bridesmaid.

The day ended with Peggy and Sam being driven in style to their cottage in Edwin's car.

'Luke's going to stay with us for a couple of nights,' Norah explained. 'They can't afford a proper honeymoon, but they deserve a bit of time to themselves.'

Twenty-Five

'How is Robert, Alice?' Pips asked her when they had a few moments alone.

'Much better. He seems to be sticking to his writing now.' She smiled. 'He's giving me an awful lot to type up and send to Dr Hazelwood.'

'But you don't mind?'

'Heavens, no. I'm delighted.'

The following day Pips returned to her life in London with a lighter heart.

'So, Mitch Hammond, when are you taking me flying? You've been promising me for months, but nothing seems to be happening.'

'Whenever you say the word. I didn't really know if you were that keen.'

'Of course I am, but I'd like to learn how to fly myself. I'm not good at being a passenger. Can I do that?'

Mitch chuckled. 'November's not really the best time of year to start lessons, but I'll talk to Jeff Pointer. He's a qualified instructor who works for me and he also takes up members of the public for joyrides. I think you've met him, haven't you?'

Pips laughed. 'Yes, I beat his sister, Pamela, in a race. I just hope he won't hold that against me. But won't you teach me?'

Mitch shook his head. 'I've made it a rule – we both have – that we don't train family or close friends. It's better that way. We take them up for joyrides, but not to teach them.'

'Yes,' Pips said slowly. 'I think I can understand that.' Then she grinned. 'You could have a nasty fall-out, especially,' she added impishly, 'if they crashed your plane.'

A few days later, Mitch sent word that Jeff would be quite happy to teach Pips to fly. *Come down on Saturday. He'll take you up then and see if you like it.*

'Oh darling, you're so brave. I don't know how you dare to go up in one of those things.' Milly giggled. 'My granny always says, "If God had meant us to fly, he'd have given us wings".'

Pips joined in. 'And my mother says, "If God had intended us to smoke, he'd have fitted us with a chimney".'

'Is George going too?'

'I think so. He did say he'd like to learn too.'

'Oh Pips, really! Can't you see that he doesn't like you meeting all those dashing young men at the racetrack and the flyers are even more handsome and devil-may-care.'

Pips shrugged. 'Then he'll just have to deal with it, won't he?'

As Jeff led her across the grass towards the plane, he said, 'This is a Vickers Boxkite – a biplane. It's what we use to start pupils on until they're good enough to graduate to a more advanced monoplane. Today, there'll be no instruction as such. I'll just take you up to see how you like it.'

Her first flight was everything Pips had imagined it would be – and more. High above the clouds, she felt a sense of freedom and lightness of spirit as if all the dreadful memories had for a little while been left behind. She revelled in the way Jeff handled the aircraft and was thrilled when he began to try out a few acrobatic moves.

When they landed, he helped her to climb out. 'Well, Pips, you are the first woman I've ever taken into the air who didn't squeal when I did a few unusual manoeuvres. I congratulate you and I'll be delighted to give you lessons.'

'When can we start?' was all Pips said as they crossed the grass to where George and Mitch were standing together. As she drew near, she could detect a frosty atmosphere between the two men, but she smiled and said, 'That was fantastic. Are you going up now, George?'

For a moment, he hesitated and then he shook his head. 'No, I'll give it a miss today, thanks. I have to get back.'

As they all walked to the clubhouse, George murmured, 'It seems as if I'll have to keep my word now.'

'What d'you mean? To take up flying yourself?'

He shook his head. 'No, to not try to stop you doing anything you want. I will keep my promise, Pips, but I won't be trying it again myself.'

'Again? You've been up before?'

He nodded. 'In the war. I was violently airsick. Flying is definitely not for me.'

'I'm sorry to hear that because I thought you said it would be something we would do together.' She paused and then added, 'You thought I'd hate it, didn't you?'

'To my eternal shame, I hoped you would.'

'Well, I'm sorry, George,' she said and her tone was tight, 'but I loved it and I *will* be taking lessons with Jeff just as soon as it can be arranged.'

Although life was exciting and fulfilling in the south, Pips could never quite quell her longing for home and the sight of her beloved niece. She vowed that whatever was happening in London or at Brooklands, she would never miss Daisy's birthday.

'Are you coming with me, George?' she asked him just before Daisy's fourth birthday.

'Sorry, I can't. Rebecca's off duty this weekend.' He didn't need to say any more.

Pips was unable to take her car north, so she took a photograph of it and brought it home to show the family. She fully expected a variety of reactions to it and she was not disappointed.

'What a monstrosity,' Henrietta declared. 'Couldn't you find something a little more refined, Philippa?'

'She's a beaut,' Robert enthused. 'I only wish I could drive something like that.'

'I want to ride in it,' Daisy clamoured. 'You promised, Aunty Pips.'

Pips picked her up. 'I haven't forgotten, but I'm not allowed to bring it home. It's just a racing car.'

'Then why don't you buy a car that you can bring home for me and Luke to ride in?'

The family laughed, but, quite seriously, Pips said, 'I'll have to think about that.'

Daisy's family birthday party was noisy and

boisterous, even though she and Luke were the only two children present. The grown-ups forgot their inhibitions and played silly games all afternoon. Three days later, it was the Dawsons' cottage that was alive with laughter.

'I'll take them out for a ride on their ponies before it gets dark, Ma,' Pips said. 'I'm sure you've had enough of all the noise.'

'Eh, I dun't mind it, Miss Pips. It's good to see Norah smiling again. There's just one thing I'd wish, but I know it can never be.'

'Tell me, Ma,' Pips said softly.

''Afore the good Lord calls me home, I'd just like to see William one more time. But I don't expect even you could make that happen, Miss Pips.'

Pips patted her hand but said nothing. She was not going to make promises she might not be able to keep but she stored Ma's heartfelt wish in the back of her mind.

With Pips riding Boxer, she took the children on their ponies around the grounds of the hall before it began to grow dark. 'Birthday or not, Daisy, I think it's your bedtime,' she said as they trotted back into the stable yard. 'Jake, I know they're being trained to care for their ponies, but would you do the honours tonight, please? They've both had a very exciting day.'

'Of course, Miss Pips. What do you think of Boxer?'

Pips patted the horse's neck. 'A great addition to the stable. Are you managing all right now you have an extra one?'

Jake's grin widened. 'I couldn't be happier,

Miss. I missed 'em when we hadn't any, but now...' He didn't need to say any more; Pips could see the joy shining out of his eyes. 'And Master Robert rides Boxer. He often goes out with the children on a Saturday afternoon.'

'I'm delighted to hear it. Now, Daisy, say "good-night" to Luke. I'm just going to walk home with him.'

'Aw, can't I come too?'

'Not tonight. It's getting late. Be a good girl and next time I come, I'll go riding with you both again.'

Luke said nothing. He was quite capable of going home on his own – he'd run freely about the village almost since the time he could walk – but he savoured some time with Miss Pips. She always treated him like an adult.

Pips had a brief word with Peggy and Sam, but she was anxious to get home; her mind was on something else.

On her return to the hall, she sought out Henrietta. 'Mother, I want you to promise me something.'

'I will if I can, dear. What is it?'

Pips told her of Ma's wish, ending, 'I want you to let me know if Ma gets ill, because when she does – and it's bound to happen one day – I want to fetch William home to see her.'

Henrietta stared at her. 'Do – do you think Len will allow it?'

'I don't think even Len Dawson would deny his mother her dying wish, do you?'

Henrietta bit her lip. She wasn't too sure, but if anyone could bring such a miracle about, then it

223

was Pips.

On her return to London, Milly greeted her. 'This weekend's party is at Muriel's. It's fancy dress with a circus theme. I've got a wonderful clown outfit. You and George are both invited, of course. Everyone knows you're a couple now.'

'I don't think it's quite my scene, Pips,' George said, when she told him. 'And besides, it's Rebecca's weekend off.'

Pips shrugged. She was disappointed, but there was no way on this earth that she was going to refuse a party just because of Rebecca Allender. 'Then I'd better get my costume sorted out,' was all she said.

'Why don't you get a clown's costume too and we'll go as a pair?' Milly suggested. 'We could get up to some high old jinks together.'

With their faces covered in make-up, the two friends were scarcely recognizable. 'We won't be able to speak,' Milly warned Pips as they took a taxi to the party. 'Or we'll be recognized right away.'

'I'd've thought you could adopt another voice. You're a fantastic mimic.'

'Oh, I could, couldn't I? What about you?'

'I'm dressed as the sad-faced clown, so all I've got to do is keep quiet and look miserable.'

Milly giggled. 'I can't see you managing that all evening.'

'That's a wonderful outfit, Pips,' Mitch said when he found her. He was dressed as a ring-master in top hat, red waistcoat and tails.

'Oh phooey! You're not supposed to be able to identify me.'

'D'you really think you can disguise yourself from me?' He glanced around. 'And where is your ardent suitor, then?'

'Couldn't come.'

Mitch slipped his arm around her waist. 'What a shame!' he murmured insincerely. 'So I shall be obliged to look after you all evening. What an absolute bore!'

They danced every dance, Mitch refusing to relinquish her to any other partner, until even Milly said, 'You know, Pips, darling, it's beginning to look a bit obvious. What would George say?'

It was the worst thing she could have said. 'If George doesn't want me to dance with anyone else, then he should be here. By the way, where's Jeff? Have you recognized him yet? I need to ask him if he'll give me a flying lesson this week.'

Pips wasn't sure which gave her the greatest thrill; careering round the racetrack or being up above the clouds, the sun glinting on the wings of the aircraft. *One day,* she promised herself, *when I've got my aviation certificate and she's a little older, I shall bring Daisy here and take her up. I know she'd love it too.*

'I'll be going home for Christmas as usual,' Pips said, 'but I expect you'll want to be with Rebecca.' She tried very hard to keep any resentment out of her tone, but it was difficult.

'As a matter of fact, she's working over Christmas and I've already told her that if you invited me this year, then I would say "yes".'

225

'And was she comfortable with that?'

'I didn't ask,' he said shortly. 'She's just going to have to get used to the idea that we're a couple and also that, as soon as you say the word, we'll be married.'

Pips wriggled her shoulders. 'George, I do want to marry you, but it's just – not the right time. I'm having too much fun and, when we do marry, I want to be a proper wife to you. Besides, I'd really like Rebecca to be happier with the idea. If she isn't, I'm so afraid it would eat away at our relationship.'

'We wouldn't let it. But do remember, I'm not getting any younger. I mean, we've never discussed having a family, but I don't want to be an old man by the time we have children.'

Pips put her arms round his waist. 'You, my darling, will never be old and children would keep you young.'

She forbore to ask what Rebecca would think of having half-brothers and sisters. She didn't think she would like the answer.

Christmas 1921 was a joyous time for the Maitland family and even the Dawsons, with Luke as their focus, managed to put their sadness aside just for a day or two. Each Christmas since their deaths, Norah's heart had ached to see the empty chairs around the dinner table. No one mentioned the missing members of the family, especially the three who could never return, but they were in everyone's mind. Every celebration, every birthday, the anniversary of their deaths and especially Christmas were difficult days to live through. But this year, Norah had insisted, for once determined to ignore any grumblings from Len, that their kitchen should be filled with guests.

'I'm inviting Sam and Peggy along with Luke, of course.' Norah ticked them off on her fingers. She stood facing Len, though she was sure her heart was beating in her chest loud enough for him to hear. 'His mam and Dad – else they'll be on their own – and Bess, Charlie and Betty Cooper an' all.'

For a moment Len gaped at her and Norah held her breath. It was Ma, from her chair near the range, who spoke first. 'That sounds like a lovely idea, Norah duck.' Craftily, she added, 'Luke'll love having all his family together. And we've all been invited to the hall on Boxing Day for what they're calling a buffet lunch. Haven't a clue what that is, mesen, but if Hetty's behind it, it'll be nice.'

Len seemed to be struggling for a moment before he shrugged and muttered, 'Aye well, if that's what the lad wants, then it's all right by me. Mind you,' he added with a smirk, 'I dun't know how you're going to fit 'em all in, Norah.'

'I'll manage,' his wife said, unable to remember the last time she had felt quite so happy. Now she had something to plan for, to bake and cook for.

When Len left for work, Norah whispered, 'That was a stroke of genius, Ma. Mentioning Luke. Thanks.'

The old lady put her head back against her chair and closed her eyes with a contented smile.

Twenty-Six

'Have you heard?' Bess could hardly contain herself. 'Miss Pips has brought home that soldier chap again. It must be serious, you know, if he's joined the family for Christmas. D'you reckon we'll hear wedding bells in the spring?'

'Oh, I don't know,' Norah said as she handed round the vegetables whilst Len, at the head of the table, carved an enormous goose. 'He's a lot older than her, isn't he?'

'What does your Alice say, Norah?'

'Just that he's a very nice feller.'

'He is,' Betty put in. Now that Peggy was married with a family of her own to care for and her baby due any day, Betty was the only one of their family who still worked at the hall. 'But he's very quiet and – oh, what's the word – a bit staid. I think he's too reserved for Miss Pips. She's always so lively.'

'Aye well, mebbe he'll settle her down a bit,' Ma put in. 'I know her mother would like to see her married.'

'You've done us proud, Norah,' Bess said. 'We're very lucky to be able to get plenty of food, aren't we? And I suppose it's thanks to Mrs Maitland. She'd never see any of the villagers going hungry, would she?'

They all nodded their agreement.

'Me an' Charlie's been talking and we'd like you

all to come to us on New Year's Day. Now we're all connected by marriage, it seems only right we get together on special occasions. You an' all, Clara and Bert. We're lucky in the country. Still got plenty to eat, but I hear times are hard in the cities.'

'So I've heard,' Len said. He'd unbent enough to play the gracious host. There weren't many people in the village he actually liked, but Charlie and Bert were all right. It was their wives he couldn't stand. Still, they came as a package, so he supposed he'd just have to put up with the two gossiping women. Like they said, they were all connected now. 'It's in the papers that there was a bit of a boom after the war finished, but now, there's a lot of unemployment as the soldiers have come back.'

There was a brief silence around the table, as if each one of them was thinking about those that would never come back, but Luke lightened the moment by saying, 'Well, I know what I'm going to be doing the rest of me life, don't I, Grand-dad?'

Len ruffled his grandson's hair fondly. 'That you do, m'lad. That you do.'

'And Sam'll always be there to help me, won't you, Sam?' It had been decided within the family that Luke should continue to call Sam by his Christian name and not 'Dad'. It was a decision that suited them all.

'I will, Luke,' Sam said solemnly.

'And soon I'll have a baby brother or sister, won't I? If it's a boy, maybe he could learn the trade as well. Would you mind that, Granddad, 'cos he won't actually be your grandson, like me, will he?'

Len shook his head and his voice was husky as he said, 'No, lad, he won't. But I wouldn't mind, because, like Bess says, he'll be one of the family.'

Luke smiled and tucked into his dinner, his future assured.

Slyly, Bess said, 'And what about Miss Daisy, Luke? Where does she fit into all this?'

For a moment, Luke paused and glanced at his grandmother. Then he laughed. 'I don't reckon Daisy will want to wield a big hammer, d'you?'

'No, but the two of you are very close, I just wondered...'

'Not the time or the place, Bess duck,' Ma said, her mouth full of potato. 'They're only six and four years old. Time enough for your matchmaking.'

Bess bent her head and concentrated on her piled plate. Even she didn't argue with Ma Dawson.

Bess's gossipy nature could not be quelled for long and, the following day at Henrietta's buffet luncheon, her eagle eyes watched Pips and George together. 'Oh there's summat going on there an' no mistake. Have you seen 'em, Peggy, just– Oh my lor', what's the matter?'

They were sitting together on one side of the Great Hall, with a plate of sandwiches and cakes on their knees. But now, Peggy's hand was shaking and before Bess could reach out and take it, the plate slipped out of Peggy's fingers. The crash and sound of breaking china made everyone turn. Now Peggy was clutching her stomach and bending forward. 'Oh!'

Edwin set down his glass and hurried towards her. Peggy seized his arm and gasped. 'Doctor, no disrespect, but I want Master Robert. He delivered Luke. I want... Aaah!' She doubled over as another contraction gripped her.

Edwin glanced around but he could not see his son. 'Alice – Alice. Find Robert, if you please. Peggy is going into labour.'

'Oh lor', we must get her home.' Bess began to panic.

'No time, Mrs Cooper. If you can walk, Peggy, we'll get you into my consulting room. We can deliver your baby there.'

Alice returned, with a reluctant Robert following her. 'Peggy, I can't deliver your baby. Not this time. You must see that.'

'But I want you there. You calm me down. You tell me what to do...' She cried out again. *'Please!'*

At once, all Robert's training and his innate sense of care for anyone in distress took over. He forgot that he had lost an arm, he forgot that he wouldn't physically be able to deliver her child, and remembered only that in front of him was a young woman suffering the pangs of childbirth and begging for his help.

'Just relax, Peggy. Try not to fight the pain. When this contraction dies away we need to get you to a bed.'

'My consulting room, Robert,' Edwin said.

'Good idea, Father. Now, Peggy, up you get. Take my arm. I've still got one for you to hang on to.' He tried to make light of it, but as the young woman stood up, her waters broke and flooded onto the polished wooden floor. 'Oh, I'm so sorry, Mrs Maitland. And your lovely plate...'

'No matter, my dear. Just let's get you onto a bed.'

On the way through the house, two more contractions gripped her, but by the time the next one began, Peggy was lying on Edwin's examination table whilst Alice scuttled around the room gathering together whatever would be needed.

Pips appeared in the doorway. 'I've only just heard. I was outside with the children. What can I do?'

Already, Robert was sitting beside Peggy holding her hand and talking to her in a low, comforting voice. Edwin rolled up his shirt sleeves and washed his hands in the basin.

'Go and reassure her family – especially Luke, if he's heard what's happening. And poor Sam. He looks petrified.'

Back in the Great Hall, the conversation was muted and, as Pips hurried back in, all eyes turned towards her.

'She's in good hands.' Her gaze sought out Luke's white face. Daisy was standing beside him gripping his hand, her dark eyes large with fear. Briskly, Pips went to them. 'Come on, you two. Jake–' Pips looked round for him. 'Will you please saddle up the ponies and we'll take them out for a little ride. George, will you come with us, please? Sam, you'd better stay here in case Peggy needs you.'

She could see that one or two people were shifting from one foot to the other, feeling as if perhaps they ought to leave. 'There's no need for anyone to go,' Pips said brightly. 'By the look of things, it won't be long and I'm sure you'd all like to hear the news. After all, you're all family.' As she turned to go, Pips added, 'And please will someone get Mrs Nuttall a stiff drink. She looks as if she needs it even before her grandchild arrives.'

Her words eased the tension and Henrietta hurried forwards to attend to Clara.

'Now, children, come along.'

'But, Miss Pips, Mam–'

'Your mam's in the best place possible, Luke dear. Two doctors and a competent nurse. She wouldn't get better attention if we were to try to take her home or to the Lincoln Hospital. We don't want your baby brother or sister born on the way there, now do we?'

Luke tried to smile and clung to Daisy's hand even harder. 'They'll – they'll come out and tell us, won't they?'

'Of course they will. The moment there's some news. Now, come along, let's go and find your ponies.'

With George leading Luke's pony, Jingles, and Pips walking beside Daisy on Lucky, they had done two circuits of the orchard and were heading back towards the house when they saw Sam appear round the corner and come running towards them, waving his arms.

'It's a boy! It's a boy!'

Luke slid from his pony and ran to his stepfather to be lifted high into the air and swung round. Pips lifted Daisy down and she ran after Luke.

Tears of joy were coursing down Sam's face as Pips and George reached them in time to hear Luke ask, 'Me mam? Is me mam all right?'

'She's fine,' Sam reassured him. 'Mrs Maitland has insisted that she stay here for a few days. She's getting a bedroom ready and then I'm going to carry her up there.'

'Can I see her – and the baby?'

'Of course you can, Luke, but we'll just give them time to get everything sorted out, shall we?'

Luke's face fell – he wanted to rush into the house to see his mother that instant – but he bit his lip and nodded.

An hour later, Luke was introduced to his half-brother.

'What d'you think we should call him, Luke?' Holding the baby in her left arm, Peggy drew Luke close to the bed and put her right arm around him. 'Sam and I can't decide on a name. We thought perhaps you could settle it for us.'

'I like the name Harry.'

Peggy glanced up at Sam standing at the end of the bed. She was unsure whether he would mind the name for his son being so close to Harold's. But Sam, ever generous, smiled and nodded. 'That's a perfect name, Luke. Harry, it is. Mebbe we could christen him "Henry" but he'd always be known as Harry. How would that be?'

He glanced at Peggy who, with tears in her eyes and unable to speak for the lump in her throat, nodded. How kind and tactful Sam was.

'And now, we must leave your mam to rest,' Sam said. 'Your grandma Dawson has invited us to stay with her tonight and Mrs Maitland says we can come back any time we like to see your mam and the baby over the next few days.'

Luke kissed his mother's cheek and gave a little wave to the baby, who slept on, blissfully unaware of the disturbance he had caused.

As they left the room, Peggy heard him say, 'It'll be a long time before he's big enough to play with me, won't it, Sam?'

''Fraid so, but you've got Daisy.'

'Yes,' Luke murmured. 'I'll always have Daisy.'

Twenty-Seven

'Fancy,' Pips laughed as she and George travelled back to London, 'another little one born around Christmas. It'll soon get very expensive.'

'You spoil them,' George murmured, 'always buying the same kind of present for Luke as you do for your niece.'

'He's such a nice little boy and he's Daisy's cousin.'

'He's very grown up for his age.'

'I expect that's being around adults all the time. He doesn't seem to have any other friends in the village apart from Daisy. When he's not playing with her, he's at his grandfather's workshops. Besides, I love buying presents.'

'And now you'll have to treat Harry the same as the other two.'

'Yes, I will, won't I?' she said happily. 'Now,

where are you going? To Milly's with me, or back home?'

George sighed. 'I'll have to go home. With working over Christmas, Rebecca has all of New Year off, so...'

'That's all right,' Pips said, forcing herself to be generous. After all, the girl hadn't seen her father all over the holiday. 'We've had a lovely time together, haven't we? So now it's Rebecca's turn to monopolize you.'

'It shouldn't be like that, though. We should all be together. Will you join us on New Year's Eve?'

Pips couldn't think of anything she'd like less. 'I'll be fine. Milly's organizing a party for the Brooklands gang. You're invited, of course, but I think you should be with Rebecca. This time, anyway.'

She risked a glance at George and saw that his mouth was tight. Deliberately, she had pre-empted his suggestions. No doubt, she thought with amusement, he was thinking that Mitch would be at the party.

But George said nothing.

'It's fancy dress again,' Milly told her, 'and we're having the party at a nightclub.'

'Is there a theme for the fancy dress?'

'A character from history, so come as anyone you like. I'm going as Marie Antoinette.'

Pips laughed. 'Just mind you don't lose your head.'

'They're all coming. It'll be such fun. What about George?'

'No, Rebecca's off duty.'

'Ah,' Milly said, understanding at once. 'You know, Pips darling,' she added, for once very serious, 'you're going to have to make up your mind about George and his daughter. If you really want to marry him, you're going to have to do something about the situation.'

'Probably, but at the moment, I'm having too much fun to bother. Now, about this party...'

They were all there; everyone who was involved in Brooklands in any way, several of whom Pips had not met before.

She was dressed as Salome and her costume seemed to attract a lot of admirers.

'I did think of coming as Lady Godiva, but I thought it was a bit cold at this time of the year,' she joked.

Mitch pretended to leer. 'I must make sure we organize a party in midsummer, then.'

'So,' Jeff said, seeking her out. 'Where's the boyfriend tonight?'

Pips arched her eyebrow playfully. 'And which one might that be?'

Jeff guffawed. 'Oh, so it's true what I've heard, then?'

'That depends on what you've heard.'

'That you're keeping one or two dangling on the end of a string.'

Pips frowned. It wasn't quite how she liked to hear herself described. 'It's more complicated than that. And it's certainly not *two*. Whatever gave you that idea?'

He eyed her quizzically and said airily, 'Oh just something Mitch said.' He paused and then added, 'George is quite a lot older than you, isn't he?'

Pips nodded. 'It isn't just that. He's a widower and has a daughter.'

There was silence between them until Jeff asked gently, 'And you're not prepared to tell me any more?'

Pips sighed. 'It's difficult. I would feel I was being disloyal.'

'Fair enough. I can respect that.' He cocked his head on one side and regarded her thoughtfully. 'I get the impression you're strong on loyalty.'

'Very.'

Now it was his turn to sigh heavily, but it was an exaggerated one. 'So, I haven't a chance if I throw my hat into the ring as a suitor, then? Because, despite what you say, there is Mitch, you know.'

Pips laughed. 'Oh him. He's not serious.'

But Jeff's tone was deadly earnest as he murmured, 'I think you'll find he is. Anyway, this conversation is getting far too heavy. Let's dance. I fancy doing the tango with you, so I have the excuse to hold you close. Are you game?'

'Of course, but first, when's my next flying lesson?'

During the second week in January, Pips received a letter from her father. She tore it open, anxious that it might contain bad news – Edwin rarely wrote to her now. Letters usually came from Robert in his shaky – but improving – left-handed writing. She read it and then read it again, more slowly the second time:

Dearest Pips, I hate to trouble you when you're having so much fun, especially the New Year's Eve party you told us about in your last letter. Even your mother just shrugged her shoulders and said, 'Well, she deserves it'. But why I'm writing is to ask you when you might next be coming home. You see, we feel we are progressing with encouraging Robert to take up his career as a doctor again. I know last time's efforts ended in failure – perhaps we tried too soon – but after he was so helpful at Peggy's confinement – she's singing his praises to the rooftops and telling everyone she couldn't have done it without his calming influence – we think he's really begun to see that he could help patients by just listening and maybe counselling them. He would probably be able to diagnose ailments, too, where a physical examination wasn't necessary. And, for the moment, I am still able to do that. Though your mother would like me to, I have no intention of retiring just yet! We all feel he needs one final push and we think you are the only person who can do that. By the way, do bring George, if he's free and would like to come. We all like him very much...

The letter continued with family news and a long paragraph about Daisy's progress, which Pips read three times. Then she sat down to write a quick note to George telling him that she'd be going to Lincolnshire at the weekend and asking him if he wanted to go with her. When she hadn't heard from him by Friday afternoon, she set off on her own, disappointed, but not surprised.

'No George?' Robert was the first to ask.

239

'Not this time. It's you I've come to sort out. I know you're still doing your research...' She grinned. 'Dr Hazelwood showed me your piece printed in *The Lancet*. You must be proud of that. We are. But what on earth are you dithering for about joining Father in the practice again? For goodness' sake get back to what you can do and stop dwelling on what you can't.'

'Ah. So who's been telling tales. Alice?'

'Heavens, no! And don't ask any more, because I'm not going to tell you. What's important is that you should give it another go.'

'I tried, if you remember, but it didn't work out.'

'Why?'

'I just haven't got the confidence any more.'

'But you were fantastic with Peggy. Holding her hand and telling her how to cope with the contractions. There's so much you could do to take the weight off Father. He'd be able to take it a bit easier. At least give it another shot, won't you?'

'But what about when Father wants to give up completely? What then?'

'He could employ another doctor. Like Sam suggested. We all thought that was such a good idea at the time, but it never went anywhere. Mainly because of your reluctance.' She eyed him with her head on one side as she thought quickly. 'Perhaps we could find a young doctor just out of medical school, who'd benefit from the experience and with advice on hand. Father will want to remain part of the practice and that way, he'd still feel useful. Or...' Now she was being even more devious. 'A doctor who'd served in the war.'

'You've got it all worked out, haven't you? You're all in cahoots.'

'No, actually, we're not. I've only just thought about the last bit. But it's a possibility, don't you think?'

He nodded and said slowly, 'All right. I'll give it another go, even if it's only to get you off my back.'

Pips kissed his cheek. 'That's more like the Robert I know, and now, where's Daisy?'

'Have you been away?' was George's first question when Pips opened the door to him on the Wednesday evening after her return.

For a moment, she gaped at him and then opened the door wider for him to step into the flat. 'I wrote to you. Didn't you get my letter?'

George frowned. 'No, I didn't.'

'Oh well.' Pips shrugged it off, though she had her own suspicions as to what might have happened to the letter she'd sent to the flat he shared with Rebecca. 'Never mind, you're here now.' She tucked her arm through his and led him into the living room, explaining the reason for her sudden visit home.

'And do you think it will work?'

'I'm hoping so.' She laughed. 'I seem to be the only one who can give him a straight talking to. Everyone else – even Father – treats him with kid gloves. I don't.'

George smiled and said softly, 'It is what he needs, though, my dear.' He sighed. 'Perhaps I should adopt the same approach with Rebecca.'

She sat beside him and took his hand. 'Still no

sign of a thaw in her attitude?'

He shook his head. 'She's on duty for the next four days. Would you come and stay?'

'There's no need. Milly doesn't mind you staying here.'

'But I do,' he said covering her hand with his. 'I want you all to myself. Milly is so gregarious. Oh, don't get me wrong, I'm extremely fond of her – but there are so many people in and out of here all the time that it resembles Charing Cross Station at times.'

'All right. For the next three days – I'm all yours.' She leaned forward and kissed him.

They were sitting in George's apartment, still in their dressing gowns, having a leisurely breakfast, when there was a rattle at the door and Rebecca came in. It would have been difficult to say who was the most startled of the three of them.

Rebecca slammed the door behind her and marched towards her bedroom, stopping only to point a finger at Pips and say between gritted teeth, 'Get that bitch out of here,' before slamming that door too.

'Oh dear. Was she expected today, George?'

He shook his head. 'No, not until tomorrow.'

'I thought that's what you said. I'd better make myself scarce.'

'And I'd better get dressed,' he murmured. 'And face the music.'

'You sound as if you're scared of her.'

He laughed sardonically. 'Let's just say I'd sooner go over the top.'

They smiled at each other before Pips kissed

his cheek and hurried to the bedroom they had shared for two nights. Half an hour later, she left the flat without having seen Rebecca again.

George tapped on his daughter's bedroom door. 'Rebecca?'

'Has she gone?'

'Yes, but I won't have you speaking to Pips like that.'

The door was flung open and she faced him, her face red with fury. 'I told you I didn't want to come home and find *her* here. It's so embarrassing finding you both in a state of undress. This is my home – or at least I thought it was. If you want me to move out, you only have to say.'

'Rebecca – please. I thought you weren't due home until tomorrow.'

Moodily, Rebecca was forced to agree. 'I wasn't, but I've developed a cold and Sister doesn't like us to be on the wards where we might spread infection to the patients – or to our colleagues, either.'

'Then, I'm sorry. Is there anything you need me to get for you?'

'No,' she snapped, then added, grudgingly, 'Thanks. I just want to go to bed and sleep.'

'You go ahead, then. I'll make dinner this evening. Perhaps you'll feel a little better by then.' He turned away, thinking to himself, *better in temper as well as physically, I hope.*

Twenty-Eight

Pips didn't see George for another two weeks and she concluded that Rebecca was spinning out her illness on purpose. In the meantime, she continued to have fun with Milly, to practise at Brooklands and to go flying with Jeff. Over the next few months she went on several visits home to see Daisy and the rest of her family. She was delighted to learn that Robert was now seeing a few patients every week in his own consulting room.

'He seems to be sticking to it this time,' Alice told her.

'Let's hope so.'

When winter turned into spring and she was able to fly more often, Pips soon completed the requisite number of hours Jeff had demanded before she could even think of going solo. But as she landed the aircraft smoothly one day in late April and climbed out, he said, 'I'm pleased to see that last week's dreadful accident hasn't put you off flying.'

The accident he was referring to had resulted in the deaths of two flyers and had cast a black cloud over Brooklands.

'Did you think it might?'

'It crossed my mind.'

'Jeff, if I allowed other people's accidents, either in their cars or planes, to put me off, I'd never do anything.'

Jeff nodded approval of her sentiment. 'In that case, then I think you can apply to the Royal Aero Club for your Aviator's Certificate.'

Pips flung her arms around his neck and kissed him soundly.

Two months later, she received a letter that had her dancing around Milly's kitchen, waving it in the air. 'I've got it, Milly. I've got it.'

Milly, emerging from her bedroom in her dressing gown, yawned. 'What have you got, darling?'

'My aviator's certificate. I can fly solo now and go anywhere I want, because it's recognized internationally.'

Milly blinked. 'That's marvellous, darling. So, all you need now is an aeroplane to fly?'

'Well, I've sort of got one.'

Milly ran her fingers through her tousled hair. *'Have* you?'

'Mitch has said he'll lend me one of his any time I want. He's got two now.'

Milly's eyes widened. 'Oh dear. He has got it bad. I'm very fond of Mitch, Pips. Please don't break his heart.'

But all Pips said was, 'Oh phooey.'

They were all there to watch on the day that Pips took her first solo flight.

'Nice take off,' Jeff murmured as the small aircraft lifted smoothly into the sky.

'Where's she going?' Milly asked. 'She won't go out of sight, will she?'

Muriel laughed. 'No knowing with that one.

245

She probably won't be back until tea time.'

'Half an hour. That's what I told her.' Jeff was like a bird watching his chick fledge.

Standing beside Mitch, George said, 'I'm surprised you didn't teach her yourself.'

'Golden rule, old boy. Never teach family or very close friends.'

'And you consider Pips a very close friend?'

There was a slight pause before Mitch said softly, 'She saved my life.'

'We have that in common, then.'

'Yes. That too.'

The underlying meaning behind his words lay heavily between them, but neither spoke again as they watched Pips circle Brooklands and then head northwards.

'Where's she going?' Milly asked worriedly.

'Lincolnshire, I shouldn't wonder,' Muriel said airily.

Milly turned frightened eyes towards her. 'Oh no, she wouldn't, would she?'

'I'm teasing you, Milly darling. I bet she'd like to, but no, she won't. For once she'll do just what she's been told.'

They watched the aircraft grow smaller and smaller in the clear sky until, just before they could no longer see it, it turned to the left and, in a much wider circle this time, flew around them. Thirty minutes later, almost to the second, she brought the aircraft down.

'That's one of the smoothest landings I've ever seen a first-time soloist make,' Jeff said proudly.

'You've done a great job, Jeff,' Mitch said, but the other man merely shrugged.

'It was easy. She's a natural.'

'Come on. Let's go and meet her,' Mitch said, leading the way across the grass. 'This calls for the champagne I've got in the back of my car.'

Although George followed them, he hung back, allowing Pips's Brooklands friends to greet her, but as she stood up in the cockpit he was gratified – and not a little smug – to see that it was to him she waved.

Pips continued to race at Brooklands and to fly whenever she could, but she could not persuade George to take part in either activity.

'Give him credit, though, darling,' Milly said. 'He comes to support you at every race he can *and* watches you fly off into the skies. And he never tries to stop you doing any of it. Lots of men would, you know.'

'He couldn't if he tried,' Pips muttered.

'Tell me – woman to woman – is it you putting off this wedding or him?'

'Both of us really. I don't want to be tied down – not just yet – and although he's all right about everything now, I just have the feeling that if we were married he'd be more likely to try to enforce the "obey" bit in the marriage service.'

'You said "both of you",' Milly prompted.

Pips sighed. 'He still hasn't tackled the "Rebecca problem" and she's never going to come round in a month of Sundays.'

As if to emphasize the fact, George did not accompany her to Lincolnshire for the children's birthdays. And then, just before Christmas when Pips invited him to join her family for the

247

celebrations, he wrote:

Darling Pips, I would love to come, but Rebecca has some time off over Christmas and she'd be on her own if I went away. So, regretfully…

'You know,' Robert said gently when she told him, 'I think you're going to have trouble with that girl.'

Pips folded the letter. 'I already have.'

Alice was kept busy helping Henrietta plan for Christmas, but she couldn't help her thoughts turning to her own family. There were always faces missing around the Dawson dinner table. If only her father was not so stubborn about William. Now she had a child of her own, she could not understand Len's unbending attitude. She loved Daisy fiercely – they all did – and whatever the girl did as she grew up, Alice knew she would forgive her anything. Perhaps now, it was Len's prickly pride rather than the fact that he still bore malice towards his only surviving son. She sighed as she washed the crystal glass that would adorn the long table in the Great Hall on Christmas Day. Sadly, she knew there was nothing she could do, but her heart ached for her mother and Ma.

'Aunty Pips! Aunty Pips! You're home for Christmas. Will you take me and Luke riding?' The little girl – just turned five – was jumping up and down in excitement when Pips entered the Great Hall by the front door.

'Of course, but let me see everyone first.'

'Can we take Luke out too? Today, instead of waiting till Saturday?'

'If his mummy says so, then yes.'

'Grandpa Dawson will say "yes". Luke spends all his time at Grandpa's workshop when we're not at school. That's where he'll be.'

Although not quite five at the time, Daisy had been able to start school in September and Robert had written to tell Pips all about her first day. Pips had not dared to go home to witness the momentous event in her niece's life. She was sure that, for once, she would have given way to tears and that would never have done.

You should have seen them, Pips, Robert had written. *Luke took her hand and led her into the playground, not caring if anyone teased him. He introduced her to her classmates and though he didn't actually say anything – he didn't need to – he made it clear that he was her protector. She's settled in very well and has made one or two new little friends, who come here to play, but of course Luke will always be her very best friend...*

Now, Daisy kept a tight hold on Pips's hand so that she couldn't escape her promise to take the children for a ride.

Half an hour later, Pips was riding through the fields, with the two children waving to everyone they passed.

Christmas once again was a lovely time of year for families and, with each year that passed, they were able to put the bitter memories a little further behind them. That didn't mean they forgot those who were missing, just that the pain of loss, though it would never go away entirely, was not quite so acute. And now they all had the younger generation to concentrate on.

Boxing Day at the hall, when Henrietta invited the Dawsons, the Coopers and the Nuttalls to a buffet luncheon, was becoming a tradition, and this year the numbers were growing as Peggy and Sam brought Harry too to celebrate not only his first birthday but also the actual place of his birth.

But this year, although it had been wonderful to be with her family, to see Daisy and especially heartening to hear that Robert was still working alongside his father in the practice, Pips was strangely restless and found that she was missing George more than she had believed possible. So she returned to London on 28 December and the next day called unannounced at his flat. Her heart was pounding as she rang the bell and waited. If Rebecca answered, she would make an excuse and leave immediately...

To her relief, it was George who opened the door. His smile and his outstretched arms told her that he had missed her just as much. He pulled her inside, shut the door and kissed her passionately. 'Rebecca's at work,' he whispered against her lips. 'We have the place to ourselves.'

'Are you sure she won't come home?'

'Positive. She thinks you're still safely in Lincolnshire.' He took her hand and led her towards the bedroom to make love with an urgency and intensity that showed them both how much they had longed for each other.

Afterwards, they lay in each other's arms. 'I was thinking,' Pips murmured. 'If it's not a problem, we could go away for New Year. To Brighton, maybe.'

'Perfect. As long as we can book in somewhere.'

'Oh, Milly will know someone with a hotel there. I'm sure she'd get us a room.'

'Is there anyone Milly doesn't know?'

Pips giggled. 'Not many people.'

'Right, see what you can do. And now, I'm taking you to lunch at Claridge's.'

Their time together in Brighton – just the two of them – was idyllic. Pips couldn't remember a time when she had felt so at peace. Although she loved the thrill of racing and of flying, it was nice to be away from it just for a little while, to be with the man she loved; to walk hand in hand, to dine together and to make love. They walked on the wintry beach, well wrapped up against the wind, and dined together by candlelight in the evening.

On their last night, George ordered a bottle of champagne, which they took to their room to toast each other in privacy.

As George took her in his arms, he murmured against her lips, 'This has been a wonderful few days, my darling. Marry me, Pips, please.'

'I will, George, I promise I will.'

But she dared not voice the question that was uppermost in her mind. What about Rebecca?

Twenty-Nine

During 1923, unrest rumbled on in Europe and the German financial situation was described as 'most desperate'. And at home, the Government was unsettled too. In May, following the resignation of the Prime Minister for health reasons, the Tories chose Stanley Baldwin to take his place, though there was not unanimous agreement in the party on the choice. But for the Brooklands Girls and all their friends the most important event was the Le Mans twenty-four-hour race and all the latest technology in racing cars on show there. Those who could not attend devoured the press for details. And, of course, for Milly and her circle, a new dance craze swept through the dance halls and nightclubs from America: the Charleston. The more fashionable women bobbed their hair. Even Pips, to her mother's horror, had her lovely auburn hair cut short, and she began to wear the straight lines of 'Coco' Chanel's fashions.

'Those clothes suit you so well and your hair looks divine, darling,' was Milly's pronouncement.

'I'm not sure George likes the new style,' Pips said. 'But he has bought me a bottle of Chanel Number Five.'

'Well, Mitch likes your new style, he told me so, but some men do like their girlfriends to have

252

lovely long flowing hair. Now, tonight we're all at Lady B's. She has a huge house in Belgrave Square and just *loves* giving parties. Is George coming?'

'Yes, he'll be here just before eight to escort us both.'

'Wonderful! And I've got a new dress I'm positively dying to wear. But first, I'm going to teach you the Charleston. Push back the furniture, Pips, and let's have a go...'

Pips picked up the steps quickly and was soon swivelling alongside Milly.

'Now, we just have to teach everyone else.'

'I just hope you're not going to have us all doing this new craze in America. "Dance till you drop", they're calling it. One couple, the papers said, were dancing for forty-five hours.'

Milly's eyes twinkled. 'Now would I, darling?'

Lady Beatrice's drawing room was crammed with young people still determined – even after almost five years – to forget the horrors of the war and yet it was impossible. Several young men still bore obvious scars; a lost limb or facial injuries, whilst others fought valiantly to push away the dreadful memories from wounded minds. This evening their hostess had hired a trio so the music was loud, but the forced laughter was even louder.

'Have you heard about the new music from America and the dance crazes?' Jeff shouted in Pips's ear.

'Yes, Milly's going to have everyone trying the Charleston tonight.'

Jeff pulled a face. 'Reckon I'll give that one a miss.'

Pips laughed. 'You won't be allowed to.'

Sure enough, when Milly organized the furniture to be moved back to the walls and a space created in the centre of the large room, no one was allowed to sit on the sidelines. She and Paul demonstrated the Charleston – swivelling their feet and flapping their arms in a dance so crazy it had the whole room in stitches.

Mitch weaved his way to Pips's side. 'Come on, we've got to try this.'

Soon everyone was dancing, even Jeff. Only George looked on.

'Not quite your thing, major?' Lady Beatrice said as she came to stand beside him and hand him another glass of champagne.

'Sadly, no.'

'A war wound.'

'No – no.' He hesitated and then was forced to admit, 'I can't actually dance this sort of thing. The odd sedate waltz, maybe...' He shook his head. 'But this is quite beyond me.'

'Me too,' Lady Beatrice chuckled, 'but the young ones love it.'

George said nothing. Unwittingly, Lady Beatrice had pointed out the age difference between himself and Pips. He watched – not without a little envy – as Pips swivelled and kicked her legs to the lively tunes. But when Mitch picked her up and threw her around him, George turned and left the room.

'We must do this again,' they all agreed as, in the early hours of the morning, they tottered home on aching feet.

'Next time we'll go to a nightclub where they'll have a full band and lots more room for the new dance. It's such fun,' Milly said as she kissed everyone goodbye. 'How about next week?'

'I'm going home next week,' Pips said firmly.

Milly's eyes widened. 'But you will come back? Promise? I'm always worried when you go home to Daisy that one of these times, you won't come back.'

Pips laughed. 'Yes, yes, I promise.'

'Then I'll put it off until you do,' Milly said, wagging her finger at Pips.

The promised visit to the Grafton Galleries took place three days after Pips came back from Lincolnshire. The Brooklands gang were all there – only George was missing.

'He went home with me, but he's had to go on to Yorkshire. The tenant in his house gave notice and he's gone to check the place out and set about finding a new one.'

'Oh dear, what a shame. Never mind, we'll still have fun.'

When they all paused for breath, Mitch, who had danced with Pips for most of the night, drew her apart from the rest into a quiet corner. 'Wait here, I'll get us a drink. Mind you, it's probably time for breakfast. It's nearly four o'clock.'

'Milly's got all that organized, if you're up for it.'

Mitch grinned. 'Ever known me to say "no"?'

When he returned, they sat down together. 'I'm going flying tomorrow afternoon,' he said. 'Well, today now. Are you coming?'

'Oh yes, please. Any chance to fly and I'll be there.'

'What would George say?'

'George wouldn't say anything,' Pips said a little sharply. 'I'm my own woman.'

Quietly, Mitch smiled into his beer.

In June, whilst Pips was at home on a fleeting visit, Alice received an ecstatic letter from William telling them that Brigitta had given birth to another baby boy.

Both are doing well, wrote the happy father. *He is just like Pascal when he was born and, luckily, they both take after their mother with fair hair and blue eyes. He is to be called Waldo.*

'We'll go and tell Mam and Ma,' Alice said. 'Please come with me, Pips. We'll go before the children come home from school. Dad will be safely at his workshop.'

They walked down the lane, arm in arm. They'd always been friends, even when Alice had been a lady's maid. But now, as sisters-in-law, they were even closer.

As if thinking about those earlier times, Alice said, 'Did you know your mother has asked Betty Cooper to be her lady's maid? And yours, whenever you're at home.' She hesitated before adding, with a little embarrassment, 'And mine too.'

'That's a good idea. I don't think poor Betty is even thinking about marriage, do you?'

'No. She was so in love with Roy, she won't even look at another feller.' Alice pulled a face. 'Not that there are many eligible bachelors about.'

Pips was quiet for a moment before asking, with deliberate casualness, 'Are you happy with that arrangement?'

Alice laughed self-consciously. 'I suppose so, but I find it difficult to have her waiting on me. I still think it should be my job to attend your mother.'

Pips pressed her arm. 'Well, don't. You've done remarkably well since marrying Robert to get all your former workmates on your side. Not one of them has an ounce of resentment against you and that's all down to your sweet nature, so let's hear no more of you feeling awkward about your position now. I can't ever imagine you being a domineering mistress.'

'I follow your mother's example. Her manner with her staff is exemplary and they all love her. As do I.'

Pips chuckled. 'As your mistress or as your mother-in-law?'

'Both, I suppose, but probably more as my mother-in-law now. She's been extremely kind to me.'

'I know she's very fond of you too. And I have to give her credit for admitting she was wrong to be against you and Robert marrying. She now says you're the perfect wife for him.'

Alice blushed. 'That's good to know. Thank you, Pips.'

They arrived at the cottage to find Ma in her usual spot, soaking up the sunshine. 'It helps my aches and pains,' she said getting up stiffly. 'But I'm guessing you've brought us some news from across the water. Come in, come in. Norah's busy baking.'

They followed the old lady into the cottage, noticing that her movements were slower these days.

'Norah, duck. Alice and Miss Pips have news for us.'

Norah looked up, her hands still deep in a bowl of dough she was kneading. 'Give me a minute. I can let this prove now.' She set the bowl on the hearth, washed her hands and sat down. Her eyes were bright and her smile wide. 'Is it news of the little one?'

'Here.' Alice handed the letter to her mother, but Norah shook her head. 'No, you read it out to us, Alice, then we'll both hear it together.'

When Alice had finished reading, Norah was wiping tears of joy from her eyes. 'How wonderful. Another little boy. Another grandson. We've got three now. Four, if you count Harry, and we always treat him just the same as we treat Luke. And a granddaughter. We're very lucky.' Her expression sobered. 'If only Len would...'

'That'll never happen, duck,' Ma said. 'He's a foolish, stubborn man and I dun't reckon he'll ever change. It'd take a miracle.'

Thirty

The proposed marriage between Pips and George kept getting put back further and further, much to Henrietta's dismay.

'Are you officially engaged or not?'

Pips shrugged. 'Well, yes, we are, but it's complicated, Mother.'

'I don't see why. I blame you, Philippa. You're so busy dancing the night away, racing and flying, that you don't want to settle down and be a good wife to a lovely man. You'll lose him, if you're not careful, and then I will be very angry. You won't get many more opportunities like Major Allender and there are plenty of spinsters just waiting to snap him up from under your nose.'

'You're right in what you say, Mother,' Pips agreed honestly. 'But there's a little more to it than that.'

'Then tell me.'

'His daughter is causing problems for him.'

Henrietta frowned. 'Rebecca?'

'Yes. She doesn't want her father to marry anyone – and certainly not me.'

'She's a nurse, isn't she? I'd have thought she'd have had more sense.'

'Whatever do you mean, Mother? Why should she feel differently about her father marrying again just because she's a nurse?'

Henrietta wriggled her shoulders and avoided

meeting Pips's gaze. 'Well – I'd have thought she'd have realized that men have...' She was embarrassed. Women of her generation just didn't talk about such matters. 'Needs. And they need a woman to take care of them too. I mean, without sounding conceited, what would your dear father do without me?'

Pips hid her smile as her mother sighed and went on, 'It's a pity. It must put the poor man into a dilemma. I just want to see you happily settled, Philippa. That's all I worry about. Who will look after you when we're gone? You can't rely on your poor brother for ever, you know.'

A sharp retort that she was quite capable of looking after herself sprang to her lips, but Pips bit back her impatience. She put her arm around her mother's shoulders. 'George loves me. I know that. And I love him and I'm sure that one day, we will be married. We just need a bit of time to readjust after what we've both been through. Don't forget, too, that he lost his wife in tragic circumstances and it doesn't sound as if it was a happy marriage anyway. He needs time to sort things out with Rebecca and the last thing I want is for him to be estranged from his daughter. Besides, as you rightly say, I'm enjoying my life far too much at present to settle down.'

Henrietta had the grace to chuckle. 'I just hope he's prepared for the fact that you will probably never "settle down".'

'Oh he is. Believe me, he is.'

Mentally, Pips crossed her fingers and hoped that what she was telling her mother was true. Although George had promised her as much, she wondered if it was a pledge he would be able to keep.

Towards the end of November, when Pips went home for the children's birthdays again, Robert asked her, 'Do you still follow world affairs?'

She was delighted to see that since he had returned to the practice alongside his father, Robert was much better. Although his black moods still occurred, they were less frequent.

Pips pulled a face. 'Not so much. It doesn't make for pleasant reading most of the time. Though I am still interested in what's happening here.' She laughed. 'Milly's granny and I have some lively political discussions whenever I go to the manor. You'd love her, Robert. Why do you ask?'

'Do you remember Field Marshal Eric von Ludendorff?'

'Indeed I do. I think he was the general who planned the attack along the River Marne in the last year of the war, wasn't he?' She smiled. 'It's where George was promoted to major, so he told me.'

'It was a last-ditch effort on the Germans' part, I think.'

'So, what's he been up to now?'

'There's an ambitious corporal who served in the war and who is the leader of an extreme national party, known here as the Nazis. A couple of weeks ago he attempted to seize power by inciting a revolution in Munich and claiming he had the support of Ludendorff.'

'Did he? Have his support, I mean.'

'It seems so. Various other supporters gave up the idea, but Ludendorff thought he was powerful enough for a march through the city to lead to success. But outside the royal palace the police were waiting. Someone fired a shot killing a policeman and after that, I think it was mayhem. The corporal fled and went into hiding and Ludendorff is now under house arrest.'

'And the corporal? What happened to him?'

'He was found and it's thought he'll be sent to prison, so I don't think there'll be any more trouble from him.'

'Let's hope not. What was his name?'

'Adolf Hitler.'

In January, when Pips had returned to London, Milly said, 'We're invited to the manor for the weekend on the twenty-fifth for a belated New Year celebration. Mummy said you can bring George if you want to. Paul's coming.' She giggled as she added, 'Though I'm afraid it will be separate bedrooms.'

Pips smiled. 'Of course. It always is when we go up to Lincolnshire. I wouldn't expect anything else and neither would George. We must respect the older generation's sensitivities.'

'Do you think they guess, but just don't say anything?'

Pips wrinkled her forehead. 'I expect Robert and Alice do, but I don't think such a thought would enter my mother's head.' She laughed. 'Well, I hope not anyway, though I can never be sure.'

'Your skirt is rather short, Millicent,' was Granny

262

Fortesque's greeting.

'It's the latest fashion, Granny. Calf length.'

Eleanor cast her eyes to the ceiling in a gesture so much like Henrietta's that Pips found it difficult to hide her laughter.

'Let's just hope it doesn't get any shorter,' Eleanor said primly.

Later, Milly said, 'You'd better go home next time in some of your older dresses, Pips darling. I'm sure your mother will think some of your latest purchases will be far too short.'

'Don't worry, Milly. I've already thought of that.'

Dinner at the manor that evening was a merry affair, with everyone pretending it was New Year's Eve and raising a glass to 1924 even though the first month of the year was almost over.

'So, what are your thoughts on this first Labour government we've got?' Henry said, glancing at George and Paul, but it was Pips who spoke up at once. 'As long as they stick to their policies and do something about unemployment and the housing problem, then I'd be all for it.'

'You do realize, Philippa,' Eleanor said, looking at her over the top of her spectacles, 'that eleven out of the twenty cabinet members are of working-class origin.'

Before Pips could reply, George said, 'I think they're going to have to ease themselves into the role gradually. Ramsay MacDonald himself has said that, being a minority government, he is in office, but not in real power. I doubt, despite their altruistic motives, that there'll be a social revolution overnight.'

'Thank goodness for that,' Eleanor declared. She glared at Pips. 'Did you vote this time, Philippa?'

'Sadly, no. I would have done, but I'm not thirty until later in the year.'

'And what would you have voted?'

'Mama,' Henry said, mildly. 'We never ask anyone their politics or their religion.'

'It's all right, Mr Fortesque. I don't mind.' Pips faced Eleanor boldly. 'This time, I would have voted Tory, but next time – when I will be able to vote – I shall consider it very carefully. It rather depends on how the Labour Party performs whilst in office. I just think that there should be a fairer society and that's what they *say* they're aiming for. After all, if the working class are good enough to lay down their lives for their country, then they should be allowed to have a say in how their country is run. Don't you think?'

'But are they educated well enough to have a properly considered and balanced opinion?'

'If they're not,' Pips shot back, 'then that is the country's fault for not educating them.'

'Mm.' Eleanor appeared to be pondering and then she added sadly, 'Of course, the cream of the middle and upper classes of a generation – the ones who would be the next leaders of our country – were taken in the war. Is that not so, Major Allender?'

'The officers led from the front, which is as it should be, but of course, because they did...' He spread his hands and said no more, but his meaning was obvious.

After the meal when the ladies retired to the

drawing room, Eleanor said, 'Now, no more talk of politics. Come and sit by me, Philippa, and tell me all about this nice young man you've brought with you. That's far more important.'

So Pips told her how and where she and George had met and even about his wife and daughter.

'Poor man,' Eleanor murmured sympathetically. 'But I can see he's very much in love with you, my dear, so don't keep him waiting too long, will you? He's not getting any younger.' She eyed Pips archly. 'And neither are you, if you want to have children. Do your parents approve of him? There's not an obstacle there, is there?'

'No, all the family love him, it's just...'

'You don't,' Eleanor said bluntly.

'Oh I do, I do.' She sighed. 'But I don't want there to be an estrangement between him and his daughter. I think it would cause trouble between us – eventually.'

'Mm, it is a dilemma for you, I have to admit. They always say that you don't marry a person's family, but I'm afraid that's not true. Of course you do.' She patted Pips's hand. 'I hope it works out for you, my dear.' Then she nodded across the room towards Milly. 'And that's another relationship I can't quite work out. Are Milly and Paul a couple, or not?'

Pips smiled. 'I can't tell you that, Granny Fortesque.'

'Can't – or won't?'

Honesty was the best policy with a formidable woman like Milly's grandmother.

'A little bit of both.'

'And that will have to do me, will it?'

'I'm afraid so.'

Eleanor chuckled. 'I like you, Philippa Maitland. Even though I might not always agree with you, there aren't many people who dare stand up to me and life can get a little boring without a challenge sometimes. I enjoy a healthy debate. Do come again very soon, won't you?'

'I most certainly will.'

Henry Fortesque kept a stable of three horses, so, whilst Milly didn't ride, the following morning, Pips, George and Paul took them for a gallop.

'You'd better have this one, miss,' the stable boy, Merryfield, said. 'Neptune there is a handful. He's the master's horse. The major should perhaps take him.'

The bay horse in question stood seventeen hands and, although a different colour, still reminded Pips sharply of Midnight. It was the look in his eye and Pips caught a glimpse of his spirit. 'I'll be fine,' she told him, stroking the horse's nose and offering him a carrot. 'And I promise you will not be held responsible if I take a tumble.'

But beneath Pips's practised hands, the horse behaved impeccably, although when Henry heard which mount she had ridden, he was horrified. 'Merryfield shouldn't have given you Neptune. I must have words with him.'

'Please don't, Mr Fortesque. He did try to stop me, but I insisted and told him I would take full responsibility. George and Paul were there. They'll tell you.'

'And did he behave? The horse, I mean?'

'Perfectly. I could tell he likes a good gallop. And, as you know, I like speed.'

'I'm glad I wasn't there to see it,' Henry said. 'I think you would have given me a heart attack.' But he was smiling as he said it. The whole family had taken to this daring and independent young woman and he had warmed to her for the way she had defended his daughter. Even he had been unaware of the bravery Milly had shown during the war, but he was glad to know now. And that was thanks to Pips. 'Well, as long as you're sure you're safe on him, please feel free to ride him any time you wish. You can probably let him have a freer rein than even I dare to do nowadays.'

'Thank you, Mr Fortesque,' Pips grinned, 'I'll hold you to that.'

Thirty-One

During the year there were two fatal accidents at Brooklands.

'However did that happen?' Henrietta asked worriedly when Pips went home at the end of September. 'I hadn't realized it was quite so dangerous, Philippa. You have to stop.'

'Normally, Mother, it isn't so bad. When you think just how many cars race there in a year, accidents aren't that frequent. In the most recent accident, the driver was trying for a new land-speed record.'

'And the earlier one that happened at Whitsun?'

'I – er – I'm not sure.'

Henrietta eyed her suspiciously. 'You were never a good liar, Philippa. Even as a child, when you'd done something wrong, you could never lie about it. And Daisy's just the same. Even when she knows she's going to be in trouble, she always tells the truth. I think you *do* know only too well, but you don't want to tell me. No matter. Racing is a dangerous game. I'm not stupid.' There was a heavy silence between them before Henrietta added, 'So, are you going to stop?'

'No, Mother, but I will promise you I'll be more careful.'

'I'm not sure how you can be "careful" when you're tearing round a racetrack.' Henrietta sighed heavily and turned away. She was not the only one to be concerned. Robert tried to talk Pips into giving up racing and he was brave enough to say, 'We all love you, Pips, and Daisy would be heartbroken if anything happened to you. Think about her, won't you?'

Pips winced. 'That's a low blow, Robert.'

He grinned, unfazed by her retort. 'I'll try anything to keep you safe.'

When she returned to London even George broached the subject. 'I know I said I'd never try to stop you doing what you want, but please, Pips, think carefully. I couldn't bear to lose you and all your family would be devastated.'

A rather cruel retort sprang to her lips – 'Rebecca wouldn't be' – but she bit it back and forced a smile. 'Not you too. I've had them all at home telling me I ought to stop. But I'm sorry, I can't. Not yet.'

The other racing enthusiasts, especially the Brooklands Girls, were in agreement with Mitch, who said, 'You need to get straight into another race and drive like the wind.'

At the next meeting, Muriel squeezed Pips's arm and said, 'I see you're entered in the next race. Good for you, gal.'

Pips smiled. 'I am quite aware of the dangers, but even crossing a road in London is getting quite precarious now.'

Muriel laughed loudly. 'And it'll get worse. The motor car is the future, Pips. Now, time we were heading to the start line.'

With her family's warnings still in her mind, Pips drove a little more cautiously than usual and finished in sixth place, but it seemed to her that everyone had been a little slower. Perhaps they were all thinking about the men who had lost their lives on this very track earlier that year.

On her next visit to Fortesque Manor at the beginning of November, she braced herself for more disapproval from Milly's family too, but, to her surprise, it was not forthcoming. Instead, the talk around the dinner table was of the recent election when the Tories had swept to a huge victory.

'Ramsay MacDonald didn't last long, then, did he, Philippa?' Eleanor said. 'It was rather foolish of him to run the gauntlet of a vote of confidence over the Campbell Case, don't you think?'

Pips frowned. 'I'm not sure what that was all about.'

'Tut-tut,' Eleanor teased. 'And there I was, thinking you were a modern young woman who kept up with all the day's news and politics. In a nutshell, my dear, charges were brought against a communist newspaper, edited by Campbell, for alleged "incitement to mutiny" by publishing a letter addressed to the military. Unfortunately, Ramsay MacDonald suspended the prosecution of the case, which brought down his Labour government after only nine months in office.'

'But wasn't there something underhand going on just before the election itself? I've been reading about this Zinoviev letter addressed to British communists encouraging a revolution.'

Eleanor waved her elegant hand. 'Oh, that's now thought to have been a hoax.'

'But it was enough for the country to turn against the Labour Party and return the Tories to power. It all seems to me like a ploy and an underhand ploy at that.'

'Well, I'm sure your Labour Party will come to power one day.' Eleanor was smiling, but there was a hint of sarcasm in her tone.

A small smile quirked the corners of Pips's mouth as she replied in the same tone, 'I'm sure they will.'

Throughout the following year, Pips kept in touch with the national and international news. At home, the Chancellor of the Exchequer, Winston Churchill, returned Britain to the gold standard as proof, he said, of the country's postwar recovery. Sixpence was taken off the standard rate of income tax and a new national insurance scheme was introduced with the State pension age reduced to sixty-five. Abroad, Leon Trotsky was ousted from the leadership of the

Soviet Communist Party, primarily by moves by Joseph Stalin; in Italy, Benito Mussolini, who had declared himself the leader of the National Fascist Party, showed an iron fist against the opponents of Fascism and in Germany, a new name came to the fore – Adolf Hitler.

'Wasn't he that little corporal connected with Ludendorff in some sort of uprising in November 1923?' Pips said to Robert when she was on a visit home.

His mouth was tight. 'The very same.'

'So it looks as if a term in prison didn't have the desired effect.'

'Sadly, no. His sentence turned out to be a joke. No more than a slap on the wrist and not a very hard one at that.'

But Pips's main focus was on her racing and her flying and, of course, on George. They met often, spent several nights each month together and were always made welcome at Fortesque Manor or at Doddington Hall, though, of course, it continued to be separate bedrooms at both places.

Much to Eleanor's disgust, Milly shortened her skirt to just below the knees.

'Have you no control over your daughter, Victoria?'

'Not really, Mother,' Milly's mother replied airily and promptly shortened her own skirts.

Daisy delighted her family as much as ever and whenever Pips was at home, the young girl monopolized her aunt's time and attention. And often, Luke, and now three-year-old Harry too, came along. Pips took the three youngsters riding, fishing or just playing games in the grounds of the hall. On cold days there were raucous games in the Great Hall and even, if Henrietta could be persuaded to turn a blind eye, games of hide and seek throughout the big house.

'I really must buy a different car,' Pips told Mitch. 'One that I can race but also drive up to Lincolnshire in.'

'Daisy still pestering to be taken out for drives, is she?'

'Yes – every time I go home.'

'Well, there is one that Michael has for sale. Like to come and see it? I'll take you, if you like.'

'Oh, yes please. When?'

'Tomorrow afternoon all right?'

'Perfect. George is busy tomorrow.'

It was indeed perfect, then, Mitch thought with an inward smile.

Pips stood in front of the blue Bugatti and fell in love with it.

'It's got headlights and a licence plate,' Michael said, 'so there is no problem about you driving it anywhere you want to go. And she'll do ninety miles an hour.'

'And it's a two-seater,' Pips murmured. 'Just what I'm looking for.'

'Take it out for a run.'

With Mitch beside her, Pips drove the car through the lanes near the farm. She didn't 'open her up', but she could feel the power.

'So?' Michael raised his eyebrows when they returned to the farm.

'Providing you can sell mine for me, I'll take it.'

Michael held out his hand. 'Done.'

The following weekend, Pips drove to Lincoln-shire. She arrived just as Daisy was walking up the drive, home from school. As the young girl turned and saw who was driving through the gate, her mouth dropped open. 'Aunty Pips! You've got a new car and it's got two seats...'

Pips drew to a halt. 'Jump in!'

Daisy did not need telling twice.

'Can we take Luke out too?'

'Of course. We'll go this minute.'

With the children squeezed into the passenger's seat, laughing and shouting with delight, Pips drove through the lanes, scattering hens and chickens, dogs and cats. As they left Luke outside the cottage where he lived, Pips promised, 'I'll take you out again tomorrow before I go back to London. And I must take Harry too.'

Daisy and Luke grimaced at each other and then laughed. 'If you must, Aunty Pips.'

Much to the disgust of the older generation, especially the women, the Charleston became even more popular and skirts were shortened to the knees to give the dancers more freedom of movement; and movement there certainly was! Now, it was the favourite dance of all classes of society. There were no barriers when it came to enjoyment.

But there was growing social unrest that even the Bright Young Things – the name given to the wild partygoers – could no longer ignore.

In March 1926, the Miners' Federation refused to accept the recommendations that their pay should be cut and the working day lengthened. The phrase 'Not a penny off the pay, not a minute on the day' became a popular slogan.

On visits home and to Fortesque Manor, Pips discussed the situation with her father and brother and also now with Henry Fortesque and his mother.

'The problem started last year,' Henry told her. 'The mines were under the control of the Government during the war, but went back into private ownership afterwards. In June last year the mine owners said they were going to cut wages and lengthen the working day.'

'Yes, I remember reading about that. Didn't the Government cave in and offer a subsidy to maintain the status quo for a few months?'

'Governments, my dear Philippa,' Eleanor said, 'do not "cave in"; they negotiate – or pass a law.'

Pips grinned across the dinner table at her. 'I stand corrected, Granny Fortesque.'

Henry hid his smile and continued. He loved to see this headstrong young woman clashing swords with his formidable mother and would often deliberately start a conversation to provoke a 'healthy discussion'. Then he would sit back and enjoy the verbal firework display!

'But I fear matters are coming to a head and we could have real trouble that will affect all classes of society in one way or another.'

Henry was right. Over the next two months as talks failed, a crisis loomed; by May, the Trades Union Congress called a strike, which split the view of the country and, as the newspapers declared, developed into a class war. Soon, the press

274

themselves were affected as a general strike began on 3 May and newspapers could no longer be printed. Over one and a half million workers went on strike. The transport systems ground to a halt, which affected all areas of life. The Government, however, during the time it had provided a subsidy, had made plans and now used volunteers, primarily from the middle classes, to run trains and buses.

Soon there were clashes between the strikers and the volunteers and, of course, with the police, who were only trying to do their job in keeping law and order.

Thirty-Two

'Darling, you don't mean to tell me that you're on the side of these dreadful strikers?'

'Of course I am, Milly. They've been treated appallingly. It's even been reported that the King has said that people should try living on their wages before judging them.'

'Well, I'm sorry for the miners and their families – of course I am,' Milly seemed to be wavering, 'but they can't hold the country to ransom like this.' She paused and then added, uncertainly, 'Can they?'

Pips shrugged. 'It seems they can.'

'What about the rest of your family? Surely they don't agree with it. I mean...' Milly flapped her hands. 'You're hardly "working class", are you?'

275

'I don't believe in the class system. We all contribute to the life of this country in some way, or at least we should do. My mother owns an estate, yes, but she gives employment to others. My father works very hard as the local doctor. And I am trying to do something useful at Hazelwood House, even if I am having fun at the same time.'

'And I suppose you think me a useless butterfly.' Milly's pretty face crumpled and tears glistened in her eyes. 'Endless partying, dancing and trailing after chaps who don't seem to have any intention of proposing and making an honest woman of me.'

'Oh Milly, darling...' Pips put her arms around her and Milly laid her head against Pips's shoulder. 'I thought you'd had umpteen proposals, especially from Paul.'

'I did, about three years ago, but recently he's stopped asking and now I realize I love him, but I think I've left it too late.'

'Do you think he's got someone else?'

'Oh no, I think he just got fed up of me saying "no".'

'Then you ask him.'

Milly giggled through her tears. 'Oh I couldn't. Granny Fortesque would be appalled. She'd say I was "fast".' It was the word the older generation now used to describe the independent young women.

'Pity it's not a leap year,' Pips said.

Milly raised her head and stepped back. 'You know, you're very lucky. You should snap George up. I don't know why you're dithering. Don't lose him. Don't you love him?'

'Yes, I do, but I just don't want to be – trapped. And then, there's his daughter. I don't want to be the cause of a rift between them.'

'I think that's for him to decide.' Milly put her head on one side and regarded her friend thoughtfully. 'What does George think about all this strike business?'

'I really don't know.'

Milly wiped her tears away. 'I do. He'll do whatever you do.'

Pips smiled thinly. 'Maybe, but I can't imagine that Rebecca will join the strike. She's a nurse.'

'Well, I shall do whatever Paul does. At least he's still around. I think he plans to drive a tram or a bus or something.'

'You can't drive.'

'No, but I could be his clippie.' Milly made the action of clipping a ticket. 'Ding ding.'

The two girls dissolved into laughter, their easy friendship restored, though Pips was left feeling a little apprehensive. She didn't want to fall out with any of her friends and yet, she had to stick to her own principles.

Pips saw George the following day and her first question was, 'What are your views on this strike? Whose side are you on?'

'Well, not the strikers.'

Pips stared at him in horror for a moment. 'So, you're with Milly and her set, are you?'

George raised his eyebrows. 'I'd've thought you would have been too.'

'Well, I'm not.'

'The miners won't win their battle, you know.'

'Why ever not?'

'Because once the country has been plunged into chaos, public sympathy will turn against them.'

'I don't think it will cause that much hardship, because Milly and her like will keep things running. Well, for people's basic needs anyway.'

'Then it still won't work, will it?'

'I see what you mean. No, perhaps it won't. How sad that we can't pay a decent wage to men who risk their lives on a daily basis, grovelling for our coal.'

'Besides, the Government will call in the army if it gets really serious. It's what we do. Pips, I'm an army man through and through. Although I won't be involved, I know what I'd be obliged to do if I was still a serving officer.'

'Blindly follow orders,' Pips said a little bitterly.

George smiled thinly and murmured, 'I suppose it must seem like that to outsiders, but it's what we sign up to do.'

Pips fidgeted for a moment before blurting out, 'If I'm completely honest, I'm torn. I don't actually know what my family think.'

'Would it make any difference?'

Pips had the grace to laugh. 'Not a scrap.' She paused and then went on, 'I was just wondering if there was anything I could do to help, but which would not be classed as strike-breaking.'

George was thoughtful for a moment before he said with a little smile, 'You could always drive an ambulance.'

'Paul says he's going to drive a bus.' Milly clapped

her hands. 'If he does, then I'm going to be his clippie.'

Pips frowned. 'He'd be better off driving an ambulance. I'm thinking of setting up a first-aid post.'

Milly blinked. 'Like in the war?'

Pips nodded. 'Some of the hospitals are closed and the police have told me that the Poplar area will be the most dangerous.' She grinned. 'So, of course, that's where I'm going.'

'Those two brothers, who were with us in Belgium – the London bus drivers – didn't they come from the East End?'

'Milly, sometimes you are just absolutely brilliant. Yes, I think they did. Now, if I could find them...'

'But – but they'll be striking, won't they?'

'Exactly, but I'm proposing to set up a first-aid post to *help* the strikers. I'm on their side. Remember?'

Milly nodded. 'I know, and I so wish you weren't.' There were tears in her eyes again as she added, 'I'm so afraid it's going to cause a rift between us and between you and George.'

'Oh phooey,' Pips began and then, seeing that her friend was genuinely upset, she hugged her. 'We're not going to let this come between any of us. It's just that we have different opinions, that's all. We're allowed that, aren't we?' She laughed. 'And just like we did in the war, first aid will be available to the "enemy" too.'

Milly dried her tears and tried to smile. 'I can see your point of view, truly I can, but I still don't think the workers should hold the country to ransom.'

'They wouldn't – if the authorities gave them a fair day's pay for a fair day's work. They're trying to make the miners work longer hours for less pay, so they're getting hit in both directions. That's hardly fair, is it?'

'I suppose not,' Milly said reluctantly.

'And other industries are only coming out in support of them. Now, I'm going to drive to Poplar and find a local police station. I'll ask for their help not only to set up a first-aid post somewhere, but also to ask if they can help me find the Enderby brothers.'

'Do – do you want me to come with you?'

Pips shook her head. 'And for Heaven's sake, don't tell George where I've gone, if he should call.'

Milly's eyes widened. 'Oh Pips, he'll wheedle it out of me. I know he will.'

Pips chuckled. 'Milly darling, you were wonderful at the front, but you would never have made a spy. Don't worry,' she added airily, as she went towards the door. 'He'll find out eventually anyway.'

Only half an hour after Pips had left, George arrived.

'Hello, Milly dear. Is Pips in?' he asked when Milly answered the door. He was very fond of the scatter-brained girl and whilst he had never met her out in Belgium, he had heard from Pips what an asset she had been to the flying ambulance corps, even though she'd not had much nursing training.

Milly pressed her lips together and shook her head.

'Where is she?'

'I – um – don't know – exactly.' Then she rushed on. 'Would you like a cup of tea or coffee?'

George regarded her thoughtfully, his head on one side. 'Milly – there's something you're not telling me. I can see it in your face. Where has she gone?'

'Oh, George, please – don't ask me.'

He took her hands in his and made her face him. 'I won't be angry – I promise.'

'No, but Pips will. She said I wasn't to tell you.'

George couldn't help chuckling at Milly's anxious face. 'But she knew you would tell me, didn't she?'

Milly smiled thinly. 'She said I would never have made a spy.'

Now George threw back his head and laughed aloud. 'That's true. So, tell me where she's gone and what she's planning.'

'She's gone to Poplar to try to find Hugh and Peter Enderby. You remember them?'

George nodded. 'Indeed I do. They were brave men. But why?'

'She's heard Poplar is one of the dangerous areas – or could be – during the strike and she wants to set up a first-aid post there.'

'Then I'd better go and find her and help her.'

'But – but you're on our side. You don't agree with the strikers.'

'Pips has been very clever. She's found a way to help in a neutral capacity. She'll give first aid to both sides, I've no doubt.'

Milly nodded. 'She said that.'

'Do you know where she was going initially?'
'The local police station there, I think.'
'Then that's where I'll go too.'

Travelling to the east of the city was difficult: there was already a feeling of unrest in the air. For the first time in his life, George was relieved that he was not in uniform. He suspected he would have been seen as an 'enemy'. At last, he found a police station.

'Ah yes, sir, there was a young woman in here a few hours ago. Inspector Kenny went out somewhere with her. The nearest bus station, I believe.'

Receiving directions from the helpful desk sergeant, George set off once more. Already the bus service was at a standstill – the depot was crammed with vehicles that should have been out on the streets. The drivers and conductors stood around in small groups, looking unsure as to what they ought to do. George approached the nearest gathering. 'I wonder if you can help me?'

'I doubt it, mate. Buses aren't running today.'

George shook his head. 'It's not that. I'm looking for a young woman – possibly in the company of a police inspector – who is looking for two of your colleagues. The Enderby brothers.'

The man's face cleared and, despite the seriousness of the situation, he laughed. 'Aye, she found 'em and they greeted her like a long-lost sister. They're around somewhere.' He looked about him and one of his colleagues jerked his thumb over his shoulder, volunteering the information, 'They all went towards the office. Over there, mate.'

As he neared the building, George could see Pips through the window talking animatedly to four men, two of whom he knew. As he opened the door and entered, they all looked up.

'Captain Allender.' Peter was the first to get to his feet and hold out his hand. 'How good it is to see you again.'

George shook his hand warmly and that of his brother too. 'You too. Are you well?'

'Very well, thanks, though we're not too happy about what's going on at the moment.' He turned towards the man sitting beside a desk. 'This here's our depot manager, Mr Bradley. We knew Captain Allender at the front, sir.'

George nodded towards the depot manager and the police inspector and took a chair beside Pips.

'It's Major Allender now, by the way,' Pips said, before turning towards George. 'I knew Milly would tell you. I hope you've not come to try and stop me.'

'If you're attempting to set up a first-aid post, of course, I wouldn't dream of trying to prevent you. Sadly, I think it will be needed.'

'But – but you don't agree with me.'

'As always, my dear, you have cleverly found a way to assist whilst remaining neutral because, knowing you, you will treat both sides of the conflict with equal care and attention.'

'But I'm not sure the locals will see it that way, major,' the inspector sighed. 'Nevertheless, I have just been telling Miss Maitland here that there is an empty shop only a short distance from here. I know the owner and I am sure he would be willing to let her use it.'

'It might suffer damage, if there's rioting,' George said.

'He'll understand that and I'll make sure that there is at least one constable on duty whenever Miss Maitland is there.'

'We'll be with her,' Hugh and Peter chorused.

'As will I,' George murmured.

'And I think some of our colleagues will join us,' Hugh Enderby said. 'Once word gets around that we're not taking sides but just helping the injured. After all, we treated the enemy with the same consideration as we treated our own lads, didn't we, Miss Pips, if we got one of their casualties? And we'll do the same this time.'

'You're talking as if we're going to war,' the depot manager murmured.

Pips turned her green eyes upon him. 'Well, aren't we, Mr Bradley?'

Thirty-Three

The vacant shop that Inspector Kenny had found for her was ideal. Not only did the frontage look out over a main street, but there was also hot and cold running water and a stove in the back rooms. Above the shop were living quarters, again with water and cooking facilities. 'I can move in,' Pips said delightedly. 'Be here on hand all the time.'

'I don't want you staying here on your own,' George said. 'I'll come too.' He glanced around the bare room. 'We'll need to get beds from somewhere.'

'I'm sure Hugh and Peter will be able to source whatever we need in the way of medical supplies, but surely,' she added archly, 'we only need one double bed.'

'Wicked woman,' George murmured, but he was smiling. They had been lovers for almost five years now and the thought of being able to spend several days and nights with her made George hope that at last he might be able to persuade her to name a date for their wedding. He was beginning to think that he'd really have to go ahead without his daughter's blessing if he wanted to marry this wonderful woman.

'And now,' Pips was saying, 'I'd better don the apron I've brought, pick up my brush and get scrubbing.' And that was how Milly, Paul and Mitch found them.

'I never thought I'd live to see the day.' Mitch grinned. 'Pips on her knees and Major Allender, with his sleeves rolled up, doing a housemaid's work.'

'She can be very persuasive,' George said mildly.

'Don't I know it,' Mitch said. 'Anyway, we've marshalled the troops. Muriel and Pattie are collecting whatever medical supplies they can lay their hands on. And we've made a start. We've several boxes in my car outside.'

Pips stood up and eased her aching back. 'You never fail to surprise me, Mitch Hammond. I thought you'd have been driving a bus or a train.'

He chuckled. 'You're right, I should be. But when we all heard what you were doing, we thought we'd help you instead.' His brown eyes looked deep into hers as he said solemnly, 'I owe my life to you, Pips, and I'll never forget it. Whenever you need help, you can be sure I'll be there. Now,' he said briskly, as if suddenly aware he was becoming too sentimental in front of onlookers, 'where do you want all the stuff?'

'In the back room – but it really needs cleaning first.'

'I'll do that, darling,' Milly said. 'I've brought my apron.'

'You'll ruin your nails,' Pips warned, but Milly only laughed, flapped her hands and, using Pips's favourite word, said, 'Oh phooey!'

They all laughed and Paul, taking off his jacket and rolling up his shirt sleeves, said, 'We'll all help. We'll follow the major's example.'

Despite the seriousness of the situation, the 'working party' enjoyed setting up the first-aid post and when Hugh and Peter arrived with more medical supplies, food and the furniture they needed for the upstairs, they were ready.

'Well, there's no point in me hanging about,' Mitch said. 'I'm no nurse, but I'll call in each day to see if there's anything else you need.'

'And I'll come every day, darling, to help where I can. I learned how to do basic dressings, Pips, so maybe there'll be something I can do, even if it's only making tea.' There was a pause before Milly added, 'Is Alice coming down to help you?'

Pips shook her head. 'I wouldn't dream of asking her. She has enough to do looking after my brother and Daisy. Besides, to be honest, I'm not sure where my family's sympathies lie.'

'I don't think they could disapprove of what we're doing,' George said mildly. 'We're not taking sides, are we?'

'True. But I don't think my mother will be best pleased.'

'Edwin – what on earth does Pips think she's doing?'

'What's that, Hetty my love?' Edwin asked as he sat down at the breakfast table.

Henrietta prodded the newspaper she was holding. 'It says here that she and a few others have set up a first-aid post in Poplar to help any casualties during this wretched strike.'

'I – um – don't quite understand your concern...'

'Good morning, Mother – Father,' Robert said as he entered the room, with Daisy and Alice following him.

'Have you seen this, Robert?' Henrietta asked.

'If that's this morning's paper, then, no, not yet. Why?'

'It's Pips.'

Robert looked up sharply, his face suddenly anxious. 'What's happened? Is she all right?'

'I really have no idea, except that she seems to have lost any shred of common sense she ever had.'

'What has she done now?'

When Henrietta had explained, Robert said, 'If you want my opinion, she has been extremely astute. She's helping, yet no one can accuse her of taking sides.'

Henrietta gave a click of exasperation. 'But we all know she'll be on the side of the strikers, don't we?'

'More than likely,' Robert said cheerfully. 'I only wish I could go and join her. Don't worry about Pips, Mother. I'm sure Milly will be with her and,' he added pointedly, 'George too.'

'Don't try to deflect my concern, Robert.' Henrietta turned towards her daughter-in-law seeking her support. 'What do you think, Alice?'

'Pips will be fine. She knows how to look after herself. For two pins, I'd go to help her.'

'Can I come too, Mummy?'

'No, darling. It's no place for you or for me now.'

'But I'd like to help Aunty Pips too.'

Alice patted the little girl's hand. 'I'm sure it'll all be over very soon and then perhaps she will come home for a holiday.'

Henrietta stood up and threw the newspaper onto the table in disgust. 'Not before she's got herself into trouble with one side of the dispute or the other. Probably with both.' And she marched out of the room.

Daisy turned wide eyes upon her grandfather, sitting at the end of the table. 'Gramps, is Granny cross with Aunty Pips?'

'Just a little, sweetheart, but don't worry. It's not the first time and I doubt very much that it'll be the last.'

'I've managed to persuade someone in the Red Cross to allow you ladies to wear their uniform,' George said the morning after they had set up the post. There had been no patients for them that first evening. 'So at least we'll look official now.

They've also lent us a car and offered a driver, but I said we didn't need one.' He turned towards the Enderby brothers, who had arrived back early that morning. 'I thought you two could manage that between you, though you must wear the Red Cross emblem too.'

'Well done, major,' Peter said with a huge grin. He turned to Pips. 'And I can't wait to see you back in your nurse's uniform, miss.'

'Come on, Milly. Let's put them on.'

When the two young women arrived back downstairs, there were two solemn-faced men in the shop. George turned to Pips as she came through the door. 'These gentlemen are from the Strike Committee. You've to go with them to explain what you're doing.'

'Can't I explain here? Besides, isn't it rather obvious what we're doing?'

The two men glanced at each other. 'Not to us, miss, nor to the locals. They fear that the troops are about to be sent in and you've set up a post to attend any injured soldiers.'

'I know nothing about the army coming, but if they do and there are injured among them, then of course we will help them.' She stepped closer to the two men, completely unafraid. 'Just as we will help anyone – strikers, strike-breakers, police officers and any other officials. In fact, anyone who needs our aid.' She gave them her beaming smile. 'Even you. Now, may I offer you a cup of tea?'

The two men glanced at each other. 'What d'you reckon, Jim?' the first one, who had seemed to take the lead, now turned to his colleague for his opinion.

Jim scratched his head. 'Don't rightly know, Percy. I say we have that cuppa and then report back to the other members of the committee and see what they say.'

Percy turned back to Pips. 'They might still want to see you, miss, but we'll do what we can.' He nodded as he glanced around. 'I believe you.'

The two men sat down and chatted in a friendly manner. But just as they were about to leave, the door burst open and a man, his eyes wild, rushed in. 'Come quick. My mate's been hurt. Hit on the head with a brick.'

At once Pips issued orders. 'Peter – Hugh, please go with him. Take the stretcher. Bring him back as soon as you can. We'll get ready here.'

Twenty minutes later, the two brothers arrived back bearing the stretcher between them. On it lay one of the strikers, holding a dirty bandage to his head and groaning loudly. The two officials looked on, lingering, as if watching for proof of Pips's declaration. Now, they were seeing her first-aid post in action for one of their own.

Hugh and Peter lifted him onto the table and Pips bent over him.

'What's your name?'

'I ain't telling you that. I'm not daft.'

Pips hid her smile. 'All right. I'll call you "Bill". Now, let's have a look at that gash on your head. Milly, bring me a bowl of warm water, please, and cotton wool. We must clean it first.'

The wound was not deep, though it was bleeding profusely. After she'd cleaned and dressed it and wound a white bandage around his head,

Pips said, 'Do you live near here? Hugh here will take you home in the car.'

'I ain't letting you know where I live. Sorry, miss, but we all reckon this place is a set-up for you to spy on us and report back to the authorities.'

'I can assure you it isn't. Whatever our private feelings, this first-aid post is completely neutral. You have nothing to fear from us.'

'Aye, well, I don't know that, do I?'

'No, you don't, I agree, but you and your colleagues are welcome to come and see for yourselves. These two gentlemen here are from the Strike Committee. They're going to report back. If their colleagues aren't satisfied, then they'll be back, I'm sure. Just so you know, we shall treat anyone who needs our help – whatever side they're on. Now, if you're sure you'll be all right, off you go.'

But as the man stood up, he wobbled and put out his hand to grasp her steadying arm.

'I really don't think you're quite ready to go home alone, are you? What if I come with you? Surely no one is going to disrespect a nurse's uniform.'

The man seemed to be struggling to decide. 'Were you in the war, miss?'

'Yes. Near Ypres.'

'Bill' bit his lip and said huskily, 'My brother was killed there. I couldn't join up. I was too young then.' He was thoughtful for a moment before nodding and then saying, 'You'll do, miss. I'll tell all me mates I reckon we can trust you–' he glanced around – 'all of you. And yes, I'd be glad of a bit of company...' Then he gave an apologetic grin. 'At least to the end of me road.'

They all laughed and Pips, 'Bill' and the two men from the Strike Committee left the post. When they had walked a short distance, George murmured, 'I think I'll follow at a discreet distance – just to make sure she's all right.'

They walked for about half a mile, completely unaware that they were being followed.

'We'll see him the rest of the way, miss,' Jim said as he took the wounded man's arm. 'We've to think of you walking back alone before we've had time to get the word out that you're not to be touched.'

Pips nodded. 'You seem to be walking more strongly now,' she said to 'Bill', 'but promise me you'll rest when you get home and if you should develop a bad headache or feel dizzy or sick, you must come straight back to us.'

'We'll make sure he does, miss, and – thank you.'

As Pips turned and began to walk back the way they had come, she saw George standing in a shop doorway.

As she drew near, she smiled. 'You followed me?'

'Of course; I'm not going to let you go wandering through the streets on your own as things are. What sort of a fiancé would do that?'

She laughed and looked up into his face. 'Oh, engaged now, are we? I don't remember agreeing to that.'

He chuckled. 'It's not for want of asking.'

They walked along in silence, but as they

neared the post, Pips said slowly, 'I don't mind being engaged to you, George, if you're sure.'

'I've never been surer of anything in my life. But are you?'

'It's not marriage and it'll give us time to see how Rebecca reacts to the news.'

George gave a wry laugh. 'I think I can tell you that already.'

Thirty-Four

For the next few days, the first-aid post was kept busy. As they had promised, they treated strikers, those who were injured whilst trying to keep the country going and members of the police force, who were valiantly trying to keep order. It was a hopeless – and thankless – task. The only time that the members of the post were really fearful was on the sixth night of the strike when a riot occurred in the street outside the post. Luckily, they were all there. There had been a feeling of unrest all day and, in the early evening, Bill visited the post. He was now fully recovered.

'I've come to warn you,' he told them soberly. 'I shouldn't, but you've been good to me an' my mates. There's going to be trouble tonight. You'd do best to leave.'

Pips glanced around at her fellow helpers. They all gave a brief shake of the head. She turned back to Bill. 'We appreciate your concern, and putting yourself in an awkward position by coming to tell us, but, no, if there's to be trouble, we'll be needed here more than ever. But our resolve is still the same. We help anyone who needs it. Is that understood?'

Bill sighed and said in a low voice, 'You were all there, weren't you? At the front. I can see it in your eyes. You've all seen far worse than a bit of a skirmish on a London street.'

Pips touched his arm. 'We're so sad to see fighting on our own soil and between our own people. This sort of thing really shouldn't happen.'

'No,' he said bitterly as he turned to leave. 'It shouldn't.'

As dusk fell, they watched groups of men forming in the street.

Pips peered out of the window.

'Don't stand too near the glass, darling,' George warned, 'in case someone lobs a brick in our direction.'

'I–' Pips began, but then she gasped in horror. 'There's a car coming down the street. I can't be sure in the half-light, but I think it's Muriel and Pattie. Oh no ... they're being surrounded. They're trying to drag them out. We must help them.'

Pips pulled open the door, rushed into the street and ran towards the mob surrounding the car. Everyone from the post followed her at once.

'Leave them alone. They're bringing us more supplies,' Pips shouted, but above the hubbub she could not be heard. She began to pull at the jackets of those nearest to her, but they just shrugged her off. Then she saw Muriel standing up in her open-topped car, gesticulating at the crowd and shouting words that Pips could not hear. Hands reached up to pull her down, but Muriel swiped them away, gesticulating angrily. Pattie, in the passenger seat, was clinging valiantly onto a large box, but in a concerted effort both women were pulled from the car and manhandled over the heads of the crowd. Then the crowd began to rock the car until, with one gigantic effort, they toppled it onto its side.

Furious now, Pips pushed her way through the throng. 'You idiots!' she railed. 'Don't you realize we're trying to help you? They're bringing medical supplies to our first-aid position.'

With a supreme effort, she pushed her way through to the car, just in time to see a man close to it brandishing what looked like a can of petrol.

'Don't you dare!' she shouted at him. 'There are medical supplies in that car.'

He paused and then glanced around at his mates for support. 'They're strike-breakers.'

'No, they're not. They're part of our team at the first-aid post. But if this is the thanks we get, we'll pack up, go home and put our feet up. Or...' she moved towards him, menacingly, her green eyes spitting fire, 'I'll drive a lorry or a bus and then I'll *really* be helping the other side.'

Another man pushed his way to the front and Pips heaved a sigh of relief. 'Bill, am I glad to see you. For Heaven's sake tell them...'

'His name ain't Bill,' the man with the can muttered.

'I know that, but when he came for treatment he didn't want to tell me his real name.' She grinned. 'So as far as I'm concerned, he's Bill.' She turned to the man. 'Just tell 'em, Bill, will you?'

'They're all right, mate, honest. This lass was at the front near Ypres driving ambulances and nursing. And this feller,' he pointed at George, 'was a captain in the army, but he ended up a major.'

'He's not on our side, then,' the man with the can was still threatening.

'I said "was", yer daft bugger. They're doing what they've done before – helping anyone in trouble. They're not taking sides. So get this car turned back onto its wheels and help carry the supplies to their post, if you've got any sense left in that daft head of yours.'

There were a few moments of muttering rippling amongst the crowd but then one of their number said, 'Come on, lads, let's give 'em the benefit of the doubt. But if we find out you're not what you say you are, if yer spying, then it'll be the worse for you.'

Pips put her hands on her hips and faced him. 'Are you threatening me, feller, because if you are...'

'No, miss, he ain't. Come on, Joe. Put that bloody can out of harm's way and help us up with this car. My, it's a Napier. You could race this at Brooklands, miss.'

'I do,' said Muriel shortly. She had pushed her way back to the front of the crowd. 'And quite successfully, thank you very much. So I hope there's no lasting damage done.'

The car was lifted and bounced back onto its wheels. There were a few dints on the right-hand side, which had hit the ground, but Bill said at once, 'I've got a mate who'll knock them out for you, miss, in a jiffy. No real harm done.' He grinned at her. 'I bet it's had a few more knocks than that in its time.'

'Are you insinuating, my man, that I'm a bad driver?'

Bill's grin broadened. 'Would I, miss? But Brooklands is a dangerous place. Even more dangerous than trying to cross a picket line. Now, let's help you unload and take this stuff to the first-aid post.'

The incident passed off without serious injury, yet it had been a warning to Pips and her helpers that it could have turned ugly, if it had not been for the timely arrival of Bill, whose real name Pips still didn't know.

'Well,' Muriel said as she, Pattie and Pips stood looking at the damage to her car. 'Despite the rather unfriendly reception, I think we should still go ahead with our idea, don't you, Pattie?'

'Of course. We'll be helping their families, not these idiots.' She gestured towards the scratched paintwork and dinted driver's door.

'What are you two planning?' Pips asked.

'We've been talking to the local shopkeepers down this street,' Muriel said. 'They're trying their best to support the local community by letting anyone who's involved in the strike have food on credit, but there's only so much they can afford to do. They still have to pay for their stock.'

Pips frowned. She couldn't guess where this was leading.

'So, Pattie and I are going to set up a soup kitchen for families who have been the hardest hit. And there're a few of them around here.'

'There's another empty shop a bit further down the street,' Pattie said. 'We've seen the owner and he's given us permission to use it.'

'Provided we make good any damage.'

'I don't think there'll be a lot of that, if you're feeding their kids.'

'Neither do I. So, Pips, when we're up and running – hopefully by tomorrow – you can start telling folks – your new friend Bill, for one. He'll soon spread the word.'

'And the Strike Committee. I'll let them know too.'

The soup kitchen was a great success and each day, longer and longer queues, mainly women and children, formed outside the former shop premises. When they weren't busy at the first-aid post, Pips and Milly went to help out too.

'Now, no pushing. You'll all get served,' Pips admonished, but her heart went out to the kids with pinched, white faces and huge, hungry eyes.

'But what if you run out of soup, miss?'

'Then we'll make some more.' She smiled, ladling a generous helping into a bowl and handing it to the boy who had spoken. 'Don't forget your bread bun. Freshly baked this morning.'

She watched the poorly dressed urchin leave the shop and squat down in front of a building across the road. He was so ravenous, he couldn't wait to carry his meal home.

As Pips watched him, she couldn't help but send up a silent prayer of thanks. But for the grace of God, it could be Daisy or Luke or Harry...

Gunshot wounds and shell-blast injuries had become cracked skulls and bloody noses. But there was little difference in Pips's eyes; the casualties still needed her skills, though in the end, there weren't as many injuries as had at first been expected.

After nine days, when the effectiveness began to crumble, the TUC called off the general strike, though the miners vowed to carry on their struggle.

'Well, that didn't last as long as we thought it might,' Pips said as they cleared away all the supplies and furniture and tidied the shop in preparation for leaving. 'And there weren't as many serious injuries as there might have been, but I feel so sorry for the miners. They're carrying on the fight on their own now, and I suspect that they won't win.'

'It isn't right, I agree with you. They feel they've been deserted.' George shook his head as if in disbelief. 'We can spend millions on fighting a catastrophic war that should never have happened in the first place, but we can't pay the men who put their lives at risk on a daily basis to provide us with coal.'

'You should stand for parliament, George.'

He laughed wryly. 'If anyone should, it ought to be you.'

'Me?' Pips was startled. 'Oh I don't think I'd last long in there, even if I got in in the first place.' She grinned. 'I'm far too outspoken and opinionated. I'd never be able to follow the party line.'

'And which party would that be?'

'That's just the trouble. I never know which to support. I agree with some things the Tories say and with others that the Liberals say. And then there's the Labour Party. I think they're going to get a lot stronger as time goes on. At least they seem to be the party for the ordinary working man. Besides, although women have got the vote now, generally speaking, it's still only for certain women at the moment, isn't it?'

'It'll come – given time. But as regards the Labour Party, they're overtaking the Liberal Party in popularity, so I've heard.'

As she glanced about her to check that everything had been done, Pips murmured, 'So, it's back to Hazelwood House for me, then, though the need for that now seems to be dwindling. I think I'll go home for a few days, George. I can't tell you how much I'm missing Daisy. Would you like to come with me?'

George hesitated, but then shook his head. 'I need to see Rebecca.' He caught and held her gaze. 'Especially if you're going to agree to marry me.'

'I do love you, George...' She hesitated and he added softly, 'There's a "but" though, isn't there?'

She bit her lip and nodded. 'I don't want to come between you and your daughter. You know that. You're all she has.'

'Hopefully not for always. She'll get married and have children of her own.'

'Will she, though? The papers are saying that there are two million surplus women now. Many of them are never going to find husbands.'

To that, sadly, George had no answer.

Thirty-Five

'*Engaged?* Oh Daddy, I can't believe you can be so blind. She's nothing but a gold-digger. Can't you see that?'

'I don't know how you make that out. She's from a very well-to-do family.' He smiled wryly. 'Maybe her parents are saying that about me.'

Rebecca gave a snort of derision. 'I doubt it. They'll have found out all about you, you mark my words. They'll know that you're not dependent on any sort of army pension you might have. I don't think that would allow you a house near York and an apartment in London, do you? Does *she* know that you were left a lot of money by your parents and about all the money you've made since the war on the American stock market?'

'I've no idea. It's never come up in conversation. Any more than I have asked her what she's worth.'

'Is she heiress to this estate you say her parents have?'

George shook his head. 'No, she has a brother, Robert, who will inherit that.'

'There you are, then. I doubt she'll have much. She'll be dependent on her parents and then on her brother, unless,' she added ominously, 'she marries.'

'So, you're asking me to give her up, are you? To have nothing more to do with her.'

301

Rebecca sighed. 'Dad, if she'd been a widow – a war widow – of a similar age to you, then it might have been different. But she's not much older than me. Whatever reason can she have for marrying someone of your age, if it's not for money?'

George's mouth twisted into something between a wry smile and a grimace. 'You don't believe she could possibly love me?'

'Do you want me to be honest?'

'Of course.'

'Then – no, I don't.'

Seated across the table from her in their favourite restaurant, George toyed with a fork. 'You're forcing me to choose between you, are you? I either lose the woman I love – or my daughter. And I don't think I need to remind you how very much I love you, do I?'

'Oh Daddy...' She reached across the table to touch his hand. 'I'm only thinking of you.'

George remained silent because he was unsure now whether or not his daughter was speaking the truth.

'You know, Pips,' Robert said as he watched his sister pacing the long drawing room restlessly. 'I really don't know why you're hesitating. George is a good man – a fine man – and it's obvious to us all he adores you. Don't you love him?'

'Yes, I do, but...'

'Don't tell me you're still hankering after Giles Kendall?'

'Heavens, no! He's the last man on my mind.'

'Then, who?' He paused and then asked incredulously, 'Not Mitch Hammond?'

Now Pips threw back her head and laughed aloud. 'Lord, no. He's nuts. Nice nuts, but nuts, nevertheless. I'd never know a moment's peace with him.'

'And that's what you want, is it?' Robert asked softly. 'A peaceful, quiet life?'

Pips wriggled her shoulders. 'No, I don't think I do. They're just so – well – polar opposites. One extreme to the other. George is almost a pipe-and-slippers man whilst Mitch – oh my goodness, why am I even talking about Mitch Hammond? I'm not in love with him.'

'Are you quite sure?'

'Absolutely sure,' Pips said firmly, but, fleet-ingly, Robert wondered if she was trying to convince herself as much as him.

'But you are in love with George?'

Pips sighed. 'I do love him dearly, but it's not that heady excitement of falling in love. D'you know what I mean?'

'I think so.' There was a pause between them before Robert said softly, 'There's something I once heard or read – I can't remember which now – but it might help you. When you marry, it's not a case of finding someone you can live with, but someone you can't live *without*.' He was silent for several moments before saying softly, 'I knew I couldn't live without Alice. I wanted to be with her for the rest of my life and that's why I was prepared even to risk upsetting my family – my dear mother in particular – to marry her.'

For several moments Pips was very still until she looked up and met her brother's concerned gaze.

'I would be very sad to think that I'd never see George again.'

'And – Mitch?'

She laughed ironically. 'Chance would be a fine thing. He'll always keep turning up like the proverbial bad penny.'

At the race meeting at the end of May, Mitch sought her out.

'I think you might have told me,' he said.

Pips blinked. 'What? What haven't I told you?'

'That you're actually engaged to George.'

'Sorry – I thought you knew. We've been together long enough.'

'You're making a big mistake.'

Pips glared at him. 'I beg your pardon?'

Mitch smiled wryly. 'You're marrying the wrong man.'

Pips gasped. 'You've got some cheek.'

'You should be marrying me.'

'Ha!' Pips forced a laugh. 'You have to be joking.'

'No. For once in my life, I'm deadly serious. You know very well I'm in love with you, Philippa Maitland. I have been ever since you dragged me from my crashed plane in no-man's-land *and* risked your life to rescue my photographs that, at that moment, I believed were more important than someone's life – *your* life.' He paused but Pips could think of nothing to say. 'I was wrong,' he went on quietly. 'And you're wrong now. George is a nice man – a good man. A soldier and a gentleman. He's solid and safe and will take care of you for as long as he lives, but...' He hesitated.

304

'Go on,' Pips said tartly. 'You've come this far, you can't stop now.'

Mitch took a deep breath. 'But for you that security will turn into boredom. You don't want a *safe* life, Pips. You want excitement and adventure – a reason to get up every morning.'

Pips shook her head. 'You don't understand him. George loves me. He won't stop me doing anything I want to do.'

Now Mitch's smile was sad. 'He won't manage it, I've no doubt, but he will try and that will then cause a rift between you.'

'And you'd muscle in then, would you?'

He sighed. 'You've got me all wrong, Pips. I love you with all my heart – more than I ever thought I could love any woman. I've always known I'm selfish. I like my own way. I like to follow my own pursuits and live my life the way *I* want to, but, d'you know, I'd give everything up in a heartbeat if you said you'd marry me.'

Pips was shocked. He was serious and all she could do was stare at him.

'Don't say anything...' he said, softly.

'I wasn't going to, because I don't know what to say, except that I'm sorry if I've hurt you. I – thought it was all banter from – from a lady's man.'

'Oh, I'm a flirt – I know that. I've had a string of girlfriends – and I'll probably go on to have several more, if I can't have you, but I've never asked any one of them to marry me and now, I never will.' He took her hand and held it. 'All I want is your happiness, Pips. If you're sure about marrying George, then you won't see me again.'

305

'I'll see you at Brooklands.'

'Probably, but I shall keep my distance.'

'But why? Can't we be friends?'

'No, Pips, it doesn't work like that. At least – not for me. It's all or nothing. That's the sort of guy I am.' He squeezed her hand. 'But I'll just say one thing: if ever you should need me, I'll be there for you.'

'Mitch, I...'

'Don't say any more.' He leaned forward and kissed her cheek, released her hand, then turned and walked swiftly away without looking back.

After their involvement with the strike, life returned to normality and the weeks passed much the same as before until Paul arrived at Milly's flat one evening in June.

'I am the bearer of exciting news.'

The two women and George looked at him expectantly.

'Go on then, darling. Don't keep us in suspense.'

'The very first British Grand Prix is to be held at–' He paused for effect and was not disappointed when the three of them chorused, 'At Brooklands.'

He beamed. 'However did you guess?'

'Because, my darling,' Milly said, kissing his cheek, 'you wouldn't be quite so excited about it if it was being held anywhere else.'

'When is it?' Pips asked.

'Saturday, the seventh of August.'

'We must all go.' Milly clapped her hands. 'I'll organize it.'

'Then you can all come and cheer me on,' Paul said.

They stared at him.

'You're going to enter?' George said.

'Of course, and I think Mitch is entering too.'

'I don't suppose they allow women, do they?' Pips asked.

'No!' the other three said vehemently.

But the day before the event, both Mitch's car and Paul's developed mechanical troubles that meant they had to withdraw from the race.

'I'll just hate watching,' Mitch declared.

'Me too, but let's keep the ladies company.'

Mitch brightened. 'At least *he's* not coming.'

'Now whoever could you mean?' Paul grinned. 'Come on, let's pick them both up and take them to Brooklands. We're meeting the other girls there.'

'How does it work, this Grand Prix thing?' Milly said when Mitch and Paul had joined them. '*Do* explain it to me, darling. I'm sure Pips understands it, but I don't.'

'There are five races in different countries decided by the International Federation and these make up the World Championship.'

'France has already won two,' Mitch said glumly, 'and seeing as now there are only three British cars left in the race...'

'Oh look. What are those sandbanks for in the middle of the track?'

'Chicanes.'

'What?'

'They're artificial tight corners to make the

race more exciting.'

'Come on, Milly,' Paul said, taking her hand. 'Let's find a good place to watch.'

Mitch's pessimism was unfortunately proved right. French cars took first and third place, sandwiching Captain Campbell's Bugatti between them. They were the only cars to finish.

'I'm not surprised,' Mitch said. 'Two hundred and eighty-seven miles is some distance. Let's hope we can do better next year.'

Thirty-Six

Pips stood with her hands on her hips facing her brother as he sat near the window in the drawing room gazing at the flat landscape beyond. She was beginning to despair that they would ever manage to coax him into going out further afield than the safety of his home environment. Although he was now practising as a doctor again, he still only visited patients locally. He never went into the city and wouldn't hear of going down to London to visit Pips, even though she had invited him to attend race meetings several times. Another Christmas had come and gone and still he clung to home, but now she thought that perhaps she had come up with a plan that he could not refuse.

'Robert...'

'Oh dear, I recognize that tone. I'm in for a telling off – again!'

Her patience was wearing thin. 'Oh for goodness' sake!' She sighed heavily, dropped her arms and sat down in a chair opposite him.

More gently, she said, 'It's the inauguration of the Menin Gate on the twenty-seventh of July and that's only two months away. I think we should go.'

'Me?'

'Don't look so startled. Of course, you. And Alice and Daisy. And I think we should take Luke too, if his family will let us. We could take him to see where his father and two uncles are buried. He's old enough now.'

'But Daisy isn't. She's only nine.'

'If it's all explained to her very carefully before we go, she'll understand.'

'She'll understand right enough, but don't you think it will be all far too emotional for her? There'll be veterans there who'll have some horrific wounds, which are still obvious. There'll be grieving families. It'll be so traumatic for everyone. And for a young girl, well...'

'Daisy has lived all her life with a wounded veteran and with her other grandparents grieving for their sons. She'll cope.' She paused before adding, 'I think it's more you who can't face it. Am I right?'

There was a long silence before Robert whispered, 'As always.'

'I think it would help you. Get things in perspective for yourself. You've shut yourself away here, cocooned by a loving family. You haven't seen the wounded in London – and, I'm sure, throughout the rest of the country – struggling to cope because they can't find work – can't support their families any more. The "land fit for heroes" is a joke.'

Robert winced. 'You mean, I'm privileged?'

'Well, aren't you?'

'I'm damned lucky. I do know that, but why would going back there make me feel better?'

'I don't know. I'm not a doctor or a psychiatrist. I just have a gut instinct that it'd be cathartic for you. Not closure, exactly – it'll never be closed for any of us, will it? – but I truly believe it would help you. I think I can persuade George to go too.'

'What does Alice say?'

Truthfully, Pips was able to say, 'I haven't talked to Alice about it.'

He was thoughtful for a moment before saying, 'If Alice thinks it would be a good idea for us all to go, then yes, we will.'

'Oh Pips, I don't know. I don't want to force him to do something he doesn't want to. What if it made him ten times worse?'

'I just think it'd help him, Alice. He'd see that Ypres is being rebuilt and that there's a wonderful memorial to all those who perished in the Ypres Salient and who have no proper resting place. He'd see that the people who live there are trying to rebuild their lives, to move on, and it might help him to do the same. And we'd be able to see William and his family bringing up the next generation who – God willing – will never have to face another Great War.' Pips paused as Alice chewed her lip. 'Are you worried about Daisy going?'

'Heavens no, she'll take it all in her stride, even though she's only nine. And Luke too. No, it's

Robert I'm concerned about.'

'If all of us go, we won't be able to stay with the Duponts. They won't have room, but we'll stay in Pop and then, if he really can't face it at the last minute, he can stay at the hotel.'

'I'll talk to him about it.'

'And don't let him persuade you to take Daisy and Luke and go without him. It's all of you or no one.'

'Yes, Miss Pips.' It had been a long time since Alice had called her former young mistress that. They both laughed and hugged each other, remembering all the times they had shared – good and bad.

After much heart-searching and talking it over with both Edwin and Henrietta, Robert agreed to go.

And now I've got Len to convince to allow Luke to go too, Pips thought. She didn't know who would prove the most difficult, her brother or Len Dawson.

To her surprise, Len leapt at the chance. 'It'd be good for him to visit his father's grave. Thank you, Miss Pips, I accept your offer gratefully, but I want to pay for his fare.'

Pips thought quickly, not wanting to offend the man's pride. 'There's no need, Mr Dawson, but if you wish to do so, then I agree.'

'He's a good lad. Already he does the work of a man. And when he leaves school in a couple of years' time, he'll be paid properly. At the moment, I've only been giving him pocket money, you might say, but he's earned his trip. That's if he wants to go, miss. I shan't force him.'

Pips laughed. 'Oh, he'll want to go, Mr Dawson. Daisy's going.'

'George, you will come with us, won't you?'

'Of course. It won't be easy, but if your brother can face it,' he laughed a little wryly, 'then I must.'

'There's no "must" about it, but I would like you there.'

He took her hand and kissed it. 'Then I shall be.'

'What about Rebecca? Will she mind?'

George wrinkled his forehead. 'I'm not planning on telling her.'

Daisy had travelled to Belgium before, for William and Brigitta's wedding, but she could remember very little about the trip.

'I can remember Uncle William,' she told Luke as they sat together on the journey. 'He's big and strong.'

'Granny Cooper's always saying I'm like him.' He was quiet for a moment before adding, 'Ma explained it all to me. What happened with him in the war and why me granddad's still so bitter about it all. He hasn't said owt, but I think he realizes we'll be seeing Uncle William and his family. Ma just said I was to be sure not to mention his name in front of Granddad when I get back.'

'It's sad, isn't it?' Daisy said. 'Aunty Pips said Uncle William was very brave.'

When they landed in Belgium and travelled

across the flat land, Daisy exclaimed, 'It's like home. It's like Lincolnshire.'

Pips, sitting with George just behind the two youngsters, laughed. 'That's just what we said when we first came out here.'

When they arrived in Poperinghe and booked into a hotel there, Daisy, as energetic as ever, didn't want to rest after their journey. 'When are we going to see Uncle William and our cousins?'

'Tomorrow. Then we'll be able to find out about arrangements for Sunday.'

Daisy pouted, but Luke said quietly, 'Leave it, Dais. Your dad must be tired and it's a huge thing for him to come back here, you know. And for Major Allender – and, I expect, for your mam and Aunty Pips too.'

Pips cast him a grateful glance. What an intuitive and kindly boy he was. Daisy punched him playfully on the shoulder. 'Trust you! Sorry, Aunty Pips, I'm just so eager to see and do everything.'

Pips chuckled, seeing, not for the first time, herself in the young girl. 'We'll make sure we do everything you want to whilst we're here, I promise.'

But it seemed that William was as eager as his niece to see his family for he, Brigitta and their two sons arrived at the hotel that evening.

'We couldn't wait,' he said, sheepishly. 'My, Daisy, how you've grown and you must be Luke.' He held out his hand and Luke took it. 'Hello, Uncle William. I'm very pleased to meet you.' He regarded the older man solemnly, looking him up and down, and then he nodded. 'I can see what

313

Granny Cooper means.'

William frowned, wondering, for a minute, what village gossip the boy had heard. All of it, no doubt, but Luke was smiling. 'She says I look a bit like my uncle Bernard, but that I'm going to be tall and strong like you.'

William smiled with relief. 'You've got nicer-coloured hair than I have, Luke, whereas mine has always been described as "mousey" and my eyes are hazel.'

'What was me dad's?' Luke asked candidly.

'My brothers all had brown hair and lovely dark eyes too. I was always a bit envious of them.' William laughed, ruffling the boy's hair affectionately. He liked his nephew. 'It's good to see you. I'm so glad they let you come. I was a bit doubtful that they would.'

'Me too, but Granddad was all for it. He wants me to visit my dad's grave and put some flowers on it.'

William nodded and said huskily, 'We'll do that, lad. On Monday. I've got it all arranged. We're all going. Now, come and meet your other cousins. You too, Daisy.'

Pascal, at six, and Waldo, at just turned four, both favoured their mother in colouring, with fair hair and blue eyes, but their stature promised to be like their father – tall and broad. They were already big for their ages.

For a few moments the four youngsters stood in awkward silence, eyeing each other, and then Daisy stepped forward and stuck out her hand. 'Pleased to meet you, Cousin Pascal – Cousin Waldo.'

She spoke in English and they replied in English too. No doubt, Pips thought, the boys were being brought up to be bilingual. With the ice broken, the four moved away from the grown-ups and were soon chattering amongst themselves, leaving William to catch up on family news with his sister. Brigitta, Pips, Robert and George talked amongst themselves.

'It is so good to see you again, Dr Maitland,' Brigitta said. 'And you too, major.'

'Oh please, Brigitta, it's just Robert now.' Robert nodded towards her sons. 'You have two fine boys.'

'I'm sorry we couldn't put you up at the farm-house, but we want you to spend as much time as you can with us whilst you are here. It's nice for William to see his family. I'm so glad you've brought Daisy – and Luke too. That was a lovely surprise.'

Robert nodded but said no more. Brigitta knew all about the family rift and there was no point in dwelling on it.

Thirty-Seven

William had organized transport for them all and, the following morning, they were picked up from the hotel and driven into Ypres. Pips craned her neck for her first view of the place that she had last seen in ruins.

'Oh my, just look at all the building work.'

'Most of the rebuilding work of private houses and the utilities has been done, but the larger buildings – like Cloth Hall and the cathedral – will take years to complete. Work on Cloth Hall is due to start next year,' William said. 'The driver is taking us to the Grand Place. From there we'll be able to walk to the Menin Gate.'

With their medals proudly pinned to their chests, George and Robert joined the long line of relatives and veterans congregating in the square.

'Come along, you lot,' Robert said. 'Walk with us. I don't want us to get separated.'

Alice glanced about her. 'Are we allowed to?'

'Of course. You're a veteran of sorts too, don't forget. Come.' He took her hand and held it tightly, but Alice was astute enough to know that he wanted her close for his own sake rather than for hers. She glanced at him anxiously, but Robert was smiling as he looked about him.

William walked beside Brigitta, clutching her hand, with their two boys on either side of them.

Pips glanced at William. 'You should have had a medal too,' she said softly. He shook his head and seemed embarrassed and Pips was sorry she'd mentioned it. But Brigitta glanced up at her husband and smiled. No doubt, Pips thought, his wife's pride in him was the only thing that really mattered to him and he certainly had that.

Pips walked between Daisy and Luke, who had both gone very quiet as they took in the scene about them.

'Aunty Pips,' Daisy whispered, 'look at all the black flags hanging from the buildings. And there are people lining the streets all the way and people hanging out of the windows from all the new buildings.'

'This is a very big day for the people of Ypres,' Pips murmured.

A procession seemed to be forming outside the town hall.

'Oh my,' Pips whispered. 'You see that gentleman there – the one next to the soldier, who has a moustache a bit like George's? That's the Belgian king – King Albert.'

'He looks very grand. And who is the other man with the moustache, the one in the fine uniform?'

'That's Field Marshal Lord Plumer. I think he's going to make a speech. And the other man. He looks like someone important.'

Overhearing their conversation, George butted in, 'That's General Foch of France. I've found out that seating has been set up on the eastern side, but that it's only for officials. We would be best going up onto the ramparts, I think, but at the eastern end, where we can see the wooden platform set up for those who will be making speeches and where we can see the military bands.'

'Are we here? The British bands, I mean?' Daisy asked.

'Oh yes. Come along.'

George steered them through the crowds and found them the perfect place where they could see almost everything. Maybe it was the row of medals on his jacket that helped.

By the time the ceremony started, there were no spare seats left or even a place to stand. As they waited, George pointed out the numerous photographers and even the loudspeakers, which would broadcast the events. 'They'll be listening to this in England on the wireless.'

Of all the speeches that were made that day, it was Lord Plumer's that Pips was to remember. Standing on the very spot where thousands of British and allied soldiers had marched out of Ypres, amidst the sound of guns and shellfire, with terrified horses and mules trudging forwards, perhaps for the last time, he spoke movingly of the terrible loss that relatives had suffered, made worse by the phrase 'missing, believed killed', which meant their fallen loved ones had no known grave that their families could visit to mourn and to lay tributes. But, he said, that had been put right. For all those who lay somewhere in Flanders fields now had a fitting memorial and, for each one, it could now be said, 'He is not missing; he is here.'

As the ceremony came to an end, women, their faces lined with grief, dressed in sombre clothes and wearing the medals of their loved ones, laid wreaths. Buglers from the Somerset Light Infantry played 'The Last Post' and, standing on the ramparts, pipers of the Scots Guards played a lament.

As the crowds began to disperse, Pips and the others stood beneath the central arch of the memorial gazing around at the thousands of names inscribed on the panels.

'So,' she said, 'the locals got what they wanted. Ypres is being rebuilt as it was and now they have their wonderful memorial. It's magnificent, isn't it, but it's so sad.'

William stood beside her. 'It was designed by Sir Reginald Blomfield.'

'The same man who was one of the architects of the Forceville cemetery?'

'Yes. And since then, he's designed well over a hundred other cemeteries.'

'They're all beautiful,' Pips murmured. 'Poignant, but beautiful.'

'Is my dad's name here?' Luke asked quietly, his voice not quite steady.

Pips put her arm around his shoulders. 'No, your dad has a proper grave. We're going to see it tomorrow. The names here are all those who perished in the fighting, but were never found.'

Daisy slipped her hand into Luke's and rested her head against his shoulder. She said nothing. Even Daisy could find no word of comfort. But as they walked away, she said in a small voice, 'All those men. Every one of them had a family. It wasn't just them that were lost, was it? It was such a lot of lives devastated and generations to come just – gone.'

For a nine-year-old, Pips thought, Daisy had amazing insight.

With her arm still around Luke, Pips said, 'Come, let's go and look at all the new buildings in the square. I especially want to see how the rebuilding of the cathedral is progressing.'

The following day, the party journeyed to the Somme.

'Your dad is buried at Ovillers military cemetery, but your uncles, Bernard and Roy, are buried near Longueval. They were killed together and they're buried side by side. We'll go to both places.'

Clutching Daisy's hand tightly and with Pips close by, Luke stood looking down at the name inscribed on the marker: the name of his father, but a man he had never known. Carefully, he stooped and laid the wreath that William had brought.

'I'll take a picture of it for you, Luke,' Pips said softly. 'I've brought my Box Brownie. I'll take one of your uncles' graves too. Your gran and ma would like to have pictures, I'm sure.'

The boy nodded, his eyes never leaving the grave. They all waited patiently for some time until Luke himself was ready to leave. He touched the marker with trembling fingers and seemed to be saying 'goodbye', then, still clinging on to Daisy's hand, he turned away.

It was William who now put his hand on his nephew's shoulder and said, 'Your dad would be so proud of you, Luke, as you have every reason to be proud of him and your two uncles too. They were very brave.'

With unshed tears shimmering in his eyes, Luke looked up. 'And you too, Uncle William. I know just how courageous you were. I'm proud of you, an' all.'

Back at the farm where Mrs Dupont had laid on a fine spread for all of them, George said, 'I've only just heard – and I'm sorry we've missed it now – but Lord Plumer laid a foundation stone some time yesterday for a church to be built as a memorial for British and Commonwealth troops on a piece of land not far from the cathedral. They plan to fill the church with furniture, plaques and even windows, donated by various British organizations like military units, schools and, of course, families of the fallen. I believe it's to be called St George's Church.'

'Is it called after you?' Daisy asked innocently.

George laughed, lightening the moment. 'No, I'm not that famous or important, Daisy. But I understand the designer is once again Sir Reginald Blomfield. It's just going to be a simple building in keeping with those being rebuilt around it. It'll be a place for families to come and remember.'

William nodded. 'I'd heard about it, but I didn't know the foundation stone was being laid yesterday. I'm sorry we missed that too. I understand that they're combining it with a school with donations from Eton. Evidently, there were three hundred old Etonians who lost their lives around here.'

'I've heard,' Brigitta put in shyly, 'that they'll be looking for embroidered hassocks with regimental emblems worked in tapestry for the church.'

Pips clapped her hands. 'How marvellous. There you are, Alice, you can do one for the Lincolnshire Regiment with the sphinx on it, like their cap badge.'

Alice smiled and blushed. She liked the sound of making something for the memorial church. She said to Brigitta, 'Let me know what is needed for the church, won't you? I'd love to do something.'

Early the following morning, before they were due to leave, George said, 'Pips, will you come to

Brandhoek with me? I want to visit my friend's grave.'

'Of course.' She smiled. 'I've already asked William if I can borrow his truck. I thought you'd want to go.'

'Just the two of us?'

Pips nodded. 'Of course.'

They set out and soon arrived at the cemetery.

'It looks so different since I last saw it,' George murmured as he helped her climb down.

'I came to visit him for you just before we left.'

'Did you? That was kind of you.'

They walked to where they knew George's friend lay and stood beside his grave looking down at the pristine white-marble marker. Pips laid the small posy of flowers she had brought near it. 'The poppies are over now, aren't they? I'd like to have seen them again.'

George gestured around them. 'There are still one or two latecomers, but no, not the profusion we saw before.' He took her hand. 'Do you remember...?'

Before he could go any further, Pips said, 'Of course I do, George.'

'And now I am free to declare my love for you openly and I do. Pips, please, will you marry me soon?'

'Yes, George, I will. And I'll even set a date.'

His eyes lit up and he seemed to be holding his breath until she said, 'Saturday, the seventh of December 1929.'

His face fell. 'But that's two years away.'

Mischievously, she said, 'Then it'll give you plenty of time to work on Rebecca.' She linked

322

her arm through his as they walked back amongst the graves towards the vehicle.

'Seriously, though, I would like another two seasons racing before I give it up.'

'Pips, I've told you I won't ask you – or even expect you – to give up what you love to do, though I shall, of course, worry.'

'Precisely, and I don't want to do that to you. No, George, give me two years and I'll give up racing, though probably not the flying. Agreed?'

He smiled wistfully. 'If I must, but why as late as December? The last races of the season are usually in October, aren't they? Or November at the latest.'

'Oh I couldn't possibly allow our wedding to interfere with Daisy's birthday. And Luke's too, of course. And now we'd better get back to say our "goodbyes".'

Thirty-Eight

'I am loath to admit it, Pips, but you were right,' Robert said. 'I never thought it would, but going back has helped.'

Pips had returned to Lincolnshire with her family, leaving George in London with the strict instruction: 'Now, don't forget to tell Rebecca about our plans. I'm going to tell my mother.' She chuckled. 'I can't wait to see her face.'

Now she said to Robert, 'I'm glad. I took a risk, persuading you to go, I know.'

'It's high time I faced up to life and realized just how lucky I am not only to have survived at all, but to have a loving family, who cares for me.'

'You are.'

Robert grinned. 'My darling sister, who pulls no punches.'

Pips shrugged. 'I never have and I don't suppose I ever will now.'

'Don't change, Pips. We all love you just the way you are – warts and all.'

Pips's eyes widened and she gave a mock gasp of surprise. 'Warts? And what are my "warts", might I ask?'

Robert held up his hand, counting off on his fingers: 'You're bossy, self-opinionated, impetuous, you like your own way, you're too daring for your own good... Ah – with only one hand, I've run out of fingers.'

Pips snorted with laughter as Robert added, 'And you can be most unladylike at times. Poor Mother, she's done her best, but she'll never be able to launch you into the upper echelons of society, I fear.'

'Well, I do have one piece of news for her that might brighten her day.'

'Do tell.'

Pips wagged her finger. 'Oh no, you must wait until dinner when I will tell all of you together. And now, I must go down the road to see the Dawsons. I have some photographs to show them that even Len will want to see.'

'Just be careful you don't show him that one of William with his arm around Luke's shoulders. He'll blow a fuse.'

Norah and Ma pored over all the photographs, lingering over the ones which included William. 'He looks well,' Norah murmured.

'He is, Mrs Dawson. And happy. And those are his two sons. Your grandsons.'

'They're big boys. Look, Ma, here are Pascal and Waldo.'

Ma gazed at the photograph. 'Fine boys.'

There was a rattle at the back door and Pips hastily gathered up any photographs of William and his family.

'It's only me,' came Bess Cooper's familiar tones.

'Don't show her them photos of William,' Norah hissed. 'She'll gossip and Len will hear.'

'Aren't you afraid Luke might say something?'

Norah shook her head. 'He knows not to. He understands now. Though I'm hoping he won't say much in front of young Harry. He's a little chatterbox.' She raised her voice. 'Come in, Bess. The kettle's on the boil. I reckon you can smell my tea mashing.'

Bess manoeuvred her large frame into the kitchen and headed for Len's chair on the hearth opposite Ma. 'It's not that, duck. I know you allus have elevenses...' She grinned. 'So that's when I come. Nah then, Miss Pips. Did you have a good trip?'

'We did, Mrs Cooper. Would you like to see some photos I took of the boys' graves?'

'Aye, I would.' Bess held out her hand to take them. It was several minutes before she glanced up. 'There's none of William and his family. Now,

I'm not daft, Miss Pips. I know you'll have seen him and brought back pictures of him, his wife and boys to show Ma and Norah. But you daren't show 'em to me, because you think I'll blab about it all around the village. Oh I know what everyone thinks of me. That I'm an old gossip, who can't keep a secret and loves to stir up trouble and, yes, in me time I've had a dig at the shenanigans in this house. But I'm very fond of Ma and I've grown closer to Norah over the years, 'specially now we share Luke as our grandson. Believe it or not, Miss Pips, I have learned when to keep me mouth shut.'

There was silence in the room before Ma said, 'Oh show her, Miss Pips.'

For the next ten minutes, Bess cooed over the photographs of William and his family, but when they heard the back door open again and Luke's voice, Pips gathered them up quickly, leaving only the ones of the graves of the three brothers for Len, who came in with Luke, to see.

He, too, studied them for some time before he looked up slowly and met Pips's gaze. From the look in his eyes, she could tell he knew very well that they had all seen William, but all he said was, 'Thank you for taking Luke with you. He's been telling me about seeing his dad's grave, and his uncles'.' He paused and seemed to be struggling, deciding whether to say more, but the moment passed and he merely nodded and held the photos out to her.

'They're for you to keep, if you'd like,' Pips said quietly.

'Thank you. Norah, you put these wherever

you want 'em. If I want to see 'em again, I'll ask you, but I'd rather not have 'em framed and on display, if it's all the same to you.' He turned away to go back into the scullery to wash at the sink before his midday meal.

As Pips said, 'I must be going. I'll call to see you again before I go back to London,' she handed the other photos to Norah, who nodded her thanks and swiftly put them all in her apron pocket.

Over dinner at the hall that evening, when the dessert arrived, Robert said, 'So, Pips, what is this announcement you have to make?'

'I think you'll all be pleased to know that George and I have fixed a date for our wedding.'

Henrietta dropped her spoon onto her plate with a clatter. 'Oh my, Philippa. When?'

'We've agreed on Saturday, the seventh of December–' She paused and drew breath before adding, '1929.'

Henrietta's face was a picture. 'But – but that's two years away.'

'I know. That's exactly what George said.'

'But why? Why need you wait so long?'

'Because, Mother dear, I have promised that when we marry, I will give up motor racing. And I just want to take part for another two years. He's not demanded it – not even asked me – but I know it will worry him every time I climb into a car.'

'And you think it won't in the intervening years? Really, Philippa, for a clever girl, you can be irritatingly obtuse at times.'

'What about the flying?' Edwin asked.

'Oh, I shall keep doing that.'

Henrietta tutted in exasperation and cast her eyes to the ceiling.

The following months seemed to fly by for Pips. It wasn't that she didn't want to marry George. She loved him and missed him acutely when they were apart, but she loved her life at the moment. She loved the tranquillity of her family home in Lincolnshire, but the bustle of London excited her. The music and dancing, the nightclubs, the live theatre and then, Brooklands; all were exhilarating and helped to obliterate sombre memories. Although she meant to keep her promise to her future husband, the nearer the day came that she would have to give it all up, the more she clung to the frenetic lifestyle. And then there was the 'Rebecca problem', as she always referred to it. George didn't seem to be making any headway with his daughter's acceptance of his forthcoming marriage at all.

Daisy, Luke and even young Harry were growing up. Each time she went home, Pips could see a subtle change in them. The three of them now went about together all the time, but Pips was unsure whether it was such a good thing.

'She ought to make other friends,' she told Alice.

'They don't spend that much time together,' Alice said. 'Luke works most nights after school at Dad's workshop and even at weekends when they're busy.'

'I was thinking more of Daisy.'

Alice smiled. 'Of course you were. Silly me.'

The two young women smiled at each other. 'I just think it'd be nice for her to have girls as friends, not just Luke and now Harry too. Has she not made any friends at school?'

'A few, I think, but she never asks to have anyone here for tea. Perhaps, when she goes to the high school, she'll make more friends there.'

'I was delighted to hear that Luke got a place at the grammar school. How's he getting on?'

'Very well. He's quite a bright lad, you know.'

'Will Len let him stay on?'

'I very much doubt it. As far as my dad's concerned, Luke's future is settled.'

'What about Daisy?'

'Oh, she'll get to the high school. No problem. She's too clever for her own good.' Alice chuckled. 'Just like her Aunty Pips.' Pips had the grace to smile as Alice went on, 'And don't be too concerned about her closeness to Luke and Harry. It'll all come out in the wash, as Ma always says.'

Thirty-Nine

'Do you have to tag along with us everywhere we go, Harry?' Luke said.

'Oh, leave him alone. He's all right,' Daisy said. 'He hasn't anyone else to play with.'

'Hardly surprising,' Luke said grumpily. 'He's a pain. He always wants his own way.'

But Harry only grinned and linked his arm through Daisy's. 'Daisy likes me, don't you, Dais?'

''Course I do.'

'I'm going to marry you one day, you know.'

'Oh no, you're not,' Luke shot back.

The two brothers glared at each other, but Daisy only laughed. 'I wasn't thinking of marrying anyone just yet. Come on, let's go riding.'

They found Jake cleaning out Samson's stable, whilst the big horse stood tethered to the mounting block in the centre of the yard. The animal harrumphed and tossed his head when he saw the three youngsters.

'Now then, old feller. Do you want a good gallop today?' Daisy said, stroking his nose and producing a carrot from her pocket.

'If you want to ride him, miss, I'll come with you.'

'No need, Jake, we'll be–'

'Oh yes, there is, Miss Daisy. Mrs Maitland'll have my guts for garters if I let you go out on Samson on yar own. To say nothing of what Master Robert and Alice would do to me. And now your Aunty Pips has gone back to London, there's only me to keep an eye on you.'

'I wouldn't want to get you into trouble, Jake, you know that, but we haven't got enough mounts for the four of us. Granny said that Lucky is getting a little old now for us to ride.'

Jake nodded. 'Mrs Maitland has suggested we put him out to pasture.'

Daisy's eyes widened. 'She's not going to sell him, is she?'

'Heavens, no. He'll just live out a very happy retirement here.' Jake grinned. 'But you're wrong about us not having enough for us all to ride. We got another yesterday from Horncastle. A bigger horse for Luke to ride and Harry can have Jingles. The new one's called Napoleon. I've tried him out and he's very well behaved.'

'I aren't having his cast-offs,' Harry said. 'It's bad enough me mam making me wear his hand-me-down clothes. They're half worn out when I get 'em.'

Jake turned to him and said sternly, 'You'll have what you're given and be thankful for it. Not all the village kids have the privilege of being able to ride the horses at the hall. Just remember that.'

Harry was immediately contrite. 'Sorry, Jake. Don't tell the missus, will you?'

Jake grinned, his sharpness with the boy forgotten. ''Course not.'

'But we are family, aren't we?' Harry was not quite ready to capitulate completely. 'Well, sort of.'

'He always has to have the last word,' Luke muttered.

'In a way, I suppose,' Jake said gently now. 'Luke is related to Alice, of course. She's his aunt. And he's your half-brother...'

'More's the pity.'

'Hush, Luke,' Daisy admonished him. 'That's not nice.'

'But you're Sam's son and so not directly re-lated to the Maitland family, but they always treat you just the same as they treat Luke, so they're very fair, wouldn't you say?'

Harry nodded, forced at last to agree.

'I think they've bought this horse so that we can all go riding together with Master Robert when

331

he wants to go. Come on, then,' Jake said. 'I'll get all four saddled up and we'll go for a nice canter. And you, Miss Daisy, no galloping. Not when your Aunty Pips isn't here.'

Daisy pulled a face, but said nothing.

'Now, come and meet Napoleon. I'll ride him today just to see how he shapes up and you can ride Boxer, Luke.'

An hour later the four of them were riding through the fields belonging to the Maitlands' estate.

Suddenly, Daisy kicked her heels and urged Samson into a gallop, leaving the other three behind her.

'The little madam,' Jake muttered and spurred his horse to follow her, but she was halfway across the field and, riding the smaller horse, he had no way of catching her. He held his breath as she neared the hedge on the far side of the field, galloping straight towards it. 'Oh no, Miss Daisy. Please don't...'

She sailed over it, landed the other side and disappeared from their view. Arriving at the point where Samson had jumped, Jake slid from Napoleon's back and ran to the hedge. He dared not set his mount to jump it; he wasn't sure of the new horse's capabilities yet. As he peered over the hedge, the first thing he saw was the horse a short distance away. He'd come to a halt and was pulling at the grass – but there was no Daisy on his back. Jake felt fear flood through him. He couldn't even see her ... then he heard a sound just below him near the hedge.

'Luke, give me a leg up. Daisy's fallen.'

The two boys dismounted and ran to help Jake scramble over the hedge. He dropped down on the other side.

Daisy was sitting on the ground, her head thrown back, and she was roaring with laughter.

'Well, that's brought me off my high horse. Don't say it, Jake. It serves me right.'

Jake had no intention of saying any such thing. He dropped to his knees beside her. 'Oh Miss Daisy. Don't move. Are you hurt?'

'Only my pride, Jake. And probably the biggest bruise you've ever seen on my bum, but no, I'm fine. Nothing broken, I promise.'

'Whatever will your folks say?' he muttered as he helped her to her feet. 'Your gran will likely sack me.'

'You're not to tell them, Jake, else I'll never speak to you again.'

Now he faced an awful dilemma. Somehow, he had to stop Daisy repeating this escapade and yet he didn't want to quarrel with her. But her safety was paramount.

'I'm sorry, Miss, but they'll have to know. I can't risk you doing that again.'

Daisy pulled a face as Luke and Harry arrived beside them.

'Is she all right?'

'Are you hurt?'

'I'm fine, honestly. Don't fuss. Just help me up.'

Jake and Luke stood one on either side of her as she stood up gingerly. Then she nodded again as if to reaffirm her own statement. 'See, I'm fine,' she repeated.

'How are we going to get her over the hedge?'

Harry said.

'No need. There's a gate a few yards down. Harry, go and catch Samson, but just lead him back, mind. I don't want any more accidents.'

They walked slowly along the hedge side, Daisy limping a little, through the gate and back to where the other two horses were chomping grass.

'Come on, let's get you home. Do you want to walk or shall we help you onto Samson?'

Daisy seemed to hesitate and then said, 'I'll ride.'

And then Jake began to worry that she had hurt herself, but wasn't telling him.

Back at the stable yard, Jake tied up the horses and took Daisy to the back door. In the kitchen he said, 'Cook, where's Master Robert?'

'In his consulting room, I think. They've both just finished morning surgery.'

'Come on, Daisy. I'm taking you to him and no arguments, and if you choose not to speak to me again, so be it.'

'What's happened?' Mrs Bentley frowned.

'She took a tumble.'

'Then you're in trouble, Jake, for not looking after her.'

'I know.'

'No, he isn't. It wasn't his fault. I won't have him blamed,' Daisy said. 'But he shouldn't be telling tales.'

'Master's got to know, Miss Daisy.'

Minutes later, Jake, with a tight grip on Daisy's arm, was knocking at the door to Robert's consulting room.

'Come in.' His tone was surprised; he thought

334

he'd seen all the patients. He was even more shocked to see Jake helping Daisy into the room, but before he could ask questions, Daisy said, 'Daddy, it's nothing, honestly. Jake's fussing.'

'I'll be the judge of that. What happened?'

There was silence until, realizing that Daisy wasn't going to say anything, Jake said, 'She took a tumble, Mester Robert. Off Samson.'

'Help her onto the couch, Jake. And would you tap on my father's door and ask him to come in here.'

'Daddy, there's no need...'

'Lie back, Daisy, there's a good girl,' Robert said firmly.

Jake scuttled out of the room, relieved that he wasn't going to be asked any more questions. At least, not for the moment.

'Now, what have you been up to, Daisy my girl?' Edwin asked jovially as he entered the room. 'Nothing broken, I trust?'

'That's what I want to find out, Father, if you'd do the honours.'

Edwin examined his granddaughter carefully. 'No, all in one piece, but did you bang your head?'

'No, Gramps.'

Nevertheless, he checked for any sign of concussion and then pronounced, 'Just a few bruises, but no harm done.' He looked at her quizzically over the top of his spectacles. 'I don't suppose it's any use us asking you not to take any more risks?'

'Not a chance,' Daisy said, grinning as she sat up.

'Just like your Aunty Pips,' Edwin murmured with a smile. 'I couldn't count the times she came into my surgery with cuts and bruises, but she never had any serious injury. Not until...' He had been going to mention her war wound, but decided against reviving disturbing memories for Robert. Instead, he said, 'Well, just be a bit more careful in future, young lady, and not so adventurous. I expect you nearly gave poor Jake a heart attack.'

'Please don't be angry with him. I disobeyed him,' Daisy said, ever truthful. 'He said Granny would have his guts for garters.'

Edwin and Robert glanced at each other and stifled their laughter. Controlling his amusement, Robert tried to say sternly, 'Then you mustn't disobey him again. You're being very unfair on him when he's trying his best to look after you – all of you. You three aren't the easiest youngsters to handle when you all get together.'

Surprisingly, Henrietta didn't blame Jake at all. 'It was Daisy's wilfulness. She's just like Pips used to be.' She sniffed disparagingly. 'And still is, if I'm honest. All this car racing and flying. Next thing, she'll be wanting to take Daisy.'

Henrietta's words were prophetic for the very next time Pips came home she asked, 'Alice, will you let me take Daisy to London during the summer holidays? She's been asking me for ages if she can come and stay with me. And there's so much in London I'd like to show her.'

Alice laughed. 'As long as you don't take her racing, yes. If Robert agrees, of course.'

Pips ran her tongue round her lips. 'Well, no, I hadn't intended to let her drive or even take her round the track, but I'd take her to watch, if that's all right.'

'Of course. That'd be fine.' There was a pause whilst Alice eyed her sister-in-law. 'Out with it, Pips. There's something else, isn't there? I know you too well.'

'We-ell, I would like to take her flying?'

'Is it safe?'

Pips cocked her head on one side. 'Do you think for one instant that I'd put Daisy in danger of any sort?'

'No. Sorry. I should have known better than to ask that.'

'I'll ask Robert, of course.'

Robert didn't need to ask his sister if it was safe; he knew how devoted Pips was to her niece. But it was Henrietta who worried. 'Oh Pips, what if she's airsick? I mean, in those tiny little planes. And you won't be able to help her if she's in a separate seat. What if–'

'Mother, I will only take her up for a very short circuit the first time.'

'The *first* time?' Henrietta almost squeaked. 'It'll be just the once, Philippa. If I had my way, it wouldn't even be that.'

Edwin, however, was more trusting. 'Pips will take good care of her, Hetty, my love, and she's just the right age for her first trip to London.' His eyes twinkled behind his spectacles. 'And for her first flight too.'

Henrietta flapped her hand. 'It seems I am out-voted as usual. Just take good care of her, Pips. She's very precious to all of us.'

'As she is to me, Mother dear.'

'Yes, well, I do know that. But you were always a little wild and I fear Daisy takes after you. I caught her riding Samson again the other day. I was very angry with Jake for allowing it after what happened last time.'

'Please don't blame Jake, Mother,' Robert said. 'He wouldn't have been able to stop her and it's much better that he should be with her than that she should try riding Samson on her own. I doubt she'd be able to saddle him up properly anyway and that *would* be dangerous. You'll have to accept that she is just like Pips in many ways. Certainly in her daring.'

Henrietta sighed with heavy sarcasm as she said, 'Why was I *blessed* with a wayward daughter and now a wilful granddaughter too?'

Robert chuckled. 'I rather think they both take after you in some ways.'

'Nonsense, Robert. I was never so rebellious.'

'Maybe not, but you are strong-willed. You couldn't run this estate the way you do so magnificently if you weren't. I don't wish to sound morbid, but I'm almost hoping that the estate will bypass me and go straight to Daisy.'

'I'm hardly in my dotage yet, Robert,' Henrietta said with asperity, then, softening, she moved to his side and put her hand on his shoulder. 'Whatever happens, the estate will be in safe hands, I know that.'

'So, may I take her flying, Robert?'

'Of course, Pips.'

Forty

Daisy was ecstatic. She clapped her hands. 'Are we to stay in a grand hotel?'

'No, Milly has said you can stay with us at her flat.'

'Oh, how lovely. I do like Milly. She is such fun. Will she teach me the Charleston?'

'I expect so, if you ask her. We may be able to take you to a *thé dansant*.'

'What's that?'

'It's dancing, but at tea time, so I think you'd be able to go.'

'But I haven't got a pretty dress. Mummy would make me one, I know, but there isn't time.'

'Then, my darling,' Pips said, hugging her niece, 'we shall buy you one from Selfridges.'

When the school holidays began, Pips travelled to Lincolnshire by train to fetch Daisy.

'I'm sorry I'm not in my car,' she explained. 'It needed some repairs in time for my next race. But I'll bring you home in it, I promise.'

Daisy was to stay for a week.

'I will miss you,' Luke said forlornly. 'Be sure to send me a postcard.'

It wasn't Daisy's first trip on a train but it was the first time she'd been to stay in London. She was so excited that she could scarcely keep still in her seat. Luckily, the other passengers smiled indulgently at the girl's exuberance but when she stepped off the train in the city, Daisy fell silent, gazing around her with wide eyes in awe of the bustling streets and the tall buildings that almost shut out the sky.

'Don't be frightened, darling,' Pips said, taking her hand, but Daisy only laughed.

'Oh I'm not frightened, Aunty Pips. I just can't take it all in at once. But it's wonderful, isn't it? So – so alive.'

They took a taxi to Milly's flat so that Daisy could see all the sights. She soon engaged the friendly driver in conversation and he was delighted to point out all the places of interest in his cockney accent. He reminded Pips so much of the two Enderby brothers. Their cheerful humour had been a tonic in difficult times.

'Here we are,' she said, as the cab drew up outside the block of flats.

'Thank you for telling me about London,' Daisy said politely as she climbed out. 'I hope I see you again.'

'It's a bit doubtful, miss. There're a lot of us taxi drivers and London's a big place, but whoever you get, you just ask 'em what you want to know. We're a friendly bunch.'

'I will.' Daisy beamed.

'Darling!' Milly threw her arms wide and Daisy succumbed to her bear hug with amused grace. 'Hello, Aunty Milly. It's kind of you to have me to stay.'

'It's our pleasure, darling. Now, come along, let me take your suitcase. I've put up a little bed for you in your aunty's room. I hope you'll be comfortable.'

It had been agreed between the two women that neither George nor Paul would come to stay whilst Daisy was there, though they would both join them on outings.

'I'm sure I will,' Daisy said. 'I sleep like a top, but I do have a favour to ask.'

'Anything, darling. What is it?'

'Will you teach me the Charleston, please?'

'Of *course* I will.'

'Aunty Pips said I might be allowed to go to a tea dance with you.'

Milly clapped her hands. 'What a perfectly lovely idea. We'll teach you one or two dances and then we'll take you. We'll get Paul to come too.' She glanced at Pips. 'And George, if he wants to, though he doesn't dance much.'

'Is Paul your boyfriend?'

'Well, I suppose so. I have lots of friends who are boys but they're not boyfriends. But Paul is rather – special.'

Daisy nodded knowingly. 'Like Luke and me. He's my best friend. And then there's Harry. He's always tagging along with us. He's only six and he's a pain.'

'Poor Harry,' Pips said. 'I expect he feels left out. I hope you're not unkind to him.'

'No, Aunty Pips. We tolerate him.'

The two women glanced at each other and smothered their smiles.

The rest of Daisy's first day in the capital was taken up with learning to dance.

'Lady B is organizing a tea dance at her house on Sunday,' Milly said, 'we'll take her to that.'

'That'll fit in nicely because I've arranged to take

her to the race meeting on Monday and then for a flight on Tuesday, if it's OK with Mitch.'

'I'd be most surprised if it wasn't,' Milly said casually.

'Now, now,' Pips said softly.

Paul and George were both there at the tea dance and made sure that Daisy danced every dance. Paul danced the Charleston with her and George took her around the floor in a sedate waltz. One or two other gentlemen asked her to dance too, so that by the end, the girl was pink faced with exertion and delight.

'You've really got the hang of the Charleston,' Paul told her. 'You swivel as if you've been doing it for years.'

'I had a good teacher,' Daisy said modestly. 'Aunty Milly.'

Gallantly, Paul kissed her hand. 'I'll see you at the race.' And knowing very well that she wouldn't be, he asked facetiously, 'Are you driving?'

Daisy giggled. 'I wish, but no, not yet.'

Paul laughed aloud. 'I like the "not yet" bit. Want to follow in your aunt's footsteps – or rather her wheels?'

Quite seriously, Daisy nodded. 'Oh yes, I want to be just like her.'

'You stand with me,' Milly said on the Monday when they arrived at the racetrack and climbed up Members' Hill. 'We'll get a good view from here of Pips winning.'

'D'you think she will?'

'I hope so, but she's got some stiff opposition

today. Both Muriel and Pattie are racing and though we're all friends, it's gloves off on the racetrack.'

Pips was entered in two races that day. She came third in the first race behind Muriel and Pattie, but won the second. Daisy jumped up and down and clapped. 'Oh I must write to Daddy tonight and tell him.' She turned to Milly. 'Do you know where I could buy some postcards? I promised to send Luke one.'

'Of course, we'll buy some on the way home, if we can find a shop that's still open. We're some-times a bit late leaving.' She leaned closer and whispered, 'We all meet in the clubhouse after-wards and it can go on a bit.'

'Will I be allowed in there?'

'I expect so. You'll want to get a few cards, though, won't you? You mustn't forget to send one to Harry too.'

Daisy pulled a face. 'No, I mustn't forget Harry.'

The following day, they met up with Paul and Jeff at the circuit, but this time it was to go flying.

'Is Uncle George coming today?'

Pips shook her head. 'No, his daughter's not on duty today, so he's having lunch with her.'

Daisy pouted for a moment. She liked George. He always treated her as if she were a grown-up. She was about to ask why they weren't both com-ing to the race meeting when a voice sounded behind her. 'Well, well, well. Who's this charming young lady? You must introduce us to her, Pips.'

Daisy turned to find herself looking into the face of a very handsome man with raven-black hair and dark brown eyes. And when he laughed, his eyes twinkled with merriment. And then she spotted a boy of about her own age standing just behind him. It must be his son, she thought, because he was just like him.

'And why would I want to do that, Mitch Hammond? I try to keep her away from bad influences.'

Mitch put his hand on his heart. 'Oh, the hurt. She wounds me deeply. But, you know, I can guess who you are. You're the famous Daisy. And this,' he stepped aside and gestured towards the boy with him, 'is my nephew, Johnny.'

The two youngsters stared at each other, whilst Pips said, 'I didn't know you had a nephew.'

Mitch moved a little away from the boy and murmured, 'He's my brother's son. An only child. My brother was killed in the war and I try to take him out now and again. His mother is seeing someone else now. Can't blame her for that – and I don't – but the new boyfriend and Johnny don't exactly get on.'

'Mitch – I'm sorry. I...'

'Oh, don't go soft on me, Pips. It won't do my reputation any good.'

Pips smiled, but couldn't help thinking she was seeing a different side to Mitch Hammond. They turned to walk towards the aircraft that awaited Pips and Daisy, the two youngsters falling into step alongside each other, whilst Pips and Mitch led the way.

'We'll wait until you've taken off, but I'm taking Johnny up today.'

'His first time?'

'Heavens, no. He's been up several times. Absolutely loves it. He intends to join the RAF when he's old enough. And Daisy?'

'Her first time.'

'She'll love it,' Mitch said confidently.

'I hope so.'

Only minutes later, Daisy, suitably dressed, was marching purposefully towards the aircraft, whilst beside her, Pips gave her some last few instructions. Daisy nodded, her eyes gleaming with excitement. All she murmured as she climbed in was, 'I wish Luke was here to see me flying.'

As Pips had promised, they only stayed up a few minutes for this first flight, but when they landed, came to a halt and climbed out, Daisy's face was glowing.

'Oh Aunty Pips – that was fantastic. So thrilling. How old do I have to be to learn to fly?'

Johnny came running across the grass towards them. He was about to ask how she'd enjoyed it, but there was no need; he could read the answer on her face. He smiled at her, that same saucy grin that his uncle had, his eyes crinkling. Behind him, Mitch sauntered up.

'Well, I see we have another would-be flyer in the family, then?'

'Oh Mr Hammond, that was glorious.'

'Hey, none of this "Mr Hammond" nonsense. It's Mitch – or, if your aunt really insists, I'll be an honorary uncle.'

'Uncle Mitch it is, then. I was just asking Aunty Pips how old I have to be to take lessons.'

Mitch frowned. 'It would be a bit difficult to learn here, wouldn't it?'

'Oh, there's an airfield in Lincolnshire not far

from us,' Daisy said, not to be thwarted. 'I'll find out if they give lessons. I bet Luke would like it too, Aunty Pips, don't you think?'

Pips laughed. 'But I'm not sure his grandfather would allow it.'

'Then we won't tell him.'

'Oh now, you know I couldn't condone deceit, Daisy.' Pips's tone was stern and Daisy immediately pretended contrition, but she dropped her head to hide the gleam in her eyes.

As the two youngsters followed Pips and Mitch back across the field, Johnny said, 'Who's this Luke, then?'

'My cousin on my mother's side. We've been friends all our lives.'

'Oh, that's all right, then. How old is he?'

'Twelve.'

'Same age as me.'

'His dad was killed on the Somme.'

For a moment Johnny's face was bleak. 'My dad was in the Royal Flying Corps, as it was then, like Uncle Mitch. It's the RAF now, of course. He was killed doing reconnaissance over enemy trenches. Just like Uncle Mitch might have been, if it hadn't been for your aunt.'

Daisy stopped and turned to face him. 'What d'you mean?'

Johnny stopped too. 'Don't you know?'

When Daisy shook her head, he went on, 'He did the same thing in the RFC as my dad – taking aerial photos of our lines as well as the enemy's. He crash-landed in no-man's-land and it was your aunty Pips and another man called William something, who rescued him. Your aunt got shot in the leg, but she saved his life – and his precious photos.'

Daisy glanced at the two adults in front of her. 'I never knew,' she murmured. After a moment they walked on. 'I wouldn't have thought that a woman would have been allowed into the front-line trenches, never mind going into no-man's-land.'

Johnny laughed loudly. 'They weren't – officially – but I wouldn't think that ever bothered your aunt, do you?'

Daisy shook her head, her gaze still on Pips. 'The other person – the man? You said his name was William something. Was it Dawson?'

Johnny wrinkled his forehead. 'Yes, I think it was.'

'Then that's my uncle.'

'The one that was killed? Luke's dad?'

'No, that was Harold. There were four brothers and a sister – my mum – in the family. William joined the flying ambulance corps with my mum and Aunty Pips as a stretcher bearer. He survived the war, but he married a Belgian nurse and lives out there now. The other three didn't come back.'

Johnny opened his mouth to ask yet more questions, but at that moment, Mitch turned back towards him. 'Right, young man. Are you ready for your trip? And be warned, I'm going to loop the loop with you today.'

If he'd hoped to make the boy nervous, he failed because Johnny only grinned. As he followed Mitch, he glanced back. 'See you again, Daisy.'

Forty-One

When Pips came home in April the following year, Henrietta greeted her, 'I'm glad you're home this weekend for your father's birthday. I want to have a family conference.'

For a moment, Pips looked alarmed. 'There's nothing wrong, is there, Mother?'

'No, and I don't want there to be, but he is sixty-nine on Sunday, Pips, and I really think it's time he retired fully. I know he's only been working part time for the past few years, helping with things that Robert can't manage, but...'

'Does he want to retire?'

'I haven't asked him.'

Pips smiled. That was so typical of her mother, but this was one occasion she couldn't argue with her. Edwin was beginning to look a little old and they all wanted him to enjoy a long and well-earned retirement. They certainly didn't want him to die 'in harness'.

'So, what are you suggesting should happen to the practice?'

Henrietta sighed. 'Robert isn't – and if I'm honest, never has been – interested in running the estate. He's never made a secret of the fact that he'd like it if I can hang on long enough for Daisy to take over.' She arched her eyebrows. 'Unless, of course, you'd be willing to come home and oversee it until Daisy comes of age?'

348

Pips hesitated. 'Only if it was necessary.' Then she grinned. 'I wouldn't worry, Mother, you'll probably outlive us all.' There was a pause before she added, 'So what are you proposing?'

'That Robert becomes head of the practice and that we should get another doctor to assist him like Sam Nuttall suggested some time ago, if you remember?'

Pips nodded. 'I do remember. It was on the first Armistice Day, wasn't it? I thought then what a good idea it was, but we never seemed to get round to doing it. Would you employ someone full-time now?'

'Yes, I think so. Dr Moses retired three years ago and his practice was absorbed into ours, so now we have a great many more patients than we used to have. That's why I'm anxious about your father.'

'Ah, I see. I remember you telling me at the time, but I hadn't realized quite what an effect it would have on Father and Robert.'

Henrietta forbore to say that Pips, although she visited frequently, wasn't always aware of exactly what was happening at home. But Henrietta didn't blame her daughter. There was nothing for Pips to do here and she seemed happy enough in London, though Henrietta was disappointed that the marriage between her daughter and the major was such a long time in coming.

'Have you anyone in mind?'

Henrietta shook her head. 'I haven't broached the subject with them yet. Philippa, I need your support. Do I have it? I know we don't always agree, but on this occasion...'

'Of course you have, Mother.'

'And there's something else too, whilst you're home. We must really start planning your wedding. You seem to me to be putting it off. I hope you're not having second thoughts.'

'No, Mother, I'm not, though it just seems to be galloping towards me. But yes, you're right. We should start thinking about it.'

'Not just "thinking", Philippa. We need to get the church booked. You're thirty-five this year and if you plan to have children, then you shouldn't leave it too long.'

For a moment, Pips's face was bleak. This was something she could not discuss with anyone and certainly not her mother. Only George knew and they hardly ever talked about it. During their times together, they never took precautions against her becoming pregnant. Pips knew that if she should find herself 'with child', George would marry her in an instant. But it hadn't happened and Pips feared that perhaps it never would.

But she could not tell her mother this; the subject was too delicate.

After dinner that evening when the family retired to the Brown Parlour and Daisy had gone to bed, Henrietta poured coffee whilst Pips handed around the cups.

'There's something I would like us to discuss as a family. Edwin, I'll be blunt.'

'When were you ever not, Hetty my love?' he said mildly, a small smile on his mouth as if he rather knew what was coming.

Henrietta had the grace to smile. 'Edwin, you are sixty-nine on Sunday. I think you should think about retiring and that we should get another doctor to work with Robert.' She glanced at her son. 'I presume you'd have no objection?'

'I've been thinking along much the same lines, Mother, but I felt it wasn't my place to suggest it. What do you think, Father?'

Edwin was quiet for a moment, perhaps struggling with the thought that his working life and maybe, in his mind, his usefulness, would be over, said slowly, 'On one condition.' He paused as his family all looked at him. 'That your mother and I go travelling. There are places in this country – and abroad – that I would like to see while we are both still active and in good health.'

Henrietta beamed. 'Edwin, that's a splendid idea. Why didn't I think of that?'

'Wouldn't you worry about the estate in your absence?'

'Not particularly. Since we decided to employ a farm manager, the day-to-day running is much less onerous on me. Besides, Robert and Alice would always be here.'

'That's settled, then. We'll start advertising for a doctor to join us.'

'Well, that was easier than we expected,' Pips said softly to her mother as they retired for the night, walking up the staircase side by side. 'You didn't even need me.'

'Just so long as he sticks to it,' Henrietta said.

There were several applications for the vacancy.

'Father, I like the look of this one,' Robert said, handing the candidate's letter across Edwin's desk. 'Could we interview him?'

351

'Of course, and I've picked out two more. They're rather young, but that might not be a bad thing.'

'The one I favour – although I do agree with your choices too – was in the war.'

'As a medical officer?'

Robert nodded. 'A very young one. Rather like me, he went out there as soon as he qualified. Of course, I need to meet him, but I think we might get on very well together. With our shared experiences out there, we'd understand each other.'

'As long as you don't think it would be too much of a reminder.'

Robert grimaced. 'Sadly, Father, the memories are always there. And it might help us both to have someone else who knows what it was like. I can't always burden Alice – or even Pips.'

'Was he wounded?'

'In the leg, but he says it has healed well and, also, he can drive, which is a bonus.'

Edwin scanned the letter. 'I see he's married, but no children yet.'

'So are the other two you picked out – though one of them has a family. I wondered if Mother could find a little cottage for whoever we appoint.'

'I'm sure that won't be too difficult. Right, then, we'll write to these three and invite them for interview.'

The interviews took place a week later and both Edwin and Robert saw all three in turn. The applicant Robert had picked out, Conrad Everton, was a year older than he was and had served with the Red Cross in the war. He was tall and thin, with fair hair and hazel eyes. He limped slightly from an injury from a sniper's bullet, sustained whilst helping to bring in wounded from the trenches.

'I shouldn't have been there, of course, but I'm sure you know how it was.'

'I do indeed,' Robert said with feeling. 'I lost my arm for the very same reason.'

'Do you regret it?' Conrad asked, bluntly.

Robert grinned. He liked the other man's straightforward attitude. He would fit in well with the villagers, people who 'called a spade a spade'.

'Being injured, yes, but not what I was doing at the time.'

Conrad nodded.

'Have you any questions?'

'Only one. How do you wish it to work?' He nodded towards Robert's empty sleeve without a hint of embarrassment.

'You would have to undertake any physical examinations that I can't manage, but I'm a very good listener to people's problems and I can still do certain things, like sound people's chests. And I have learned to write with my left hand. My wife, Alice, has learned to make up prescriptions under my guidance, although you could help out there too, if you would.'

'Understood. My wife was a Red Cross nurse at the front. That's how we met. Since then she's trained as a midwife so she would always be willing to lend a hand if needed, I know. And home visits?'

'We can share those. We have a young man who's worked for us for many years – Jake. He drives me around and will continue to do so. You have a small car, I understand from your letter, so you wouldn't need a driver. Is that correct?' When Conrad nodded, Robert asked, 'Anything else?'

'I don't think so.'

'As you know, we've interviewed three people today. We've both seen each of you, so now my father and I need to confer. I see from your letter that you are on the telephone, so we will let you know our decision as soon as possible.'

Robert stood up and held out his left hand. 'Thank you for coming.' He was on the verge of saying, 'I'll see you soon', but knew he mustn't give the young man any false hopes. Perhaps his father would not agree, but Robert hoped that he, too, would prefer Conrad out of the three men.

'Well, for me,' Edwin said, as they sat together after the three candidates had left, 'it's the young man you picked out. Conrad Everton.'

'I'm delighted, Father, because he's the one I really want. The other two were fine candidates, but there was just something about Conrad. He has a dry sense of humour and wasn't afraid to speak his mind. I liked that. And as he has been in the war, I think the villagers will take to him and he will understand them too.'

'I agree. We'll give him time to reach home and I'll telephone him this evening. Now, let's go and give your mother the good news.'

'And I'll write to Pips tonight and tell her too – provided he accepts our offer.'

'Oh, I asked each one of them,' Edwin said, 'whether, if they were offered the post, they would accept. They all said "yes".'

Forty-Two

'Now, there's someone I really want you to meet,' Edwin said as he drove Conrad around the village on his second morning. He had taken up the post a month after the interview and he and his wife, Florence, had moved into a cottage on the estate. Florence was an energetic young woman, with dark hair, brown eyes and a ready smile.

'Mrs Dawson senior,' Edwin explained, 'always known as "Ma", has never been quite sure of her age, but she must be in her mid-nineties by now. She was born in the days when a year or so was added onto a child's age when they were ten or eleven, so that they reached working age all the quicker.'

'Really? I hadn't heard that before.'

'Oh yes, it was quite common.'

'But wasn't their birth registered?'

'Not officially until 1837, and many slipped through the net even after it became law. And unless a child was sickly, they weren't necessarily baptized until they were a few months old. If at all.' Edwin halted the car not far from the Dawsons' cottage. 'That's her, sitting in the sunshine with her clay pipe. Winter and summer she sits out here for a short time each day – longer, when the weather's fine. Before we meet her, I must tell you a little about the family...'

Edwin went on to explain the Dawsons' family

history to the newcomer, ending, 'William – like you – fell in love with a nurse out there, a Belgian girl, and made his home in her country. Besides helping Brigitta's grandfather to run their farm, he now tends the local war cemeteries.'

'And he's never come back. Not even to visit?'

'His father disowned him at the time and has never relented. But it's Ma and Norah I feel for. They've as good as lost William too. I just wanted you to know the family's background before you meet them.'

'Thank you. It is helpful.' He smiled. 'Even if it's only so that I don't put my size tens right in it.'

They climbed out of the car and walked the short distance to where Ma was seated.

'Nah then, Dr Maitland. Come to show us the young man who's tekin' over from you, have you?' She nodded towards Conrad. 'We've heard all about you, young feller. The village grapevine, in the shape of Bess Cooper, has been busy.' She gave a toothless grin and cackled with laughter at her own joke.

Edwin sat down beside the old lady. 'Will he do, then, Ma?'

She squinted up at the newcomer. 'From what I hear, doctor, he'll do very nicely. Be a good companion to Master Robert, I reckon. Pleased to meet you, young feller.'

Conrad held out his hand. 'And I'm very pleased to meet you, Mrs Dawson.'

'Nah then, none of that "Mrs Dawson". I ain't been called that in years. It's "Ma" to everyone. Mrs Dawson's me daughter-in-law, Norah. Ah, now here she comes with a tray of tea.' She laughed again. 'Funny how the teapot allus comes out the minute we have visitors. Now, sit down and tell me all about yourself, at least the bits that Bess Cooper couldn't find out.'

The four of them sat in the sunshine for almost an hour with Ma reminiscing and filling Conrad in on all the locals.

'Well,' Edwin said as they climbed back into his car and headed for home, 'you've made a conquest there. She's taken to you and the rest of them will follow her lead like lambs.'

'She's a wonderful old lady. I hope she'll be around for a few more years yet.'

'So, Philippa, I presume you're going to vote in the forthcoming election?' Granny Fortesque's mouth twitched and her eyes sparkled with mischief. 'The one they're calling the "Flapper Election", because of all the women who will be voting for the first time.'

'I most certainly will be.'

'And for whom will you be voting?'

'Mama,' Henry interrupted from the end of the dinner table, 'you really mustn't ask anyone their politics.'

'Of course I must. I need to know that Philippa is going to cast her precious vote – which has been hard won by some very gallant women, I might add – sensibly. If she is not, then I shall seek to instruct her.'

Sitting beside Pips, Milly giggled. 'Darling Granny, no one *instructs* Pips to do anything. They couldn't even stop her going into no-man's-land

357

in the war, so I'm afraid she's not going to take a scrap of notice of you.'

'That was different.' The older woman bridled. 'She was saving lives. This is hardly in the same category.'

'Actually, Granny Fortesque, I'm not even sure yet,' Pips said. 'I'm reading the manifestos of all the three main parties and then I shall decide. But vote I certainly will. You can be sure of that.'

'Mm.' Granny Fortesque tried to purse her lips and appear disapproving, but she failed miserably and everyone around the table ended up laughing together.

Pips did not tell anyone what she voted, not George, not even Robert, though they both tried to prise it out of her, but she scoured the newspapers after the election to analyse the results for herself.

'It's what they call a hung parliament,' Robert explained.

'Mm, I know,' she murmured, only half listening.

'Ramsay MacDonald's Labour Party has won the most seats, but he has not got an overall majority. David Lloyd George's Liberal Party will hold the balance of power.'

'Oh well, I don't doubt, they'll soon call another one,' Pips said, folding the newspaper. 'Now, where's Daisy? I want to go riding.'

'Milly, will you come to Lincolnshire with me next weekend? I have something very important to ask Alice and I may need your help.'

Milly's eyes widened. 'Of course. Am I allowed to know what you're going to ask her?'

Pips smiled. 'You'll see.'

'Is George coming?'

Pips shook her head. 'I don't want him there this time.'

Milly's mouth formed a round 'O'. 'Then I think I can guess what this is about.'

They travelled north together in Pips's car, Milly tying a silk scarf firmly around her hat.

'It's wonderful to see you all again,' she said as she hugged each member of the family in turn.

'It's lovely to see you too, my dear,' Henrietta said. 'You don't visit us nearly often enough. I expect the country is too boring for you.'

'Oh no, please don't say that. I love it here, but this time we're on a special mission.'

'And what might that be?'

Milly's eyes were full of mischief. 'I'm not supposed to know, but I think I've guessed.' She leaned closer to Henrietta and whispered, 'I think it's to do with wedding outfits – and Alice.'

'Ah! Then I think I can guess too. I'll give my husband the tip that we ladies might need a little longer in the parlour on our own after dinner. Would that be a good idea, do you think?'

'Perfect, Mrs Maitland. I've brought some pictures to give Pips some ideas, though maybe she won't need them. Maybe she has her own ideas.'

Henrietta laughed. 'Pips has never been very interested in clothes. She'd sooner be riding – or driving.' She patted Milly's hand. 'But with your help, we'll find something just right for her.'

When the four women were sitting together over their coffee, Pips turned to her sister-in-law.

'Alice, please would you make my wedding dress for me?'

Alice gaped at her. 'Oh Pips, I'd love to, but I – I couldn't. I wouldn't be good enough.'

'Nonsense, Alice,' Henrietta said. 'You make most of Daisy's clothes and your own and some of mine, so let's have no false modesty. Besides, Rosemary Fieldsend has a wonderful dressmaker in Lincoln. I'm sure you could always go to her for advice, but I don't think you'll need it.'

'Oh, but Mother, a *wedding* dress!'

'I've brought some pictures to show you all,' Milly said. 'At least have a look. I thought this one would suit Pips perfectly.' She giggled and glanced at Henrietta. 'And you'll be pleased to see, Mrs Maitland, that the hems have dropped again to a discreet ankle length.'

'Thank goodness for that. And the dropped waists have gone too, I see. I never did like them. It made women look such a peculiar shape. What do you think, Pips?'

Pips studied the pictures. 'I like that one,' she said, pointing. 'Do you think you could have a go at that, Alice?'

Alice bit her lip. 'Well, just so long as, if it doesn't work out and you're not happy with it, you'll tell me.'

'I promise,' Pips said.

Now Alice beamed. 'Then I'd love to make your wedding dress, Pips.'

'You'll need some white satin shoes,' Milly said. 'And a veil. Oh darling, just look at this picture of a pearl headdress.' It was like a close-fitting cloche hat decorated with pearls, but with a waist-length veil. 'You'd look absolutely beautiful in it.'

'And would you be able to make a bridesmaid's dress for Daisy?'

'Actually,' Alice said shyly, 'I had already wondered about offering to do that, but I hadn't even thought about making *your* dress.'

'What's her favourite colour?'

'Rose-pink.'

'Perfect,' Milly said, and she clapped her hands.

'This is going to be a catastrophe,' Robert said, prodding the newspaper.

Pips was at home for a fitting of her wedding dress, which was always done in the utmost secrecy. No one else, not even Henrietta, had seen the results, for Alice had insisted working in a room away from the main part of the house and she always kept the door locked. 'No one else but Pips and me must see it before her big day,' she had decreed firmly.

But, this morning, they were all sitting in the Brown Parlour having morning coffee and biscuits. Conrad was always included now. It was a brief oasis in the day for the two doctors to relax and yet to compare notes if they needed to do so. And even to involve Edwin, if they felt they needed his advice. Pips had taken to Conrad on sight and had liked his wife just as much.

'She'll be such an asset,' she'd said. 'A friend for Alice and a midwife for the area. No more of these unqualified village women with their unhygienic ways, thinking they're indispensable.'

361

As Pips had predicted, Alice and Florence soon became firm friends. They shared confidences that Alice did not feel able to share with her mother-in-law or indeed with her own family. And Florence, new to the area though she was, knew she had to keep her counsel amongst her husband's patients. Gossip was not in Florence's nature, but she valued Alice's quiet friendship.

'What is?' Pips asked her brother as he rattled the newspaper, turning the pages impatiently.

'This Wall Street crash in America.'

Pips frowned, set her cup down on the low table, and went to stand behind her brother's shoulder to read the articles.

'There was a bit of a panic last Thursday when some companies revealed disappointing results, following which, investors decided to sell their shares. At that stage, financiers tried to prop up prices by buying, but by last Tuesday, the twenty-ninth of October – Black Tuesday, they're calling it – share prices fell by forty billion dollars in one day.'

'What! That's impossible, surely?'

''Fraid not,' Robert said gloomily.

'But how has such a situation been allowed to develop?' Henrietta asked.

'There's been a boom through the twenties and it appears to me – though I have to admit I'm not an expert on this – that shares had an inflated value.'

'It won't affect Britain, will it?'

'Not immediately, perhaps, but I think it will have a knock-on effect in time. Maybe the whole of Europe too, eventually. Much of our trade is linked to America. And, of course, anyone with investments in America will feel it straight away.'

'Oh my,' Pips breathed. 'I think George has a lot of his money tied up in American companies.'

Robert and Pips exchanged an anxious glance.

Forty-Three

'Well, Daddy, I expect you won't see m'lady for dust now.'

George stared at his daughter and then a bleak expression came into his eyes as he realized exactly what she was implying. Slowly, he said, 'I shall of course give her the option of ending our engagement, even though the wedding is only a few weeks away now.'

'Oh, she'll cancel, as sure as eggs is eggs. Or her parents will. They won't want their daughter tied to an old man with no money to keep her in the manner to which she is obviously accustomed.'

George glanced away, hurt beyond words to see the smug expression on Rebecca's face. He could tell that she wasn't bothered at all that he'd lost his money, only that it served her purpose in separating him from Pips.

She crossed the room and put her arm around him. 'Don't look so forlorn, darling Daddy. You can sell the house in Yorkshire and come and live here. The apartment is paid for, isn't it? And I'm earning enough to pay the bills.'

George eyed her sceptically. 'My dear girl, my

363

father had a saying, "you don't see the chickens scratching for the old hen". It really wouldn't be right for me to be living off you. Besides, one day, you might want to get married.'

Rebecca pulled a face and said wryly, 'Hardly likely, Daddy, is it?'

'But you're a pretty girl...'

She shook her head. 'That makes no difference. There just aren't enough men of my age to go around now. No, I'll be quite content to continue with my career as a nurse and to care for you. Maybe I'll end up as a matron one day. Who knows?'

George smiled thinly, but the worry never left his eyes. He didn't know how on earth he was going to broach this subject with Pips.

Making a decision, he said, 'Well, I'm not quite bankrupt yet. I'll go up to Lincolnshire and see Pips at the weekend.'

'George!' Pips's face lit up as he was shown into the Brown Parlour, where she was sitting with her mother finalizing the details of her wedding day – 7 December. She jumped up and went towards him, her arms outstretched. He took her hands in his and kissed her on both cheeks.

He shook hands with Henrietta and smiled down at her, but the smile never reached his eyes. Henrietta, quick to notice, rose and said, 'I'll leave you to it, then. We can talk again later, Pips. Have you eaten, George?'

'Yes, thank you.'

'Then I'll have tea brought in for you both and I'll see you at dinner.'

As her mother left the room, Pips wound her arms round George's waist and lifted her face to be kissed properly. Though he kissed her, it was not with the same ardour that she was used to. She pulled back and looked up into his face. 'What is it? What's wrong?'

George sighed heavily. 'Sit down, my dear. We must talk.'

'George – darling – you're frightening me.'

'There's no easy way to say this, my love, but I have to release you from our engagement.'

Pips's eyes widened and then narrowed suspiciously. 'You've met someone else?'

George was actually able to laugh at the absurdity of such a thought, but he knew in a moment why Pips would think that. She had been hurt before. 'Heavens, no! I love you with all my heart, Pips, and I always will. You must know that.'

'Well, I thought I did, but – then why?'

'I've lost almost all my money.'

'In the Wall Street crash, you mean?'

He nodded. 'Do you remember me telling you that at the time I received my promotion, I was posted to join our troops launching a counter-attack alongside the French and the Americans?'

Pips nodded.

'I became great friends with an American officer. His father was a stockbroker – a reputable one, I might add – in New York. On Wall Street.'

'Oh dear. I think I know where this is heading. Go on.'

'He survived the war and when he went back home, he joined his father's firm. We kept in touch and he offered to handle my financial

365

affairs, if I should think of investing in American stocks and shares. Pips, through the twenties, America has experienced a boom. I have made a lot of money through his sound advice. I was paid handsome dividends. Some of it I used to supplement my other income, but most of it I ploughed back into shares. So, I suppose, you can guess what's happened now. I've lost almost all my money.'

'George,' she gripped his hands. 'I'm so sorry, but why should that affect us getting married?'

'I can't support you in the way you've – er – been used to.'

Pips frowned. 'But my income's quite safe. We, as a family, don't have investments in stocks and shares. Everything we have is tied up in the estate and that's how we make a living for all of us. Well, most of it, anyway. Until recently, Father still insisted on running his practice, but that's always been more because he wanted to rather than because he had to. And now that Robert runs it, it's still part of our overall income.'

'And you think I'm the sort of man who would be happy to live off his wife?' George said stiffly.

Pips stared at him. 'When you put it like that, no, I don't, but you see, I'm one of these irritating modern women who thinks that a husband and wife should be equal partners in a marriage. What's yours is mine and what's mine is yours.'

'I don't think that your parents – or your brother – would see it that way.'

'Then we'll ask them,' Pips said simply.

As the family, apart from Daisy, sat down for

366

dinner, George was nervous – more nervous than he'd ever been in his life. Leading his troops 'over the top' had never been as frightening as this.

As forthright as ever, Pips came straight to the point. 'George has offered to release me from our engagement because he has lost most of his investments in the Wall Street crash.'

'Oh dear,' Henrietta said, glancing anxiously from one to another and then turning to Edwin. For once in her life she was at a loss as to what to say.

But it was Robert who took the lead. 'I'm sorry to hear that, old chap – about your finances, I mean, but why would that mean you can't marry Pips?'

'I won't be able to support her in the manner in which I would wish to do,' George said stiffly.

'Is that the only reason you're asking to be released from your promise?'

'Of course it is.'

Robert nodded. 'I respect and admire you for that, but if this had occurred *after* you were married, you wouldn't have abandoned her, would you?'

'Of course not, but that isn't the case.'

'So, in true army fashion, you're falling on your sword, are you?'

George had the grace to smile. 'Something like that, I suppose.'

'I don't know what our parents think,' Robert said, glancing at them both, 'but I think this is a load of nonsense. You've been together for several years and it's high time you were married and Pips settled down.'

367

'What d'you mean, "settled down"?'

'Stop all this daredevil stuff. Poor Mother has kittens every time she knows you're racing or flying.'

'Oh phooey!' Pips said, making them all smile – even George. 'I've already promised to give up motor racing, though not the flying, and George has agreed to that.'

Robert chuckled. 'I don't suppose you gave him much choice, did you? And, if I'm not much mistaken, we have another member of the family following in your footsteps. Daisy already rides her pony like the wind – and Samson, when she can. Even Jake can't keep up with her. Anyway, enough of that for the moment.' He turned to Edwin. 'What d'you say, Father, about George's problems?'

Edwin glanced at his wife before smiling and saying, 'Well, apart from the little bit of money that my practice brought in, I've been a "kept man" all these years.'

'Oh Edwin, nothing of the sort. Everything we have is *ours*, not mine.'

'Exactly!' Pips said triumphantly, as Edwin touched his wife's hand and said, 'I know, my dear, but perhaps George doesn't see it that way.'

Henrietta turned towards George and said spiritedly, 'Well, he should. Tell us just how bad things are. Have you nowhere to live?'

'I have the apartment in London, but my daughter classes that as her home when she's off duty.'

'That's understandable,' Henrietta murmured. The family knew all about Rebecca's animosity towards her father's marriage to Pips, but they were too courteous to allude to it. 'Have you any other property?'

'A house near York which I can sell, though I don't think I'll get its true value in this climate.'

Edwin cleared his throat. 'Have you actually sold any of your shares yet?'

George shook his head. 'No, not yet, but...'

'Then don't be too hasty, at least not with the companies that are still in business. You won't receive dividends for some time, probably, but surely things will recover eventually – apart, of course, from companies that have actually gone bankrupt. You can't do anything about them. Take advice from your stockbroker in America. If you trust him, that is.'

'Oh, I do. None of this is his fault. It seems that he was trying to get in touch with me after the twenty-fourth, when the panic first started, to discuss what I wanted him to do, but was unable to do so.'

'Since the war,' Robert put in, 'I've dabbled a bit in the stock market. Oh, not in a big way, but just to give myself an interest. Something to do, you know. But if you'd like a second opinion...' He smiled at the allusion to his own profession. 'I have a very good stockbroker, if you'd like to talk to him.'

George glanced around the table. He still wasn't sure what their answer was. 'So...?'

'I think what we're saying, old chap,' Robert said, 'is that it's all up to Pips. She's the one marrying you, but we'll support her – and you – in whatever decision she makes.'

'And if you've nowhere to live,' Henrietta smiled, 'there's a cottage on the estate about to become vacant. You could have that. You could spend your time between here and London, if that's what you want.'

There was silence around the table until Robert said, 'You're still not comfortable with it, George, are you? I expect you see it as charity.'

George winced. 'Not exactly, it's just that I don't want to live off my wife's income.'

'If you marry Pips, you'll be part of this family and you've heard what Father has said.'

'But he worked right up until this year. He did a very useful job. I don't. And to be honest, I don't know what I *could* do. I've only ever known army life.'

'We'll give it some serious thought,' Henrietta said, 'but for now all we need to know is – is the wedding still going ahead?'

'As far as I'm concerned, yes,' Pips said at once and, in an effort to lighten his mood, she added, 'and George, you really can't disappoint Daisy. She's so excited about being my one and only bridesmaid and wearing her pretty frock.'

As they prepared for bed that night, in the privacy of their bedroom, Henrietta whispered, 'Edwin, is there anything else we can do to help George?'

Edwin climbed into his side of the double bed. 'Leave it with me, Hetty my love. I have an idea, but please don't say anything to anyone. It will have to be very hush-hush.'

Henrietta switched off the bedside lamp and climbed in beside him. 'Dear me, you make it

370

sound like something Basil used to confide in us during the war.'

'Hetty my love, sometimes you are just far too astute for your own good. Now, go to sleep and try not to worry. You'll still see your daughter walking down the aisle, I'm sure.'

Forty-Four

'I really don't understand what their motive is.' Rebecca frowned when George told her about his trip to Lincolnshire. 'Her family must be absolutely desperate to see her married. And why does she still want to marry you if you can't keep her in the lap of luxury?'

'You're very cynical, Rebecca. Can't you believe that we love each other?'

'Oh, I can see you're besotted with the woman, but as for her...' She met her father's troubled gaze. 'Daddy, I adore you, you know that, but I'm not blind. You're in your fifties now and what is she? Early thirties, I'd guess?'

George didn't answer. He wasn't exactly sure of Pips's age. It was something he hadn't really wanted to know. All he knew was that he loved her and couldn't bear to think of spending the rest of his life without her. And yet, he loved his daughter dearly too.

Huskily, he said, 'Rebecca, Pips and I are going to be married in a month's time. Can't you try to get along with her for my sake? Please?'

Rebecca was silent for a moment, glaring at him resentfully. Through gritted teeth she said, 'Never in a million years. I can't stop you coming here, to the flat – it's yours. But I'd be obliged if you'd let me know when the two of you are going to be in residence and I'll make other arrangements. I'm absolutely appalled that a man of your moral uprightness should be prepared to be kept by a woman.' She turned on her heel and with a parting shot over her shoulder, added, 'But if you're determined to go ahead with it, you can tell them that I won't be coming to the wedding.'

George slumped into his chair, still anguished over his decision. The war, with all its horrors and tragedies, had been much simpler than family feuds.

Pips was due back in London the following day and after a restless night, when he had barely slept, George rose, washed, dressed and went to Milly's apartment.

Milly opened the door in her silk dressing gown. 'Darling – what a nice surprise. Do come in, but Pips isn't back until later today. She's driving back. Actually, I thought you were up there with her.'

'I was, but I came home on the train yesterday. I needed to talk to my daughter.'

Milly made coffee and they sat at the kitchen table. 'You know, I know everyone sees me as this empty-headed chatterbox, but I can keep confidences when I need to.'

'I have never thought of you like that, Milly. Although we never met out there, Pips has told me just how valuable an asset you were at the front. You're anything but empty headed, my dear.'

'Sweet of you to say so, but what I'm trying to say is that if you need someone to talk to, then I'm always here for you. For both of you. Nor would I tittle-tattle from one to the other, if you know what I mean.'

George smiled thinly. 'There are no secrets between Pips and me.' He sighed heavily.

'But you have got a problem of some sort, haven't you? A big one, by the look on your face. Is it your daughter?'

George nodded. 'Partly. She just can't – or won't – come to terms with Pips and me marrying.'

'Well, she's leaving it a bit late in the day. The wedding's in a month.' Milly paused and then asked softly, 'And what's the other part?'

'I've lost most of my money in the crash.'

Milly pulled a face. 'Daddy's lost quite a lot too, but he thinks the secret is not to panic. Just hold tight and don't sell. I don't know if he's right or not, but that's what he thinks.'

'Yes, that's what Robert and his father suggested too.'

'The markets will recover, I'm sure, but it'll take a while.' With a shrewdness that few people gave her credit for, Milly said, 'But you're a man of honour – a true gentleman – and you can't bear the thought of marrying Pips when you can't support her in the way you'd wish to. Am I right?'

'Absolutely! Her family have been very good – very magnanimous and, when I was there, I sort of agreed to their suggestions, but now I'm back here and – to be honest – after something that Rebecca said, I've changed my mind. I have to tell Pips today that I can't marry her. At least, not now.'

'I see,' Milly said quietly. 'Then I'd better get dressed and make myself scarce, but can I ask you something, George?'

'Of course.'

'Do you intend to break it off completely or just to postpone the wedding?'

'That will be up to Pips.'

'I'd be quite happy for you to move in here, if you wanted to. I love having Pips here. We get along so well and, even if we don't always agree, we seem to have found a lovely way of working things out.'

'I wouldn't want to make things – well – awkward for you.'

Milly shrugged. 'You wouldn't. I'm a modern woman. I'm sure you know that Paul and I are lovers. He stays some nights and it never bothers Pips. The apartment's quite big enough for all of us. Anyway, the offer's there. And now, I'll get out of the way...'

Pips was surprised to find George waiting for her at Milly's home when she arrived back. 'Is everything all right?' she asked anxiously, seeing his solemn face.

'Not really, my darling. I have to ask you to postpone the wedding or – if you so wish – to release me from our engagement. My principles will just not let me go through with it whilst my finances are in such a chaotic mess.'

She moved to him and put her hands on his chest and looked up into his troubled eyes. 'George – be honest. Do *you* want to break it off all together?'

'Of course not,' he said hoarsely.

'Then we'll just carry on as we are now. I'll write and tell mother to put the wedding plans on hold and we'll see how things go.'

'Your family were so generous. I feel I'm throwing kindness in their faces.'

'They'll understand, I promise.'

'I talked to Milly this morning – before you came home. She's offered for me to move in here too, but I don't feel it's a good idea, do you?'

'Good old Milly.' Pips laughed. 'She's a darling, but I agree with you. It might feel a bit crowded. Besides, I feel you need your independence. You'd be feeling as much in her debt as in my family's, don't you think?'

'Yes, yes, I do.'

'So, we'll carry on as we are, as I said. We'll meet at your flat when Rebecca's not around and here when Milly's away.'

But George was still frowning. 'I still don't like these clandestine meetings. I want to make an honest woman of you.'

Pips threw back her head and laughed. 'Too late for that, my darling. Besides, I like the intrigue and the excitement and leaving people guessing just what the truth might be. Now, stop looking so worried and kiss me.'

'Have you heard?' Bess Cooper stood in front of

375

Ma on the hearth rug. The old lady had not ventured out into the cold today and was sitting huddled near the fire in the range.

'Don't know till you tell me, Bess. Go on, then, what choice bit of gossip have you got for us today?'

'Miss Pips has been jilted – again.'

Ma glanced up. 'No! A' you sure?'

'It's come from our Betty. Wedding's off. Well, they're saying "postponed", but we know what that really means, don't we? Fancy, I'd've thought that if anyone would have been able to hold on to a man, it'd've been Miss Pips. Even in these times.'

Ma made no comment and Bess looked down at her. 'You all right, Ma? You look a bit peaky.'

'She's not been herself for a few days now,' Norah said anxiously. 'I wanted her to stay in bed this morning, but she insisted on getting up.'

'Have you seen the doctor?'

Norah shook her head. 'She won't have him sent for, though...'

'I am here, you know. Stop talking about me as if I wasn't. If I tek to me bed, I'll never get out of it again and I'll tell you when I need a doctor.' Her toothless mouth worked and her voice was unusually shaky as she said, 'But I'll tell you what I do need. I want to see William just one last time. I'm not long for this world and I want to see him afore I go. So there, now you have it.'

Norah gasped and her eyes widened as she stared first at Ma and then at Bess. 'Len'll never allow it,' she whispered.

Bess stood for a long moment, looking down at

the woman she had known all her life. The woman she'd always been able to run to with her troubles, who'd never shunned her like some of the villagers did. If Bess Cooper loved anyone outside her own family, then it was Ma Dawson and she felt a lump rise in her throat to think that soon, perhaps very soon, this woman would no longer be here.

'You leave Len to me, Norah.'

'Oh Bess, I don't think...' she began, but Ma raised a hand that trembled slightly to stop her.

The old lady's eyes were on Bess as she said, 'Just don't make trouble for Norah, Bess, that's all I ask. She's been the best daughter-in-law anyone could have wished for and she's still got to live with him once I've gone. There'll be nobody here then to stand between her and him. I know he's my son and he's been good to give me a home all these years, but I have to admit, he's not the easiest of men to live with.'

Bess squatted her huge frame down in front of Ma, took her hands and looked deep into her eyes. 'I promise I'll always watch out for Norah, Ma. When your time comes – and I hope it's not yet – I'll be a friend to Norah.'

Ma nodded and a tear slipped down her wrinkled cheek. Both Norah and Bess were shocked. They couldn't remember ever seeing Ma shed tears, not even when news had reached them that three of her four grandsons had been killed on the Somme. Now, only William, the black sheep of the family, remained and Ma wanted to see him once more before she died.

Bess marched down the lane towards Len's

workshop. She could hear her son-in-law, Sam, at the anvil, but it was Len she wanted to see. She found him in the carpenter's shop putting the finishing touches to a coffin. Luke was nowhere to be seen, though; at fourteen, he had left school at the end of the previous term and was now working full-time with his grandfather in the workshop that would one day be his.

''Morning, Len. Who's that for, then? Someone round here?'

'An old boy in Skellingthorpe. Passed away two days ago. Funeral's early next week.'

'Sad to say, Len, I think you'll be making one soon for Ma.'

Len stopped sanding down the oak and glanced up at her, frowning.

'She's not well. I've seen a change in her this morning.'

'Has Norah sent for Dr Maitland?'

Bess shook her head. 'Ma won't hear of it. Not yet. But, Len, there is something she wants before she passes and you'll just have to accept it.'

His frown deepened but he said nothing and Bess wondered if he had an inkling as to what she was going to say next. She took a deep breath. 'She wants to see William one last time.'

Len growled in his throat and turned back to start rubbing vigorously at the coffin again. 'Never! I won't have that coward in my house.'

Bess folded her arms across her ample bosom and faced him fearlessly. There was no one in the village she was afraid of and there were only a few folk she respected enough to treat them with deference. Len was not one of them, though his

378

mother was.

'You're a selfish man, Len Dawson, and stubborn as an old goat carrying on this feud all these years with the only son you have left, but I didn't think even you would deny your own mother her dying wish.'

Len continued to sand the woodwork, his mouth tight.

'I'll tell you what I'm going to do, Len. When the time comes – and I don't reckon it's going to be long, she'll be lucky if she sees Christmas this year and that's only a few weeks away – I'm going up to the hall to see your Alice and Mrs Maitland.'

'You'd do best to mind your own business, woman, and keep your nose out of matters that don't concern you.'

'Ah, but it does concern me.' She took a step forward. 'Your mam has been a good friend to me all me life.'

'More fool her, then. You're nowt but an old gossip.'

Bess laughed raucously. 'Oh, I know that. You can't insult me, Len Dawson. Anything you say has all been said before.' She paused, giving him the chance to change his mind, but when he remained silent, she added, 'So, if you've nothing more to say, then that's what I'm going to do.'

With that parting shot, Bess turned on her heel and marched back up the lane towards her own cottage, her mind firmly made up.

Forty-Five

Probably because of her own willpower, Ma lived to see Christmas, but in the New Year of 1930 she could no longer get out of her bed and downstairs to sit in her favourite chair by the range.

'Well, Norah duck,' Bess said, 'time's come. I told your Len afore Christmas exactly what I was going to do and now I'm going to do it.'

'Oh Bess, please...' Norah began, but Bess had already marched out of the scullery and into the lane towards the hall where she was sure of a welcome and a sympathetic ear. She knocked on the rear door and waited until the kitchen maid opened it.

'Come in, Mrs Cooper,' the young girl said politely. 'Have you come to see your Betty?'

'No, duck. I've come to see Alice.'

'Come in, then. I bet Mrs Bentley'll find you a cuppa.'

As she stepped into the kitchen, Bess was greeted warmly by the cook. 'Now then, Bess, what brings you here? Have you come to fetch Harry? He's playing with Miss Daisy somewhere in the garden, but don't ask me where. She's keeping him amused now that Luke's a working man, though they'll both be back at school next week. I'll send Jake to find 'em. You sit down at the table and I'll make tea for us both. I could do with a sit down.'

'No, leave 'em be. It's Alice I've come to see. She needs to know that her grandmother isn't well.'

Mrs Bentley looked startled. 'Ma? Oh my! I never thought to hear it. I thought she'd last all of us out. Has Master Robert or Dr Everton seen her?'

Bess shook her head. 'She refuses to have a doctor, but she has made one request and that's why I'm here. She wants to see William one last time.'

'I bet that's set the cat amongst the pigeons in the Dawson house, hasn't it?'

Grimly, Bess nodded. 'You could say that. I've had a go at Len, but he's as stubborn as a mule. Says he won't have William in the house.'

Mrs Bentley shook her head sadly. 'He'd even spite his own dying mother, would he?'

'Seems like it.'

The cook turned to the kitchen maid. 'Rosie, duck, go and find Miss Alice and ask her to come down here, would you?' She turned back to Bess. 'We still call her Miss Alice, even though she's now Mrs Maitland. We tried calling her that when she first married Master Robert, but it got so confusing, she herself suggested we just call her "Alice" like we always had, being as how she was once one of us, but we all felt we should give her a bit of a title, you know. So, Miss Alice it is.'

'I bet it was difficult for all of you, her being a servant like the rest of you and then suddenly becoming your mistress.'

Despite the seriousness of Bess's visit, Mrs Bentley chuckled. 'We all thought it would be, but

381

d'you know, Bess, the girl herself was so diplomatic. She still treats us like she always did – as her friends. Besides, none of the Maitland family have ever referred to us as "servants". We're their employees, certainly, but they treat us with kindliness and respect. Always have done.'

Bess opened her mouth to say more, but at that moment the door opened and Rosie came into the kitchen followed by Alice.

'Hello, Mrs Cooper. How can I help you?'

Mrs Bentley pulled herself to her feet, murmuring, 'I'll get you some tea.'

And as Alice said, 'That'd be lovely, Mrs Bentley, thank you,' Bess saw and heard for herself the easy relationship between the former lady's maid and the rest of the staff.

'It's more I've come to help you, duck,' Bess said. 'I've been to your mam's this morning and Ma's not well, but before you say anything, she don't want the doctor. Adamant, she is.'

Though there was concern in her eyes, Alice said, 'Well, we'll see about that.'

'There's summat else, though. She wants to see William just one more time, she said.'

'Ah, now I see.' Alice sighed heavily. 'I don't think that's going to be easy. I don't expect my father...'

She got no further as Bess shook her head. 'I've been to see him and his answer was "never". But you see, I thought that if you wrote to William, he'd come anyway and maybe – somehow – he could see her.'

Alice chewed her bottom lip thoughtfully and then said, 'I'll need to talk it over with Robert –

see what we can do.'

As Mrs Bentley placed a cup of tea and a plate of biscuits on the table, she glanced at each of them in turn. 'Well, there's one person who could sort all this out.' They both looked up at her, the same question in their eyes. Though not a word was spoken, Mrs Bentley answered it herself. 'Miss Pips, of course. She'd go and fetch William home – and she'd sort that old devil out.'

Alice and Bess glanced at each other and then smiled. 'Of course,' Alice said. 'It's Pips we need.'

'But isn't she – well – I mean...?' For once in her life Bess was flustered. 'We've all heard the wedding is off. Mebbe she won't feel able to help us.'

'The wedding has just been postponed, that's all,' Alice explained. 'Poor Major Allender has some problems in his life, which need to be sorted out first. I can't go into details, it wouldn't be right – but believe me, they are still engaged.'

Bess smirked. Now she had a fresh piece of news to impart and it was straight from the horse's mouth, as she was so fond of saying.

Mitch had been as good as his word and Pips flew his plane often. It felt glorious to be up above the clouds and being able to fly solo was even more liberating. She felt so carefree, but in January came news from Doddington that would mean she could put her newfound skill to good use.

She wrote a swift note to George.

I have to go home. Ma Dawson is evidently quite ill

*and as she's in her nineties, we have to treat it as
serious. Robert has suggested that I should go out to
Belgium and bring William back. She's asking to see
him one last time. Take care, my darling, don't worry
and I'll see you soon. P xx*

She arrived home late in the evening.

'How is she, Father?' Although Edwin had officially retired, Ma had asked for him to attend
her.

'Not good, I'm afraid. She's failing fast but she
must be a big age, Pips. I don't know if there's
time for you to fetch William.'

'I'll drive back tomorrow and I already have
permission to borrow a plane. Perhaps I should
have gone straight away, but I wanted to come
home and see for myself how bad she is.'

'A – a plane?'

'Oh yes,' Pips said airily. 'Mitch Hammond's. I
can borrow it any time I want, so I can fly out to
Belgium and bring William back.'

Edwin shook his head. 'You never cease to
amaze me, Pips.'

'Now, if Cook can find me something to eat, I'll
get to bed. I have a long day ahead of me tomorrow.'

Her visit to the Dawsons' cottage early the next
morning left Pips feeling very sad. Ma Dawson
had been a part of her life – an important part.
No one – not even Henrietta Maitland – had Ma's
shrewd wisdom. She'd seemed indestructible, but
now she was a frail old lady lying in her bed unable even to get down the stairs, though her mind

384

seemed as sharp as ever.

'Open the window for me, Miss Pips. I must get some fresh air even though I can't get outside no longer.'

Pips pushed open the casement window, which, despite its age, worked surprisingly easily. She guessed that Ma had it open every day.

Pips stood looking down at her for a few moments. She cleared her throat and said, in the tone that brooked no argument, 'Ma, I'm going to Belgium to fetch William home to see you. I know it's what he'd want and I think it's what you want too, isn't it?'

Ma's rheumy eyes filled with tears and, not trusting herself to speak, she nodded.

Pips patted her wrinkled hand and left the room before she should break down herself. Pips never cried – at least that's what she always told herself – but there were times when tears were very close and this was one of those times.

Back in the kitchen, she met Norah's gaze. 'I'm going to Belgium to fetch William home to see his grandmother. And if you want me to deal with Mr Dawson for you, then I will.'

For a moment, Norah hesitated and lowered her head. Then she straightened her shoulders. 'No – no, I'll tell him. For once in me life, Miss Pips, I'll stand up to him. Surely...' She shook her head as if unable to believe what she was obliged to say. 'Surely, he can't begrudge his mother – his dying mother – the chance to see her only surviving grandson one last time?' She met Pips's gaze again as she added in a whisper, 'Can he?'

Pips shrugged then added, 'William'll have to

come here to see her, of course, but he can stay at the hall with us.'

Pips drove back south and went straight to Brooklands. Coming straight to the point, she asked Mitch, 'Would you trust me to fly your two-seater to Belgium to pick up William Dawson and bring him home?'

Without hesitation, Mitch grinned at her. 'Of course. I don't know of a safer pair of hands.'

Pips smiled at the compliment. 'Thanks.'

His face sobered. 'Besides, I remember William and what he did. He was the one who helped you pull me out of the wreckage, wasn't he? When do you want to go?'

'As soon as possible. His grandmother's dying and it's her wish to see him one last time.'

'I'm sorry to hear that, Pips. Of course, I'll be glad to help. Do you know of somewhere you can land safely over there?'

'The area where he lives wasn't badly shelled and his father-in-law is a farmer, so there should be a reasonably smooth grass field somewhere nearby.'

'Right. We'll get her ready for you and you can go whenever you want.'

'Tomorrow morning, first thing?'

'Fine. I'll make some contacts, sort out any permissions you need and get some maps ready for you.'

The flight across the Channel was uneventful and she landed in a field not too far from Mr Dupont's farm where William and Brigitta now lived. Farm workers stopped their work in the fields and hurried towards the plane as Pips climbed out. She greeted them in English and asked how far she was from the farmhouse. One fair-haired youth, with a hoe in his hands, began speaking to her in halting English and gesticulating. She understood a few words, mainly that he would take her there. She smiled her thanks and began to follow him across the field, leaving the other workers milling around the plane.

The boy led her out of the field and down a lane. After only a few moments the farmhouse she remembered came into view. He waved his hand towards it and said, 'Here.'

'Thank you,' she responded and, with a nod and a wave of thanks, entered the farmyard. At the far end, William, about to enter the house, paused.

'My goodness,' he said as he came towards her, his arms outstretched. 'I never expected to see you here.' He frowned as he added, 'And you've no luggage. What on earth is going on, Pips?'

'I've an overnight bag in the plane.'

'Plane? Don't tell me that was you just now flying overhead and landing over yonder?'

Pips grinned. William hadn't quite lost all his Lincolnshire sayings. 'It certainly was.'

'So why are you here? Just out for a joyride and got lost?' He chuckled.

Pips's face sobered. 'I've come to fetch you home for a visit, William. Your grandma is very ill and – to put it bluntly – not likely to live much longer. But she wants to see you one last time, she said.'

Pain flitted across William's face. 'What about me dad?'

'Never mind him. You'll stay with us at the hall and visit your grandmother when he's out of the way.'

'If he finds out I've even been in the house, he'll give my mother a hard time.'

Pips pulled a face. 'Possibly, but your mother even said that – this time – she will stand up to him.'

William grunted. 'She'll suffer for it, if she does.' He sighed heavily and was quiet for a few moments.

'William, I am not going back without you, so you'd better get your bag packed.'

William smiled wryly. 'Well, there's no argument then, *Miss* Pips, is there?'

Pips laughed. 'Not really, William, no. Now, where's your lovely wife and those handsome sons of yours?'

Forty-Six

It was, quite literally, a flying visit, but Pips was made so welcome and the whole family pressed her to come again in happier circumstances, that she promised she wouldn't let so much time elapse again.

'Now you can get here so easily, you've no excuse,' William said as they walked back to the plane very early the following morning. 'This field is always left as a meadow. Is it your plane, by the way?'

'Heavens, no. I borrowed it from Mitch. I learned to fly at his flying school at Brooklands.'

By the time they'd landed and driven all the way to Lincolnshire, they both felt it was too late to visit the cottage that evening.

'I did think about trying to find an airfield near Lincoln,' Pips explained as they drew up in front of the hall, 'where we could have landed, but the time it would have taken me to get permission and so on would probably have been longer than landing at Brooklands and driving up.'

William nodded. 'But me dad'll be at home by now. I don't want to run into him, if I can help it.'

'Come along in, then. I'll show you to your room.'

'I can bunk in with Jake, Pips. He's still here, I take it.'

'Oh yes, but you'll do no such thing. You're Robert's brother-in-law and my good friend, so I'll hear no more of that nonsense.'

William laughed. 'You don't change, Pips, I'm glad to say.'

'I don't think my mother would agree with you, though.'

She led the way in through the front door and into the Great Hall where the maid was just laying the finishing touches to the dinner table.

'Sarah, lay another place for William, would you, please?' She turned back to their guest. 'Come, I'll take you up to the guest room and then you must come and see all the family. They'll be in the parlour awaiting dinner by the time you're ready.'

Half an hour later, William was ushered into the Brown Parlour. Henrietta rose at once and came towards him, her hands outstretched. But before she could reach him, Daisy catapulted across the room and flung herself against him. 'Uncle William, Uncle William.'

He lifted her up and swung her round before setting her back on the floor and kissing her forehead.

Henrietta reached him and, to his surprise, kissed him on both cheeks. 'It's good to see you again, William, though I'm so sorry for your sad errand.'

Alice hugged her brother and Robert shook his hand. Edwin, too, stood up to welcome him and William was shocked to see how the doctor had aged since he had last seen him.

'I'm sorry about your grandmother, William. I saw her this morning and I'm sad to say that she is failing fast now. You have come not a moment too soon.'

William turned to Robert. 'Ought I to see her tonight? I – I really wanted to visit in the daytime, but – if you think…'

Edwin shook his head. 'No, no, I'm sure tomorrow will be fine. She sleeps a lot now and your best time to visit would be mid-morning.'

'Now, come along,' Henrietta said. 'We'll all go into dinner. I'm sure you must both be ravenous. All that travelling!' She nodded at Pips with a look that said, 'Well done, Philippa'.

They tried to steer the conversation away from Ma Dawson, yet her imminent death hung over them all. The family wanted to know all about

William's life in Belgium, about Brigitta and their two boys.

'Besides helping on Brigitta's grandfather's farm,' William told them, 'I now have a permanent job as one of the gardeners looking after the Lijssenthoek war cemetery and the one at Brandhoek too.'

'That's wonderful, William,' Robert said, 'but doesn't it revive bitter memories for you every day?'

William smiled. 'Everyone living in Belgium and, I presume, other countries that were occupied, especially France, have to try to move on. To be honest, I think it helps me. I was lucky to survive – we all were,' he added, glancing around the table, 'and I think it still helps me to come to terms with the fact that I refused to fight. I feel I'm still helping those that did give their lives by tending their graves.'

'Your work as a stretcher bearer was just as dangerous as the soldiers'.'

'But I didn't have to go over the top and run towards a barrage of gunfire, did I?'

'No, but you went into no-man's-land every day to pick up the wounded and the dead,' Pips reminded him. 'And snipers were always active. Look at Robert. He was a doctor, but he was still badly wounded and could have been killed.'

'If it hadn't been for the three of you – well, four, if I'm honest...' Robert glanced at Pips apologetically for reminding her briefly of Giles, for he, too, had braved no-man's-land to help Robert. 'I would have died out there. Never forget, William, you did exactly what you said right from the start that you wanted to do. You saved countless lives instead of *taking* them. There should be recognition for stretcher bearers and I hope one day there will be. You should at least have received a medal.'

Colour flooded William's face. 'Actually,' he said quietly, 'I did.'

Pips's eyes widened. 'Really? Why ever didn't you tell us? You didn't wear it at the Menin Gate ceremony.'

'I – I suppose I didn't feel I deserved it.'

'Of course you did, my boy,' Edwin said. 'Believe me, they don't hand out medals for nothing. What was it?'

'The DCM.'

'Oh my,' Pips said. 'The Distinguished Conduct Medal. How perfectly marvellous and so well deserved. Do your family here know?'

William, his face still red, shook his head. 'And please, Pips, don't tell them.'

Softly, Henrietta said, 'You should tell Ma, William.'

He was thoughtful for a moment before nodding and saying, 'If I get the chance, I will.'

'She'll go peacefully, then, knowing your courage was officially recognized.'

'Oh my boy, my little boy.' Ma held out a trembling hand towards him as he entered her bedroom. William sat down at the side of the bed and took the wrinkled, blue-veined hand into his. He was shocked at the change in her. She had shrunk visibly. Her cheeks were sunken and her eyes dull. She was no longer the woman he remembered. He felt the lump rise in his throat, thinking of all the time he'd missed with her over the last few years.

'Tell me all about yourself and your family. I want to hear it all.'

For the next hour or so, William talked softly, pausing occasionally when he thought she had drifted off to sleep, but her eyes would flutter open and she would whisper, 'Go on. I'm listening.'

At last, he said, 'The Maitlands think there's something else I should tell you, though I find it difficult.'

'Go on, lad. Spit it out. You've nowt to fear from me. Never did have.'

'No, I know that.' He took a deep breath. 'At the end of the war, I was awarded the Distinguished Conduct Medal for my work as a stretcher bearer.'

'Quite right too,' Ma said, mustering what little strength she had left. 'Me and your mam know what you did. We saw pictures in the papers. Terrible, it was. Let's hope it never happens again.'

'How – how is Dad?'

'Huh! Him! I suppose I should be grateful that he's let me live under his roof and die in me own bed, but life's not easy living with him. I worry for your poor mam when I'm gone. But, as for him, he's all right. He's pinning all his hopes on young Luke now to take over his business. Anyone would think he's leaving a huge concern, but it's only a little village industry.'

'But it's important to him.'

'Aye, well, I suppose so.'

'I'd like to see Luke again, but I don't suppose I'll get the chance. I don't really want anyone else knowing I'm here.'

Ma chuckled weakly. 'It'll not have escaped Bess Cooper's notice, you mark my words. And if she knows, everyone else in the village soon will.'

'I understand it's because of her that I'm here, but I don't want to bring trouble on you and Mam. Pips came here with me. She's downstairs talking to Mam.'

'Is that how you got here? Did she fetch you from Belgium?'

'Yes. She got her pilot's licence some years ago. Did you know?'

Ma squeezed his hand. 'Not afore now, but it doesn't surprise me.'

'You're doin' fine, Ma. Hang on in there, won't you?'

She moved her head a little on the pillow. 'Nah, lad. It's my time. I'm tired, an' now I've seen you...' Her voice faded away and then came back strongly just for a moment. 'Thank Miss Pips for me. She's a grand lass.'

Then she closed her eyes and slept.

William sat a little while longer before tiptoeing out of the room and down the stairs.

'She's asleep,' he told his mother.

'You'd best go, William. Yer dad might be home any– Oh!' Her hand flew to her mouth as the back door in the scullery rattled and they heard voices; a young boy's voice and a deeper, man's voice.

Luke came into the room first and stopped in surprise. 'Uncle William...' Then he stopped short as the thought struck him as to why his estranged uncle should be standing in his grandmother's kitchen. His eyes darkened. 'Is it Ma? Has she...?'

'No, no, love.' Norah reached out a trembling hand, but her eyes went to the man who now stood in the doorway. 'He's just going, Len. He's just been to see Ma. He won't come again.'

'Aye well, best not, though I wouldn't deny me mam her dying wish.'

'Uncle William–' Luke said again and was moving towards him when Len snapped, 'Come away, lad. You're to have nowt to do wi' 'im, else I'll want to know the reason why.'

But it seemed that the young boy was not as much in awe of his grandfather as Len would have liked to believe. He took a step towards William and held out his hand. 'I'm glad you came. Ma's been asking for you this past two weeks. She'll go easy now.'

William took Luke's hand and smiled down at him uneasily. 'I'd best be off,' he said softly and Luke nodded. 'I'll walk out with you.'

There was a low growl from Len, who turned on his heel and left the scullery, slamming the back door behind him. With his departure, Norah sagged and sat down heavily in a chair near the table.

William moved and put his hand on her shoulder. 'Are you going to be all right, Mam? I don't want to leave you with him in that mood.'

'She'll be fine,' Luke said. 'I'll watch out for her an' if he lays a finger on her, he'll have me and Sam to deal with.'

William nodded. There was no one William would rather see bringing up his nephew than

395

Sam and he smiled. Huskily, he said, 'Thanks, Luke. You're a grand lad. Now, I really must go.'

Outside, Len was nowhere to be seen, but William could hear the distant crashing of his heavy hammer against the anvil.

Forty-Seven

The family – including William and Daisy, as a special treat to see a little more of her uncle – had just sat down to dinner, when a knock came at the front door,

'Who can that be at this time of night?' Pips murmured as she rose from her place, gesturing to Wainwright that she would answer it, but before she opened the door she had guessed and was not surprised to see Luke standing there.

His eyes were wide. 'It's Ma. She's gone. I – I thought I should come and tell you and Uncle William.'

Pips reached out and touched his arm. 'Come in, Luke. Have you eaten?'

'Yes, Miss Pips. We'd just had supper when me granddad came to tell us she'd gone. He said she went peaceful, like. They never heard nothing.'

He stepped into the hall to face the sympathy on all their faces.

'Wainwright,' Henrietta said quietly to their butler, who, as always, was hovering close by. 'Fetch Luke a cup of tea, will you, please? I'm sure he could do with one. And just ask Cook to hold back dinner for half an hour.' She rose from her place at the table and came down the long room.

'At least come and sit with us, Luke, for a few minutes. We're all sorry to hear the news. Ma was a huge part of the village. She was much loved and will be greatly missed. You will let us know if there's anything we can do, won't you? Tell your grandmother I'll come and see her tomorrow.'

Still a little bemused, Luke glanced around the table and then seemed to remember another message he'd been entrusted to deliver. 'Granddad asked for the doctor to go to see her. Something about a certificate.'

'Of course.' Edwin rose from the table. 'I'll come back with you, Luke. Just ask Cook to keep my dinner warm, Hetty, if you please. It's not fair to keep these poor folks waiting. I'll just get my bag whilst you drink your tea.'

There was silence around the table. No one knew what to say, but it was Daisy who broke the awkwardness. She pushed back her chair and walked round to Luke to stand beside him. She put her hand on his shoulder. Her voice was shaky as she said, 'I am sorry, Luke. I loved Ma too. She was always so kind – and so wise. She always treated me like a grown-up – not as if I was a silly little girl.'

Luke smiled weakly up at her. 'Yeah. I know what you mean. Me too.'

As Edwin returned to the room carrying his medical bag, Luke drank the last of his tea and stood up.

'I won't be long, Hetty. It'll be quite straightforward.' He turned back to Luke. 'We'll walk back together. I don't want to trouble Jake to get the car out.'

'Then let me carry your bag, doctor.'

After they'd left, Pips said, 'William, you'll stay for the funeral, won't you?'

He hesitated only a moment before his mouth hardened. 'I will, though I don't expect I'll be wanted there.'

'You are most welcome to stay here with us,' Henrietta said. 'And as for the funeral, you can sit with us, if it would be easier for you.'

'Thank you, Mrs Maitland. You're very kind.'

In the small community, it didn't take long for the funeral to be arranged, especially when Len made the coffin for his mother. Everyone in the village attended; even mothers with young children, who had no one else to look after them, stood in the churchyard and listened to the prayers and the hymns floating out through the open door. They stood in respectful silence as the coffin was carried from the church to Ma's final resting place beside her husband.

As the mourners turned away at last to go to the hall for a spread which Henrietta had laid on in the Great Hall there, Sam Nuttall approached William and held out his hand. 'I'm sorry we have to meet again on such a sad occasion, William, but it's good to see you. How are you?'

Before William could even open his mouth to answer, an angry roar rose above the murmur of voices and Len lumbered towards them. 'Don't you be shaking his hand, Sam Nuttall, else you'll find yoursen without a job come the morning.'

Sam turned to face his employer. Slowly and clearly, so that those around could hear, he said, 'Mr Dawson, I respect and admire you in many ways and I'm grateful that you employ me, but that does not give you the right to dictate whose hand I can shake. You're a foolish man to carry on this – this vendetta against your own son.' He raised his voice and glanced swiftly around, making sure that more folk than just Len heard his words. 'I never had the privilege of being in action where William was but I saw what the stretcher bearers did, all day, every day and often through the night. William did exactly what he said he would do. He saved lives out there – most likely hundreds of them. And I'll tell you summat else you might not know, there's a rumour going round the village that he was awarded a medal, the DCM, for his courage.'

'Oh aye? And what does that stand for?' Len sneered. 'The Dirty Coward's Medal?'

Sam shook his head as if unable to understand the man's thinking. 'No, it doesn't. It's the Distinguished Conduct Medal and if I had my way, he'd have had a lot more. I don't mean to belittle your great loss, Mr Dawson. Your three lads were all brave and gave their lives in what they thought was an admirable cause, but, once they'd volunteered, they just did as they were told. William chose to go out into danger every day and bring back the wounded. He didn't have to go, he didn't have to stay, but he did, through four long years of Hell. So, yes, I'll shake his hand and if you sack me tomorrow, so be it.'

With that, he turned his back on Len, put his arm about William's shoulders and led him out of the churchyard and up the driveway towards the hall.

'How did you know about me medal?' William asked. 'I've never told anyone until the other night at the hall.'

Sam chuckled. 'That's one thing about servants in a place like the hall, they become invisible. Wainwright was just leaving the room when you told them, but he overheard you.'

'And he told the rest of the staff?'

'Aye, and Betty couldn't wait to tell us.'

'And so now they all know.'

'Aye, an' so they should.'

William sighed. 'Well, there's one thing I am glad about. I did tell Ma before she – left us.'

Sam squeezed his shoulder. 'Good.'

'But I wish you hadn't put your job in danger for me, Sam.'

Sam guffawed. 'Don't you worry about that, William. If I know Len Dawson at all, nowt more will be said about it. Besides, I don't want to sound big headed, but Luke'd never let him get rid of me. We've got our future all mapped out, Luke and me – and young Harry.'

'Mam, would you mind if I went to stay with Gran for a bit?'

Peggy stared at her son. 'Why, Luke?'

The boy shrugged, but avoided meeting her gaze now. 'I reckon she'll be lonely now Ma's gone.'

'But your granddad's there.' Peggy was mystified.

Sam, sitting by the range, rattled his paper. 'I think the lad wants to be sure his gran's all right.'

Peggy glanced from one to the other as the man and the boy exchanged a look of understanding. 'What? What is it? Tell me.'

Sam got up, threw down his paper and put his arm about his wife's shoulders. 'Your son, my love, is a very sensitive and caring lad.'

'Aw, Dad,' Luke said, squirming with embarrassment, but Sam only smiled and went on. 'We all saw how Len was with William today at the funeral. He's never forgiven him and it seems now that he never will. Norah agreed to William coming into their cottage to see Ma before she passed away and Len will blame her for that. And now the old lady's no longer there, there's no knowing how he will be with his wife. I think Luke wants to go to live there – just for a little while – to make sure that – well – he doesn't treat her badly. Am I right, Luke?'

The young man nodded.

'Oh Luke...' With tears in her eyes, Peggy reached out a trembling hand and touched her son's face. 'You are a thoughtful boy. I'm that proud of you. Of course you must go, but come and see me every day, won't you?'

Luke hugged his mother. ''Course I will. Thanks, Mam.'

'We'd better get to bed now,' Sam said. 'I've to be up early tomorrow, seeing as we've lost a full day's work today. Mind you, that's if I've still got a job to go to in the morning.'

Peggy snorted with wry laughter. 'Len Dawson might be a stubborn old man but he's no fool. He couldn't carry on his business now without you or Luke. You mark my words, no more'll be said about you being sacked.'

'Aye, that's what I told William, but it was more to reassure him than being positive mesen. Still, we'll know in the morning.'

Peggy was right; Len made no reference to their quarrel nor did he make any comment when Luke moved a few belongings into the bedroom where his biological father had once slept. 'I've started to call Sam "Dad" now, Gran, but I'll never forget who me real dad is.' He nodded towards one of the photographs on the mantelpiece. 'While I'm here, I want you to tell me all about him – and me other uncles, an' all – if it won't upset you too much.'

Norah wiped her eyes with the corner of her apron, but she was smiling through her tears. 'I'd love to talk to you about them. Ma used to let me talk to her sometimes, but your granddad doesn't like to speak of them now. It's too painful for him.'

'And Uncle William?'

'Now, that's one name you must never mention in his hearing again. I think you've seen for yourself now just why, but I'll tell you about him, an' all. It's caused a bit of a ruckus, him being here for Ma's funeral, though I'm glad he was.' She put her arm round him and rested her cheek against his shoulder. Already the fourteen-year-old was taller than his grandmother. 'It's good to have you here, Luke. Thank you. And guess what? I've made your favourite apple pie for tea.'

Pips flew William home the day after the funeral and, once again, stayed the night at the Duponts' farm.

The following morning, she said, 'I'd like to visit the cemetery near Brandhoek where George's friend is buried.'

William smiled at her. 'I'll take you in the truck. Can the boys come with us? It'll get them out of Brigitta's way for a while. Her grandmother isn't too well these days and Brigitta has more of the housework to do.'

'Of course. That'd be lovely. Perhaps I could bring Daisy to see them again sometime. Luke, too, if you wouldn't mind and if we could wangle it.' She laughed. 'They're all first cousins to each other in one way or another, aren't they?'

Pascal, now eight years old, was quiet and thoughtful. His brother, on the other hand, was outgoing and boisterous. Although two years younger than Pascal, Waldo was already taller than he was and seemed to take the lead in every-thing. But, on this outing, they were both sub-dued and respectful when they arrived at the cemetery.

In silence they stood around the grave of George's friend.

'I brought my camera,' Pips said. 'I'll take a picture to show George.'

'Perhaps he'd like to come out here with you again some time. You'd be very welcome to stay with us. You'll always be welcome, Pips, any time.'

'I'll ask him, but George doesn't like flying. He gets airsick. But if we all came together, we could stay in Pop again and see you often. We wouldn't want to impose, especially if Madame Dupont isn't well.'

As they turned to leave, Pips took one last glance at the grave and silently sent up a prayer for all those buried there. She touched the brooch on her left shoulder, remembering...

'You're doing a wonderful job here, William, tending all these graves.'

'We get a lot of visitors now. Folks coming to see where their loved ones are buried. It can be heart-breaking but, like you say, they seem so glad that we're looking after them.'

'They're beautiful, peaceful places, especially now the cemeteries are all getting the lovely white stone markers.'

'There's still a lot of work to do, but we're slowly getting there.'

She knew it was a sensitive subject, but she had to ask. 'Have you been to see your brothers' graves again since we were here?'

'Yes, I have. Tell Mam I go as often as I can and take flowers for her.'

'That'll be a huge comfort to her, I know.'

William nodded as if he had a lump in his throat. 'It was good to see her again. It was just a shame it was under such circumstances.'

'I know, I know.' She gave him a swift hug and then turned to find the boys staring at her, solemn faced.

'Now, boys,' she said brightly, speaking to them slowly in English. She knew they were being taught it as their second language. Just like their mother and their great-grandparents they spoke it well, but with a strong accent. 'It's been wonderful to see you both again. You take care of all your family. They're very special people. And maybe one day, I'll bring Daisy and Luke to see you again.'

'We'd like that,' Pascal said quietly.

'Dad drew us a family tree so we could understand just how we're related to them,' Waldo piped up.

'Perhaps one day we'll have a big family party and all get together. How would that be?'

Waldo clapped and skipped alongside her as they made their way back to the farm truck. 'I love parties,' he said gleefully.

But Pascal, the serious one, said, 'It'd be very nice, but not easy when we live in different countries.'

'We'll find a way,' Pips promised and, listening, William knew that if Pips Maitland said it would happen, then one day it would. 'And in the meantime I will certainly bring Daisy again and Luke too, if I can.

Back at the farm, Pips made her farewells to the family as they all came out to the field to watch her take off.

'What a remarkable young woman,' Mr Dupont said. 'I hope we see her again.'

'You will,' William said, with his arm round Brigitta's waist. 'We all will.'

Forty-Eight

The following months passed by quickly for Pips. She was enjoying racing and flying whenever she got the opportunity.

'D'you know,' she said to the family when she was home in May on one of her frequent visits – this time, George had come with her and, despite his wish to postpone the wedding, had been made as welcome as ever – 'there's sand racing at Skegness next month. I think I will enter.'

'Won't it ruin your car? Sand isn't the best thing if it gets into the engine or even other parts,' Robert warned.

Pips wrinkled her forehead. 'I'll talk to Paul – or Mitch. They'll advise me.'

'Oh, is that tiresome young man still around?' Henrietta said, though she said it with a fond smile now. She didn't intend to let her daughter know – and certainly not George – that her feelings towards Mitch had softened.

Impishly, Pips said, 'Who? Paul? Oh, he's rather nice. You'd like him, Mother, but he's Milly's boyfriend.'

Henrietta clicked her tongue. 'You know very well that I mean Mitch Hammond.'

'Oh – yes – right. Yes, he's still around, but don't forget I have him to thank for taking me racing *and* flying.'

Henrietta frowned and pursed her lips. 'That's

no recommendation,' she said tartly and this time she meant it. She was rewarded by a grateful look from George.

'Are you sure they'll allow women to enter?' Robert asked, trying to steer the conversation away from Mitch.

Pips stared at him. 'Oh, I hadn't thought of that. I'd better check.'

'Have a word with Basil,' Edwin said. 'I believe he goes to watch every time they have such an event there.'

'*Does* he? Every year? Why have we never heard of it before now?'

'I expect he never thought you'd be interested.'

'He's known about me racing at Brooklands, hasn't he?'

'Of course, but I expect he thought that was rather different from beach racing.'

Pips folded the newspaper. 'Then I must have a word with him.'

'You can telephone him, if you like, from my surgery.'

Pips stared at her father. 'The telephone? You've got the telephone?'

'Oh yes,' he said. 'And the wireless. Since we had electricity installed a couple of years ago, we've been able to have all sorts of new-fangled inventions.'

'Why ever didn't you tell me before now? I can ring you up from London.'

Edwin chuckled. 'It was only put in last week and we wanted to surprise you.'

Pips rose from the table and kissed the top of her father's head. 'Well, you've certainly done that. I'll go and telephone old Basil right now.'

'His number's in the little black book at the side of the instrument.'

'Give him our regards,' Henrietta said, 'and ask him if he and Rosemary are free to dine with us tomorrow evening.'

A few moments later, Pips was saying, 'Major? It's Pips Maitland.'

'My dear girl, how lovely to hear from you. Where are you?'

'At home for the weekend. Major, before I get to the reason I'm telephoning you, Mother wants to know if you and Mrs Fieldsend are free for dinner tomorrow?'

'Of course we are, my dear, especially if you're going to be there. And have you brought that nice Major Allender with you?'

'Yes.'

'Capital, capital. I'd very much enjoy a chat with him. Now, how can I help you?'

Swiftly, Pips explained her reason for telephoning him, ending, 'Father says you often go and I wondered if you knew if they allow women to race?'

There was a pause whilst Pips could imagine the major wrinkling his forehead. 'Well, I can't remember ever seeing women in a race, but as far as I know there are no rules against it. Look, Pips, leave it with me. I am acquainted with the organizer. I'll get in touch with him and ask if he'll permit you to enter. I'll try to get an answer for you by the time we visit tomorrow evening.'

Pips met their guests at the front door, eager to hear if Basil had news for her. 'Mr Brown will allow you to enter the Novices' Race, my dear. I told him you were no novice and that you raced at Brooklands, but to no avail, I'm afraid. "We don't normally allow women to race," he said. Very snootily, I thought, and I told him so. But, I'm sorry, my dear, that on this occasion he was adamant. It's the Novices' Race – or nothing.' Basil leaned closer to her and whispered, 'You'll just have to show him how good you are. Novice, indeed!'

Pips laughed, her own indignation soothed by the major's outrage on her behalf. 'Thank you, major. I will certainly give them a run for their money, if I can. Now, tell me, what do I have to do?'

'I got him to put your name down, so you just have to turn up on Skegness seafront on Friday, the thirteenth of June, so, I hope you're not super-stitious.'

Pips roared with laughter. 'Not a bit, major. And thank you. I'll look forward to seeing you there.'

As they all discussed the matter over dinner, Robert suggested, 'Why don't we hire a chara-banc and have a family outing to watch Pips race? Even better, why don't we make a weekend of it?'

'There's a nice hotel there – well, several – but the one we always stay at is The Vine.'

'Oh yes, Daddy, yes. Do let's,' Daisy enthused. Now twelve years old, she had been allowed to join the grown-ups for the first time this evening when there were guests, under strict instructions from her grandmother that she should be 'seen and not heard', but at the thought of such an outing she could not contain her excitement.

'Daisy...' Henrietta began sternly, but Basil only laughed and Rosemary smiled indulgently. 'Don't scold her, Hetty dear. She's delightful. Just like Pips was at the same age.'

'Well, yes,' Henrietta said drily, still eying her granddaughter, 'but I'm not sure that's such a good thing.'

'Of course it is,' the major boomed. 'I like a youngster with spirit. You follow your aunt's example, Daisy, and you won't go far wrong.'

Henrietta looked none too sure. She frowned and pursed her lips but said no more. Basil had always championed Pips and it looked as if he was about to do the same for the next generation.

As the ladies rose from the table to go to the parlour, leaving the men to their port and cigars, Alice quietly reminded Daisy that she should now go to bed.

Sensibly realizing that objecting would not be a grown-up thing to do and would only incite her grandmother's displeasure further, Daisy smiled and prettily bade everyone goodnight.

As she kissed her father's cheek, she whispered, 'Daddy, may Luke and Harry come on the outing to Skegness too?'

'I don't see why not, as long as their mother agrees. Of course, Luke will have to ask his grandfather too, now that he's a working man.'

'Oh look, Harry, it's the sea.' Daisy took the younger boy by the hand and led him onto the sand. She and Luke had been on day trips to the seaside before, but this was Harry's first time.

'It's big, isn't it?' he said in a quiet voice.

'D'you want to paddle before the races start? They've got to wait for the tide to be right out so they can drive on the hard sand,' Daisy explained. 'So we've plenty of time.'

Harry shook his head. 'Not – now. Mebbe tomorrow.'

'Of course,' Daisy said understandingly.

Beside them, Luke smirked and was about to tease his younger brother, but at the sight of Daisy's frown he closed his mouth. Instead he said, 'Let's go and collect some shells to take home to Mam and Grandma.'

After a while, bored of collecting shells and pretty stones, they watched the organizers rushing to mark out the course as soon as the tide had retreated far enough.

'There's Aunty Pips over there with her car. Let's go and say "hello".'

'I don't think we'll be allowed to, Dais,' Luke said, glancing around him. 'I reckon spectators have got to stand behind that fence they're putting up.'

'What's that line of stakes they're digging into the sand in line with the shore?' Harry asked.

'Dunno,' Luke said.

'I think it's to mark out the track. I think the cars will come down that side and then back up the other,' Daisy suggested. 'Let's go and find Major Fieldsend. He'll know.'

Basil was happy to explain the layout to the children. 'Spectators must stand behind this fence for safety, but we should be able to see everything. The cars will start on the outside of the course and then come closer to the spectators, where

411

they'll reach the greatest speeds. The course isn't too bad today, though I'm told there's some water at the north end and at the opposite end the sand is a little soft, so they'll be forced to slow down there. Still, it could be worse.'

'Where's Aunty Pips?'

Basil leaned close to Daisy and pointed. 'Over there. Look, she's lining up with the other cars. Hold on to your hats – they're about to start.'

Daisy giggled. 'I'm not wearing a hat, major.' Instead, she clung on to Luke's hand, holding her breath as Pips set off. Up and down the course the cars raced until someone waved a flag and it was over.

'Did she win?'

'No, she was third,' Basil said. 'But that's good enough to be in the Novices' finals tomorrow.'

'Is she in anything else today?'

Basil shook his head. 'Sadly, no. That's the only race they'd let her enter.'

'I hope she wins tomorrow,' Luke said stoutly. 'That'll show 'em.'

'Quite right, my boy.'

When the tide began to encroach upon the racing area, the cars left the beach and the spectators dispersed.

'Right, you,' Luke said and grabbed Harry's arm. 'You're going in the sea.'

'Dais,' Harry wailed plaintively.

'It's all right. We'll all go – just for a paddle. No bathing today.'

The horrified look on Harry's face made her dissolve into a fit of giggles.

The day trip to Skegness had turned into a week-end holiday as Robert had suggested and the family were booked into The Vine Hotel, a very old building which was said to have been one of Alfred, Lord Tennyson's favourite places to stay. The family were well cared for and the food was excellent.

'We'll come here again, perhaps for summer holidays,' Edwin declared. 'Daisy loves the sea and she's even managed to get Harry to bathe.'

'Is there anything that child *can't* get those two boys to do?' Henrietta said, smiling.

'Nothing that I know of, Hetty my love,' Edwin chuckled. 'Now let's go and watch the racing.'

They all stood to one side watching the cars hurtling round the track marked out afresh on the sand.

'Look, look,' Daisy clutched Luke's arm excitedly, 'Aunty Pips is in front. She's going to win.' The two children jumped up and down and cheered loudly even though they knew Pips wouldn't hear them.

'Well done,' Robert congratulated her when the racing was over. 'But you didn't half churn up the sand. It was flying all over. I'd get your car to a local garage if I were you and get it thoroughly washed underneath before you drive back home.'

'Sound advice,' Pips agreed. 'I'll do that.'

It had been a wonderful outing for all the family. Even Henrietta had enjoyed it and she said so as she linked arms with Rosemary to walk back to the hotel. It was about a mile from the seafront but the two women insisted they would enjoy the walk.

'Now that we're alone, Hetty, tell me, is there any news of the wedding?'

Henrietta shook her head sadly. 'George has had no good news as regards his investments, I'm afraid, and from what Robert gleans from the press, it looks like this country is going to be affected by a depression too. It's all very sad. Whilst I respect his decision, I can't agree with it. He's letting his pride get in the way, I fear.'

'Mm,' Rosemary said thoughtfully and murmured, 'I must talk to Basil.'

Henrietta, lost in her own thoughts, did not think to question her.

Forty-Nine

Through the summer of 1930, Pips continued to race and to fly as often as she could. George attended regularly and though Mitch was often at the circuit, he now seemed to be keeping his distance from them both. Although he knew their wedding plans were 'on hold', he noticed that Pips was still wearing her engagement ring. Whilst Mitch was – as Henrietta had described him – a lovable rogue, he did have principles and one of those was not to pursue a married or even an engaged woman. He wined and dined and squired a string of pretty young girls, one or two of whom he became quite fond of, but not one of them could ever match his love for Pips. He'd decided that, if he could not have her, he would enjoy his life, but he would never marry.

No one else knew this and so adoring and ever-hopeful young women continued to fall at his feet.

Towards George he had ambivalent feelings. He admired the major: he was a true gentleman, upright and honourable, and he recognized that he too loved Pips devotedly, but, of course, he couldn't help envying him. At the track, he tried to avoid them, for seeing them together almost broke his heart, though not, to his eternal credit, his resolve.

At the end of August, Pips travelled to Lincolnshire to spend a week with Daisy before school re-opened. Daisy was now at the high school in Lincoln, coming top of her class in both term time and examinations.

'I do hope you're not going to stand in the way of her doing whatever she wants in life,' Pips said to Robert when she caught him alone in the parlour just before dinner on her last night.

He grinned at her. 'Of course we won't. Within reason.'

Pips raised her eyebrows. 'And what exactly does that mean?'

'Well, if she decides she wants to be a pilot or something equally as dangerous. A joyride with you is one thing but to take it up as a profession, I don't think either her mother or her grandmother would be too happy.'

Pips sniffed contemptuously. 'I don't think that's likely to happen. Not easily, anyway. We've only just got the vote for all women, for Heaven's sake.

What about university? Would you allow that?'

'Oh, most definitely.'

'Has she ever mentioned wanting to become a doctor?'

Robert shook his head. 'No. Actually, she's never mentioned any particular ambition.'

'Not like me, then,' Pips murmured.

'She's only twelve, Pips. She hasn't seen what's out there yet. All the different possibilities.'

Pips laughed. 'Maybe she just wants to take over running the estate when Mother steps down or...' She left the words unspoken.

Robert wrinkled his forehead thoughtfully. 'Maybe so, but she's never said.'

'She wouldn't. It would be incredibly tactless. But she must have heard you say countless times that you're not that interested in taking it on. That all you ever wanted was to be a doctor.' She glanced at him. 'Thank goodness we've got you back doing that.'

'It took a while,' Robert admitted. 'But you were all right. It's working well with Conrad and I can honestly say that I'm the happiest I've been since before I was wounded. And that's thanks in no small part to you, my dear sister.'

'Oh phooey!' she said and they both smiled.

'Maybe you're right about Daisy,' Robert went on. 'I hadn't thought of that.'

'But do let her go to university, Robert. It would be so good for her and she's so clever. It would be such a waste of a good brain if she didn't.'

'I'll make sure of it. I promise you that she'll at least have the opportunity, if that's what she wants.'

As the rest of the family joined them – including Daisy – they changed the subject of their conversation.

When she arrived back in London the following day, George had left a message with Milly that he wanted to see her urgently.

'Oh dear. Is something wrong?'

'I don't think so,' Milly said airily, seeming to be avoiding Pips's gaze.

'Milly Fortesque, you're grinning like a cat that's got the cream. You're hiding something. I can tell.'

'Please don't ask me, Pips. I've been sworn to secrecy.'

Pips laughed. 'And when could you ever keep a secret?'

'Oh, I can. Sometimes.' She wriggled her shoulders. 'Just go and see him, there's a dear.'

'You know I can't "just go and see him". *She* might be there.'

Milly giggled. 'You talk about his daughter as if she was the other woman.'

Pips sniffed. 'It feels like that sometimes, believe me. I almost wish she was. I'd know how to deal with that situation.'

'Just go and see him, Pips. It'll be all right. Rebecca is away on holiday this week. She won't be there, so pack your little suitcase again and *go*.'

Two hours later, Pips was ringing the doorbell to George's flat. He flung it open and pulled her inside and into his arms.

'Darling Pips, we can now marry, if you'll still have me?'

Pips gasped. 'Of course I will, but why – I mean – what's happened to make you change your mind?'

'You're not going to believe this, but I've been offered the most marvellous job. It's got to be kept quiet, but I've been appointed as a military advisor to the War Office.'

'Oh, how...?' Pips was about to ask how it had come about and then, her mind working with lightning speed, she knew. Good old Basil! Swiftly, with only the merest hesitation, she changed her words to: 'Oh, how absolutely wonderful.'

She kissed him soundly and they hugged and then, as they sat together to marvel again at his good fortune, Pips couldn't help asking, 'But what about Rebecca? Don't tell me she's come round at last?'

George's face sobered. 'No, not exactly, but I have told her that now things are better, I mean to marry you. She's just going to have to come to terms with it. I've waited long enough – far too long – to make you my wife and as long as *you* agree, that's the most important thing, wouldn't you say? I'm not going to wait any longer. Please, Pips darling, say you will.'

'Of course I will.'

'I know you've only just come back, but let's go up to Lincolnshire at the weekend and tell your family.'

Pips giggled. 'Yes, let's. I can't wait to see my mother's face.'

'At last!' Henrietta clasped her hands together. 'I can hardly believe it.'

'We thought we'd fix the date as Saturday, the sixth of December, just after the children's birthdays.'

Henrietta frowned. 'We could be ready before that, Philippa. We just have to pick up all the plans we made before and put them into action. I know we need three weeks to have the banns read, but we're only in September. We've plenty of time. Why not the middle of next month? The weather could still be quite nice then.'

'Because there are two race meetings I want to take part in during September and although I won't be competing in October, there are three meetings then and it would mean that a lot of our friends wouldn't be able to come to the wedding.'

'Oh Philippa, really! It's high time you gave up all this racing nonsense.' She glanced at George. 'I hope you're going to put a stop to it once you're married.'

George smiled. 'I wouldn't dare to try, though as you know, Pips has said she will.'

Henrietta shook her head in exasperation. 'And you a former major in the British Army...'

'I couldn't even control her out at the front and, believe me, I did try.'

Henrietta stared at him and said softly, 'You tried to stop her going into no-man's-land to pick up the wounded?'

'I did, but then it was Pips, along with one of my soldiers, who rescued me when I was wounded. If it hadn't been for her, I doubt very much I'd be here now.'

Henrietta nodded and said softly, 'And neither would her brother.'

'In his case, most definitely he would have died out there.'

'Then I suppose,' she said tremulously, 'I'd better not be too hard on her.'

'I am here, you know,' Pips laughed.

'All right. Have your races, Philippa, but please, just be careful.'

Fifty

It was the last race that Pips planned to take part in. Plans for her wedding in the church close to her home were almost complete and the only thing to spoil her happiness was Rebecca's refusal to attend. George was tight-lipped and refused to discuss the matter with his daughter any more. Although they were still speaking to each other, there was a frostiness between them that had never been there before. But now he was determined that nothing and no one would stop him marrying Pips. Not even Rebecca.

They were all there: George, Milly, Paul and Jeff, to watch their protégée. Even Mitch, who had deliberately kept his distance since their conversation about her marriage, had not been able to stay away. He watched anxiously as they lined up at the start. He saw Muriel, Pattie and Pips all wave at each other, their rivalry evident.

'She should do well in this race,' Paul declared as they watched from Members' Bridge. 'She has the fastest car.'

'And she knows how to handle it,' Jeff agreed.

The race began well. Muriel took an early lead, but Pips was soon on her tail and then passing her. She was coming round the bend below the bridge and onto the banking, when Jeff said, 'Oh Hell, her front tyre's shredding...'

They watched in horror as the car began to spin and then to slide down the banking.

'Oh my God! She's hit the fence,' Milly breathed and they all began to run.

Despite being the oldest amongst them, George reached the smoking wreckage first, but Mitch was close behind him. Pips lay with her head on one side and her eyes closed. Blood spurted from a nasty gash on her hairline and she was unconscious. George pulled at the door, but it was buckled and wouldn't open.

'Steady on, old chap.' Mitch reached his side. 'We must be very gentle getting her out or we could do her more damage.'

'But the car might go up...' George said. The brave, usually calm and controlled army major was frantic.

'If it does, then we'll pull her clear double quick.'

The two men exchanged a glance, each knowing what the other was feeling. In that moment, they both acknowledged their love for this woman. Now the others reached them, Milly bringing up the rear. She had taken off her heeled shoes and thrown them aside. She ran in bare feet, not caring if the rough ground cut her.

'Is she...?'

Jeff, leaning into the car, felt the pulse in her

neck. 'No, she's alive, but we must be careful. If she's broken her neck...'

'There's a stretcher coming,' Paul said, 'and the doctor.'

The current Clerk of the Course always insisted that a doctor be present at races.

Under his instructions, they worked together to ease Pips out of the vehicle and to lay her very gently on the stretcher, but she did not open her eyes. The race had been stopped and an ambulance had come hurtling round the track. Now she was lifted into the back of it and as they watched it move away, George asked, 'Where are they taking her?'

'I've suggested they should take her straight to the London Hospital,' the doctor said. 'The local ones are very good, but they haven't the facilities for what Miss Maitland might need.'

George shook his head and allowed himself a humourless smile. 'The London,' he murmured, and wondered what his daughter would think when she found out who the most recent admission was.

He felt someone grip his arm. 'I'll take you there,' Mitch said simply.

'What is it? What's happened?' Henrietta demanded as Edwin replaced the telephone receiver and turned with a solemn look to face her. He went to her and took her hands into his. 'Hetty my love. There's been an accident at Brooklands.'

Henrietta drew in a sharp breath. 'Oh no. Pips?'

'I'm afraid so. She's been taken to the London Hospital.'

'So she's not – not dead?'

'No, no,' he said swiftly, 'but she is badly injured. I think we should go down. I'll talk to Robert.'

He found Robert and Alice in Robert's surgery. They both looked up as he entered and, just like his wife, at once noticed his solemn expression.

'Pips has been in an accident at Brooklands. She's alive, but quite badly hurt. She's been taken to the London Hospital. Your mother and I would like to go down. Can you manage everything here, Robert? Your mother said to tell you not to worry about the estate. Her farm manager is very competent.'

'I'm sure I can. Conrad will step in. I'll speak to him and explain the situation. You and Mother go as soon as you can. Jake can drive you both to the station. Off you go, but promise me that you'll let us know how Pips is.' For a moment, his face was bleak. He couldn't contemplate life without his beloved sister.

Edwin was about to leave when he turned back to Alice. 'I almost forgot. Hetty told me to ask you to postpone the wedding, Alice. We very much doubt Pips will be well enough by then.' His voice was husky and Alice moved quickly to his side and linked her arm through his. 'We'll look after everything here, Father. You just go to Pips.'

Edwin covered her hand with his. 'You're such a comfort, Alice. I don't know what we would do without you.'

The house was quiet after the flurry of their hurried departure. Even Daisy, who had been so excited to be bridesmaid for her aunt – the only bridesmaid – was subdued and anxious.

'Daddy, Aunty Pips will be all right, won't she?'

'Of course she will, darling,' Robert said, putting his arm round her waist as she stood beside him in her dressing gown on her way to bed. 'She's as tough as old boots. I expect she's had a bit of a bump on her head and will have to take it easy for a few days. But if I know my sister, you'll still get to wear that pretty dress hanging in your wardrobe, though perhaps not as soon as we hoped.' He kissed her forehead and said, 'Now, off to bed with you.'

'You will tell me if you hear any news, won't you? Even if it's in the middle of the night.'

'I promise.'

'Can I go to London too?'

Robert stroked her hair. 'No, darling. Gramps will keep us informed and I promise I will tell you everything.'

Safe in the knowledge that none of her family ever broke a solemn promise, Daisy went to her bed. As he watched her go, Robert was not quite so optimistic as he had made out to his daughter.

'Have you heard?' Bess said, coming in through the Dawsons' back door and through the scullery. Now there was only Norah to hear her gossip but Bess never failed to bring the latest news to her.

'What is it now, Bess?'

Norah was a little impatient. It was Saturday evening and there were all the vegetables to prepare for the big Sunday roast she always did. Luke, although no longer staying with his grandmother, was coming and he had asked if he could

424

bring Daisy, so Norah wanted to make it a special meal. Len was in the back garden, tending his vegetable patch.

'Miss Pips has had a serious accident in her racing car.'

The news stopped Norah instantly and she gaped at her visitor. 'No!' she breathed. 'Is she bad?'

'Seems so. Still unconscious, our Betty says. Doctor and Mrs Maitland have rushed off to London. That's where she's been taken. To a big London hospital.'

Norah sat down suddenly in a chair, her busy hands suddenly idle.

'You sit there, Norah duck. I'll mek us a cup o' tea. Allus good for shock.'

Bess bustled about the kitchen, almost as familiar with it as her own, whilst Norah sat quite still, stunned by the news. It brought back to her the times she had heard terrible news about her own boys. 'Oh, I hope she'll be all right.'

'Don't we all,' Bess said, 'and I expect the wedding will be off – *again!*'

They sat together, speaking if they felt the need or just in companionable silence, old friends who were now joined together by their mutual grandson, Luke.

'It's times like this that I miss Ma the most,' Norah said. 'She'd seen so much of life that she was always able to bring comfort. She was a very strong woman, you know.'

'I do know, Norah duck. I turned to her a lot mesen when times was hard. I reckon the whole village misses her.'

425

As she pulled herself up, Norah said, 'Let me know if you hear owt else, won't you?'

'I will. Betty'll keep me up to date.'

There was no more news that night. Edwin telephoned briefly to say that he and Henrietta had arrived safely in the city and had booked into a hotel as near to the hospital as possible. 'We can't see her until visiting hours tomorrow, but we've been in touch with Milly and she says that George is breaking every hospital rule in the book and demanding to sit by her bedside all the time.'

'I'm surprised some dragon of a matron hasn't come along and shooed him out,' Robert said.

There was a silence at the other end of the line until Edwin cleared his throat and said, 'Perhaps that's because of who's been assigned to nurse her round the clock.'

'What d'you mean, Father? Who's looking after her?'

There was another pause until Edwin replied, 'Rebecca. George's daughter.'

'Dad, there's no need for you to stay. You should get some rest. It's getting late. Besides, you could get me into awful trouble.'

'Rebecca, I'm staying here. If they want me out, they'll have to carry me out forcibly.'

'They might well do that,' Rebecca muttered. She glanced from her father to the white-faced woman in the bed and back again.

'Why don't you go and book in at the hotel where her parents are staying? It's closer to the hospital than our flat. Even they're not insisting on visiting until the proper time tomorrow.'

'What they do is their business, what I do is mine,' he replied stiffly. 'And as for you getting into hot water, I'll make sure everyone knows that this is entirely my fault.'

'But...'

'No "buts", Rebecca, I'm staying.'

She sighed. 'What with you here and all the Brooklands mob sitting in the waiting room...' She glanced at him. 'Dad, don't you trust me?'

'Good Heavens, Rebecca. Of course I do.'

'I'm not her biggest fan, but you must know that she is my patient and I will do my very best for her.'

'My darling girl, I know that. It's just that...' For a moment, his face crumpled and Rebecca saw, possibly for the first time in her life, her father close to tears.

Fifty-One

Quite unaware of the conversation between father and daughter in the small ward where Pips lay, Milly, sitting in the waiting room with the others, said in a low voice, 'Well, I don't trust her any further than I could throw her. And considering that I couldn't even pick her up, that's not far. She's been positively vitriolic towards darling Pips. It's Rebecca's fault they weren't married years ago.'

'Really?' Muriel said. 'I rather thought it was because of all her activities. Men don't relish their wives being – well – so *busy.*'

'I would say it was because of the danger she put herself in,' Mitch said, pausing for a moment in his restless pacing up and down the room.

'For goodness' sake, sit down, Mitch,' Muriel snapped. 'You make the place look untidy and besides, you're giving me the jitters.'

'Sorry.' He sat down beside her, but jiggled his leg up and down. Muriel had never seen the ebullient Mitch Hammond in quite such a state. She bit her lip as realization struck her. He was in love with Pips himself, she guessed, but she held her tongue.

'Look,' she said, glancing around at the other five people in the room, 'why don't just a couple of us stay here and the rest of us go home? We could even do it in shifts, if you want, just till we hear how she is.'

'That's a good idea, Muriel,' Paul said, jumping up and holding out his hand towards Milly. 'I'll take you home. You ought to wash and bandage your feet. They must be sore.'

Milly glanced down at her torn stockings and grubby feet. 'Perhaps you're right.'

'I'm staying,' Mitch said abruptly.

'I'll stay with Mitch,' Muriel said, 'but I'll keep you all informed. I'll telephone you, Milly, and you can let the others know.'

'When do you want us to come back?'

Muriel glanced at her watch. 'I suggest we do four-hour shifts in pairs. How does that sound?'

'Good idea,' Paul said. 'Milly and I will get something to eat and come back at midnight.'

'That's only two hours.'

'True, but we've all been here several hours already. You'll be ready for a break.'

'Right, Pattie and I will come in at four a.m. and take over,' Jeff said.

With a plan in place, the others left and Mitch and Muriel were on their own. For some time they didn't speak much; then, when Mitch resumed his agitated pacing, Muriel said, 'Tell me, Mitch Hammond, are you in love with that girl in there?'

With his back to her and looking out of the window into the darkness, he stood very still for a moment. Then slowly he turned and looked down at her with a solemn expression. It wasn't often, Muriel couldn't help thinking, that she'd seen such a serious look on Mitch's face.

''Fraid so, old girl, but don't you dare tell anyone. Wouldn't do my playboy image any good at all.'

'Have you told her?'

Mitch sighed. 'Foolishly, yes, and I had the audacity to say she was marrying the wrong man. I expect she hates me now,' he added dolefully.

'Nonsense,' Muriel said briskly. 'Pips isn't the sort to bear malice.' After a pause, she asked, 'Does George know?'

'I expect he's guessed. Now, if not before. I just couldn't help myself when I saw her in that mangled car. I expect everybody's guessed now. You have, haven't you?'

'Well, yes, but I'm a nosey old bird. I'm sorry, Mitch, because I think she really is going to marry George.'

'I know,' he said gloomily, 'but I still say he's

not the right one for her. Even if I'm not either, she needs someone to bring a bit of excitement into her life. He's so much older than her, he'll soon be ready for pipe and slippers.'

Muriel laughed. 'The thing is, Mitch, I think he loves her so much that he'll never try to stop her doing whatever she wants. He'll just be happy to sit in the sidelines and watch.'

'You think so after this? I'm not so sure. I don't even know if *I'd* want her to race again now if – if she was my wife.'

'Perhaps you have a point,' Muriel agreed quietly.

On the Sunday morning, Daisy walked down the lane towards the Dawsons' cottage. Luke, expecting her to come to his grandparents' for dinner, was sitting outside on what had been Ma's favourite seat.

As she drew near, he stood up and came towards her. 'Dais, what's the matter?' He put his arm around her.

Daisy scrubbed her tears away, but fresh ones welled immediately. 'It's Aunty Pips. She's had an accident racing at Brooklands.' She hiccupped. 'She's in hospital in London. Unconscious. Didn't you know?'

Luke turned white and, for a moment, he couldn't speak. He shook his head and then tightened his arm around her shoulders. 'Mam and Dad obviously don't know yet. They'd've said. And I've only just got here. I haven't been in to see Grandma and Granddad yet. I was waiting for you. How – how bad is she? Do they know?'

'If they do, they're not telling me. Though I've begged Daddy to tell me everything and he said he would.'

'Then he will.'

'Granny and Gramps have gone to London. Jake took them to the station and Gramps telephoned late last night, but they can't see her until today.'

'D'you want to go?'

'I asked if I could, but Daddy said "no". I think he thought it would upset me too much to see her if – if...'

Luke squeezed her shoulders again. 'But you'd like to go, wouldn't you?'

'Yes, I would.'

'Then we'll go. I'll take you.'

'Oh Luke, would you? But – but how? I've no money.'

'I have. We'll go on the train.'

'They won't let me go.'

'Then we won't tell them. Just pack a small bag and we'll hitch a lift into Lincoln very early tomorrow morning. There're always lots of folks going into the city at that time.'

'I'll be in awful trouble.'

'Which is more important? Being in trouble for a bit or seeing Aunty Pips?'

She smiled through her tears, but before she could speak he said, 'You don't need to tell me; I know the answer. So, when you go home after dinner, get yourself ready and meet me at the end of your drive at six o'clock tomorrow morning. And don't tell anyone.'

'But they'll be so worried.'

'You could leave a note, I suppose, but they might not find it.' Luke was thoughtful for a moment. 'I'll tell Harry so he can tell them when we're well on our way. Now, we'd better go in for dinner, else Grandma might start asking awkward questions.'

Daisy tried to eat the lovely meal Norah had made, but her appetite had deserted her. Luckily, Norah, who knew about Pips, understood.

Edwin and Henrietta arrived at the hospital on the Sunday morning and were granted special permission to see Pips outside the normal visiting hours. They found George still sitting by her bedside. He had dark shadows under his eyes, but he was still sitting ramrod straight in his chair, his gaze never leaving Pips's face.

Edwin put his hand on George's shoulder. 'How is she?'

George stood up stiffly and offered his chair to Henrietta. 'No change, I'm sorry to say, though she's no worse.'

'Is your daughter still here?'

George shook his head. 'No. She was ordered to get some rest, but there's a sister who keeps popping in and I've been given instructions to call someone if – if…'

'You ought to get some rest, too. We can stay whilst you do and, yes, before you say anything, we'll come and find you if necessary,' Edwin promised. 'Where will you be?'

'Just in the waiting room. There are some comfortable chairs. I should be able to catnap.'

'Off you go, then. I'll find another chair and

we'll sit here with her.'

In the waiting room, George found Muriel and Mitch there. For a moment, the two men stared at each other before Muriel leapt up and asked, 'Any news?'

George, recovering from his surprise at seeing them there, shook his head and sank into the most comfortable chair in the room. 'Her parents have arrived and insisted I took a break.'

'I'll see if I can find you some coffee,' Mitch murmured. 'How do you like it?'

'Black and strong, thanks.'

When Mitch had left the room, George asked, 'Have you been here all night?'

Muriel shook her head and explained the arrangement the friends had made. 'We're back here for our second shift. We're all very fond of her.'

'Especially Mitch, I think.'

Muriel avoided meeting his gaze and shrugged. 'She saved his life, by all accounts, and you know what they say when someone saves your life. You're beholden to them for the rest of yours.'

George smiled wanly. Muriel wasn't very good at lying, but he wasn't going to challenge her about it. Instead, he murmured, 'She saved mine too. As she did for countless other young men. It just won't be fair if she loses hers.' He rubbed his hand wearily across his eyes as Mitch came back into the room carrying a tray with three cups of coffee on it.

'There's still no change,' Edwin told Robert when he telephoned that evening. 'She's still unconscious, but the doctors say she's no worse.'

'Is George still with her?'

'He only leaves her side when someone else is there and he's forced to take a nap. How he keeps awake for the long hours he does, I don't know.'

'His army training, I expect.'

'And the rest of her Brooklands friends are taking it in turns to stay in the waiting room around the clock. We'll go back in the morning and I'll ring again tomorrow night. Sooner, if there's any news, of course.'

'Everyone's anxious to know. When Jake drives me on my rounds, we have to stop every few yards with someone flagging him down to ask about her.'

'I can imagine.' There was a pause before Edwin asked, a little tentatively, 'Is Daisy all right?'

'Upset and anxious, as we all are.'

'Anyway,' Edwin said, a little huskily, 'I'd better ring off. This call will be costing me a fortune. Goodnight, Robert. Try not to worry.'

As he replaced the receiver, Robert muttered to himself. 'You might as well tell me not to breathe.'

Fifty-Two

'Now, listen, Harry. I've something important to ask you to do. Can I trust you?' Luke whispered in their shared bedroom that night.

'Of course,' the eight-year-old said, feeling important.

'Me and Daisy are going off tomorrow morning to London to see Aunty Pips.'

Harry's face brightened. 'Can I come?'

'No, but I want you to go up to the hall late morning and tell them where we've gone.'

'You'll be in trouble. Dad might take his belt to you.'

Sam had never so much as raised his hand to either boy – a look of disappointment on his face was always enough to bring them into line – so the thought of his stepfather thrashing him caused Luke to smile, though, to be fair, he'd never tested Sam's patience as he was about to do now.

'Will you do it?'

''Course, but I wish you'd let me go with you.'

Daisy had never been up this early before as she stood shivering at the end of the drive. It was cold and frosty and only just getting light. By the time Luke came running towards her, her teeth were chattering.

'I've found someone to give us a lift. He'll be here in a minute on his cart.'

When the farmer pulled up beside them five minutes later, they clambered aboard. Daisy sat next to the driver, Luke in the back.

'Now, what are you two scallywags up to?'

'Just going into Lincoln,' Luke said swiftly. 'Daisy needs to be at school early this morning.'

The farmer flicked the reins and they were on their way.

'Sarah,' Alice said as breakfast was being cleared away, 'have you seen Daisy?'

'Not this morning.'

Alice frowned. 'Neither have I, but her bed's made.'

'Perhaps she's gone out riding before school.'

'She shouldn't have. It's very frosty. The ground will be too hard to be safe. She knows that. I'll speak to her father.'

Alice found Robert and Conrad discussing the day's list of surgery appointments and home visits and dividing the work between them. Not required to run the household – that was still in Henrietta's hands – Alice now acted as reception-ist for the two doctors, but at the moment she had other things on her mind. 'Sorry to interrupt, but I can't find Daisy. No one seems to have seen her. D'you think she might have gone riding?'

Robert glanced at the window. 'I doubt it, but she might be down at the stables. Have you tried there?'

'No. I'll go and find Jake.'

Not unduly worried, Robert returned to dis-cussing their patients. 'If you're ready, Conrad, we'd better open the surgery.'

'Harry, whatever are you doing here?' Sarah, the housemaid at the hall, said when she opened the back door to find the boy standing there.

'I've come to see if there's been any news of Aunty Pips?'

'Not yet that we know, but come in, duck, and I'll see if Cook can find you summat to eat and drink. Yer aunty Betty's here. D'you want to see her?'

'Not if she's busy working,' the boy said. He

didn't want to see her; she might wheedle the message out of him. Harry had now decided that he was not going to deliver the message at all. He was going to do something entirely different. But first, he wanted to find out just what they knew at the hall.

'Maybe she'll spare a minute for you,' Sarah said, pulling the door open wider for him to step inside. 'And how's yer mam and dad and Luke?'

Harry grinned. 'He's fine. Bossing me about, as usual.'

Sarah laughed. 'Mebbe he needs to. I heard about you going missing the other day and being found here in the orchard. That's trespassing, you know. Dr Maitland could have called the copper.'

'I was only building a den. Jake said I could.'

'Aye, well, I don't expect the doctor'd mind. After all, you both come every week to ride the ponies with Miss Daisy, don't you?'

The Saturday-afternoon rides had continued through the years and whenever she was home, Pips always rode out with them on the stallion. On her most recent visit home, Pips had talked about Luke – and even Harry – riding a horse more often too. A lump rose in the boy's throat as he thought about her.

'The whole village want to know how Miss Pips is, Sarah,' he told her as she led him through to the kitchen. 'Everybody – likes her.'

'Loves her, I would say.' Sarah smiled. 'Now, here we are. Cook, we have a visitor. A hungry young man from the village.'

'Hello, duck. Come in. I'll make you a sandwich.'

'I just came to ask if there was any news about Aunty Pips,' he said, sitting down at the square, scrubbed kitchen table and tucking into the ham sandwich which Cook made for him.

'Nowt yet and I know they'd let us know if there was,' Cook said. 'If we hear owt, lad, we'll be sure to send word to you all. By the way, have you seen Miss Daisy this morning? We can't find her. D'you know where she is?'

Harry took another bite of the sandwich. 'Sorry,' he mumbled. 'I don't know nothing.'

By the time Robert and Conrad had finished their Monday-morning surgeries and come through to the parlour for a light lunch, Alice was almost frantic with worry. 'I've checked with the school and she's not there. Oh, Robert, where can she be? Jake hasn't seen her. Whatever can have happened to her?'

He put his arm about her and Alice wept against his shoulder.

'Look, I'll cope with all the home visits,' Conrad said. 'There aren't many and I've my own car, so you get Jake to take you out looking for her.'

'That's good of you, Conrad, thank you. But, to be honest, I don't know where to start looking.'

Alice raised her head. 'Luke! Why didn't I think of him before? If anyone knows where she is, it'll be him.'

'Let's have some lunch first...'

'I couldn't eat a thing.'

'You must, Alice, even if it's only a little. Come, sit down and we'll discuss calmly what we should do.'

'Call the police?' Conrad suggested.

Robert nodded. 'If we can't find her ourselves, then yes, we will.'

Half an hour later, Jake drove them to Len's workshop. Sam came out to greet them.

'Is Luke here?' Alice asked at once, hardly waiting for the car to stop before she jumped out. 'Daisy's missing and we thought–'

Her voice faded away as Sam shook his head. 'He's not here and Harry's not at school either, though we think he might be playing truant. He's done it before, but if you say Daisy and Luke can't be found either...'

Len came up behind Sam. 'Luke wouldn't go off without telling me.' He jabbed a finger towards Robert. 'That little madam of yours has led him into mischief, I'll be bound.' He seemed to be forgetting, for the moment, that Daisy was his grandchild too. 'She can twist him round her spoilt little finger.' He glanced at Sam. 'And I bet young Harry's with 'em. He'll do owt they tell him.'

'Oh, Dad, please,' Alice whispered, but Robert, ignoring the older man's accusations, said, 'Can you think of anywhere they might be?'

Now they all looked at each other, but not one of them could make a useful suggestion.

It was Jake who said, 'I'll round up all the farm workers and organize a search party,' prompting Robert to add, 'And I'll go home and telephone the police station.'

Having hitched a lift into the city, Harry felt lost standing amidst the bustling travellers on Lincoln railway station. He had thought to empty his

439

money box, but he had no idea what he ought to do next or how to find the right train to London and he dared not ask a railway employee. He was sure they would not allow an eight-year-old to travel to London on his own.

He sidled nearer to a family of four, mother, father and two children – a boy and a girl – who looked about his own age.

'Now,' the father was saying, 'this is the right platform and the train is due in about ten minutes. When we get there, we'll check in at the hotel. Then, what do you want to do first?'

The two children both spoke at once.

'See Buckingham Palace.'

'Go on a boat on the Thames.'

The father was smiling. 'We'll do both.'

Buckingham Palace, Harry thought. He'd heard of that. It was where the King lived and it was in London. He lingered near the family, not near enough to attract their attention but close enough to seem to an observer that he was part of their group.

When the train came in, he followed the family into the same carriage, earning himself a curious glance from the mother. No doubt she was thinking that he was young to be travelling alone, but he kept his eyes averted and concentrated on gazing out of the window until her attention was diverted by the demands of her own children.

As the train began to move, Harry breathed a little more easily.

As they stepped off the train, Luke said, 'Now, what hospital did your dad say she was in?'

'The London Hospital.'

'Right, now I'll ask a porter how far away it is. There's one. Wait here, Dais, and don't move. I don't want to lose sight of you.'

When he came back, he said, 'It's too far for us to walk. He says we'll need a taxi.'

'Have you got enough money?'

'Yeah. We'll be fine,' Luke said, taking her arm. He wasn't so confident inside. The two train tickets and the cab fare would probably take all the money he had been able to bring.

As if sensing his thoughts, Daisy squeezed his hand. 'I know they'll be cross with us, but Gramps will give you the money back.'

'Don't worry about it, Dais. As long as we get to see Aunty Pips, I don't really care.'

Fifty-Three

'Tickets, please.'

Harry felt his stomach turn over when, at the next station, the ticket inspector opened the door into the carriage. Hoping not to be noticed, Harry continued to stare out of the window, but now he was not seeing the view before him; he was only aware of the conversation behind him. He heard the rustle of paper, a pause and then the man's voice. 'You're a ticket short, sir.'

'I don't think so,' the father of the family said. 'Two adults and two children.'

Harry felt as if all eyes were turned towards him

441

before he heard the father say, 'He's not with us. I don't know who he is.'

The burly figure of the inspector loomed beside him. 'Now, lad, have you got a ticket?'

With a sigh, Harry turned to look up at him. 'Sorry, no.'

'Then you'll have to come with me, son.'

Knowing he was in trouble now, Harry followed the man with his head down. He didn't even glance at any member of the family as he passed them. The ticket inspector led him across the platform towards the stationmaster's office. Swiftly, he explained the situation to his superior, ending, 'I'll have to leave him with you, sir, I can't hold the train up.'

When the inspector had left, the stationmaster looked at Harry severely over the top of his spectacles. 'Now, m'boy, you tell me the truth and I won't have to call a bobby in. What's your name?'

'Harry, sir.'

'Harry – what?'

Harry clamped his jaws together and stared at the man in front of him, but not another word would he say.

After ten minutes of trying to coax the information out of him, the man sighed and said, a little sadly, Harry thought, 'I'm sorry, but you leave me no alternative. You haven't got a ticket...'

Harry fished in his pocket and brought out a few coins. 'I can buy a ticket.'

The man looked at the coins in his hand. Perhaps there was another way to get the little lad to talk. 'Where are you trying to get to?'

'London. My aunty's in hospital an' I want to

see her.'

'What's her name?'

Harry opened his mouth and then closed it quickly, guessing what the stationmaster was trying to do.

'I'm sorry, m'boy, but you haven't got enough money to go any further. But we're not a heartless bunch. I'll send you back to Lincoln without charge. How would that be?'

Harry, at eight – nearly nine, as he was fond of saying – knew when his luck had run out. If he argued any more, the police would be called.

'I'll put you in the care of the guard on the next train back to Lincoln. That's the best I can do, I'm afraid.'

'Thank you, sir. I'm sorry I did wrong. I didn't know about buying a ticket. You can take all this money though.'

The man got up from behind his desk and ruffled Harry's hair. 'That's all right, m'boy. Now let's see if I can find you a cup of tea and a bun before your train's due.'

'This must be it, Dais.'

'Let's hope so,' Daisy said, clinging to Luke's hand. They had run out of money for taxis and had now been walking for over an hour, asking the way every so often. Though he didn't say so to Daisy, Luke had the horrible feeling that they had been going round in circles. It was late afternoon and already the city streets were turning to dusk.

'It's not like the skies we've got at home, is it, Dais?' Luke said, looking up at the tall buildings all around them that seemed to the country boy

443

to block out all the light.

They entered the hospital and approached some form of reception desk.

'Excuse me,' Luke said politely, 'could you tell me if a Miss Pips Maitland is a patient here?'

'They'll likely call her "Philippa",' Daisy butted in.

The woman looked down her lists. 'Oh yes, here she is.' She told them the ward name and gave them directions. 'You'll need to ask someone if you can see her. Visiting is almost over for today.'

'Thank you,' they both said hurriedly and scuttled away before she could change her mind about letting them even go to the ward. They found the right floor, but were completely lost when Daisy caught sight of someone she recognized.

'Mitch!'

She left Luke's side and ran down the corridor and into his outstretched arms. Luke, not knowing him, approached more slowly.

Daisy glanced back and beckoned him. 'Luke, this is Mitch, one of Aunty Pips's friends at Brooklands.' She turned back to Mitch. 'Have you seen her? How is she?'

'Come into the waiting room. Milly's here.'

This time it was Milly and Mitch keeping vigil together.

'Oh darling!' Milly said and hugged Daisy. 'Have you seen your granny and grandpa? They're with Pips now. And George is here somewhere, but I think he's just gone to get something to eat.'

Daisy shook her head. 'We've only just got here.

We got a bit lost. It's a big place, isn't it? Can we see Aunty Pips?'

'We're only allowed in two at a time – or three at a push – and George insists on staying most of the time, so... Here, let me take you to her room.'

They walked along the corridor and into the room where Pips lay white-faced and motionless.

Daisy stopped. 'Oh my!' she breathed and tears sprang to her eyes.

At the sound, Edwin and Henrietta glanced up. 'Daisy! Whatever...?' Edwin rose and came towards her, enfolding her in an embrace. 'Are your mother and father here too? They didn't tell me they were coming when I telephoned last night.'

'Gramps, don't be cross. Luke brought me down.'

'D'you mean they don't know where you are?'

'They will now. Luke told Harry to tell them.'

'Let's hope he did, or they'll be frantic.'

Edwin went to Pips's bedside and kissed her forehead. 'We'll leave you for today, my darling, but we'll be back tomorrow. Daisy and Luke have just arrived now, too, so they'll be here as well.'

'Can she hear you, Gramps?' Daisy whispered.

'We don't know, but the doctor encourages her visitors to talk to her.'

'Can I?'

'Of course.' He moved aside and allowed Daisy to come close to the bed.

'Aunty Pips! Aunty Pips!' She took hold of Pips's hand. 'It's Daisy. Please wake up. We've come to see you. Luke's come with me. He wanted to see you too.'

To the girl's disappointment, there was no

445

movement, not even a flicker of her eyelids.

Edwin put his arm around her shoulders. 'Come along, my dear. We'll go now, but we'll come and see her again tomorrow.'

'But we can't leave her on her own.'

Edwin smiled. 'George is somewhere close by. He'll come back as soon as we go. We'll tell him we're leaving.'

As they made their way along the warren of corridors, Edwin said, 'We'll telephone home and tell them you're staying for a night or two at the hotel with us. Will that be all right for you, Luke?'

The young man – for, at almost fifteen, tall and broad shouldered from his work at the anvil, and deserving of the title – grinned sheepishly. 'I expect I shall get a roasting from me granddad, but...' he glanced at Daisy before adding, 'I wanted to see Aunty Pips too.'

Edwin respected him. He could have blamed Daisy, could have said she'd persuaded him to bring her, but he hadn't. He was taking the responsibility for their escapade firmly on his young shoulders.

But Daisy was not going to allow him to take the blame. 'It's my fault, Gramps. You must tell Daddy that. Luke found me crying.'

'You? Crying? Good Heavens!' Edwin exclaimed.

Daisy smiled. 'Yes. Me. Actually crying.'

'But you hardly ever cry. Not even when you hurt yourself.'

'I know. That's why Luke knew I was really upset and worried.'

Henrietta, who had been listening to the exchange, said, 'You should have asked your father, Daisy. He would have arranged something for you.'

Daisy hesitated and dropped her head, but her perceptive grandmother guessed. 'Ah, I see that you did and he said "no".' Henrietta sighed. 'What you both did was wrong, Daisy, but if you did ask your father and were refused, then...' She pulled in a deep breath and put her arms around both youngsters. 'I have such mixed feelings about the pair of you. You were wrong to sneak away – so I'm angry with you – but at the same time, I'm so proud of you. It's just–' her voice trembled – 'the sort of thing Pips would have done for someone she loved.'

'Oh Granny, I'm sorry to have made you angry, but I'm not going to apologize for coming. I – we – just *had* to see her.'

Henrietta hugged them both. 'Then we'll say no more about it. Edwin, you must telephone Robert the minute we get back to the hotel.'

Edwin booked two rooms for Daisy and Luke and then tried to telephone the hall. After three attempts, he said, 'I can't get through, Hetty. The line seems to be permanently engaged.'

'Leave it for a while. Let's take them down to dinner and try again later. Another hour or so isn't going to make a lot of difference.'

'But what if they don't know where they are?'

'Harry will have told them, I'm sure. Come along, those two must be starving.'

Daisy, who had enjoyed the high life with Pips on her previous visit to London, took everything in her stride, but Luke was over-awed.

'Isn't it grand, Dais?' he whispered. 'I see what me granddad means now.'

'What about?'

'About you being "above me", as he's always saying. It's not so noticeable at home. The difference between us, I mean. It's just normal, but my family could never afford to stay in a place like this.'

Daisy giggled. 'Then you'd better enjoy it while you've got the chance.'

After dinner, Edwin tried telephoning again. Already, the streets of London were dark and the street lamps were lit. This time, his call was answered.

'Robert?' Edwin shouted down the receiver. 'Can you hear me? This line isn't very good? Are you all right?'

'We're worried sick, Father. Daisy and Luke are missing. But, how's Pips?'

'They're here, Robert,' Edwin said. 'The little rascals have come all the way to London to see Pips.'

'What did you say?'

'I said, "They're here". They're safely with us at the hotel.'

'Oh, thank God,' Robert breathed and then he raised his voice and Edwin heard him shouting: 'Alice! Alice! They're safe. Daisy and Luke. They're with Mother and Father – I'll explain in a minute.' He turned back to the telephone. 'Father?'

'I'm here. But didn't you get their message? They told Harry to tell you what they'd done.'

There was a moment's silence before Robert said flatly, 'But Harry is missing too.'

Fifty-Four

Pips felt as if she was fighting her way through a dense fog. She could hear someone calling her name – a young, light voice.

'Aunty Pips! Aunty Pips!' Someone was holding her hand. She tried to squeeze it, tried to open her eyes, tried to answer, but nothing would work. She couldn't move, she couldn't speak, she couldn't even force her eyelids open – and then the mist closed in again...

Harry arrived home after dark, cold, wet and very hungry. All his bravado had deserted him as he had walked most of the way from Lincoln, hitching a lift only for the last mile. As he opened the back door, tears flooded down his face. Peggy flew towards him, pressed him against her in a fierce hug and then stood back and smacked his face all in one swift movement.

'Where have you been, you bad boy? We've been worried sick. Are Luke and Daisy with you?'

Harry rubbed his cheek and sobbed harder.

From behind Peggy, Sam appeared and, for a moment, Harry shrank back, but all his father did was put his arm around him and lead him towards the fire. 'You're soaked through. Peg, get him some dry clothes and a hot drink. He'll catch his death, else.'

'But where are the others?' Peggy wailed. 'I

want to know where they are.'

'They've gone to London.'

'London!' Peggy and Sam both spoke at once. 'Whatever...?'

'Oh, I understand,' Sam said, before Harry could say any more. 'Daisy wanted to see Miss Pips, I bet, so Luke has taken her. He should have told us, though.'

Harry hung his head and mumbled, 'He told me to tell you.'

'So, why didn't you?'

'Because I wanted to go too and they wouldn't take me, so I tried to follow them. I got on a train, but I hadn't got a ticket, so the man at the next station sent me back to Lincoln.'

'Oh Harry, old chap, you should have told us.' Sam's tone was full of disappointment, not anger, but Peggy was not so sympathetic.

'Those two on their own in London. Anything could happen to them. Sam, you'll have to go up to the hall and tell them. They'll be frantic, just like we've been.'

Sam rose at once. 'I will, but get this lad out of these wet clothes, Peg. I reckon he's learned his lesson.'

'I wouldn't be too sure about that,' Peggy muttered and began to pull Harry's clothes off, none too gently. 'You're lucky I don't give you a good hiding.' Then, as Sam left the cottage, she pulled her son into her arms and held him close. 'Oh Harry, don't ever do anything like that again.'

The boy clung to her and, muffled against her, said. 'I won't, Mam. I promise.'

The fog was clearing – just a little. She fought against the drowsiness, struggled to open her eyes. Where was she? She listened for the noise, but all was silent. The shelling must have stopped for a while. She should rouse herself. There'd be casualties who needed her help. But she felt so bone-weary. If she just rested a little while longer, perhaps... She could feel someone sitting beside her. George. It was George. He'd found her, hadn't he? Huddled near the Ypres canal when she'd run away from the first-aid post. Why had she run away? She couldn't remember, but George had found her, wrapped her in a blanket and taken her back to his dugout in the trenches. And he'd watched over her through the long night. And he was still sitting beside her now...

'Robert – tell me quickly,' Alice said, clinging to him.

'They're safe. The little monkeys have gone all the way to London to see Pips.'

'You're sure they're all right?'

'Positive. They're with Mother and Father and he's booked them in at the hotel to stay a night or two. They said they'd left a message with Harry.'

'But we never got it and now he's missing too.'

'I know,' Robert said grimly. 'I wonder if the little rascal tried to follow them. You know how he likes to do everything they do.'

'Why didn't Daisy say she wanted to go to see Pips? We could have arranged something...'

Robert looked shamefaced for a moment. 'She did, Alice, and, to my bitter regret, I refused her. I'm so sorry. I should have realized how anxious

451

she was.'

Alice stared at him for a moment, then nodded and glanced away. 'Well, at least they were together and they're safe now. I must go and tell Peggy and Sam – and my mam and dad – that they've been found.'

'We still have Harry to worry about, though at least we know where to start looking now. You go to your parents and tell them and I'll go to see Peggy and Sam.'

'I'll get our coats. It's still raining.'

They were halfway down the driveway, just passing through the gatehouse, when Sam's bulky figure, coming towards them, loomed out of the darkness.

'Sam,' Alice said at once. 'We're just coming to tell you. Daisy and Luke are safe – they're in London with Robert's parents – but we've no news of Harry.'

'He's safe. He's just arrived home.'

Swiftly, Sam recounted the boy's escapade and then Robert explained why Daisy and Luke had gone to London, ending, 'Don't be too hard on Harry, Sam. He's only young. They were wrong to put such a responsibility on an eight-year-old.'

'To be honest, Master Robert, none of them are blameless in this. The older two should have known better and Harry – even at his age – should have realized how important the message was.'

'Maybe we're to blame a little as well.' Robert was not afraid to admit his own mistake. 'Daisy did ask me if she could go to see Pips, and I said "no".'

Sam nodded. 'We've just to be grateful it's all

ended well. Though I shall have a few stern words to say to Luke.'

'And I to Daisy.'

'I'm just glad they're all safe,' Alice murmured. 'I know it was very naughty of them all, but – they're safe.'

Robert put his arm about her.

'Sam, would you do me a favour? When you've told Peggy, will you go and tell Mr and Mrs Dawson too? I must get back to the house and telephone London. They'll still be worrying about Harry.'

'Of course, Master Robert.' Now that all the youngsters had been found, Sam chuckled as he added, 'And I promise I really will deliver the message.'

'Father?'

'Yes, Robert. Have you news?'

'Harry's back home. He'd tried to follow Daisy and Luke and didn't pass on their message. He got on a London train, I understand, and reached the next station, but was sent back because he hadn't got a ticket. He's just got back after walking most of the way from Lincoln.'

'That's wonderful news. I'll tell the others straight away.'

'No more news on Pips, I expect?'

'Not tonight. I'll ring again tomorrow after we've seen her.'

Now she remembered. It had come to her in the night. She'd just come back from England and had seen Giles – the man she loved – kissing

Rose, another nurse. She had turned away from the sight and had run and run into the night, not knowing or caring where she went.

And then George had found her...

The fog was lifting and she was aware of light. It must be morning. The soldiers would be standing to on the fire step or cooking breakfast in the trenches. She should get up, but her limbs felt so heavy and there was no one beside her now.

'George?' she whispered, and then a little more strongly, 'George?'

Her eyes flickered open, searching for him.

Someone was bending over her and she heard a woman's voice. 'He's here, Pips. I'll get him for you.'

Pips closed her eyes again and a small smile played on her lips. In a moment, he'd be here. George would be with her. He'd never let her down...

Fifty-Five

Rebecca hurried out of the ward and down the corridor. Pausing in the doorway of the waiting room, she saw her father asleep in one of the chairs whilst another man and woman were sitting on the opposite side of the room. The man, whom she had recently been introduced to as Mitch, stared at her for a moment and then leapt to his feet. His eyes still on her, he nevertheless crossed the room and shook George.

'Wha...?' Instantly he was awake and struggling to his feet. 'What is it?'

'She's stirring,' Rebecca said. 'She's asking for you, Dad. Go to her, but I must fetch the doctor.'

He pushed past her and tore down the corridor, breaking every rule in the hospital book. Her eyes were turned towards the door as he entered the room and she smiled. George thought his heart could not be filled with any more love for her than it always had been, but at that moment, it over-flowed. Willing himself to be quiet and patient, he sat down beside her and took her hand.

'My darling,' he whispered, but before she could form an answer, the doctor arrived with Rebecca close behind him. The doctor, a kindly and understanding middle-aged man, put his hand briefly on George's shoulder, though his gaze was on his patient. 'Just give me a few minutes, Major Allender, if you please, then you may come back, I promise.'

Reluctantly, knowing he must obey orders once again in his life, George left the room and went back to the waiting room. Mitch almost pounced on him as he walked through the door. 'What's happening? Is she all right? Is she talking?'

'She's awake, but she hasn't spoken to me yet. The doctor came in and, of course, I had to leave.'

'Why? Is something wrong?'

Muriel touched Mitch's arm. 'He'll want to examine her, Mitch. Do sit down, there's a dear. It must be good news.' She glanced at George. 'Your daughter said she'd asked for you. Sit down, the pair of you, and I'll see if I can rustle up some tea. Oh, here's Dr and Mrs Maitland – that's good timing.' Muriel smiled at them as they came in, followed by Daisy and Luke, clutching each other's hands. 'She's just this minute woken up, but the doctor's with her. We don't know any more, other than that she said George's name. Oh hello, Daisy – and is this Luke? I'll get you all something too.'

At Muriel's words, Henrietta gasped and swayed and Mitch leapt to her side. 'Sit down, Mrs Maitland. Make that tea hot and sweet, Muriel. We've all had a bit of a surprise, but let's hope it's a nice one this time.'

It was an agonizing half an hour before the doctor came into the waiting room. He glanced around the anxious faces and said at once, 'She's awake and lucid. I'm sure she's going to be fine, but of course, I cannot discharge her yet. She needs to rest and I need to keep a close eye on her. She's had concussion, so we must be careful.'

Henrietta struggled to her feet. 'But you're sure she will make a full recovery?'

Daisy buried her face against Luke's shoulder and wept tears of thankfulness.

'Yes, I am, but she will have a nasty scar just here on her hairline.' He touched his own forehead, then he smiled. 'And I forbid any strenuous activities for a while. Although I understand she's getting married very soon.'

His glance went around the room and came to rest on Mitch, but, to his surprise, it was an older man – the one whom he'd seen sitting beside her bed for the last three days and nights – who stepped forward. He should have guessed, he supposed, but he'd thought at first that it was her father.

'It was supposed to be in December,' George said, 'but, of course, we'll wait until she's fully recovered.'

'I would postpone it at least until the New Year. You may go in to see her now, but, please, only two at a time.'

'I'd just like to see her for myself,' Edwin said, 'and then I must go back to the hotel and telephone home.'

'You may use the telephone in my office,' the doctor said. He and Edwin had had a long chat about Pips and talked frankly as doctor to doctor. 'It's just down the corridor on the right-hand side. Please – if I'm not there – help yourself.'

'That's very kind of you. Thank you.'

The line crackled, but Edwin shouted into the receiver. 'She's awake and talking, Alice. She's going to be all right.'

'Oh, that's wonderful. I'll let everyone know. Give her our love, won't you?'

'Of course, but Alice, I'm afraid the wedding won't be going ahead as planned. Her doctor said New Year at the earliest.'

'I'll see to all that. Don't you worry. How are those two little rascals? Are you sending them home today?'

'Maybe we'll give them until tomorrow, seeing as they're here now. If that's all right with you.'

'Of course, though they don't deserve it after the worry they've caused us all.'

'Don't be too hard on any of them. They were all as worried about Pips as we were. We should

457

have realized.'

'Anyway,' Alice said, 'give Pips all our love and make sure she does as she's told.'

Edwin chuckled, able now to feel the burden of worry lift from his shoulders. 'And just how am I to do that, Alice, my dear?'

'You'll all have to band together and try, and – if all else fails – I'll send Robert down.'

The village's grapevine spread its branches far and wide and soon everyone knew that Miss Pips was going to recover.

'How many more times is that wedding going to be postponed, I'd like to know?' Bess asked Norah.

'Just be thankful there's going to be one at all,' Norah said sharply. 'She could've been killed. You should have seen poor Daisy when she came to dinner with us on Sunday. She hardly ate a thing and Luke wasn't much better. I'm not surprised they both sneaked off to London to see for themselves. They must be so happy now everything's going to be all right.'

'Aye, well, Daisy'll still get to be bridesmaid now, won't she?'

Tartly, Norah said, 'I'm sure that isn't uppermost in her mind.' Sometimes, good hearted though she was, Bess could be very irritating.

But the other woman only grinned at Norah's admonishment. 'Sorry, duck. That didn't come out the way I meant. Just me being my usual tactless self.'

Whatever else Bess Cooper was, she recognized her own faults and acknowledged them.

'When are they coming home? Dr and Mrs Maitland, I mean. And the children? Len's fretting about Luke being away so long.'

'They're sending the children home tomorrow, so our Betty says, though Dr and Mrs Maitland'll no doubt stay a day or two longer. It'll be a while before Miss Pips is out of hospital, never mind being able to travel home.'

'I expect her friends will look after her and Major Allender is there.'

'Betty said he never left her side all the time she was unconscious.'

'Aye, well, that's love for you.'

'Dad, I need to talk to you.'

'Rebecca, if it's about what's going to happen when Pips comes out of hospital, it's all arranged. She's going to Milly's and I'm going to kip down on the sofa to be near her and to help.'

'No, it's not that. Well, it is in a way, but...'

Rebecca was fidgeting with her handkerchief, twisting it agitatedly between her fingers. Then her words came out in a rush. 'Dad, I'm so sorry. I've been beastly to you and to Pips and I was so wrong. Can you ever forgive me?'

For a moment, George stared at her. He had not expected this. He held out his arms and, with a little sob, his daughter flew into them.

'Oh my darling girl, of course I forgive you, but – can I ask – what's made you feel differently?'

For a few minutes Rebecca clung to him and wept against his shoulder. Then she drew back and wiped away her tears. 'It was seeing you sitting beside her all that time – so devotedly. The look on your face as you watched over her, willing her to get better. You'd have changed places with her in an instant, if you could have done, wouldn't you? I could tell how very much you love her, and then – when she began to come round – it was your name she said first. It was you she asked for. Not a member of her family or one of her other friends – but you. I've been wrong to try to keep you apart and I bitterly regret it. Like you said before, Mummy was a very poorly lady, only I wouldn't see it, didn't want to see it. And when she – you know – I blamed you and then I blamed myself, but I see now that neither of us was to blame.' She smiled wryly. 'At least, being a nurse, I've learned that much. Mental sickness is just as bad as physical illness. Worse, in a way, because it can't be seen and people don't understand it.'

'One day I hope people will. Pips's brother is doing research into the effects of shell shock. It's a kind of mental breakdown, I suppose. I saw a lot of it.'

His arms were still around her and she laid her head against his shoulder again. 'Daddy?' she said in a small voice, using her childhood name for him.

He stroked her hair. 'Mm?'

'Please may I come to your wedding?'

His arms tightened around her and he said huskily, 'That would make our day perfect.'

'But will Pips want me to be there?'

'Of course she will. She's not one to bear malice. It's all she's ever wanted. For you both to be friends – and I hope, one day, you will be.'

She drew back again and smiled up at him. 'I'm

still helping to nurse her and I must talk to her when she's up to it. I'm certainly willing if she is.'

It was what George had waited years to hear.

Fifty-Six

Rebecca sat on the edge of Pips's bed, breaking yet another of Matron's strict rules. She'd broken quite a few over the last few days whilst she'd been nursing her special patient. But today was important for them both. Pips was sitting up and eating almost normally. She had been lucky that no bones had been broken, but it had been her head injury that had caused the doctor concern. Today, however, she was to get out of bed for the first time and sit in a chair, just in her dressing gown, but it would be a start. But first Rebecca had something she wanted to say to her.

She took a deep breath. 'Pips, I am so sorry for the way I've treated you.'

Whatever Pips had been expecting the young woman to say to her, it wasn't this. She was un-prepared and didn't know how to respond. Rebecca rushed on. 'I've watched my father over the last few days, devotedly sitting beside your bed, never leaving you until we *made* him get some rest. I've seen the drawn look on his face, the anguish in his eyes and then, when you started to regain consciousness, the very first word you said was his name.' She paused a moment, but Pips said nothing. 'I – I've met your lovely parents

461

and all your friends, who have been so anxious about you. I was so wrong about you, Pips, and I'm desperately sorry.'

Pips started to frown but winced when the wound on her forehead hurt.

'I'm not quite sure I understand you. What did you think about me?'

Rebecca blushed. 'I'd rather not say.'

'Go on. If we're to move forward, Rebecca, we have to be honest with each other.' She grinned and found that the movement of her face didn't hurt. 'I'm a big girl, I can take it.'

'Well, first, I didn't want Daddy to marry anyone. I didn't want anyone taking Mummy's place.'

'I can understand that,' Pips said gently. 'No one can take another person's place and I certainly don't want to be a mother to you.' She giggled. 'I'm not much older than you anyway.' She paused and then added, 'Was that part of the problem too? That I'm so much younger than your father?'

Rebecca shook her head. 'No, not really. It was – it was just that I thought you were...'

'Go on.'

Rebecca's words came out in a rush. 'A gold-digger. Dad had been left some money and so, when he left the army, he was reasonably wealthy. But I didn't know about your background.' She smiled wryly. 'I didn't know that your family could probably buy and sell him ten times over.'

Pips laughed aloud and then winced. 'Ouch! I must stop doing that.'

'It's just the dressing pulling when you move. I'll redo it for you in a minute.'

'So, how do you feel about me now? About us getting married?'

'I was being insufferably selfish and I want you to get married and be happy. And – I'd so like us to be friends, if you can ever forgive me for being such a – such a–'

'Cow,' Pips said bluntly.

'Harsh, but I have to admit it's a fair comment.'

Pips touched her hand and said huskily, 'I'd like nothing better. And will you come to the wedding?'

'Oh yes – *please.*'

It was the 'please' that undid Pips. Suddenly, tears were flooding down her face and Rebecca was hugging her.

And that was how George found them when he walked into the room at that moment.

After leaving hospital, Pips stayed with Milly for a few weeks, then on the last day of November, she went home to Doddington Hall to recuperate, while George, with his new appointment, had to stay in London.

'I can't possibly miss the birthdays,' she told him.

As George and Rebecca saw her onto the train, Rebecca hugged her and said, 'Come back as soon as you're well enough. You know you can stay at the flat any time you want to and I promise not to throw a tantrum. Pips, I'm so sorry...'

Pips put her finger against the girl's lips. 'Rebecca, no more apologies. It's over and done with. We start afresh from now on.'

With tears in her eyes, Rebecca said, 'Thank

you. You're a very generous woman. I don't think I'd be as forgiving in your shoes.'

'I just want us all to be happy together. Look after your dad and yourself. And now, I must go. I have a wedding to plan.'

'I've seen the vicar and we're suggesting Saturday, the twenty-fifth of April,' Henrietta said, as they sat together in the parlour the day after Luke's birthday. Pips was glad to have been able to come home, but she had found the two celebrations so close together exhausting. Henrietta had noticed and said now, 'I know it's quite a while, but we want you to be fully fit.'

'That sounds perfect. George has already said he'll be able to get the time off whenever I fix the date, but maybe I should check with all the Brooklands set.' She consulted her diary. 'I don't think there is anything important happening on that date, but I'd still like to make sure.'

'Of course. We want them here. They were all so concerned when you were injured. They obviously think a lot of you, Philippa. Now, Alice is getting on splendidly with your dress.' Henrietta's mouth twitched with amusement. 'So she tells me.'

Pips stared at her. 'You mean, you haven't seen it?'

Henrietta shook her head. 'It's a closely guarded secret. She locks the door of the little room she uses as her sewing room and won't let anyone in, not even the housemaid to clean it. She insists on doing that herself.'

'What about Daisy and her dress?'

464

'She brings that out for her to have a fitting, but even Daisy isn't allowed in the sewing room.'

'Oh my! What about me? Do you think I shall be allowed to see it?'

Henrietta laughed. 'If you didn't need to have a fitting, no, I don't think you would be.'

A little later, Pips knocked on the door. 'Alice, it's me. May I come in?'

There was a scuffling and then the door opened a crack. 'I'm not quite ready for you to try it on, Pips. Another day or two, then we'll have a proper fitting.'

'Can't I see it?'

Alice pursed her lips. 'Not yet.' And, firmly, she closed the door in Pips's face.

'Well!' Pips said, pretending to be in a huff, but silently, she was laughing. 'Bless her,' she murmured as she went back downstairs.

Two days later, Alice said, a little nervously, Pips thought, 'If you're free this afternoon, Pips, we'll have a fitting.'

'May I come too?' Henrietta asked.

Alice turned pink and stammered, 'Er – I'd rather – I mean – I just want Pips to see it – at least for now.'

Henrietta smiled. 'It's all right, my dear. We'll respect your wishes. I can see it means a great deal to you and you want us all to have a lovely surprise on the day.'

Alice's blush deepened. 'I hope so, but I am anxious that Pips will like it.'

'You've certainly spent enough hours on it. Even Robert is beginning to grumble that he never sees you.'

'Oh dear...' Alice began, but Henrietta added swiftly, 'I'm teasing you, Alice. If he wants you, at least he knows where to find you.'

That afternoon Pips stood quite still with her eyes closed as requested, whilst Alice unwrapped the gown from its protective tissue paper.

'Keep your eyes shut, but just put your arms up and I'll ease it over your head.'

Pips felt the dress being pulled gently over her arms and head and then fall softly down towards her feet.

'Now, I've done tiny buttons all the way down the back, so it'll take me a moment. Don't open your eyes yet.'

After what seemed an age and with a little adjusting here and there, Alice guided her to stand in front of the full-length mirror. 'There. You can open your eyes now.'

For a moment, Pips didn't recognize herself. 'Oh my, Alice, is that really me?' She swished the full skirt from side to side, watching the fine fabric swirl around her. Her eyes brimmed with tears as she studied her reflection. It truly was the dress of her dreams. 'It's beautiful. However have you made it?'

'I had a little bit of guidance from Mrs Fieldsend's dressmaker at the start over the pattern, but since then it's all my own work. Do – do you really like it?'

'It's magnificent, Alice. You're so clever. Thank you – a million times.'

Alice looked over her handiwork with a critical

466

eye. 'It needs taking in a little on the bodice, but I suggest we leave that until nearer the wedding. I think you've lost a little weight since the accident, but you might well put a bit back on before April. It's always easier to take it in than to let it out.'

'Whatever you say,' Pips murmured, unable to take her eyes off her reflection.

'Now, try the headdress and veil on. This has taken me nearly as long to make as the dress, with all these seed pearls.'

The headdress and veil was exactly like the one in the picture which Milly had picked out. It fitted perfectly.

'It's a shame it covers almost all your glorious hair, but it does look lovely, even though I say it myself.'

'It does,' Pips agreed and then giggled. 'And the latest fashion too. Fancy me, being at the height of fashion. I can't wait for Milly to see it.'

'Not a word to anyone, Pips,' Alice said firmly. 'Please. I so want it to be a surprise for everyone – a nice surprise, I hope – on the day.'

'It'll certainly be that. Mother will be ecstatic. It's the first time, Alice, that I've ever looked ladylike. How very clever you are.'

When they'd gently removed the dress and hung it back on the wall, carefully covered with tissue paper again, Alice said, 'Now, this is Daisy's dress. What do you think?'

'It's lovely. What a pretty shade of rose-pink. I'm running out of superlatives.'

'She's happy with it and can't wait for the day. I've left it a little on the big side at the moment, because she could well grow a bit in four months. She seems to be shooting up. Perhaps you'd help me with a fitting with her, whilst you're here.' Alice laughed. 'She wriggles a lot.'

'I can't believe she's thirteen now.'

'And Luke is fifteen. My father has promised him a motorcycle as a combined birthday and Christmas present next year. A second-hand one, of course, but Sam will ask around for him.'

'Are you and Robert happy about that?'

Alice sighed. 'Not a lot we can do.'

'But you know what it means, don't you? Daisy will soon be riding pillion.'

Alice nodded. 'Or riding it herself.'

'Well, she won't be old enough to for two years yet.'

Alice smiled wryly. 'And you really think that will stop her, Pips?'

Fifty-Seven

'It's good of you to ask me, but no, I won't be coming to your wedding,' Mitch said stiffly. 'I don't really need to explain why, do I?'

The big day, as everyone called it, was galloping towards them. It was February and, back in London to be with George, Pips was checking that all her southern friends would be free to travel to Lincolnshire at the end of April.

'Oh Mitch,' Pips sighed. 'Then I'm sorry. I really hoped we could still be friends, but I feel as if you have been avoiding me. You didn't even come to visit me in hospital. All the others did and they're travelling up to Lincolnshire to come to the wedding. Will you really not come? You could bring Johnny, if you like?'

She'd tracked him down to the Brooklands airfield, where, as the doctor had advised her not to fly for a while, she liked to watch the planes take off and land and to meet her friends. And, of course, she went on race days.

Mitch was surprised that she was unaware of the vigil they had all kept at the hospital when she had been unconscious, himself included. He thought someone would have told her, especially Milly.

'Dear Pips,' he murmured, 'please try to understand that I really couldn't bear to see you marrying someone else, good man though George is. But always remember, that if ever you need me, you only have to say the word and I'll be there for you.'

She looked into his eyes and knew that for all his teasing and his joviality, for once in his life, Mitch Hammond was deadly serious.

'I'll remember, Mitch. I promise. But I'll see you around. I do intend to give up the racing, although I'll still come to meetings and cheer the girls on. And I'll still be flying whenever I can.'

Now he was the old Mitch again as he raised a sardonic eyebrow. 'You really think so? You really think George is going to let you carry on, even flying, after what has happened on the racetrack? It's still dangerous, you know. And you might not survive an aeroplane crash.'

'If you think anyone – including my husband – is going to be able to stop me doing whatever I want, then you really don't know me very well, Mitch.'

He eyed her sceptically and murmured, 'We shall see.'

'Mitch won't come to the wedding, Milly. I do wish he would. Can you persuade him?'

'Darling, I wouldn't even try. It's not fair on him when he's in love with you and it's not really fair on George either, is it, knowing that there's someone sitting in the congregation who wants to swap places with him?'

'Oh Milly, you exaggerate. I don't think Mitch is the marrying kind, anyway. I think it's all a lot of flannel – all part of the playboy image he likes to foster. I mean, he didn't even come to visit me in hospital, yet everyone else came.'

Milly stared at her. 'Pips, Mitch was there day and night when you were unconscious. We worked out a rota system amongst us, taking it in turns to do four hours at a time. Even through the night so that there was always someone there. Of course, we all had to be in the waiting room most of the time. Only George – as your fiancé – and your family were allowed in to see you. Though we did get a peek now and again. We all care about you, darling. Especially Mitch.'

'Oh dear,' Pips said. 'I didn't know that. He never said.'

'He wouldn't. When you came round he stopped coming to the hospital, but he telephoned me every night for a daily report.'

'I'll have to apologize to him.'

'Please don't. He obviously doesn't want you to know.'

'All right,' Pips promised reluctantly, but she was touched by what Milly had told her and contrite about her treatment of Mitch.

'Don't worry, darling,' Milly said gaily. 'The rest of us are all coming to your wedding.'

'This really is a beautiful part of the world,' Muriel said as she, Milly and Pattie walked through the grounds of the hall the day before the wedding. They had been invited to stay at the hall by Henrietta and had come for two nights. 'I've never been to Lincolnshire before.'

'Aren't the rest of her family as delightful as she is?' Milly said, linking her arms through theirs as they walked across the croquet lawn and through the orchard.

'The doctor's a darling, as you would say, Milly, but I bet her mother can be a bit of a tartar.'

Milly laughed. 'Oh, I don't mind her. She's like my Granny Fortesque, so I know just how to deal with her. And Robert, what do you think of Robert? And of his wife? She was lady's maid to Mrs Maitland and Pips, but Robert fell in love with her when they were out at the front. Isn't it romantic?'

'I bet that caused a bit of a stir.'

'It did at the time, but the whole family love her now and Daisy's so adorable.'

Muriel laughed. 'She is, but she's another Pips. No one will ever get the better of Daisy Maitland.'

'Did you know Pips took her flying at Brooklands?'

'Really? And did she like it?'

'She was thrilled. She was asking how old she has to be before she can learn to fly.'

'Not so interested in the racing, then?'

'I don't think so, though I don't think Pips has taken her round the track yet.'

'We'll have to put that right the next time she comes to stay with Pips,' Muriel said. 'Now, are you going to teach us to play this croquet game?'

'Of course, but before I do, I have some news. I haven't told Pips yet – this is her big day – so you must keep it secret for now. Paul has proposed again and we'll be getting married in the autumn.'

'Darling Milly,' Muriel's eyes were suspiciously moist, 'I'm absolutely delighted for you. We'll all be there – that's if we're invited.'

'Of course you are. I wouldn't dream of getting married without all of you there. Whatever happens, we'll always be the Brooklands Girls.'

'Is Johnny coming with his uncle?' Daisy asked on the morning of the wedding as she and Alice helped Pips to dress before Daisy put on her pretty rose-pink taffeta bridesmaid's dress. It was the perfect colour for the young girl's dark hair and blue eyes.

'Mitch isn't coming, darling,' Pips said, 'so I'm sorry, neither is Johnny.' She smiled and caught the girl's glance in the mirror. 'But you'll still have two handsome young men dancing attendance on you and vying for your favours.'

Daisy laughed. 'Luke and Harry, you mean? But they're my cousins, Aunty Pips. They don't count.'

'Luke is, but Harry isn't. He's no blood relation to you, is he?'

Daisy wrinkled her forehead thoughtfully. 'No,' she said slowly. 'I suppose he isn't, but being Luke's half-brother, I always think of him as my cousin.'

'You're far too young to be thinking about boys in those terms, Daisy,' Alice said a little sharply. 'Now, let me do your hair and we're done. I need to go and get ready myself and help your father with his tie. We mustn't keep the bride waiting.'

Pips stood alone in her bedroom in front of the mirror. She hardly recognized herself, but pinned just below her left shoulder, as always, was the red poppy brooch. It looked a little incongruous against the white dress, but it held such significance for both Pips and George that she couldn't *not* wear it today of all days.

For the few moments she had to herself on this busy day, she spared a thought for those who would not be here for one reason or another. She was sorry that William and his family could not come. She had invited them, but William had said, tactfully, that it would not be possible. He hadn't given a reason, but Pips knew he didn't want to cause any awkwardness for her on her wedding day. Len was still intractable. And then there was Ma. How she would have loved to have seen Ma sitting in the church. And she even spared a thought for Mitch. She realized now that he did love her in his own madcap way. She had to admit that, since her official engagement to George, when Mitch had 'kept his distance', she had missed the lively banter between them.

The door opened and Edwin came into the room. 'My darling girl, you look absolutely beautiful. Now, it's time we were leaving. It's a lovely day, so we can walk down to the church.' He chuckled. 'I should warn you that the driveway is lined with villagers and I expect the church is crammed.'

'How sweet of them.'

'They all love you, Pips.'

'Oh phooey. It's not just me. It's the whole Maitland family.'

'Well, whatever – or whoever – it is, they're all here to see the wedding of the year. Now, are you ready? We mustn't keep your mother waiting.'

Pips laughed. 'I thought you were going to say George.'

'He'd wait for ever, but this is a big day for my darling Hetty. This is the day she has dreamed of since the day you were born. Let's not keep her waiting a moment longer. So, shall we fire the starting pistol or wave a flag – or whatever it is they do at Brooklands?'

'Yes, let's.'

Fifty-Eight

'It's been a long time coming,' Bess said to Norah as she and the rest of their two families took their places in the church. 'I was beginning to think we'd never see the day. Wouldn't Ma have loved to have been here?'

'Aye, she would,' Norah said, as Len slipped into the seat beside her. They were all there: the Maitlands, the Dawsons and the Nuttalls – all joined now by marriage. And the rest of the village was there too. They'd all turned out for the wedding of Miss Pips and her handsome major.

After the service they all crowded into the marquee that had been erected in the grounds of the hall. Even the Grand Hall wasn't big enough to accommodate their families, friends and the whole village as well.

Speeches were made and champagne drunk and then Pips and George mingled with their guests. Pips sought out Major Fieldsend and kissed him soundly on both cheeks. 'Thank you, dearest major.'

'Whatever for, my dear girl?'

'I think you know that without your help, this day might not have happened.'

For a moment, Basil looked startled. 'Dear me. Your father shouldn't have told you that I recommended George to the War Office. I swore him to secrecy.'

Pips chuckled. 'He didn't say a word, major, but you have just let the cat out of the bag.'

He blinked and then let out a bark of laughter. 'You little minx! If ever there's another war, my dear, which God forbid there ever should be, you should offer yourself for some kind of secret war work. Not only are you extremely bright, but you're devilishly clever too.' He tapped her nose playfully. 'No one's ever got the better of me before.'

Circulating amongst their guests, Pips found herself in front of Rebecca. For a moment the two young women stood facing each other. Then Rebecca smiled tremulously.

'I'm glad I came. Thank you for inviting me, Pips. After all I've done and said...'

Pips took hold of her hand. 'Hush. Like I said before, that's all in the past and forgotten. I'm very glad you're here.'

Rebecca glanced across to where George was talking to Robert. 'He looks so happy. I can't remember when he last looked so happy, not even when Mummy – sorry, that was tactless of me – today of all days.'

'Nonsense. We will always remember your mother and talk about her whenever you want to. You do know, Rebecca, that although I'm legally your stepmother, it's not a position I want. I would never, ever, try to take your mother's place in any way. It's not necessary anyway. You're a grown woman now, but I do hope we might be friends.'

'I'm sure we can be.' Rebecca smiled wryly.

'Now I've come to my senses. Perhaps you'll have children that I can spoil.'

'Wouldn't you mind?'

Rebecca wrinkled her forehead. 'To be honest, I haven't given it much thought, but no, I don't think I would. It might be rather nice to have half-brothers and sisters. I doubt I'll ever have children of my own.'

'Of course you will. Haven't you got your eye on a handsome doctor or two at the hospital?'

Rebecca pulled a face, but laughed. 'There aren't enough to go round.'

'I'm sure you'll meet someone one day. Don't tell me you haven't had half your male patients falling in love with you.'

Now Rebecca laughed out loud. 'Oh yes, but we all know not to take that too seriously, though–' She glanced away, suddenly embarrassed, her cheeks a delicate shade of pink.

'Go on,' Pips prompted gently.

'There is one patient who has kept in touch since he was discharged. He's sent me flowers and chocolates and asked me to go out with him to dinner when he's fully recovered.'

'There you are, then.'

'But I don't know if it's allowed. I mean, I don't want to be dismissed or even reprimanded.'

'I can't see why it would be frowned upon, certainly not once he's left the hospital. Go and talk to a senior member of staff. The matron, if necessary.'

Rebecca's face brightened. 'Thanks, Pips, I will.'

They were still standing together when George crossed the grass towards them and put an arm around each of them.

'Everything all right?' he asked, a little worriedly.

'Everything's fine, Dad,' Rebecca said, and she kissed him on the cheek. Then she kissed Pips too. 'Have a wonderful honeymoon. Where are you going, or is it a closely guarded secret?'

'Absolutely.' George smiled. 'Even the bride doesn't know yet.'

It was time for the bride and groom to leave. Pips stood near the car with her back to all her guests and threw her bouquet over her head. It sailed high in the air, with the eager hands of all the village maidens reaching up to catch it. But the bouquet kept on flying over their heads until it began to drop and then it fell into Daisy's arms.

Pips turned and gave her niece a little wave and a broad wink. Then she climbed into the car beside George and they set off down the driveway with their guests waving and calling 'goodbye'.

'And who's the lucky chap going to be, then?' Luke grinned. He and Harry were standing close to Daisy, one on either side of her.

Daisy's gaze followed the car as it passed beneath the archway of the gatehouse, down the rest of the drive and into the lane. 'Ah, now that,' she said, with a mischievous smile, 'would be telling.'